OPERATION ARCANA

★ ★ ★

EDITED BY
JOHN JOSEPH ADAMS

BAEN

OPERATION ARCANA

Copyright © 2015 by John Joseph Adams

Copyrights of Stories
Introduction © 2015 by John Joseph Adams.
Rules of Enchantment © 2015 by David Klecha & Tobias S. Buckell.
The Damned One Hundred © 2015 by Jonathan Maberry Productions, LLC.
Blood, Ash, Braids © 2015 by Genevieve Valentine.
Mercenary's Honor © 2015 by Elizabeth Moon.
The Guns of the Wastes © 2015 by Django Wexler.
The Graphology of Hemorrhage © 2015 by Yoon Ha Lee.
American Golem © 2015 by Weston Ochse.
Weapons in the Earth © 2015 by Myke Cole.
Heavy Sulfur © 2015 by Ari Marmell.
Steel Ships © 2015 by Tanya Huff.
Sealskin © 2015 by Carrie Vaughn, LLC.
Pathfinder © 2015 by T.C. McCarthy.
Bone Eaters © 2015 by Glen Cook.
Bomber's Moon © 2015 by Simon R. Green.
In Skeleton Leaves © 2015 by Seanan McGuire.
The Way Home © 2015 by Linda Nagata.

A Baen Books Original

Baen Publishing Enterprises
P.O. Box 1403
Riverdale, NY 10471
www.baen.com

ISBN 13: 978-1-4767-8199-0

Cover art by Dominic Harman

First Baen mass market printing, October 2016

Distributed by Simon & Schuster
1230 Avenue of the Americas
New York, NY 10020

Library of Congress Cataloging-in-Publication Data
2014048261

Printed in the United States of America

10 9 8 7 6 5 4 3 2 1

MORE THAN A MIRAGE

★ ★ ★

The demon, like all the others before it, appeared first in the form of a horizontal plume of rust-red grit and vapor. Almost a kilometer away, it moved low to the ground, camouflaged by the waves of hot, shimmering air that rose from the desert hardpan. Lieutenant Matt Whitebird watched it for many seconds before he was sure it was more than a mirage. Then he announced to his squad, "Incoming. Ten o'clock from my position. Only one this time."

But even one was deadly.

Their combat training had neglected to cover a situation in which they were alone in an unmapped desert with no GPS, no air traffic, no vehicles, no goats, no sheep; where the radios worked, but there was no one to talk to; where the enemy emerged from churning dust wielding glittering, lethal swords—but they were learning.

Seconds passed, and then the skein of sand drew itself upright, a snake raising its head.

"Here we go," Cabuto whispered. "Show yourself, dust bunny."

To Whitebird's shock, the demon's sand form shot up the cliff face. It burst over the top between him and Cabuto, showering them in a storm of grit that crackled and pinged against their helmets and eyewear.

Whitebird rolled onto his side, his weapon aimed up as the demon congealed from the cloud.

It came dressed in a gray-brown desert combat uniform, with an M4 carbine clutched in its long, black-clawed fingers.

That was new.

—From "The Way Home" by Linda Nagata

EDITED BY JOHN JOSEPH ADAMS

CONTENTS

★ ★ ★

OPERATION
ARCANA

Arrows thick as the rain came whistling over the battlements, and fell clinking and glancing on the stones. Some found a mark. The assault on Helm's Deep had begun, but no sound or challenge was heard within; no answering arrows came.

The assailing hosts halted, foiled by the silent menace of rock and wall. Ever and again the lightning tore aside the darkness. Then the Orcs screamed, waving spear and sword, and shooting a cloud of arrows at any that stood revealed upon the battlements; and the men of the Mark amazed looked out as it seemed to them, upon a great field of dark corn, tossed by a tempest of war, and every ear glinted with barbed light.

—J.R.R. Tolkien, *The Lord of the Rings*

INTRODUCTION

★ ★ ★

John Joseph Adams

Soldiers are trained so that when they are faced with danger—so that when they must *initiate* danger—they don't have to think; they simply react. And though their superiors do what they can to prepare them for what the enemy is capable of, their training must essentially prepare them to deal with anything—the unknown. So who among us would be better prepared to suddenly come face to face with what we thought was impossible?

When I conceived of this anthology, the only guidelines I gave the authors were that I wanted stories with an equal emphasis placed on both of the words *military* and *fantasy*, and I turned them loose. As a result, the anthology ended up with a wide variety of approaches to the idea of military fantasy.

When you think of that term, you might initially picture big epic fantasy battles like J.R.R. Tolkien's Battle of Helm's Deep or George R. R. Martin's Battle of Blackwater. And indeed this anthology contains plenty of that. There's "Bone Eaters," a new story from one of military fantasy's masters, Glen Cook, set in his Black Company milieu; there's Elizabeth Moon's "Mercenary's Honor" (a Paksenarrion story), which pits two mercenary forces against each other with the fate of a town hanging in the balance; there's Yoon Ha Lee's "The Graphology of Hemorrhage," in which the pen—or in this case, the brush—is truly mightier than the sword; and then there's Jonathan Maberry's tale of "The Damned One Hundred," who must make a questionable alliance if they are to save their people from the rampaging horde of invaders at the gates.

But there are also stories where fantasy and the real world collide; in some, the real world has infiltrated fantasy: in Linda Nagata's "The Way Home," a squad of modern army soldiers suddenly finds themselves in a strange otherworld where they are beset by an unrelenting, demonic enemy unlike one they've ever faced before; or Tobias S. Buckell and David Klecha's story "Rules of Enchantment," in which a band of modern-day soldiers finds themselves in an epic fantasy world with an epic quest to fulfill.

In others, it's fantasy that infiltrates the real world (instead of the other way around): "Heavy Sulfur," by Ari Marmell, which takes us to WWI, where wizards are in the trenches and on the front lines; or Genevieve Valentine's "Blood, Ash, Braids," about the female Russian pilots in WWII known as "The Night Witches"; or Simon R. Green's "Bomber's Moon," in which angels side with the Allies and demons are with the Axis powers; or T. C. McCarthy's Korean War-era, elegiac "Pathfinder."

But not all of the fantasy-invades-reality stories are historical; there are contemporary works as well, such as Weston Ochse's "American Golem," which takes us to the current war in Afghanistan (which the author actually began writing during a recent tour there), and tells a fantastical revenge story against the backdrop of that conflict.

Although battles are obviously at the forefront of many military fantasy stories—and indeed many of the stories in this volume do portray some epic engagements—I didn't make battles a requirement because I think there are a lot of interesting stories to tell *surrounding* the battles, stories about the struggles of military personnel not only on the battlefield but off of it as well. So some of the stories do focus on other aspects of the military life: such as Myke Cole's "Weapons in the Earth" (a Shadow Ops story), which deals with prisoners of war; while Carrie Vaughn's "Sealskin" is about a soldier who finds himself lost after his service is over.

Other stories in the book don't quite fit into the above-mentioned categories but are still military fantasy stories to the core: there's Seanan McGuire's "In Skeleton Leaves," which tells the tale of neverending war in Neverland; there's Tanya Huff's story, in which a team of special forces soldiers—*extra* special you might say—lead an assault against the enemy's "Steel Ships"; and then there's Django Wexler's action-packed apocalyptic-fantasy-steampunk-epic, "The Guns of the Wastes."

All told that's sixteen tales of soldiers living in impossible worlds, dealing with impossible situations, or fighting impossible foes.

Though many of the contributors to this anthology are (or were) soldiers, I am not and never have been. But as the editor of this anthology you could say I'm the commander of an elite unit of professionals—and our primary objective with *Operation Arcana* is to entertain readers with tales of military fantasy.

To conclude, I'll just leave you with these words of wisdom that I passed along to the authors before we launched *Operation Arcana*, in which I paraphrased the legendary general of Gondor, Dwight D. Isengard, as he spoke to his troops on D-Day prior to launching Operation Dark Lord:

> You are about to embark upon a great crusade. I have full confidence in your courage in creating fantastical plots, devotion to evocative prose, and skill in creating fictional battles. We will accept nothing less than full manuscripts! Good luck! And let us all beseech the blessings of the Valar upon this great and noble undertaking.

RULES OF ENCHANTMENT

★ ★ ★

David Klecha & Tobias S. Buckell

You'd think arrows are pretty silent compared to gunfire, but there's no mistaking that bristly whistle as it whips through the air just past your head before it thwacks into someone's Kevlar. Everyone eats dirt, and you're checking your ammo with your back against a tree trunk wondering how the wood elves flanked you when you realize how stupid a question that is: this is their territory.

You're new to the squad, so you're still nervous. Every crack in the brush and shaken leaf has you jumpy. We've all been teasing you. Rookie this and rookie that.

I'm about fifteen feet away. I can see that your face is pale and shaken, but you have your rifle cradled and ready, looking for orders. The rest of the squad is spread out. Diaz is pulling an arrow out from his body armor and looking a bit chagrined. Orley is slowly crawling through dirt; he's got a bead on the shooter. "Sergeant: got eyes on the woodie," he reports.

"Hold," I order.

This is the rendezvous point. But we're dressed in robes that make us look like peasant travelers. I can feel Orley objecting already to the suspicion in my head, but even though our minds are all linked up into one single group mind via the Spell of Tactician's Weave, only one of us is still in charge.

Me.

"Ditch the robes," I order.

"Sergeant Cale . . ." Orley really doesn't want to do this. He wants to engage.

Diaz forms up a memory. A story he was told about a couple of African-American special forces who stumbled in out of the night with bows and arrows. Scouts setting out to blend into the local land. They ended up getting shot by jumpy sentries on the way back in who thought they were orcs.

Diaz is half-black. The realization that some people see black skin, bows, and right away think orc and go straight to trigger-pulling leaves a bad taste in all our mouths.

Teachable moment about making assumptions aside— and believe me, Diaz has laid plenty of those thanks to the intimacy of the Tactician's Weave—Orley gets Diaz's point and eases up. Now everyone's on board with my line of thought: that the elves are looking at us and seeing the Enemy, not US Marines.

We all shrug off the cloaks, displaying our standard Marine Corps digi-cammies and gear. My staff sergeant insignia is quite visible, making me the high-ranking target. I narrow my eyes at the shadows.

A bird whistle from the tree canopy pierces the air. They'd had us marked from the get go.

Shit.

If it wasn't for body armor, Diaz would have been a bloody piñata. And you, rookie, would have gotten a nasty surprise from up above.

Yeah, look above your head, rookie. That grinning visage looking down the bark of the tree is a wood elf. Remember what they taught you about high ground? That includes firs. You need to be better about your situational awareness; clear up and down, not just the two dimensional plane.

But I have to smile, because the challenge-and-answer is rolling through your mind like a mantra. At least you kept calm and didn't forget that.

"Cheshire!" I shout.

"Alice," comes the reply, in purring tones, from the wood elf above you. Good to go.

"Hello the shooters!" I shout. "First Battalion, Ninth Marines." You should know by now I always say something different. You should look up 1/9 and the stand at the Low Gorge Keep when we get back to the world. "You're expecting us? We're here for the Lady Wíela."

The new silence stretches on for a bit. You fidget, glancing away from the wood elf crouched on the tree above you into the foliage. More of the elves' small, childlike humanoid forms melt out from the shadows, their small bows slung on their backs, their hands resting on the hilts of knives. They are skeletal and lean, chiseled teeth glinting as they look us over with cold eyes.

"I'm Achur. I have protected the Lady this far. Do you have the writ?" The elf above you speaks again, dropping nimbly from the tree.

I hold up the papyrus, and the symbols on it glitter, then blaze as the elf's eyes pass over them. Achur swallows, then nods. "The Lady is in your care."

And just like that, they melt back away. All that remains is a young woman in a cloak as black as the shadows, her green eyes peeking out from under the hood.

Lady Wíela.

Diaz and Orley bow deeply toward her, as they've been taught by battalion S-3 and the cultural liaison gurus. I'm about to do so when your radio crackles. It's First Squad—Stormcrow—laid out two miles farther into enemy territory. "You've got three trolls, Longshanks," they report. "Headed your way like they know something's up."

None of us had heard anything, but we'd been focused on the attacking wood elves and could have missed the distant popcorn sound of gunfire. "Engage and slow them down, we have the package," I say into the handset, then strain to hear their reply.

"They're already past us, Longshanks," First Squad reports. "Two dead. I've already called for a med-evac, and we might be pinned down. I'd be calling you for help if—"

A brief burst of static.

"Stormcrow?"

Nothing. Dead or moving, but it doesn't matter to us just now.

Orley thinks he can hear the sound of wood cracking. Diaz is sure he can feel a distant thudding. I'm half convinced I can as well.

"It's dusk," says Lady Wíela, speaking up. "We'd better start running, unless any of your machines can hurt a troll."

"Trolls," you say, trying to remember your all-too-brief training before suiting up and coming through the breach.

"They'll be weak in the daylight. We just have to make it through the night," Lady Wícla says, as if reassuring us. Or maybe it's herself she's trying to convince. It's hard to say: her face is buried deep in the shadows of her cowl. None of us find it easy to get a good look at her features.

"Right," I say. "Get them to daylight." But the whole squad, linked to your mind, can tell exactly what you're thinking: that it'll be a miracle if we all make it through the night.

Antoine taps you with a Wand of Night Seeing and we're off, rolling through the woods at double-time. You're on point, like a good little newbie, your rifle half raised as you scan the woods in front of us. You'll never be a night elf—none of us can ever be that good—but the bottled spell gives you a good look at the terrain as we bust through it.

At this point, we have to figure anyone with half a lick of sense knows we're dragging a shit ton of trouble behind us in the shape of three trolls. Anyone in front of us basically *wants* to get trampled, if they're hanging around. Doesn't stop you from jumping at every flickery shadow, though.

Plus, we can all sense you're feeling the sting of letting that wood elf get the jump on you and you're itching to prove yourself.

"*Jotun*," I mutter to you. Be cool.

Cool as a frost giant.

The woods open up in front of you, which we all know is both good and bad; we have better visibility, but then so does anyone looking for us. And whatever advantage we had flitting between the trees where the trolls had to crash through would be lost in the more open ground. But if anything could make up for it, it was the view.

As you hustle down off the ridgeline, running along just below the crest, the trees thin out and you can see the Medju Gorge, the twisted frontier between the wood elves' home and the land of the orcs. I'm glancing at the tortured rock formations rising up like blackened souls trying to escape Hell, each larger, more misshapen, and unnatural than the last. The gorge deepens and widens, and the formations grow more massive. *Almost anything could be hiding in there*, Orley thinks.

The ridge you're running along slopes down toward the rim of the gorge, and the plan forms in our minds almost at once. Pros and cons shoot back and forth without the need for pleasantries or protocol as fast as the thoughts form. Within moments we're moving into position for a hasty ambush.

You stop and curl back, the rest of first team following you; you have the unenviable job of bait. But you're going to start in the beaten zone, so we think your run to safety will be short and the trolls will be distracted with other things—like stampeding off a cliff. As the ridge slopes down, the flat ground between it and the edge of the gorge narrows, and you and your team start trotting in small circles in an area where there's only about fifty meters of flat, sparsely treed ground between the ridge's steep slope and the gorge.

You feel them before you hear them, and hear them before you see them. The ground shakes and thuds first, the earth itself reacting to the trolls. Then you hear it— the trees cracking, metal jangling, grunting and snorting of the biggest, dumbest animals on two legs. Trees wave and topple, and then they lumber into view, massive arms and legs swinging through the foliage, then huge bodies tearing through. Your mind has a hard time with it, even through the unreal vision of Night Seeing. Videos from the first Rangers through the breach was one thing— gunsight cameras another—but this almost burns out your brain.

Good thing we're here too. Other than coordination, this is the thing Tactician's Weave is good for. We push you through the initial shock. As one your team raises their weapons and fires. You're not trying to bring down the trolls—only enrage them, draw them right into the beaten zone.

It works, of course. They're big dumb animals. But we all notice just *how* ineffective your fire is, and the plan starts to make less sense. Still, we're committed.

"This is a bad idea," Lady Wíela hisses just as you and your team start to.move, spraying three-round bursts back at the lumbering beasts.

"Yep, we know," I say and bring my rifle up. There's a HEDP—High Explosive, Dual Purpose—grenade in the tube slung under the barrel, and I'm hoping it does the trick.

"You won't get me back to your world this way," Lady Wíela says.

"We won't get you anywhere if we don't try to shake these assholes."

They cross the line, and whatever else she might be saying is drowned in a cacophony of fire. Our three automatic weapons open up, concentrating on the closest troll. Actual night-vision goggles help us, but they're not as good as the spell you're under. We see greenish lumps, fragments of huge bodies, and the bright, actinic sparks of tracer rounds seeking them out and pinging off their impossibly thick hides.

One staggers into view and I take the shot, angling up my rifle and popping off the grenade. The rifle butt smacks me in the shoulder, and I admire the shot for a moment—just like they say you shouldn't—but it's a perfect arc and nails the troll in its squat neck.

We all admire it, and then we scatter like camouflage cockroaches when the light turns on.

The trolls wig out, big time. The one I hit, he finally breaks and does a runner right toward the gorge. The other two start flailing around, maddened, completely lost. While that's great for us trying to boogie out, it's shit for us trying to do so in one piece. Tree limbs and rocks and clods of dirt the size of your chest start flying through the air. Marcel gets hit by a shattered tree trunk and goes down, run through with a couple of big shards of bole wood.

You grab him by the drag strap on the back of his vest and start to move through the woods. You might have been one of the biggest Tolkien nerds in your boot-camp platoon, but you were also one of the strongest.

We like you like that.

"Leave him," Wíela hisses as we try to regroup. She's stayed by my side through the ambush. "He will only slow us down, and the trolls' madness will pass. They will hunt us again."

"We do not leave a Marine behind!"

"You jeopardize this mission!" she cries. "And the whole war besides! Your people have stopped the invasion into your world, but you are barely keeping your enemies from staying on this side. I am the key to the alliance your forces need."

There is no denying that we've been stuck in a morass ever since pushing through to the other side, and you know it as well as any of us. You watched it on TV, on the Internet, through shaky YouTube videos and live Tweets. When the rifts opened, we didn't even know it was happening. At first, it was just tiny pockets where two worlds touched. But they grew wider, reaching beyond the woods and back alleys and caves where they first appeared. And just as we started to investigate, *they* poured out.

You wouldn't think—no one thought—that a bunch of creatures out of the storybooks could stand up for long against cops, much less the Army or Marines, but they made a fight out of it the world will never forget. Or maybe the world will, given enough time. Maybe it will fade to legends and fairytales and great big hairy operas by the descendants of the Germans.

One thing's for sure: everyone started looking at those

old stories differently when orcs started beheading joggers in Central Park and trolls destroyed the Empire State Building.

When we stopped the invasion and pushed through the fissures, we allied quickly with beings like the wood elves and humans like Lady Wíela, who were our allies and friends in the old stories.

Which is why we were on the edge of the wood elves' territory, running from trolls.

"We know what's at stake," I tell her. "We know you have information the brass is hot and heavy for." She seems to be some sort of royalty on this side of the rift, and we're the anonymous security team delivering her to the safe location. We know our role.

We don't stop moving, trying to form back up as we leave the thrashing noise of the trolls behind us. We take advantage of the bond that Tactician's Weave brings us and keep moving generally toward the objective.

"You don't know what's really at stake," she says, her voice rising in pitch and volume. "You haven't the first idea."

"You could just tell us," Orley says, interrupting.

"I can only speak to your leaders. And if you knew why, you would know we have no time to drag around the dying."

It's clear she's not going to tell us peons anything. "He's not dying; he'll be fine if we get him to a surgeon soon." We figure she has no idea that people could actually recover from wounds like that, much less survive them, without some intense magic. But still, the charitable understanding is hard to come by.

"We will all die if we do not get to safety and soon."

I smile as you come across a deep draw cutting across our path that drains down into the ravine. "We'll get there," I say.

You pick your way down the near slope of the gully, checking left and right like a good newbie should. You're rattled from that first encounter with the trolls, but you're also taking pride in having survived it, and having had the presence of mind all on your own to grab Marcel and drag him out of the killzone. Heath and Lomicka are carrying him now, groaning on one of our collapsible litters. They'll have a tough time getting down and back up the other side, but they can see your steps, your route, and pick their own way down from what they've seen through your eyes.

The sounds of the trolls still behind us somewhere spooks you, and you nearly squeeze off a round in panic. But we steady you again, remind you we want the trolls to follow us, and you press on. You pick your way across the gully floor slowly, eyeing the sharp rise on the far side. Lady Wíela has graciously informed us of a dry streambed that rises more gradually out the other side, and you pick up her landmarks and start moving toward them. The direction takes you down and west, closer toward that nightmare rift, where the draw empties out. Some of us think we can hear shrieks . . . or maybe it's just the wind whistling over those rock formations.

"Fuckin' eerie," Ysbarra mutters. She spits at the ground and hefts her SAW, taking comfort in the cold metal of the light machine gun in her hands.

This could, really, be anywhere on Earth. Back home. Back in the world. The same sorts of weeds and scrub poke up through the same sorts of rocks. The air, we all think, smells a little sweeter in the forest we just came from, and a little fouler up ahead where we don't want to go.

So as long as there aren't any invisible caves, or crystal staircases, or anything else weird, we should be good to go for the next attempt at an ambush. It's not that we want to stop and fight the trolls, it's that we don't have much choice. From here it's a straight shot back to our bivouac, and little else but open ground between us and the relative safety of the Forward Operating Base. Either the trolls run us down in the open ground, or we drag them all the way back to the FOB with us and hope the Marines there are up to the task.

It's a bullshit buffet, and we've got to pick something to eat.

"Wish we had a couple Gamgees with us," I mutter.

"What?" Lady Wíela asks.

"SAMs," I explain, realizing she isn't following. "Surface to Air Missiles."

But she's no less mystified.

"Think they'd stop a troll?" you ask.

I shrug. "Couldn't hurt . . ."

We follow you down, keeping up our dispersion, all of us trying to ignore the thudding in the distance. The trolls have gotten their shit together and could well be on our trail again. The sound of them certainly isn't growing any fainter.

The good Lady is chirping at my shoulder about

moving faster, but she answers the questions I put to her, however reluctantly. She sees the wisdom in our plan, however far short of ideal it may be, but she is not happy about it, and her nervousness grows with the sound of the trolls.

You set up in overwatch once you reach a shallow enough part of the streambed, scrambling up the side and back toward the steep edge of the gully. You perch on top just as the litter bearers make it down the far slope with Marcel between them. Sighting through the scope on your rifle, the landscape is laid out, the trees thinning to nothing on the opposite side, and treetops swaying as the trolls plod through.

We start setting up while we watch through your eyes, measuring distance and time and need. It's easier this time, picking out their flailing limbs and misshapen bodies, the thinning of the forest giving you more space to see. Still, the fully glimpsed form of them is just as terrifying as the half-glimpsed pieces.

"Damn," you mutter.

They are almost as broad as they are tall, but not fat as such—just thick. Squat necks with lumpy heads atop them, huge swaying arms that brush the ground as they lope along. Their hands are barely hands at all, almost just clubs on the ends of their arms. But it's not like they need much more than that.

You can only see two, which gives you hope that one of them did, indeed, panic himself right off a cliff. We're preparing for three anyway, not that it makes much difference: more than one stretches our resources to the breaking point. We have six kilos of C4, two collapsible anti-tank rockets, a dozen or so grenades, and a dwindling supply of regular ol' bullets. We arrange things as best we can, and once again dangle some bait for them.

This time, Lady Wíela herself volunteers. I tell her no, but she is insistent. We'd hate to do all this just to lose her, but she won't be put off. "You have the weapons," she points out. "If any of you steps away from your post, you reduce our fighting power. I'm your best option."

She's right. And if the trolls don't bite, we're fucked either way. We've been calling for backup—air support, or advice from up the food chain. But there's static in the air. Errant spells. Energy from the rift. Who knows? We seem to be on our own.

So we set up and there is no mistaking it now; the ground is shaking, the trees are swaying and there is no chance that it's a column of tanks rolling through to pick us up—they're still having problems stockpiling enough diesel on this side of the rifts to make it work.

We hustle to improvise some claymores and set up Brust and Antoine on the opposite side of the dry streambed from you with their anti-tank rockets.

Lady Wíela paces through a small section of cleared ground in the middle of the gully. You keep looking from her to the treeline and back again, feeling personally responsible for her safety even though we've taken that on as a squad. You still haven't worked out that team-mind thing, but we know you will; we all had to work at it at one point or another.

A lot of fantasy nerds got it in their heads that they were the next Aragorn—the movie Aragorn, no less— hacking their way through legions of orcs with a big fucking sword and a bad shave. Lotta assholes got killed that way, in and out of uniform. You're not one of those assholes. You're a solid part of the team. You've been through the training, paid some dues. Now it's time to see how it really gets done on the ground.

So you don't let yourself linger on the Lady, however good she looks in that gown-and-cloak number. No Cate Blanchett, but still easy on the eyes. Besides, when your brain wanders like that you can feel Ysbarra's annoyance at the off-mission male-gaze focus like a swift ruler crack to the knuckles. *Save that shit for your bunk.*

And when the trolls break through, you're all business. You estimate the ranges and we read them right off the top of your consciousness. Too close. Far too close.

"Lady Wíela!" you shout, and the Lady looks at your pointed hand. They're at the crest, near where we came down, towering above.

She screams, getting their attention, and starts to run.

We make a decision and Brust pulls the trigger. An unguided rocket lances out in a tight spiral. It blossoms orange just under the armpit of one of the trolls, causing it to bellow in rage.

"He ain't too fucking happy about that," I say.

From what Brust can see, we're thinking we seem to have finally injured one of them—slightly.

"Nah," you report. "I think we just really, really pissed it off."

It bellows again, and an answering roar comes from down toward the ravine.

Fuck, I think, spreading alarm out through everyone. We scope the end of the gully and see the big dark shape of the third troll lumbering up the gully toward us. It must have gone down into the ravine but continued to follow us and climbed up to try to flank. We would not have given them that much credit for coordination, and maybe it was just a happy accident (for them). "Who cares if it's an accident," Antoine hisses. "We are supremely fucked."

And the Lady is close to being trapped. "Reel her up," I order. We're not going to lose her.

You grab the 550-pound test-cord loop from your gear and fling it over the edge of the gully after tying off one end to your vest. If she can get to that, she can climb up, maybe, and you're torn between firing at the trolls to drive them off and trying to make like a bump in the grass, hoping they get more excited about Brust and his spent rocket launcher.

We solve it for you when Antoine fires on the other troll, hoping to draw them away. But no matter what we do, we've got more trolls than we can deal with and a lot of open ground behind us.

Antoine's distraction works, though that means all three trolls are now keying on Brust and Antoine. They are theoretically out of reach on the lip of the gully, but suddenly the walls don't look so high.

And then the radio crackles. Fuzzy and fractured, but recognizable.

"Longshanks, Longshanks, this is Windlord, we are one mike out from your beacon, what's your sitch?"

We somehow refrain from cheering.

"Windlord, this is Longshanks actual," I shout into the radio handset. "Three brutes, danger close, bring the thunder!"

"Thunder, aye. Hold on to your butts, Longshanks. Windlord out."

You look up and to the west, and you can see them, a flight of four sparks in the distance, but closing, growing quickly. You scramble to the lip of the gully and shout down at the Lady. She hurries toward you, broken from her fear, and starts scrambling toward the dangling cord. She finds it and loops it under her arms, tying it off in front of her. Then she starts to climb, and you take up the slack, taking weight off of her.

"What is it?" she shouts, seeing that I'm looking over my shoulder into the air. "A dragon?"

"Even better," I shout down at her. "Warthogs!"

She frowns—not sure how a pig might be able to save our bacon right now—as the Warthogs arrive.

They're ugly and beautiful-almost-ancient jets made for a different war. Their huge rotary cannons, mounted under the cockpit, were designed to plow 30mm depleted-uranium rounds into Soviet tanks and armored vehicles in support of ground troops like us. The planes themselves are actually armored, and as they dive on the gully you can see the cluster bombs and anti-armor rockets slung under the wings.

The trolls look up just as four gouts of flame erupt from the planes, each stream of phosphorescent rounds looking like a laser beam. Two of the Warthogs loose rockets, and explosions rock the gully. We all drop flat, and you're thrown down, back as you come to an appreciation of what "danger close" *really* means. The heat of the explosions washes over you, singeing the grass, reddening your exposed skin, and the weight on the line goes heavy.

The trolls bellow and cry and scream, and it all mingles with the cacophony of the Warthogs' attack. They seem to be stampeding to the ravine, to the frontier with the dark lands, and two of the Warthogs overfly them while the other two circle back around and strafe them again to make the point. One of the trolls actually falls and does not stir.

"Fuck yeah!" someone says. Or maybe we all do. Hard to tell.

You grab hold and start hauling on the line again. Lady Wíela is still on it, but heavy, not assisting you. Fantasy nerds who'd been through boot camp knew that their gaming stats had real world counterparts, and you went in big on your Strength and Constitution. Hand over hand you pull her up the side of the gully.

We all pick ourselves up, several limps and cuts and bruises, but nothing to keep us from hoofing the last few miles. We hurry over to where you are, where you're pulling the Lady Wíela up over the lip of the gully.

I'm hoping she's not dead. Really, really hoping. But you see her as you drag her over the lip and relax slightly. She's unconscious, blood down the side of her face, but she takes several deep breaths as we watch. Antoine gets down to check her out and pronounces her alive, but he's muttering, "This ain't right," over and over again.

We all take in the state of her cloak and gown, torn and shredded by the trip up the rocky wall of the gully. Her skin is gray and mottled beneath, no match for the pale face and blond hair showing above her shoulders.

Not human.

Her face and hands are a glamour, I realize. A magical disguise meant to fool us.

Or someone.

Orley draws his sidearm, ready to put two between her eyes, but you grab his wrist and push the weapon back.

We see it clear in your mind. Diaz's story about the two black Special Forces guys riddled with bullets because the sentries had mistaken them for orcs. The lady's disguise was not going to survive a trip to Washington, so she knew she would be unmasked long before she got anywhere the surprise might do her any good.

"She's an orc, but she's here to help us," you say aloud. "I don't think she dangled herself out there as troll bait for nothing. She's a friendly. And, I'm guessing, an important one."

After a moment, Diaz nods and grabs the second collapsible litter off of Antoine's back and unfolds it. We get Wíela on it, and, as the Warthogs make one final strafing run along the gully, we start hoofing it for friendlier territory.

Forward Operating Base Hammerhand sits perched on a bare sweep of rocky soil, just on the frontier of the High Elves' sacred forest. Dawn breaks as the big Osh-Kosh truck crawls up from the Entry Control Point down on the plain proper. As we crest the rise, we can see the Seven Sisters Falls, sparkling in the morning sun, pouring out from the sacred forest and into the river we all call "Binky" because none of us can pronounce its real name.

As soon as we're stopped, Antoine hauls Marcel off the back of the truck and two more corpsmen come running up. Together, they all hustle off to the Combat Support Hospital. An aircrew and some officer, meanwhile, come fetch Lady Wíela. The officer, at least, doesn't look surprised at the mottled gray skin showing under her torn clothing.

"Fucking figures," you say. And for once, we don't give you a hard time. That's hard-won knowledge—the fact that sometimes you're a mushroom: kept in the dark and fed orders.

Tactician's Weave is wearing off and we're all starting to fall back into our own heads, but we don't really need it to make some decisions together. Dropping off the back of the truck we haul our weary bodies out to the eastern end of the FOB, looking out over the forest and falls and the faint hint of golden spires away over the forest canopy.

We shuck our gear, bodies steaming with sweat evaporating in the cool morning air. As we settle in, the CH-53 Sea Stallion lifts off its pad at the western end of the base and forms up with two Cobra gunships already orbiting the base. They leg it north at top speed, and we wish them luck. Flying through the rifts is nowhere near as easy as walking or driving.

"It ain't D&D rules, that's for sure," you say, leaning back on your gear. Like some salty vet, you've already broken down your M-16 and gotten out your cleaning kit, the pieces settled on your lap. We're all following suit, of course, even those of us who didn't get off a shot.

"Yeah," Orley says, stretching his back, "I wish I could ignore encumbrance."

We all laugh. We're all nerds of some stripe or another, and most of us rolled those dice before taking the chances we do now. But reality's not as simple as those worlds we conceived. All of those guys *did* tap into something real, as it turns out, some ancient memories of the world when those rifts opened and the weird and scary and monstrous poured out, populating our nightmares and fairy tales for millennia.

"So did those elves sell us out?" Ysbarra asks, leaning over her SAW to disassemble the light machine gun.

"What do you think?" Diaz replies. "Those trolls were aimed right at us. They delivered their package, got paid, and then got paid for telling the other side where the package was."

"That's jacked up," you say. You're still too boot to say "fuck" sometimes.

"It's fucking complicated," I say. "Just like the 'Stan, just like Iraq. I was in both places. I saw how fucked up it could be, even back there. No surprise it's the same here."

You look over the sacred forest, the lands of our allies, frowning a little. We can read the thought on your face, don't need to see into your mind.

"And no—no guarantees they can be trusted, either," I say. "But if *we* trust each other and think things through, we'll be alright."

That's how it's been done through all the long years, you figure, since trolls and goblins first walked out of our nightmares, and the many wars since. If we hold off the darkness together, that's how it'll go this time, too. Maybe this time we won't forget it all to legend.

★ ★ ★

ABOUT THE AUTHORS

David Klecha is a science fiction writer living in West Michigan with his wife, three children, and no cats. After graduating from university, he skillfully parleyed his degree in History and fuzzy mastery of Russian into an enlistment in the Marine Corps and a series of entry-level IT jobs. A deployment to Iraq brought the opportunity to start a milblog, and when Dave returned home he began writing professionally, as well as climbing the IT ladder, putting his combat experience to good use. Dave's short fiction has appeared in *Subterranean Magazine*, *Clarkesworld*, and the anthology *Armored*.

Born in the Caribbean, **Tobias S. Buckell** is a *New York Times* bestselling author. His novels and over 50 short stories have been translated into 17 languages, and he has been nominated for the Hugo, Nebula, Prometheus, and John W. Campbell Award for Best New Science Fiction Author. He currently lives in Ohio.

THE DAMNED ONE HUNDRED

★ ★ ★

Jonathan Maberry

★ **1** ★

"If the Gate falls, we fall!" Kellur yelled at the top of his voice.

The iron doors remained shut. Silence was the only voice that spoke to him beyond the ghost echoes of his own words.

"They won't answer, Father," said Kan.

"They'll answer," growled Kellur, then added, "They must."

Kan looked away, and Kellur immediately regretted his words. He knew that his son was unable to meet his father's eyes. The boy was embarrassed, and for good reason. His words were weak. They were a house of straw built in the wind. *They must* was many weary miles from *They will*.

Kellur squared his shoulders and stepped up to the doors. They were twenty feet high but narrow, and every inch of each bronze panel was set with carvings of demons and gods, heroes and monsters. The whole of the scriptures were there. The birth of Father Ar in the endless fields of the Summerlands. The last of the old gods blowing her last breath into Ar's lungs, making him immortal, beginning the age of the New Faith. And all of the parables and stories of the six Books of the Faith. All of the wonders and miracles, all of the treachery and bloodshed upon which their beliefs were built. The sacred and the profane, recorded here in thousands of tiny metal figures carved from solid bronze doors. The works of a hundred nuns for a hundred years.

The great doors were set deeply into the living rock, the metal work perpetually in shadows. Kellur knew full well that no sunlight ever touched those doors. No sunlight touched this side of the mountain pass at all. It was why these witches had chosen this spot to build their cathedral.

"Open the door and hear me speak," bellowed Kellur. He pounded the side of his fist against the bas-reliefs of Mother Sun and the hero twins. "I come in the name of the Chosen. I come as defender of the faithful. Open!"

The sound of his pounding fist coaxed echoes from within.

"They will not answer," repeated his son. Kan was sixteen winters old. A fine, strong boy with his father's face and the hard, clean build of his grandfather. Blacksmith shoulders and scholar's eyes. Like all the men of their line. Warrior artisans. Poets and fighters. And like all of them, stubborn.

"Hush, boy," snapped Kellur. "They'll answer if I have to knock these doors down."

The boy opened his mouth to say something, then shut it. He looked away again, facing east toward the howling wind. The road down from this mountain pass twisted like a snake. The bones of ten thousand times ten thousand men littered the hollows at the foot of these mountains. Bones of heroes, bones of soldiers who had marched along that path toward the Red Gate that blocked the way one mile to the west.

No one walked through those broken rocks. Not yet. But far, far away, the sound of drums could be heard. It was like thunder from a coming storm. Kellur knew that his son was listening to that sound more than he was watching the road. The mountain passes amplified distant sounds and carried them for freakish distances. To someone who didn't know this, those drums sounded like they were no more than five or eight miles away. In truth the vanguard of the Hakkian army was more than fifty miles away. *Days* away.

That distance was not a comfort. The Hakkians were marching as fast at the treacherous pass would let them go. As fast as the whips of their sergeants would make them march. As fast as the war songs of their trumpets would impel them.

They would be here in two days. Three, if they paused to rest before they assailed the Red Gate. Soon the lumber carts bearing the components of their siege engines would roll up the long slope toward this spot. There the army would pause and build its towers. The towers that had brought down West Aylia and Goshtan.

The towers that had allowed the Hakkians to flood like ants over the walls of Betheltown and Vale.

Then the Red Gate would fall, and the whole of the west would be laid bare to the enemy.

The fear of that, the horror of that, put steel into Kellur's fist, and he spun around and hammered the door until pain exploded in his flesh and sent shocks up his arms.

"Open the door, you damned witches. Open the door to the Champion of the Faithful. In the name of Ar I demand this!"

He staggered back, chest heaving, hands pulsing with pain, mind ablaze.

Despair was a black scorpion that crawled through his mind.

Then, from far above, a voice spoke. Old, creaking, leathery. Nasty.

"You dare invoke the name of the usurper god when knocking at our door?"

Kellur and Kan looked up to see that a section of the rock wall above the door had swung out on iron hinges. A woman leaned out to stare down at them. She was so comprehensively wrinkled that she appeared to be little more than a mummy. Wisps of gray hair clung to her yellow scalp, and her eyes were so deeply set that they seemed to be the hollow sockets of a skull. She craned her head forward to study them, but she still stayed within the shadows.

"Woman," said Kellur, "if woman you be, then yes, I dare invoke my god. But if that is an evil thing to you, then tell me by whose name I should call, and I will be on my knees in prayer if that will get you to open these damned doors."

She studied him, her lips writhing as if preparing to speak, but for more than a minute she said nothing.

"Will you not speak to me?" demanded Kellur.

"You would bend a knee to the true goddess?"

"Father . . ." whispered Kan, "what are you *doing*?"

Kellur ignored his son. "Name her and I shall sacrifice a thousand spring lambs on her altar."

"Even to the point of forsaking the false god, Ar?"

"Even then."

She narrowed her eyes. "You wear the coat of a Knight of the Faith. You call yourself the champion of that religion. Why would such as you forswear his beliefs? What calamity would make you do this? Or do you come here with lies, as so many have before?"

"What choice have I? The wolves are at the door, and the hour of our doom is at hand. That is not poetry; I am not quoting a song. This is real, and it is happening. I am the Champion of the Faithful, loyal son of Father Ar, this is truth. But the greater truth is that I am charged with protecting all of the Faithful, with protecting everyone west of the Red Gate from their enemies." He pointed toward the eastern road. "Those enemies are coming. Do you not hear the thunder of their drums? Do you not know the doom they bring? You ask me if I would forswear my religion to save my nation? Let me in so that you can look into my eyes and know the truth of my heart. You are witches; surely you have some spell that will assure you that I speak the truth. Ensorcel me. Spill the entrails of a kid and read the secrets of its blood."

The witch watched him for a long, long time. She said nothing, but those thin lips twitched and writhed like worms.

Then she withdrew and pulled the stone trapdoor shut, leaving Kellur and Kan Kellurson standing on the doorstep.

Kan shook his head. "Oh, Father—I told you this would not work."

"Hush."

But the boy pointed a finger at his father. "You spoke heresy to that crone. You promised to betray everything you believe in. I . . . I . . . don't know what to say. I am . . . ashamed for you."

Kellur took a single step toward his son, but it brought them to within a finger's breadth of each other. Kellur, taller and broader, looked down at the boy.

"And what would you have me do? Leave without their help? Would that raise me in your esteem? Should I go back to the wall and try to hold it with a scant thousand men? If there are even a thousand left. The soldiers of the Faithful desert in the hundreds. The walls are half bare. Will Father Ar send twelve legions of angels to fight alongside us? Isn't that what the prophecy says? Well, lad, those legions are slow in coming, and the enemy marches with great haste." He took another step forward so that his son was forced to yield ground and step back. "You tell me what you would do to save our homeland. What will save your mother and sisters? What will save that girl you fancy? What will save our people from being wiped from the face of this world?"

The boy stared up at his father, but though he tried to speak, he could not. In the end, he turned away and walked ten paces toward the Red Gate. Then he stopped, and his shoulders slumped.

The wretched silence that followed was broken by the sound of rusted metal hinges screaming in protest. Kellur and his son both turned to see the doors of the witches' cathedral opening inward.

The witch who had spoken to them stood inside the arch, her skeletal hands clutching dark red robes to her bony frame. Behind her, the shadows within the cathedral seemed to twist and move as if there were a hundred demons hiding from the sun's pure light.

Kan cried aloud and drew his sword, but Kellur held out a warning hand. "Sheathe your blade, boy," he growled. "We are guests here."

The boy frowned but did as he was bid. The witch smiled. Her smile was an ugly thing. If disease and sickness were embodied in the form of a woman, its smile would be like that. It lacked warmth and promised awful things.

The witch beckoned. "Of your own free will and heart's desire, I invite you to enter."

Kellur straightened his shoulders and nodded. "And with free will I shall enter."

With his son trailing uncertainly behind, the Champion of the Faithful entered the great church of the Red Religion.

★ **2** ★

The witch said nothing, but instead turned and led them

down a long hall with vaulted ceilings. Fires burned in buckets hanging from the rafters and thousands of candles dripped from sconces mounted without pattern on the brick walls. Between the sconces hung rich tapestries of great antiquity, their faces covered with embroidered women of surpassing beauty. And yet as Kellur passed, those women seemed to turn to ponder him and his son. It was a trick of the light, he knew—though he was not certain of that knowledge. This was an abode of witches, after all.

They approached another set of doors, and these were even more massive than the outer ones. They rose in a graceful arc to stand fifty feet tall and were banded with steel set with rivets as big as his fist. Across the doors and along the walls was a single carving of a woman in repose, her gowns flowing around a voluptuous body, her hair coiled like serpents. The sculptor had captured a vulpine intensity in the woman's smile. And he'd fashioned her arms across the doors in such a way that as they opened it was as if she were opening her arms to embrace whomever entered.

It was beautiful and intensely unnerving.

"Father—?" began Kan, but Kellur waved him to silence.

The hag stopped outside the doors and gestured for them to enter. As they passed her, Kellur saw the pernicious smile that twisted her weathered face.

He stopped. "Do you have something to say to me, old woman?"

Her only reply was a chuckle. She held out her hand, indicating the room beyond. Kellur took a breath, then walked past her. Kan followed quickly, his hand on the hilt of his sword.

The room beyond those doors was vast. The walls and ceiling were lost in shadows, and the roof was supported by scores of ornate pillars. At the far end—seated like a queen on a throne—was a woman. She was as different from the withered crone as it was possible to be. Dressed in silks that were blood red and snow white, the woman was young and ripe and beautiful—easily the most beautiful woman Kellur had ever beheld. Her face was exquisite, heart-shaped and framed by masses of curling black hair. Her eyes were a vivid green, the green of summer sunlight on newly unfurled leaves. Her lips were as red as all the sin in the world. The silks she wore were translucent, and Kellur could see the womanly curves beneath, and the dark circles of her nipples on each full breast. She wore no jewelry except a dagger on a leather girdle, the handle slanting across her taut stomach, the tip pressed against the silks through which he could see the dark triangle of her pubic bush.

He was instantly flushed with a desire to hold this woman. To kiss her. To tear away those silks and plunder those loins.

And at the same moment he wanted to drop to his knees before her and worship her. As a queen. As a goddess. As a woman in the full richness of her power.

He heard a sound, almost a cry, and turned to see Kan gazing at her with glazed eyes, his face twisted with lust and fear.

The woman wore a knowing smile, clearly aware of the effect she had on men. On *any* man.

"Welcome to my hall," she said. "I am Celissa, eldest of the Red Sisterhood."

Eldest, thought Kellur. Surely an honorary title. This woman could not be older than two dozen winters.

"What do I call you, Lady Celissa? Are you a queen?"

"Lady Celissa will do. Anything more would be ungainly, Kellur Hendrakeson of Argolin, Champion of the Faithful, defender of the Gate."

Kan gasped, but Kellur bowed. "I am pleased that you know me, my lady. If you know this, then you must know of the danger that approaches."

"I know many things," she admitted, "but many of my sisters do not look beyond our walls. Tell them what brings you here to our church."

"Sisters?" echoed Kan, but as Kellur and his son looked around they realized with cold horror that the shadows that filled the great room were not merely lightless air. Figures stood there, hunched and misshapen. Vaguely womanish, vaguely human. They stood as still as statues, many covered with robes and cowls, hands clasped to their bosoms, eyes as dark as those of the witch on the wall.

"Father," whispered Kan, "we have walked into a trap. These witches will drink our lives."

"Be silent, boy," snapped Kellur. "We are guests in this house, and by Father Ar, you will respect . . ."

He let his voice trail away, aware of the sharpening of attention from the watching figures. There was a hiss of conversation, but he could make out none of the words.

Kellur cleared his throat. "Be quiet, boy."

He turned to face Lady Celissa. Her mouth still smiled, but there was heat behind her gaze. "You swear by a name that is never spoken in these halls," she said in a voice that was softer than her eyes. "You come here to ask our help, and you stain the air with that name."

Kellur placed a hand over his heart and bowed low. After a moment Kan did so as well.

"I spoke in haste and from habit, my lady," said Kellur. "I am ashamed of my clumsiness and beg forgiveness."

"Forgiveness," said Celissa slowly. "You ask much."

He said nothing.

"Rise and face me, soldier of Argolin," she said. "And you, too, child."

They stood, father and son, and looked up at this beautiful woman on the throne.

"Tell us all what would make no less than a *champion* of your religion come to us, the Red Sisters."

Kellur took a breath, nodded, and gestured backward, indicating the world beyond this chamber and this church. "The Hakkians march on the Red Gate. They are already in the foothills of these mountains and in two or three days they will be here. Right here. They will burn everything in their way, my lady, and then they will lay siege to the Gate."

"Why should we care?" asked a voice from the shadows. It sounded like the woman from the wall, though he couldn't really tell.

"Do you not know the history of the Gate?" he asked. "This pass, this cleft in these mountains, was placed here by the grace of . . . of whatever god or goddess you believe rules this world. This mountain pass that has been fought over for six thousand years until the Red Gate was built." He shook his head and once more gestured to the world outside, as if it could be seen through stone and shadows.

"The Red Gate. Do you ever look beyond your walls? You never venture outside, as far as we know, so maybe you don't care about the pass, the Gate, and everything beyond it. On the other side are fertile valleys on whose slopes and in whose plains grow the wheat and corn and apples and garlic that feed the people of half the world. Lose the Gate and lose the crops. Lose the Gate and starve fifty thousand people. Lose the Gate, lose the war. This is not complicated math, even for those who do not study war."

"The Gate is strong," said another of the shadowy women.

"Strong, yes," admitted Kellur. "But it can fall. It *has* fallen. I know. I fought to hold this pass on three separate occasions."

It was true, and he told them of it. The first time had been when he was sixteen, the same age as Kan, barely able to hold a light straight-sword. Too small yet to hold anything with real heft. He'd staggered along through the valley to the Gate, groaning and sweating inside the furnace-hot weight of his father's old armor. The metal was too heavy, the chainmail bit and burned him, and the helmet was a full size too big. And he'd gone to that fight carrying the added burden of knowing that he was only a body. Nothing more. Something to cram a narrow pass. Something to soak up arrows or weary the arms of the enemy soldiers. He was not expected to fight with any skill. He was not expected to kill a single one of the enemy. He was not expected to be anything more than obstructive meat that would slow the enemy so that they would be spent when they met the real soldiers.

That Kellur did not die was more luck than skill. He'd picked up a dead soldier's pike and an enemy lieutenant had fallen off his horse and landed on the tip of the blade. Perhaps the gods were having a grand old time messing with the lives and fates of their worshippers. The punch line of that cosmic joke was that the lieutenant was important. The son of a priest, and a man—though quite young—who everyone believed was graced by the God of War.

To see him fall, speared by a boy, his blade unbloodied, his mettle untested, was a worse blow than anything a thousand soldiers with sword and spear could have accomplished. The heart went out of the enemy, and the Gate held.

The second time was different.

Kellur was a sergeant then. Older, bigger, in the heat of his twenties, with all of the boundless energy the young are granted by gods who are strangely generous at all the wrong times. Kellur had stood with a hundred other men, each of them village champions or veterans of the coastal wars. They'd each drawn lines across their chests above their hearts with a thrice-blessed dagger and then taken sips from a cup of commingled blood. They'd sung the old war songs that had lyrics whose meanings were lost to the ages. They'd locked shields and laughed as the enemy cavalry rode toward the Red Gate.

Of the hundred blood-brothers, nine survived.

Those nine spent the next four years as slaves to the invaders. The valley and the lands beyond? It took ten years for them to recover even after the invaders were driven out.

Then there was the third time.

Kellur was forty then. Older, slower—jaded—but wise.

That was the first time the Hakkians had come out of the east. Five thousand of them had come. Lightly armored but heavily armed, and they threw themselves against the Gate. Kellur was captain of the guard. He pitted his two thousand soldiers against their numbers, and after three days of wholesale slaughter, he took the head of the Hakkian captain. It had been a costly win, though, and both of his brothers and fourteen hundred of his men had gone to the Summerlands. If the Hakkians had been better prepared or had come in greater numbers, the Red Gate must surely have fallen.

They tried it again, and again, each time with small armies that were nonetheless large enough to drain the resources of the defenders. Kellur, now elevated to general, took five thousand heads during the last battle, but it was at the cost of three thousand men. And the Gate itself was badly damaged from fire and battering ram. It had been hastily repaired, but the army was strained and weak. The new recruits came and enlisted by the thousand, but they were green. The Hakkians were a vast empire, and their soldiers were hardened from years of endless warfare and heartened by conquest everywhere but here.

"Now," he told the gathered witches, "the enemy comes again, and this time they are prepared. They've learned from their defeats. They do not send a few thousand lightly armored scouts against us, nor do they waste a legion of light cavalry. My spies have gone mad trying to count their numbers. They come up the mountain with a hundred thousand soldiers. An ocean of spears comes to take the Red Gate. And this time they bring more than rams and torches. This time they bring siege engines and mineral fire and all of their weapons of war. This time they come like an ocean, and the Red Gate will be swept away."

The hall was utterly silent.

The lady on her throne regarded him with hooded eyes and a secret smile.

"You talk of an inevitable defeat, Champion," she said. "If this is already written in the book of fate, why come to us?"

"Because, my lady," said Kellur, "there is only one thing the Hakkians fear. There is only one enemy they will not dare to attack."

She raised an eyebrow, and the curve of her smile tilted upward. "And what is that?"

Kellur said, "This cathedral stands outside the Gate, as it has stood for ten times ten thousand years."

She nodded.

"No army has ever taken it," he said, "because no army dares. Each time an army has come up the mountain road to assail the Red Gate, they march past this church. They do not look upon it. They do not speak as they pass. They will not speak of it. Any man who dares name it or even call attention to it is cut down by his own fellows lest that transgression offend those who live within these walls."

Celissa leaned ever so slightly forward. "And do you know why?"

Kellur met her level stare. "I know, my lady. I know

why this church is left untouched. I know why the churches in Hestria and Vale have also been passed by despite centuries of war and conquest."

Her eyes flicked to Kan and back. "Does your son know?"

"He knows the rumors, the campfire talk. Like all of the children beyond the Gate he thinks that this is an abode of demons. You are the things he was taught by his nursemaid to fear when he would not eat his greens or do his chores. You are the monsters of our nighttime."

Celissa sighed and looked away. He caught an emotion on her face. Was it sadness? Annoyance? Some commingling of both? The other witches murmured and whispered.

"And yet you come here, to this *abode of demons*." It sounded like those words hurt her pretty mouth.

"I do, and I come with humility."

"Why? If you know what we are, Champion, you know that we will not venture from our halls to fight your wars."

"I know that you won't," he agreed, "and I know that you can't. Not the oldest of you, for the kiss of Mother Sun would turn you to dust."

They hissed at the mention of her name.

"I know that you cannot abide the light. Only the youngest of you can endure it, but only for a day or a few days."

"A few days," she said softly. "You *do* know us."

"I do."

"Once more I ask, why come to us? If the invaders will pass us by, and if we cannot come to your aid, then how is this anything but a wasted trip for you? And a dangerous one."

"My lady, when was the last time you heard from the Red Churches in Hestria and Vale? When was the last time your sisters there sent word to you here?"

There was more whispering in the shadows, but Celissa held up her hand for silence. "If you ask that question, then you must know the answer. We have not heard from either church for seven moons. But that is not strange. Sometimes years will pass before word is shared between the churches. We expect them to send word to us before the solstice."

Kellur once more placed his hand over his heart. "I would not willingly cause you hurt, my lady, but I fear that you will never again hear from your sisters in those churches."

"And why is this? What makes you think you can speak for them?"

Kellur opened the flap of the pouch tied to his belt. He removed a handful of ash and, kneeling, let it fall to the floor. It rained down like sand.

"This is all that is left of the Red Sisters of Vale," he said. Then he took a second handful of ash from a second pouch. "And these are the ashes of the Sisters of Hestria."

He knelt there, head bowed, hands wide, fingers and palms stained with ash.

The witches screamed.

They screamed and screamed so loud that Kellur and his son clapped their hands to their ears and cried out in pain. Even Lady Celissa screamed. Tears boiled from the corners of her eyes, and as she wept, her eyes changed from vivid green to a dark and terrible red. She rose from her throne and pointed an accusing finger at them.

"What insanity is this? What lies are these? Do you want to die screaming? Do you want to see your son torn apart and consumed? I will eat your heart and—"

She stopped, cutting off her own words as she staggered and darted out a hand to catch the arm of the throne. Sobs wracked her whole body, and in that moment it seemed to Kellur that she was not a young and beautiful woman, but a hag far older and more wrinkled than any of the other witches. Ancient beyond the counting of centuries. Everything—her youth and beauty—was nothing more than a glamour.

Had this been another day, Kellur would have screamed and run from this place. He'd have run straight to the nearest shrine to Father Ar and begged the mercy and protection of his god.

But this was not another day.

"My lady," he said. "I am sorry for your losses. On my life I am. But the blood of your sisters is not on my hands, nor on the hands of any of my kinfolk. The Hakkian armies laid siege to those churches and tore them down."

"They cannot have done this," she snarled. "They fear us."

"They fear you, but they hate you more. And they *know* you. They know that you cannot abide the sunlight, and so they brought their siege engines to batter down the walls of the churches in Hestria and Vale. They brought those cathedrals down, and they burned the forests of Hestria to let the light in. They tore down the mountaintop of Vale to chase away the shadows. This they have done with their machines of war. And in the sunlight they hunted your sisters down and watched them burn." He shook his head. "Were there none of them who were young enough to endure the sunlight? None who could stand and fight them?"

Celissa wiped at her tears and shook her head. "No. Not in either church, and none here. The youngest of us is a thousand years old. We . . . we cannot step into the light. Not for a moment. Not even to kill. Not even to *feed*."

She put such hate into that last word that it seemed to burn in the air.

She looked toward the doors, to the east.

"They are coming here to do this to us?"

"My lady," he said, "they will do this. This time they will not pass you by. This time they won't ignore this church as if it is nothing but a bad dream. This time they will tear down your walls and let the sun burn you. And then they will throw their weight against the Red Gate, and it, too, will fall. In a week the Hakkian flag will fly over the graves of both our peoples, and then we will be no more."

The murmuring around the room was like the hissing of a thousand snakes. Celissa sat down. Her glamour was back in place, but the face she wore was filled with grief.

"Then the world we know is at an end. How funny to learn, after all these years, that immortality is not a passage into eternity. There would have been a poem about hubris there, but it will never now be written. The Hakkians have no art, no poetry. They are barbarians."

"They are *human*, my lady. They can bleed."

"But we cannot fight them, as you have so told us with such brutal clarity."

Kellur smiled. He could feel the way that smile cut his face. He knew that it was an ugly smile. Humorless, grim. Kan looked at him and then quickly looked away.

"Why smile?" demanded Celissa. "Is this all some joke? Is that the purpose of your visit?"

"It is not, my lady. It's just that there is one thing we can do. There is one tactic we have not yet employed."

"What? Do you propose moving your army into our church? They would be killed when the walls fell, just as we will."

"No, my lady," he said. "I have read all of the old books, and I have consulted our priests and mages. Before I dared come here I learned everything I could about the Red Sisters. This is how I know what I know."

"To what end?"

He got to his feet and walked to the foot of the throne. As he came to a stop he jerked aside his scarf and bared his throat. "Take my blood."

She was so surprised that she laughed. The other witches chuckled.

"Father!" cried Kan. "What are you doing?"

"You came here to commit *suicide*?"

Kellur shook his head. "Only in a manner of speaking. I want you to make me what you are."

"You're insane," laughed the lady. "Or you haven't read enough? Did the books not tell you that men cannot become what we are?"

"I believe they can. There are tales of men who were

bitten and were thereafter transformed into monsters. They gained such power."

"And they *died*," she countered. "The magic does not work on them. They become like us for a few days only. Then the blood pours from their eyes and mouths and their bodies begin to burn."

"I know."

"They die in terrible pain. In agony. They die screaming, driven mad from pain before the sun burns them to ash."

"I know," repeated Kellur. He jerked his scarf off and threw it to the ground. "And I come here asking for that."

"Father," pleaded Kan, grabbing his arm.

"You are insane," said Celissa.

"Perhaps. But those old stories spoke of what happened before those men died. They were like the titans of old legend. They had the strength of fifty men. Arrows and spears could do them no harm. They fought without swords or spears, and none could stand before them. And they could stand in the sunlight."

"For how long? A day? Two at the most?"

Kellur nodded. "Yes. For that short a time." He put a foot on the lowest step of the throne. "Give me this gift. Give it to my son. We will then give it to the hundred strongest of my soldiers. This we will do on the eve before the Hakkians reach this pass. They will come in their thousands and we few, we hundred of the damned, will meet them there. Each of us with the power of fifty men. Each us indifferent to their swords. They will march against us, and here, right outside of the walls of your church, we will meet them One hundred monsters to defend your witches and our own folk."

Celissa was listening now. All of the witches were.

"If the Hakkians feared you before, imagine how they will fear you once a hundred of your demon soldiers go howling among them, tearing them limb from limb. Smashing their siege engines. Killing them. Washing this mountain in blood. How long do you think they will press their attack? How long do you think their courage will hold?"

Celissa watched, eyes bright as blood.

"All we need do is hold them here throughout the daylight hours. One day. And then when night falls, you can come from these halls to avenge your fallen sisters." Kellur bent and took her hand, kissed her fingers. The glamour that made her beautiful was for the eyes only and none of the other senses; his lips could feel the withered fingers and taste the ageless dust of her.

Behind him, he heard his son weeping. It broke his heart, but this was the end of the world.

"And your son?" asked Celissa gently.

"He is a soldier of Argolin. He will die either way. As a man, he would be swept away and forgotten. As a vampire . . . he will live forever in the histories and songs."

Celissa got to her feet and descended the steps until she stood eye to eye with him. She was a tall woman and, in her magicks, so beautiful. Her eyes blazed with such intensity that he could actually feel the heat on his skin.

"They say that the age of heroes has passed," she murmured, brushing hair from his face. "It has been generations since we sisters met a man we could admire.

A man with whom we would gladly share our gift if we thought he could share eternity with us."

Kellur said nothing. His heart was hammering in his chest.

"Neither our goddess nor your gods are kind to us, Kellur, Champion of the Faithful. They bring you to us, and now we must cast you into the dust of history."

"Yes, my lady, but at least this way there will *be* history."

She nodded.

Kellur reached back toward Kan and took his son's hand.

"Can you promise me that this will not hurt him?"

A fresh tear fell down Celissa's face. "No," she said. "I respect you—and him—too much to lie. Not now. Not at this moment."

Kellur heard his son sob. Just once. Then Kan's hand squeezed his. He believed that it was not the desperate clinging of a child but rather the firm grip of a man.

"Then let us write the next page of history," said Kellur.

★ **3** ★

Three days passed.

On the morning of the fourth, the Battle-King of the Hakkians rode his chariot into the pass. Behind him were the knights of his host and behind them the legions he commanded. The cathedral rose above them, and beyond that stood the Red Gate.

The Battle-King had expected the massed ranks of the Argolins to be waiting. He expected archers on the wall in their hundreds. He expected more than the hundred men who stood in a line across the throat of the pass.

The sun was hot above them, but the day was cold. Steam rose from the hundred men, as if they stood on the smoking ashes of some great fire. But the ground beneath them was dirt and grass.

Two men stood before the waiting hundred. A tall man and a boy. They looked like father and son, and they wore matching armor.

A general reined his horse beside the chariot. "What is this, my king? A party to sue for terms?"

"Who cares?" said the Battle-King in a bored voice. "These fools think they're going to get into one of their songs."

He spat upon the ground.

Movement caught his eye, and he turned to look up. On the walls of the cathedral several small windows opened, and the faces of old women watched from the shadows.

"Witches," he sneered. "Pass the word to begin assembling the siege towers."

The general nodded, then pointed his sword toward the Red Gate. "And what about those fools?"

The Battle-King waved a hand. "Oh . . . kill them all. Bring me their heads. We'll build a pyre with them. Let the witches and those behind the gate enjoy the smell."

The general grinned and spurred his horse toward his waiting captains. All of them laughed as they arranged their men for the charge. Only one of them did not. He frowned instead and when the general asked what was wrong, he nodded to the waiting hundred.

"None of them are wearing swords, sir. Have you noticed?"

The general shaded his eyes and looked. His smile flickered, but only for a moment. "Idiots. Ah well, it will be that much easier to cut them down. Signal the attack."

The call went out, and the knights moved aside to let the pikemen advance. Thousands of them.

The general raised his sword and then slashed down. The pikemen broke into a run, each of them yelling the name of their king.

The tall man and his son smiled at them as they came.

Only the front line of the pikemen saw those smiles as they closed in to kill. They saw how wide those smiles were.

And then they saw the teeth.

Oh gods, they saw those teeth.

By the time the general called up the heavy cavalry to try and rescue the pikemen, everyone had seen those teeth.

The Hakkians were no longer chanting the name of their king.

They were screaming it.

And they were damning it.

From the high walls, the witches of the Red Sisterhood watched the slaughter. And they waited for sunset.

★ ★ ★

ABOUT THE AUTHOR

Jonathan Maberry is a NY Times bestselling author,

multiple Bram Stoker Award winner, and Marvel Comics writer. He's the author of many novels, including *Assassin's Code, Flesh & Bone Dead of Night, Patient Zero* and *Rot & Ruin*; and the editor of *V-Wars: A Chronicle of the Vampire Wars*. His nonfiction includes books on topics ranging from martial arts to zombie pop-culture. Since 1978 he has sold more than 1,200 magazine feature articles, 3,000 columns, two plays, greeting cards, song lyrics, poetry, and textbooks. Jonathan continues to teach the celebrated Experimental Writing for Teens class, which he created. He founded the Writers Coffeehouse and co-founded The Liars Club, and is a frequent speaker at schools and libraries, as well as a keynote speaker and guest of honor at major writers' and genre conferences.

BLOOD, ASH, BRAIDS

★ ★ ★

Genevieve Valentine

1943

It didn't take them long to find a name for us; almost as soon as they knew it was women inside the rickety biplanes they couldn't catch, the Germans called us witches.

It was because of the sounds our idling planes made from the ground, the story went, as if the German soldiers had spent a lot of time with brooms and knew what they sounded like, engineless and gliding fifty feet above them in the dark.

(The wires holding the wings in place made the whistle. The canvas pulled taut around the plywood made the hush. I still suspect the thing that sounded supernatural was the whirr of our engines starting up again, as they realized we had already struck them, and it was too late to escape the blasts.)

The officer who told us had half a smile on his face; he'd thought of the job as a demotion—most of them did, at first, to be in a camp full of girls—but if the Germans were already bleating back and forth about bounties for the heads of the Night Witches, then maybe he had real fighters on his hands.

Popova cracked a laugh when she heard, turned to me with grin that was all teeth. "I like that," she said. "Should we start screeching when we sail through, do you think?"

"I think not," I said. "The best witches know not to give away their position." And she laughed a little louder than she had to, as if she thought it was actually funny.

A couple of the girls glanced over from across the runway. They never took Popova's cue in being kind to me, but they were never cruel, and that might have been all Popova could hope for.

"*She'd* love being called a witch by the enemy; she might already be one," Popova said after a second, sounding circumspect, sounding a little reverent.

(*She* was Commander Raskova; at some point, she hadn't needed a name any more.)

But Raskova was elsewhere now, with only her shadow cast over us. Bershanskaya was the commander who lined us up and sent us out. She was as steady as they came, and her humor was thin and dry as air.

The first time Bershanskaya heard the name, she raised an eyebrow, and glanced quickly at me before she turned to Popova. Then she nodded, hands behind her, and said, "Let them call us what they like, if it suits them."

"Suits me, too," said Popova.

It suited all of them, I think, even if I was the only witch the 588th ever had.

One of the important things about the 588th was how little it cared where you came from. If you could take the recruiter's withering stare and the doctors' lingering hands and the open loathing of the men who ran you through your paces, and you managed to crawl under the stalled train cars to reach the station from the farthest set of tracks they could find to park your train, by the time you got to Morozovsk they had no doubts about your nerves, and that was all they needed to know about you before they put you in a plane.

I'd come to the 588th out of necessity; my village had reached the end of their patience for someone who seemed always to know when it was going to rain and yet couldn't call it down for you even if you paid her. Easier to go find an open fight than to wait for the one that was brewing back home.

There was no way I could have accommodated village needs. It's too hard to do small magic.

From a one-room farmhouse or a palace in Moscow, anyone you ask will talk to you until their tongues turn blue about all the magic they've seen or heard of, even if they say they don't believe in it. They'll all know how it's being used against them even as they speak, and the hundreds of whispers shared in the depth of the forest by the witches, who gather there for market days and trade in secret spells in a currency of dirty looks.

It's all very well to keep people out of the woods at night, but it's foolish.

There are only three kinds of magic: water, ash, and air. For ash to work, you give blood. For water, you spill tears. For air, you give your breath. They all run out; our gifts are designed to be spent.

The woods will never be a gathering of witches. We don't live long enough.

Our planes were crop dusters, wood frames covered in canvas, held together with metal cords. They were the leftovers of aviation, planes given to people for whom no one had much hope.

But they were so flimsy, and so slow, that they made a kind of magic—gold out of hay. The German planes couldn't drop down to our speed or they'd stall out and plummet, so when they aimed for us we turned and they hit nothing but air; their anti-aircraft bombs would pop right through our canvas wings and keep going, bursting a hundred feet above us as we banked a turn and the explosion illuminated our path back home.

Raskova courted us with those planes, showed us how to make them spin and make lazy loops in the air like the plaits of a braid, leapt down from the cockpit with her dark eyes glittering behind her goggles, and you could hear her heart pounding even from where you were standing.

It was easy to want to go to war, to make Raskova proud.

And once you learned them, those planes were kinder to us than horses, and to sit inside one was to feel strangely invisible, a thrill crawling up the back of your neck like a ghost every time you settled in.

You settled in four, five, eight times a night: the plane couldn't carry more than two bombs at once, and you had work to do.

"You go out at sundown," says Bershanskaya.

Her lips are drawn thin, her hands folded behind her, her buttons marching a straight line to her chin.

(She didn't want to lead, when Raskova appointed her. She hated sending us out to die.)

It's a bridge; we all know why it has to disappear—the Germans can't be allowed to move anything else into place.

But they've stopped underestimating us, witches or not. They're prepared to throw us a flak circus now, every time they see us coming.

It's rows of guns blooming outward from the ground like flowers made from teeth, and searchlights by the dozens that flood the sky for fifty miles in each direction, and you can't get free of it no matter how you try; when you twist long enough this way and that way like a rabbit, you start to panic for your life.

We lost a team that way, not long back. Their cots are still folded up on the barracks, two thin mattresses for girls who won't be needing any more rest.

"You'll go in three planes at once," says Bershanskaya.

Next to me, the muscles in Popova's jaw shift as she realizes what Bershanskaya means.

Decoys. We'll be drawing fire in our little ghost planes.

We lost our hair to be here.

They made us cut it when we were first preparing for combat; for practicality, the commander said, though I had seen one or two of the training men glare at a line of girls walking off the field those first days, their long glossy braids swinging at their waists, and I always wondered.

I didn't mind, for myself—my hair was the watery brown of old deerhide, and there was no husband or want of a husband to stay my hand from the knife. For me to cut it just meant fewer pins I'd have to scramble for every time the sirens went up. But you can't tell girls for a hundred years that her hair is her crowning glory and then one day tell her to hack it off and not have her pause before the scissors.

We all did it, in the end, every last one of us submitting to the shears, slicing one another's braids off to the jaw.

Recklessly, I offered to burn the hair for any girl that wanted. It was forbidden to leave the base alone—it wasn't safe—but some things go deeper than regulations, and some superstitions aren't worth testing.

You never leave so much hair where anyone can take it from you; petty magic has uses for that, and none of them are good.

I was an odd fit in the barracks, just strange enough that we all knew I was strange, but this superstition was so well-known that not even Petrova looked twice at me as they each thanked me and handed me their braids of brown and black and gold.

As I headed for the woods with three dozen braids draped like pelts across my arms, Bershanskaya saw me.

She was standing outside, near the engineers who were patching the planes. Her hands were behind her, and she had the narrow-eyed look of someone who had been watching the sunset longer than was wise.

I held my breath and kept going. If she called out to stop me, I'd keep walking until she shot. Some orders are holy; I had a duty deeper than hers.

She didn't say a word, but she watched me carry the plaits like a sacrifice into the cover of the trees.

In the woods, I built a fire and burned them—one at a time, until there was nothing left. I didn't start a new fire for each plait (we were tied close enough to withstand a little ash), but it was powerful enough that I was careful. I breathed steadily in and out; I thought carefully about nothing at all.

When I came back after dark, stinking of singe, Bershanskaya was standing outside the barracks and scanning the edge of the woods, waiting.

"Commander," I greeted when I was close enough, and waited for whatever she would do to me.

For a long time she looked me in the eye until it felt like I was canvas stretched across a wooden frame, and I could feel the question building on her tongue in the space just behind her front teeth, where people's worst suspicions lived.

If she asks me, I thought, she'll have her answer.

(I could cut myself deep enough to bleed. Blood and tears would summon something, I could hope I had enough willpower to make her forget what I'd done.)

She stepped aside, eyes still on me, and as I passed she said my name low, like she'd checked my name off a very short list; like a spell.

Raskova would have asked me.

I don't know if that's better or worse.

In 1938, when I was still in school, Raskova had flown across the country for glory with Polina Osipenko and Valentina Grizodubova. When they were recovered after their landing, the news was everywhere: that she and her copilots had broken flight records in the *Rodina*, that it was a marvelous feat of flying, that they were heroes of the nation.

I didn't find out what had really happened until Raskova told me herself.

They had overshot in the mist, and when it parted they were suddenly over the Sea of Okhotsk, where the water in winter is the milky flat of a corpse's eye, and they didn't have enough gasoline left for the crossing—they'd flown too high to avoid being shrouded by the fog for a day and a night. They had to turn around and pray for landfall before they dropped out of the sky.

The navigator's seat—a glass bauble at the front of the plane—would be torn to shreds in a crash, and they were hurting for altitude and out of fuel and gathering too much ice to carry.

Raskova marked a map and jumped for it.

Her copilots crashed into the taiga, the bottom of the plane in shreds from the landing, and waited for her. Even after the rescue crew got to them, they refused to budge. They took watch by the plane for two more days, until Raskova staggered out of the woods.

It had been ten days. She'd had no food or water with her, and no compass when she jumped.

(There was no magic in her—not the sort that I had—

but you wonder about witch blood in some people, when they manage things that no one should have managed.)

But more amazing to me even than her ten-day journey was the ten-day vigil the other two had kept, sheltering with the plane that had tried to kill them, without enough supplies, without knowing if she would ever come.

Doubt gnawed at me whenever I thought about it, more doubts than I ever had about being shot at, more doubts than I had about my chances of loosing a bomb just where it needed to go.

How long would they have waited beyond ten days?

How long would I wait when it was my turn?

Would I walk ten days in the wilderness rather than lie down and die?

Osipenko was dead. (Wasn't even a strafing run; she'd just been going from one place to another, and her plane had turned on her.)

Grizodubova had been sent elsewhere for the war effort. None of us had ever seen her. She was leading a defense and relief outfit near Leningrad, with real bombers and not crop dusters. She was commanding men.

I wondered if she and Raskova ever saw each other, or if they wrote—if it was safe to write. It would be easy to forgive if they had parted ways; it was wartime, and their duty to the nation lay before them.

But sometimes the nights are long and dark, and you feel so alone that you think everyone else must have someone closer than you do, and you think: if they don't still speak, it's because they're both waiting for death, and can't bear to come close and then be parted.

Then you stare up at the leaking roof and wonder if all each of them carried now was a phantom. When something wonderful or terrible happened, did one of them sometimes glance over her shoulder to look at the other before she remembered she was alone?

Sebrova volunteers to be one of the three planes against the flak, and Popova volunteers second, and before I can do more than glance at Petrova for her agreement (she's already nodding at me) I'm volunteering, too, because I have few enough friends here. Where Popova is going, I want to go.

It's a foolish thing to do, volunteering to die on a German gun, but I volunteered for that a long time ago. I'm a quick draw on the controls, so I'll be of some use, and anything's better than sitting around waiting, wondering if Popova made it out.

Outside, I smoke a cigarette I won off Meklin at cards and watch the sun going down. I wish I had time to do everything that needs doing.

Popova sits next to me on the fence, lets out a breath at the streaks of gold and pink suspended just above the grass. When she taps me on the shoulder I hand her my cigarette.

She's a marvelous pilot—light and nimble—but you'd never know it from the way she smokes a cigarette, single loud pulls that leave a cylinder of ash that drops wholesale to the ground.

After a little while she hands me a piece of chocolate from inside her pocket, grainy and already melting across my fingertips. I pop it into my mouth and lick my fingers clean, flushing a little at the bad manners, but Popova only winks. I wonder how long she's held on to it, doling out to herself one piece at a time on nights she thinks she's going to die.

"You'll be all right," she says.

"Oh, I'm sure I will," I say. "It's you I worry over."

She casts me a look and half smiles.

My lungs are acrid, suddenly. I pinch off the end of my cigarette to preserve the rest.

She shrugs. "We never let them get any sleep," she says, jamming a pin into her cropped hair and wrenching her cap on over it.

(Petrova sometimes reaches behind her to smooth a braid that isn't there. I've never seen Popova do it.

I wonder what became of Raskova's dark brown braids, gleaming and pinned to her head as she spoke to us and made us into soldiers.)

Golden hair sticks out just at the edges, half curls below her ears. "I'd hate to see us coming, too. Let's hope they're too tired to aim."

I want to smile or laugh, but I'm staring at my plane and feeling ice down my spine. Why this should be so different I don't know—slightly more impossible than impossible isn't a measurement that has much meaning—but I look at the trees instead, after a moment.

"How did you decide to do this?"

I don't know why I ask. We're all meant to be without a past, and equal. They were carpenters and secretaries and farm girls, but they're pilots now, and it shouldn't matter how they got here.

Popova raises her eyebrows at the setting sun like it's

the one who'd asked the rude question. There are only a few minutes left until it's dark enough to load up and set off. I should be going back to barracks and getting my gear.

She says without looking at me, "A plane landed near our house, when I was young."

Young—she's nineteen now, I think, but I don't say anything. Rude to interrupt. Not that it matters; she doesn't elaborate. It's the biography of a masterful pilot who knows better than to waste a gesture.

She glances over. "And you?"

"Oh, I'm a witch," I say. "Flying comes naturally." And she grins as she drops from the fence, snaps her goggles into place.

"Good thing it can be taught," she says and takes off for her plane.

It can't, not really. You can teach the mechanics of a plane, but either you have the flight inside you or you don't.

Her strides kick up puffs of dust in her wake that cover her footsteps; at nightfall she casts no shadow, and for a moment she looks like I'd imagined witches to be, before I knew better.

When she's gone, I unroll the cigarette and scoop up her ashes from the ground with the blade of my knife.

It's a sharp blade; I never even feel the cut I make. When the paper gets wet enough, I use the tip of the knife to mix it and drag a line of blood and ash under the nose of Sebrova's and Popova's planes.

I do it quickly, my eyes stinging, my heart pounding.

Then they're coming from the barracks, and I'm out

of ashes and out of time and have to step away and get my gear. We'll need to make sure the altitude gauge is fixed before we're off the ground.

Petrova, my navigator, is already there, frowning underneath the propeller and tapping our windshields. As I haul myself onto the wing, I press one bloody thumbprint into the canvas just behind her seat, where she'll never see.

Blood magic doesn't work as well when you're asking for yourself, but I'll protect who I can, however it comes.

Each of us carries two bombs. It's decided in the last seconds before leaping into our planes that Sebrova will be first, I'll be second, and Popova will make the final drop, after they're already on to us.

I don't like it, but I keep my hands on the controls as we enter the flak zone.

The engines sound impossibly loud—three of them, and we don't dare cut them with what we have to do, so there's nothing for it but to go closer and closer, knowing they know we're coming, waiting for the bullets to start.

(I miss the sound of the wind through the wires; it had always sounded to me like an owl on my shoulder, and it was a comfort as you were moving in for the drop.)

The first floodlight is almost a relief—it's something to *do*, at least, instead of just something to be afraid of—and I wait two seconds longer than my instincts scream to, just enough that the nose of the plane catches the light, that it can almost but not quite follow me when I snap a turn to one side, dropping out of their sight. A spray of bullets arcs behind me, whistling clean and hitting nothing.

I don't look for Popova. It's not safe.

Instead I drop steeply so the searchlights casting at my prior heading can't find me, and pull up at the last second with my heart pounding in my throat and the engine grinding underneath me. I cut through three lights at once, a dead hover for a moment as gravity gets confused, the blinding flashes underneath us reminding me to bank left and out of the line of fire.

I hear a series of dull thunders, then a thudding rip—a wingtip's been struck. Nothing serious, it's a lucky hit for them, that's all, but my lungs go so tight I have to wrestle them for breath as I circle back. There's already ice on my tiny windshield; there's ice in my throat when I breathe.

Then I see Sebrova's plane arcing up to meet us. She's done it; the thunders were her bombs hitting home.

It's my turn.

Petrova gives me the all-clear, and I do a big, lazy loop well out of the scope of the spotlights—I glimpse Popova, barely, practically cartwheeling and vanishing into the dark—breathe deep through my nose as we sail over the iron garden. Sebrova's been kind enough to mark the way (a fire's already started next to the drop site), but I want to be careful, and only when Petrova gives the sign do I tilt us five degrees closer to the Earth, no more, and let the unfastened bombs slide forward, hurtling toward the ground with a cheerful whistle.

I sweep up and to the left, taking my place on the flank, and the plane shakes for just a second as the payload explodes, a warm burst of orange in the black night. Petrova whoops; I grin for as long as I can stand the wind in my teeth, which isn't long, and then push through the acrid scents of fire and guns and panic toward my secondary position.

Popova's plane drops so fast I think for a second, my grip seizing on the controls, that she's been struck, but it's just the way she handles a plane—I hear the whirr of her engines above the tuneless wind as I cut straight across and through the searchlights, distracting them from her, letting them waste two arcs of ammunition trying to pin me as I drop and spin out lazily, letting the wind pull us the last few inches to the top of the arc.

But it's too bright when I get there, far too bright, and I realize with numb panic that they've got me locked, and the next round of bullets will hit home.

I try for more altitude, already knowing I'm too late, and I wonder wildly if I can point the plane at the ground so hard that Petrova and I die without pain. We have to die—we can't let the Germans take us—but she shouldn't suffer.

Really, the way to go out is a bullet through the heart. The Germans could oblige. It would keep them from wondering where Popova's gone.

Better this than ten days in the wilderness, I think; better this than to wait at the Sea of Okhotsk.

I let out my breath until there's nothing left (blood-ash-air, I think dimly, someplace with no hope left, blood-ash-air), and bank the turn straight into the center of the circling lights.

I die that way, the way Raskova died—in combat, with a strike and a tailspin and then nightfall—but not on this run.

On this run, the spray of bullets never comes, because Popova's plane soars straight in front of me.

The Germans are only tracking two of our planes, and with the interruption they can't tell whether or not they've tricked themselves into a double image with the swinging searchlights, and in the few seconds where the lights freeze in place as they try to decide what to do, I bank as hard as I can and cut down and out and back into the dark, fingers aching, pointed for home.

We're the last to get back. When I climb out of the plane I can barely stand; I don't know where all my blood's gone. Bershanskaya's come to meet us. When she nods, I find it in me to straighten up and nod back.

Popova's leaning against her plane, a few feet back from the mark of my blood and her ashes that she'll never see. There are three bullet holes through one of her wings, like a smattering of freckles at the tip of someone's nose, but she's there.

She grins around a square of chocolate, calls over, "What kept you?"

I put blood and ashes on every plane that goes out after that.

Once I duck out between the planes and see Bershanskaya watching me, her hands behind her. She doesn't ask what I'm doing there. I never say. It doesn't matter. It's what I've given over, and you can't call it back.

It's on my plane, too, the night I go down, but I never expected that to protect me for long. They all run out; our gifts are designed to be spent.

★ ★ ★

A little while from now, Popova will go on a raid and get caught in German fire. When she makes it back to the base, there will be more than forty bullet holes in the plane. There are bullet holes in her helmet.

No one will understand how she survived it; no one can imagine what protected her.

★ ★ ★

ABOUT THE AUTHOR

Genevieve Valentine is the author of *Mechanique: a Tale of the Circus Tresaulti*, which won the 2012 Crawford Award; her second novel, *The Girls at the Kingfisher Club*, came out in 2014, and will be followed by the political thriller *Persona*. Her short fiction has appeared in *Clarkesworld, Lightspeed, Nightmare, Fantasy Magazine*, and *Strange Horizons*, and the anthologies *Armored, Federations, Teeth*, and *The Mad Scientist's Guide to World Domination*, among others, and has been reprinted in several Best of the Year anthologies. Her nonfiction has appeared at NPR, The AV Club, LA Review of Books, and io9.

MERCENARY'S HONOR

★ ★ ★

Elizabeth Moon

Ilanz Balentos looked at the wall around Margay and nodded his approval. It wasn't the best city wall he'd ever seen, but it was a start, a good start for a town that had been under Vonja's so-called protection for many years. The town's leading merchants smiled. A wall—a defensible wall—had been one of his requirements before he would commit to living here the rest of his life and protecting people as they should be protected.

"You will sign the contract?" asked Ser Unglent, head of the local council.

"I will. You have done well. What did the Vonja militia think of it?"

"They told us we could not have a wall and were going to make us tear it down. We gave them wine, and when they slept the lads took their weapons and next day—"

"Did you kill them all?"

"Kill? No! But we showed them we were more than they, and held their weapons, and they went away."

Ilanz winced inside. Civilians. If they had killed Vonja's militia rather than shaming them, Vonja might have let them alone. "Vonja will send more—perhaps even another mercenary company."

"But you are here."

"Yes. And we will protect you." That was the bargain: Margay to become his domain, and his own home, and his troops—or some of them, the ones who would stay when there was no promise of plunder—would protect them. Margay independent, as it had been once, rather than paying taxes to a distant city that never bothered to care for it. "Did you find that wizard you spoke about last time?"

"No . . . we sent an envoy to Sorellin's fair, and he asked, but the wizard said we were too small and could not pay enough."

Bad news, but not too bad. Vonja never took wizards on campaign anyway. Ilanz could protect Margay without a wizard's tricks.

He signed the contract, stamped it with his seals—the seal of the company he had commanded for thirty-one years, and the new seal he'd had made, naming him Count Margay. The merchants had already signed, and then there was handshaking and talk and food and drink until at last he could climb up the stairs to the bedroom in the house he had chosen.

The long plan had come to fruition. He gave a thought to the mercenaries Vonja had hired this year to do the work their own militia should be doing: protect farmers from brigands and incursions from neighboring lands, policing traffic on their sections of the Guild League trade roads. Halveric Company had been in Aarenis only five campaign seasons, but already had a good reputation. Ilanz had no doubt he and his could defeat Halveric, if it came to it, if the Council at Cortes Vonja sent them this way, but he hoped it would not come to that. He had met the young man in Valdaire several times and liked what he knew of him.

The wall was an arm's-length higher by the time Ilanz's scouts saw Halveric Company marching up the road from Pler Vonja. Ilanz wondered what Vonja had told him about Margay. Almost certainly not the whole truth, knowing Vonja's history.

The younger commander had sense: he stopped a prudent distance away and sent two scouts forward at night, both circling wide of the town. One was captured after he stumbled into a large bramble patch and made so much noise Ilanz's own militia could not resist "rescuing" him. They sent him back to his own camp. The other was seen only as a shadow in shadows, heading for the Sorellin border. Of course the young commander would want to know if Sorellin backed Margay. Perhaps his men would catch this one on the way back.

Perhaps he could send a message to young Halveric that way. If they come to battle, it would be a bloody business, killing a lot of good mercenaries for the profit of Vonja in the Guild League . . . and maybe that was what Vonja planned. Some realms hated and feared mercenaries, even if they hired them. If that was Vonja's plan, weakening or destroying two competent mercenary companies —then not only Halveric but other companies were at risk. He paced his office, on the second level of his new house, thinking out the possibilities, and finally sat down to write a message. He would send it even if his people didn't catch that scout. For the rest of the day, he went out in the town, chatting with his citizens and his own soldiers. At dinner, he told his captains his plan to attempt a truce with Halveric.

"I'm not sure, Commander . . . my lord, I mean."

Ilanz waved his hand. "Never mind formalities. This is a military conversation. What's your assessment of young Halveric?"

"Smart, tough, increasingly competent, and . . . a very solid sense of honor. I cannot see him breaking a contract, even with Vonja."

"He has presented himself as a man of honor, that is true," Ilanz said. "But there is more than one kind of honor. If, as I suspect, Vonja has lied to him, has broken faith with him, I think—I hope—he will see that keeping faith with the faithless is foolish and merely teaches our employers that they can break their word to us with impunity." He spread his hands on the table, the scarred hard hands of a man thirty years a mercenary. One finger missed a joint, two had healed crookedly from being broken. "If he does not, we will have to fight him, and that will cost us. And him. And possibly the town as well, not only from the losses to our force, but . . . well . . . nothing in war is known until the battle's over."

Finally, late that night, he went to bed, leaving the single lamp burning as always. He had to know, the instant he awoke, if he still had sight in one eye or had gone completely blind. He set his town shoes by the table, his boots at the end of the bed, his sword in the fold of blanket. Then he slept.

He woke facedown in his bed, a weight on his back and his wrists already bound. Whoever was there breathed heavily, had sweaty hands and a very sharp knee, and smelled of blood and unwashed male. He tried to twist his wrists free, and the weight shifted. A dagger tip lay under his right ear, just firm enough to make it unmistakable.

"Be quiet."

He nodded. By the feel, the bindings on his wrist were no thicker than shoelaces. He could break those later, when the dagger was not so near his life. Weight left his back as whoever it was climbed off the bed, but the dagger's touch never left his neck. Someone with experience, then. A thief in his town? He was incensed; even a thief should recognize that Ilanz was the town's only hope of freedom.

"Who are you?" the voice demanded. "Tell me true. Will they ransom you?"

Ransom? What was this?

"Sit up!" the voice went on. "I want to see your face." A hand grabbed his shoulder, tugged. Ilanz rolled with the tug, giving momentary thought to the attack he could make as he rolled over and up to sitting, but the first glimpse of his assailant put that out of mind. He saw a stripling boy, his face disfigured by a rapidly swelling bruise from brow to cheekbone on the right side, but on the left—he knew that face, though the boy's sweat-darkened hair looked more brown than red in the lamplight.

"You're Halveric's squire," he said, keeping his voice low. "The redhead."

"You're Commander Balentos," the lad said. "I saw you in Valdaire."

Ilanz sent a quick prayer of thanks to Simyits; the trickster god had favored him once again. He could see now that the squire had one sleeve of a peasant shirt half torn off, and blood marked it.

"Did you come to kill me?" he asked. If Halveric had sent an assassin, he had misjudged Halveric's character and would have to change his plans.

"No!" That sounded genuine, disgust and anger mixed. "I didn't know you were here until I . . . well, I was running away from them."

From Ilanz's own troops, presumably. "Why did you come into town?"

"They made me. I had to get away—"

"Well . . . what are you going to do now?"

He could practically see the thoughts running through the boy's head, the kind of thoughts any young squire would have. The boy had found and disabled the enemy commander . . . which in some circumstances would make him a hero . . . or dead. Glory, danger, fear, pride. What next? Would he think to kill Ilanz, threaten him and demand his own freedom, or—

"I will take you to my commander," the boy said.

Of course. Ilanz almost grinned; instead he nodded, keeping his expression serious. "That is a sensible thing to do."

"Sir—I mean—"

"Your commander needs to know what he faces here. I am the best person to tell him. You think clearly, young man. What is your name?"

A moment of silence; the boy started to scowl, then winced at the pain. How bad was that injury? Would the boy lose that eye? Then he answered. "Kieri Phelan . . . sir."

Mannerly, intelligent . . . Halveric must be a good teacher, as well as a good commander. And the boy himself was far out of the ordinary. High-born, almost certainly, and possessed of something very like the magery that cropped up now and again in Ilanz's own family.

"We cannot just go down and out the front, Kieri," Ilanz said. "My soldiers are too many for you to hold me at hazard if they see you. They would kill you to free me. How did you get in? Can we get out that way?"

"I . . . think so. Yes."

"Good. We should start. Only . . . I need something on my feet. I cannot walk to your camp barefoot." He looked at the floor beneath the table . . . there were his shoes, and sure enough the laces were missing. "Let me stick my feet in those—"

"You won't try to escape?"

Ilanz managed a shrug. "I have been wondering how to contact your commander. And here you are, offering to lead me. Although, as part of your education as squire, Kieri, you should not trust me. I might, after all, turn on you, grab that dagger, tie *your* hands, and march you straight up to your commander, which would be a disgrace, would it not?"

The boy's mouth quirked. "It would . . . and I do not intend to let that happen. There's a sword in your bed; I felt it when I climbed on—"

Ilanz shook his head. "Advice, and I swear by Tir it's true: do not take my sword. It is much easier to disarm a man with a sword than a man with a dagger, if you have my experience. Everything in this room is a weapon to me, were I free. Also—just to show my honesty in this— if I should stumble, do not out of pity unbind my hands. There is no one in all Aarenis who could govern my movements were I unbound." He watched the boy's face, saw comprehension as quick as he'd hoped. "Of course, that means you will have to help me put on those shoes." He stuck out one foot, and waited.

Another pause he did not quite understand, then the boy knelt, keeping his gaze on Ilanz's face, and picked up both shoes. Far more deftly than Ilanz expected, he slipped one shoe on the foot, then—as Ilanz put that foot down and lifted the other—put the other shoe on the other foot. For a wonder, he had them on the correct feet. Not everyone wore such shoes, but Ilanz had a bony growth on one foot that made them necessary.

"May I stand?" Ilanz asked.

"Make no rash moves," the boy said. "Over there, where a panel is open, stairs go down. Quietly . . ."

The night air was more chill than Ilanz expected, and somewhere in the walk to Halveric's camp he got a small sharp stone in his left shoe. Simyits's price for the help earlier, he supposed. He'd paid more, in the past. Halveric's sentries were alert; he approved the way they reacted to the discovery of an enemy commander, barelegged in a nightshirt, being guided and guarded by a boy. No smirks, no laughter, but an escort to Halveric's tent.

Halveric was awake by the time they got there, boots on his feet and his shirt at least partly tucked into his trousers. Ilanz saw Halveric's eyes widen as he recognized Ilanz. Ilanz inclined his head.

"Commander Halveric," he said.

"Commander Balentos. I am . . . surprised."

"So would I be. Of your courtesy, if I give my pledge, could your men unbind my hands? I am, as you see, without weapons. And there is a stone in my left shoe."

"Donag," Halveric said. "Free Commander Balentos."

Ilanz stood still as two other soldiers stepped forward, swords out, and one moved behind him. He felt the cold edge of a dagger slide between his wrists and the thongs that bound them.

Halveric spoke to someone inside the tent. "Garris?"

A boy's voice answered. "Yes, m'lord?"

"Light us a lamp in the tent, and set up another chair."

Ilanz's hands fell free; he rubbed his wrists. Halveric's soldier put the cut pieces of shoelace in his hands and saluted, an unexpected courtesy. Halveric, he saw, had looked past him to his captor.

"Kieri, I am sure you have a report to give, but see the surgeon first, clean up, and dress."

"It's not my blood, m'lord," the boy said. "Or most of it isn't."

"That was an order, Squire." The boy bowed and left them. Then, to Ilanz, "He wasn't supposed to go into the town after you—he was supposed to go around the town to the border and find out if Sorellin troops were waiting to move in. Please—come into my tent and take some refreshment." He pulled the tent flap aside.

"He told me how he came to be sitting on my back tying my wrists," Ilanz said, limping forward. "I do not blame you; I did not think you were the sort to send an assassin. As it is, I am glad to have a chance to talk to you; there's a letter to you on my desk back there, which I had meant to send you tomorrow."

Halveric's tent was the size Ilanz's captains used—just one large room, with two cots on either side and room for a table and chairs in the middle. Ilanz sat down on one chair and kicked off his left shoe; the stone fell out. He looked at his foot—no blood, just a sore spot—and put the shoe back on.

Halveric poured wine and then water into two mugs and nodded to Ilanz. Ilanz picked up one; Halveric took the other, and they both sipped. "Would you like a robe?" Halveric asked.

Ilanz laughed. "Would I like a robe? I tell you, Commander Halveric, what I would *like*. I would *like* to be asleep in my own bed, wake up tomorrow after a full night's sleep, send you my letter, and hear in return that you agreed there was no profit in an assault on my town. That is what I would *like*."

Halveric looked back at him. "I have a contract," he said.

"Yes, of course you do. You contracted with Vonja— everyone in Valdaire knew they had come to you, and I would almost lay odds—though Simyits has been

generous to me already tonight—that I know what they
offered and what you argued them up to. I suspect they
called you in when their troops came home empty-handed
and offered you a bonus to put down a rebellion up here
in Margay."

"They did." Halveric nodded. "But they did not tell me
you were here. I had suspected your presence, and while
we are being so open, I know you have more troops, and
archers, than you had last year."

Ilanz chuckled. "I knew you were good. A squire like
that red-haired lad is more useful picking information out
of gossip than a trained spy, isn't he?"

"Several of them are," Halveric said. He got up and
pulled a box out from under a cot with the covers all in a
jumble. His, no doubt. While he rummaged inside,
Balentos looked at the others: one squire snoring, a much
younger one sitting up bright-eyed and curious on the
most distant cot. The tent was orderly, but spare. Halveric
had, he suspected, poured every nata of profit into his
men's equipment and supplies. A good way to start, but
now he should be learning to show his status.

The robe Halveric brought was broad enough—
Halveric was his match in shoulders and chest—but short.
Still, he looked and felt less like a beggar and more like a
guest with it on.

"So," Halveric said when he sat down again, dropping
two long leather thongs on the table in front of Ilanz.
"What was in your letter?"

Ilanz picked up a thong and threaded it through the
slits in one shoe. "I will be brief. Years ago, when I myself
held a contract with Vonja, I was sent up here to deal with

a border issue with Sorellin, and first saw Margay. Just such a place, I thought, as I would like to retire in, but very badly governed. They saw the tax collectors and the militia escorting them twice in the year, but no help whatever with Sorellin incursions or brigands down from the mountains." He picked up the other thong and refastened his other shoe.

Halveric nodded but said nothing.

"So a few campaign seasons ago, when I heard rumors of the town considering rebellion, I made a short visit. By myself. They remembered me; I had occasionally visited before. I talked to their town council, and we came to an agreement. The protection I could give, in trade for their allegiance to me as a lord. I advised them on fortifications—how to build new houses, how to arrange the town a little differently, how to build a wall. We set up regular courier contact."

"You . . . *encouraged* them to rebel?"

"They were going to anyway. And in this location they would be constantly harassed by Vonja and Sorellin squabbling over them. You know where that leads."

"Yes," Halveric said. "Destruction, ruined crops, dead civilians."

"I can prevent that," Ilanz said. He straightened, easing his back. "Maybe even long enough for it to last, though I can't promise. Didn't promise. And I will tell you what I think, from your expression, you have already seen in the light of this lamp: I am going blind. One eye already—and all the gold I spent for wizards' potions and spells and the prayers of every priest who would listen only slowed the blindness. They tell me the other eye will go as well, and cannot tell me how long—a few years, perhaps ten. That's why I decided on this, a place I could stay and defend. I don't need two good eyes for that. So—you said Vonja lied to you about the situation up here?"

"Greedy merchants who didn't want to pay taxes, maybe gulled by Sorellin, which has sought to encroach before. Small town, hardly more than a village, just a waystation on the north trade route, no war experience, no fortifications, should be simple." Halveric said that in a mincing falsetto. Then he grinned, showing teeth. "I don't believe it when someone says it will be simple."

"Mmm. Have you seen Margay since your own last visit—four years ago, wasn't it?"

"No."

"We now have a wall well over man-high, with appropriate reinforcement at the gates. Streets redesigned for defense, with some fortified buildings. Ample stores and water to withstand a siege . . . and my troops."

Halveric uttered something in a foreign tongue that crackled with anger.

Ilanz didn't need to know the words; he knew the tone. "You run a good company, Commander Halveric," he said. "I do not think it is as good as mine—that comes with more experience—but on some days you might defeat us. A battle between us could be—would be—ruinous for us both." He paused. Would Halveric get the point? Would he say it if he did?

"You think Vonja wants us to destroy each other?"

"I wish I knew Sorellin's role in this," Ilanz said, stretching his legs. "Do they want Margay for themselves?

They did once. Or do they agree with Vonja that there's a danger of mercenaries becoming too powerful?"

"Their envoy said they had no interest in Margay, but refused to say Sorellin would not let Margay in if it won free of Vonja."

"They still want it, then. And if Margay is weakened enough by a battle between your people and mine, they may come and take it."

Halveric sat forward. "Look here . . . it's clear you want me to break my contract and just go away—"

Ilanz shook his head. "No. You are smart enough to know Vonja will have spies out in the hills—Sorellin will, too. I think you should proceed as you would have, up to a point: send out scouts, discover that the town is heavily fortified and defended, and—what would you do then?"

Halveric shrugged. "My contract requires me to try to take it, reduce the rebellion, and bring the guilty parties to Pler Vonja."

"Yes. And if they had told you the truth about what you faced up here, would you have accepted the additional assignment?"

"I . . . probably not. We've never fought you, but we've heard from those who have. . . . You need a twenty percent advantage to win and fifty percent to win cleanly. And that's at the size you were before you hired more men last winter."

"So Vonja's lies put you in a situation where you must either break a contract—risking your reputation—or fight a battle against a superior force—risking not just lives but your company's existence. Because you know, as well as

I, how many you would lose in a direct confrontation. Do you know what Guild League law says about parties to a contract?"

"Does it say if one lies about its part the other can wiggle out of an obligation?" Halveric's jaw muscles bunched.

"More than that. The party misrepresenting serious danger may be brought before the Guild League's High Court and may be judged fraudulent, penalized with high fines, some portion of which comes back to the injured party. At least, I would think, the amount of your bonus and the unpaid part of your base contract." Ilanz took another swallow of the watered wine. Halveric's face had gone blank, his eyes mostly hidden beneath lowered lids. "And yes, a mercenary company has brought such an issue before the High Court and won. It doesn't make friends of the employer, but it does make the point that we are not mere sword-wheat, to be scythed down for profit." Another swallow, another glance at Halveric's face. The eyes were open now, watching him, the expression wary. "I know a judicar in Valdaire familiar with the law involved."

"*You* did that?"

"I was much younger and very, very angry. I lost a cohort of good men. So whatever Vonja really meant by this—was it just laziness and cowardice, or actual malice?—you should be aware of the legal situation."

"I have never broken a contract." Pride in that, but pride overlaying anger. No man could be happy with employers who lied to him, who knew a danger and did not reveal it.

"That is a good thing," Ilanz said. "A very good thing, but—" He raised a finger. "But you have another contract, do you not, with your men? And if you have a conflict of contracts, the one no commander should ever break is the one with his men. You are their only safety, their only hope. They depend on you in a way no employer does. You stand between them and an employer who would abuse them."

Halveric said nothing, staring at him, or through him; it was hard to see in the lamplight. All at once Ilanz felt old, exhausted. He felt the soreness where the stone had been; his back hurt; his eyes burned. Halveric was young and had his pride, a young man's pride; perhaps he himself had pushed too hard. His stomach rumbled suddenly, loud enough to be heard, and Halveric glanced at it, then back at Ilanz's face.

"I am sorry," he said. "My hospitality failed—and I am hungry, when I wake this time of night. I will send for food." Halveric's voice was gentle, courteous, but carried no other meaning, agreement or disagreement. Before Ilanz could think what to say, Halveric was already standing, moving to the tent door, speaking softly to the man outside. When he came back to the table, Halveric spoke to the boy still sitting on his cot. "Go to sleep, Garris. Tomorrow will be busy." The boy scrambled back under his covers and rolled over.

"It won't be much, this time of night," Halveric said, in the same easy tone. "But we will both be better for some ballast to the wine, watered as it was."

"Your squire who brought me—Kieri, he said his name was—is that your son?" The boy looked nothing like

Halveric, but perhaps the mother was very light. Ilanz wondered if she had also been a mage, or even perhaps an elf.

"No."

"He is . . . unusual. Remarkable, I would say, for a boy his age. There is power in him. He will be a fine commander some day, I judge, if he does not have a domain to take over when he inherits."

Halveric's expression sharpened. "Why do you say that?"

"What he said to me—how he was captured, how he escaped, and then how quickly he took advantage when he found himself in a room with a strange man asleep. From the way he carries himself, I would think his father a rich man, possibly even a king."

For a moment Halveric said nothing, then: "No, alas. If he . . . if he had an inheritance, it was lost to him. He came to us—to my home in the north—as a waif, homeless and hungry."

"Even more remarkable, then. You have done very well, to take such a one and turn him into this. May you have many sons, for you deserve them."

Even in lamplight, he could see a flush rise on Halveric's cheeks. "I did no more than any man would."

"My lord, here is food—" Kieri entered with a tray piled with raggedly-cut bread and pots Ilanz hoped contained honey or jam or even pan drippings.

"What did the surgeon say, Kieri?" Halveric asked as the boy put the tray on the table and stood back.

"I am fine," the boy said. When Ilanz looked at his face, his eye had swollen completely shut now, and the bruise on that side of his face had darkened more. "I am not to get hit in the face again for four hands of days, he said."

Halveric handed a slice of bread drizzled with honey to Ilanz and another to the boy. "Here, Kieri—you must be hungry. Eat this and lie down, get some rest."

The boy took his slice of bread to his cot and ate. Ilanz bit into his slice and had finished that and another one before Halveric spoke again. The food settled his stomach and cleared his head.

"It is getting toward dawn," Halveric said first. "Cooks will be starting breakfast—there'll be more than just bread and honey then." He finished his own slice of bread, took a swallow of the watered wine, cleared his throat. "I . . . understand what you said. And I am trying to think clearly. And admitting to myself that you are my elder, who—assuming you to be honest, and I have no reason to think you are not—knows more of Aarenis and war than I do, young as I am. About honor—yes, my people deserve my care absolutely. And yes, Vonja lied to me. But the contract—it is not a matter of law only, you see. I must feel that my gods agree."

Ilanz nodded. "I understand. That is exactly what a man of honor must do. I do not know what gods you follow . . ."

"I am Falkian. Do you know of Falk?"

"Indeed—the story is well-known in Aarenis. He served in place of his brothers, and they repaid that sacrifice with scorn."

"Yes. And so keeping a promise means a great deal to Falkians. To break one for any reason is a serious matter."

A pause Ilanz did not dare to break. Then Halveric sighed. "And yet I believe that you have the right of it, that my duty to my people is far greater than my duty to Vonja, who lied to me. So tell me what it is you were thinking of—though I admit I am not happy if that means us turning tail and running away."

"It is not that," Ilanz said. "Here is what we might do instead."

Ilanz rode up to the gates of Margay on one of the captains' horses, wearing clothes borrowed from one of Halveric's soldiers and his own shoes with new laces. The guards at the gate gaped and wanted to ask questions.

"I haven't time," Ilanz said. "I've been to parlay with Halveric, and there's much to do. Send someone to fetch the captains; meeting in my office in half a sun-hand."

Halveric would be meeting with his captains by now, he was sure. He wished he could have stayed for that, but he was needed here. Already people were on the street, startled to see him riding an unfamiliar horse, wearing unfamiliar clothes. He smiled at them, greeted the ones he knew, but did not stop.

At the door of his own house stood a cluster of people with worried faces; they turned at the sound of hooves. "Sir—my lord—where you been?" Kemin, retired sergeant and now his servant, sounded half frightened and half angry.

"Preventing disaster, I hope," Ilanz said. He dismounted. "This fellow needs a bit of grain and a rub-down. I need breakfast, a bath, and my own clothes—I have a captains' meeting very shortly."

Someone came to take the horse; Kemin followed him into the house and upstairs. "Sir, please—"

"I had a busy night," Ilanz said. "But I'm here now, and you're welcome to sit in on the captains' meeting. Right now—a bath."

Bathed, dressed again, a platter of stirred eggs and ham consumed, he went down to his office and met the worried gaze of his captains. Before they could speak, he held up his hand. "We have a rare opportunity," he said. "And we must prepare at once. Halveric Company's commander has agreed to my proposal."

"They're leaving?"

"Not immediately." Ilanz outlined the situation— Vonja's lies, Halveric's contract, the certain presence of Vonjan spies—and his own solution.

"A mock battle?" Meltarin, his senior captain, scowled. "You trust them to hold to the bargain? Halveric hasn't broken a contract yet, and they're a good company."

"He has more reason to distrust me than I to distrust him. And he took my point about his honor being tied to his men as well as to his employer. Now—here's the plan." Ilanz outlined it quickly; his experienced captains understood at once, and he released them to complete their parts of it, then instructed his majordomo to block up the entrance Kieri had used, posted two guards outside his bedroom, and went back to sleep for a few hours.

By the morning of the battle, two Vonja and two Sorellin spies had been caught and isolated in the town, high enough in the other tower house to see beyond the wall, but with only one small slit window to look out of.

Ilanz had inspected the view from that window. It would have been easier to fake a battle if he'd been able to hire a wizard, but a narrow window high up would do. The local rag-picker had been paid for his entire stock of old clothes and ripped blankets; the local farmers had moved their flocks away from the designated field of battle, and the local butchers, though puzzled, contributed offal, skins, and jugs of blood.

Ilanz woke well before dawn, dressed and armed himself, and came down to find his men all in place, having eaten a battle meal just after the turn of night, as usual. He ate his own breakfast, then—as the sun rose through layers of mist—climbed to the top of the wall. Yes. There was Halveric Company's vanguard, exactly as agreed. Someone on a gray horse—Halveric himself, he thought—rode along the line.

Ilanz grinned, then walked along his own defenses, reminding his men to keep their swords scabbarded unless he himself gave the order to draw them or they were attacked with bare steel. They grinned back at him. Then he spoke to his council, reminding them that everyone but troops must stay indoors. "Do not mind the noise," he said. "There will be yelling and screaming and other noises. If they get so far, there may be pounding at the gates. Do not worry. I know all that is happening, and you will be safe."

They nodded, not looking particularly confident except for a group of young men who had staves in hand and had been—he knew—part of the group that had sent the Vonja militia home weaponless. "I'm sorry," Ilanz said now to that group. "You also must stay out of this. These are hardened soldiers come against us, not the Vonja militia. We will defeat them, but you are not, forgive me, a match for them. Later, you may join the militia here. Go home and protect your own houses from within."

Halveric's vanguard advanced, then halted suddenly, as if noticing the town's fortifications for the first time. Four men on horseback rode closer, halting outside bow range and peering at the wall, hands up to shield their eyes from the sun. Three rode away from the one on the gray horse, parallel to the wall around the town, then rode back to report. Arms waved. Hands pointed. It was, Ilanz thought, a masterful job of acting out disagreement in command and the senior commander's power to settle it.

He noticed also that Halveric had figured out which wooded rise Ilanz had placed several tens of archers on, and avoided giving them a close, easy flanking shot. Good thinking . . . but he had not anticipated the second trap. Ilanz's half-cohort of mounted archers swept in on Halveric's vanguard from the sun side, and in seconds the battle was truly joined; instantly the morning quiet shattered into the sounds of battle: screams, bellows, horses' whinnying, hoofbeats, the thud of weapons on weapons and bodies. Flocks of birds burst from every tree and bush, adding to the confusion.

Halveric responded with an instant half-turn, facing three ranks of the vanguard cohort into the sun . . . excellent training and practice, Ilanz thought, and glanced up at the prisoners' window. They would see only part of that, which was exactly what he wanted. And then Halveric's surprise took his own in the flank—up from the tall grass sprang Halveric's own archers. Riders fell, infantry fell, and Halveric Company marched on, nearer, fending off the flank attack. The noise grew louder, the familiar sounds he had known so long. So far it seemed both sides fought with blunted weapons, not bare steel, but the prisoners should not be able to tell that at this distance.

Another cohort came into view. Ilanz signaled his nearest captain, lowered his own helm, and nudged his mount—Halveric's captain's mount—forward. His senior captain would lead the other half of those in town out the gate on the other side of town, supposedly out of Halveric's sight, though he knew the gate was there. Would he think of it?

Along with Ilanz's troops came both two-wheeled handcarts and wagons bearing his physicians and their gear, spare weapons, and the rags and offal and sheepskins and pots of blood he had ordered collected, all positioned on the far side of the troops from the prisoners' window.

As the sun climbed up the sky, the battle raged, noise and confusion, dust and smoke. At times the two armies pulled back, and water carriers ran up and down the ranks. Scattered bodies lay in the grass, some moving feebly and others motionless. Overhead, scavengers appeared, wheeling high over the battlefield, then swooping low to check out any unmoving body. A few even landed to start pecking.

Cohorts and parts of cohorts maneuvered, struggling for advantage, but as midday passed, it was clear that Halveric could not advance all the way to the walls, and had, indeed, been pushed back half the width of the big pasture. In midafternoon, they began a disciplined withdrawal; Ilanz's forces made short dashes at them, but did not press the pursuit. It looked as though the Halverics had lost almost a third of their force, leaving the brown-clad troops in command of the field, and well before dusk the Halverics had returned to the previous night's camp, helping their wounded. War-crows and vultures descended on the motionless figures. A half-glass later, Halveric appeared again, with a red flag, and Ilanz met him mid-field. He was glad to see that Halveric looked as dirty and tired as he himself felt. Practice or not, it had been a long, hard fight.

"A good training exercise," Ilanz said. "I had good reports of your company before, and now I know those were not exaggerated."

Halveric nodded. "I learned from you. You nearly took us at the start—I knew you had archers, but not mounted ones. Where did you hide the horses last night?"

"Two hills back." Ilanz pointed. "But your counter-flanking movement was excellent. I knew you had anticipated my archery contingent in the woods—"

"May I just ask how many extra troops you got last winter? Were we really outnumbered, or are yours that much better?"

Ilanz laughed. "You were outnumbered. I hired fifteen tens, sent ahead in small groups, over the winter. No shame to you for needing to withdraw."

"Well, that's good to know." Halveric grinned back. "I thought we could hold longer than we did at evens."

"How much damage?" Ilanz asked. "We had some broken bones and a lot of bruises—outnumbered or not, your troops fight very well."

"Much the same, but for one death. Hit square in the throat on a backswing—choked—"

"That's bad . . . did you get him back?"

"Yes. Carried as wounded."

"Good. We can let the scavengers do their worst, then. Will you come to supper tonight?"

"Tomorrow, I think. Frankly, all I want now is a bath and a good sleep."

"I, also. Tomorrow, then."

The Captains' Banquet had been a great success; Halveric's captains and his own had exchanged names and stories, congratulated one another on the performance of their cohorts, and at a nod from Halveric had excused themselves to go back to the camp, picking up any stray Halverics along the way. The prisoners would not be able to see any of the festivities.

Now Halveric and Ilanz had the terrace to themselves as the long summer twilight lingered and a fresh scent of green leaves and fruit came from the lower end of the house's walled garden. Ilanz sent thanks to Simyits and Tir, that they dined as friends, that only one had died in the training exercise. And thanks also that he would have, for the rest of his life, a place of his own. No more need to spent half a year in a tent, the rest in rented lodgings. When his sight failed, he would have this place, where he would know every wall, every door . . . and a sweet-scented garden. He drew a deep breath and let it out slowly.

He felt gratitude to Aliam Halveric as well, and hoped the younger man would accept a little more advice. Two things, in particular. He glanced over. Aliam, as he now called him, leaned back in his chair, legs stretched out before him. He looked like someone contemplating both success and a new worry.

"If I may," Ilanz began.

Aliam gave him a lazy smile. "If you're going to offer me more advice, Ilanz, go ahead. Your advice has been to my advantage so far."

"Well, then. You need a new tent, a tent fit for the commander you are, and will become: in your own colors, at least three rooms, and the front one kept for the reception of visitors. Table or two, chairs, your weapons on display, space to store maps and so on."

"I thought you were looking down your nose at my tent."

"No—I understood you spent first on your men and their needs, and that is good. So did I, when I began. But to deal with merchants who care more for gold than anything else, you must make a show."

Aliam nodded. "I'll take your advice, and, as soon as I can, I'll order such a tent."

"And . . . one other thing."

"Yes?"

"In Valdaire, I have four more years' winter lease— Evener to Evener—of a caravanserai large enough for your company. I know you asked about it. But now, I will not need it. If you still want it, I will give you a note to the owner's factor: you can take over the lease." Aliam opened his mouth, and Ilanz shook his head before Aliam could speak. "I want nothing back for it. By the gods, man, you could have killed me and did not. You kept to our bargain about the battle. You have acted, dare I say it, like the son

I wish I had had, but never sired. And so, in this one thing, being a mercenary commander, I see myself your father, and give you what I would give a son."

To his surprise, Aliam's eyes glistened, as if tears were near. "Thank you, Ilanz," he said. "I am honored to be able to accept."

Ilanz thought of telling him more, but reflected that every man had his limits, where advice and gifts were concerned, and it was best to let the young learn for themselves.

★ ★ ★

ABOUT THE AUTHOR

Elizabeth Moon, a Texas native, is a Marine Corps veteran (Vietnam era) with degrees in history and biology. She has published twenty-six novels in both science fiction and fantasy, including Compton Crook Award winner *Sheepfarmer's Daughter*, Hugo-nominated *Remnant Population*, and Nebula Award winner *The Speed of Dark* (also nominated for the Arthur C. Clarke Award), as well as three short-fiction collections, including *Moon Flights* (2007) and the e-book collection *Tales of Paksworld* (2014). She received the Heinlein Award for body of work in 2007. Over forty short-fiction pieces have appeared in anthologies and magazines. Her latest novel is *Crown of Renewal*, fifth and final volume of Paladin's Legacy, a return to the world of *The Deed of Paksenarrion*.

THE GUNS
OF THE WASTES

★ ★ ★

Django Wexler

The six days it took the mail cutter to traverse the pass at Rusthead were the longest of Pahlu Venati's life. The slope and the rocky ground cut the landship's speed to a crawl, her eight fat tires bouncing and shuddering in their pods at the ends of her long, articulated legs. The ceaseless chug of the engine was his constant companion, faster than a heartbeat, broken every so often by the whistling hiss of venting steam.

Vegetation petered out as they gained altitude, the scrub woods along the side of the road turning to weedy grass, which became patchy and finally disappeared altogether. At night, shielding his eyes from the ship's lanterns, he could see a great wheel of stars marching overhead, far outshining the handful he'd been able to make out from his window at the Academy. They seemed distant and cold, and he would have gladly traded the view for the smoky, overcast sky of home.

On the fourth day, they began descending again, the cutter's engines straining to keep her from careening wildly down the rock-strewn slope. Pahlu was surprised to see grass on this side, too, and even a few stunted trees; this was the edge of the Waste, after all. But of course it was only the *edge*, and few of the Enemy ever made it as far as the passes.

Pahlu had always been careful to think of them as the *sraa*, since that was the official designation. When his turn came to stand night watch, waiting with a rifle in his hand by the rail and staring out into the darkness, he thought he understood the impulse to make them sound more mystical. The Great Enemy. The Plague. He imagined them gathering just outside the circle of light, circling around the little landship and waiting for their chance to strike.

Silly, of course. Even if a sraa made it this far east, it would be a small one, and more likely to hide from a Grand Alliance ship than attack it. But Pahlu could not seem to prevent his hands sweating, however much he wiped them on his brand-new uniform trousers. He decided to chalk it up to anticipation. After all, his whole life—since the day he walked out of his home forever, his father's anger still ringing in his ears—had been preparation for this moment.

When the sun rose on the sixth day, the captain of the cutter gave a sigh of relief at the sight of the *Marilei's Wrath*, nestled quietly against a low hill. Taller and wider than the cutter, the light cruiser's proportions made her look squat by comparison. On each side of the warship, two heavy struts arched down to connect to a single long pod wrapped around a caterpillar track, while two forward legs bore conventional wheels. Her hull looked like a fat cigar cut in half, rounded side down, with the struts disappearing into long vertical slots. A tall, blocky superstructure amidships was topped by the bridge tower, and she carried two six-inch guns in fore and aft turrets.

Colored lights flashed from the shutterbox attached to *Wrath*'s tower, too fast for Pahlu to follow. The cutter flashed the ACCEPT signal, three green lights, and powered across the flat ground to draw alongside the larger landship. It wasn't until they came close that Pahlu appreciated how much bigger the cruiser was. She towered above them, so much higher that she had to lower a rope ladder to reach the cutter's deck.

He was ready by the time she did, his few possessions gathered into a backpack, his red uniform unfaded by sun or weather. His black leather cap—slightly too large, if truth be told—still had the factory shine, and the single bar at his collar gleamed. He'd spent the past night polishing all the brass on his uniform, feeling simultaneously embarrassed and unwilling to look less than his absolute best.

The cutter captain, a civilian in a faded blue greatcoat, emerged onto the deck and looked at him with an unreadable expression. The man had wings of gray in his close-cropped hair, and Pahlu wondered how many young officers he'd delivered this way, and how many of them had come back. For a moment he thought the captain was going to offer some worldly advice, but he merely grunted and turned away, walking to where a couple of his men were fastening a hooked line from the cruiser to the knot atop a sack of mail.

Pahlu waited a moment longer. When no one seemed inclined to tell him what to do, he turned around and took hold of the ladder, climbing hand over hand toward his new life.

The deck of the cruiser was corrugated steel instead of old, stained wood, and everyone in sight was wearing the familiar red and black of the Grand Alliance Navy. Pahlu swung his legs over the rail, straightened up, and found two women approaching him from the direction of the bridge tower. On sighting the pair of stripes denoting a first lieutenant, Pahlu drew himself up and saluted, fist pressed against his heart.

They made for an odd pair. The lieutenant was Kotzi, like most of the crew, with a tight fuzz of curly hair under her cap and deep brown skin several shades lighter than his own. She was tall and broad-shouldered, with a formidable air of solidity, and she stared at him with an expression that said she was not pleased with what she was seeing.

The other woman was a head shorter, with the paler, nut-colored skin and delicate features of a Remnant, descended from the people who had once lived in the Waste. Her hair was straight and hung past her shoulders, and instead of a uniform she wore a long khaki coat, thick with buttoned pockets and stained at the edges. She was, to all appearances, a civilian, and so Pahlu was surprised when the lieutenant stopped a half-step behind her and let her take the lead.

"Hmm," she said, staring at him. Instead of a military-style cap, she wore a band of dark fabric across her forehead, with variety of odd things sticking out of it. Pahlu saw several pencils, a ruler, and some sort of optical device on a hinged metal clip. The woman's hand went to the latter, apparently out of habit. The lieutenant cleared her throat.

"He's not a specimen, Rev," she said. "He's our new officer. Remember?"

"Oh yes." She blinked big, watery eyes. Pahlu held his position, hand pressed against his chest. His back was starting to ache. "What's he doing?"

"Standing at attention," the lieutenant said, with an air of exasperated patience.

"Why?"

"It's customary. You ought to welcome him and tell him to relax."

"Sir," Pahlu said, overcoming his hesitation to interrupt a superior. "I think there may have been an error. I was ordered to report to—"

"To the *Serrianople*," the lieutenant said. "I know. I sent for you. You *are* Second Lieutenant Pahlu Vitali, correct?"

"Sir, yes sir." His eyes were drawn toward the shorter woman, who had flipped down a complicated arrangement of brass and lenses and was fiddling with dials around the edges. The lieutenant, following his gaze, sighed.

"You may as well relax," she said. "I'm Lieutenant Sark Elb. This is Professor Revya Ahldotr."

"Yes?" Revya said suddenly, looking at the lieutenant.

Her movement set the device hanging in front of her face to swinging and clicking. "What? I'm here."

"And I'm to report to you?" Pahlu said.

"That's right," Sark said. "I've got all the paperwork down below, if you want to look it over."

"Understood, sir." Pahlu saluted again. "It will be an honor to serve!"

"If you say so," Sark muttered, looking Pahlu up and down. "Well. Come along. We'll get your things stowed."

"Of course." He turned to the professor, only to find her already walking away, one hand on her lensed device as she stared at the horizon.

"Don't mind her," Sark said. "She's always like that."

"It's not that she means to be rude," the lieutenant explained as they negotiated the cramped corridors of *Wrath*'s underdecks. "She just doesn't *care*, you see. Her attention span for anything that doesn't involve the sraa is about thirty seconds. It's best to warn you going in, so you don't think it's personal."

"Can I ask," Pahlu said, turning sideways to let a pair of ratings hurry past, "in what capacity she's . . . serving?"

"I'm not sure how the Admiralty classes her on the official books. Hell, I'm not sure she even gets a salary, not that she'd know what to do with one. She's out here as a sraa expert, gathering intelligence. Some kind of secret project."

"And you, sir?"

"I'm here to keep her alive. Which is a challenge even

when we're in port, let me tell you. And since we lost our last second lieutenant, I've been short a pair of hands."

"Was there an enemy attack?"

"What?" Sark looked back at him and chuckled. "Oh, no. She just couldn't stand to be around Rev anymore, so she petitioned the Rear Admiral for transfer. I asked the Academy to send us a replacement. I assume this is your first posting?"

"Yes, sir."

"And you're Querbi."

"Yes, sir."

"Are we going to have any religious problems?"

Pahlu winced. The only thing that most Kotzi seemed to know about his homeland was that it produced more than its share of fanatics, clinging to their weird, singular god. For a moment he saw his father's face, purple with anger. *Domus will not forgive you for venturing among the heathens!*

"No, sir. No problems."

"Good." They reached a doorway, half covered by a thin curtain, that led into a narrow room. The walls and floor were all gray metal, and two wooden beds took up nearly all the floor space. "You're in here with me until we get back to the *Serrianople*. Rev's next door, when she can be bothered to sleep."

"Will we be returning soon, sir?"

As though his question had been an invocation, the ship shivered, rolling slightly as the legs shifted on their springs. A new vibration thrilled through the decking, and Pahlu felt a slight lurch as they started forward. Sark shifted her balance to compensate, automatically, and he found himself envying her unconscious ease.

"We're headed that way," she said. "But we've got a stop to make first. Do you need a few minutes?"

Pahlu tossed his backpack onto one of the narrow beds and squared his shoulders. "No, sir!"

Sark gave him a broad smile, with only a hint of malice at the edges. "Oh, good. A nice *keen* lad."

Several hours and a few minor lacerations later, the edge of his keenness was a bit dulled.

Sark had sat him down in an empty room, with a big, leather-strapped chest and a canvas sack that clanked when she pulled it across the deck. The sack, it turned out, was full of scrap metal, scraped up by the crew from the site of a past engagement. Most of it was junk, but mixed in were bits and pieces of sraa, which needed to be sorted out and wrapped in linen for transport back to the Collegium in Kotz. She'd given Pahlu a pair of thick leather gloves for his hands, but he'd manage to nick his forearms a couple of times handling some of the larger pieces of shrapnel.

He set aside a chunk of twisted armor the size of a dinner plate and reached carefully into the bag for the next piece. It was a real find—a whole sraa leg, practically intact. Pahlu held it up to the lamp, marveling at how light it was. Fully extended, it was nearly as long as his arm, and it could bend inward through six different joints, giving it a marvelous range of motion. The steel-gray struts were wrapped in a complicated network of tiny brass rods and pistons, with intermeshing gears where they met. When he moved it, the parts all clicked and turned in an absolutely smooth ballet of mechanical perfection. At the "foot" end, there was a polished sphere, a flawless steel bearing in a universal mount, flanked by a pair of long, curved blades.

Pahlu folded the leg up, until it was curled in on itself like the limb of a dead insect, then reached for the roll of linen wrapping. He was just getting it stowed away when the lieutenant rapped at the doorframe behind him.

Sark looked at his progress and gave an approving sort of grunt. Pahlu jumped to his feet and thumped a salute.

"Making progress, sir!" he said. "Another few hours."

"Leave it," she said. "You can finish later. We're coming up on Old Gotterlak, I want you on deck with me in case Rev decides she needs a sample. Here's your first standing order: *don't let her jump off of anything*. I swear, that woman thinks she can fly."

"Yes, sir!" A bit relieved, Pahlu followed the lieutenant back down the corridor to the main stairs, then up into the open air of *Wrath*'s deck.

The ship was buzzing like a hive, men and women in red-and-black uniforms hurrying across the deck in all directions. Both guns—small enough that they were set on hand-cranked swivel mounts rather than motorized turrets—were manned and ready, and both rails were lined with riflemen.

Beyond the ship stretched the Waste, an endless, uniform expanse of red-brown earth, swelling here and there into low hills. Patches of sparse grass grew here and there, and the occasional shrub protruded from a rocky cranny, but there was nothing larger, and no animal life at all. It was so utterly unlike the foggy, riotously green landscapes of Pahlu's youth that it seemed as though it belonged on a different planet.

The lieutenant touched his shoulder, and he realized he'd been staring. He turned, embarrassed, and found her holding out a rifle.

"I assume you can use one of these?" she said.

"Yes, sir." Pahlu took the weapon, popped out the five-round clip in the butt to make sure it was loaded, then worked the bolt with a satisfying *snick-snack*. "I won a first-year prize for marksmanship."

Sark chuckled. "Let's hope you won't have to show off."

She led him up toward the bow, past the forward gun crew and several lookouts. It felt odd to be sauntering casually along the deck while so many ratings were clearly intent on important work, but the lieutenant didn't pay the enlisted men any mind, and Pahlu followed her example. At the forward rail, Revya was staring into the distance through the brass scope clipped to her headband, now swiveled into position in front of her right eye.

"Anything interesting, Rev?" Sark said.

Revya turned around. A bit too quickly, it turned out— her view through the eyepiece must have swung disorientingly, because she lost her balance and took a step back against the rail. Sark lunged forward immediately and grabbed her by the arm, yanking her back and pulling the scope out of the way.

"Not yet," Revya said when she regained her footing, ignoring the entire incident. "But I still think this is a bad idea. These patrols are too predictable."

"We have to check for oxcarts," Sark said.

Pahlu, looking out at the Waste, had a hard time imagining *any* sort of animal living out here, much less a team of oxen. His confusion must have been obvious, because the lieutenant rolled her eyes.

"An oxcart is a sort of sraa transport," she explained. "They load it up with salvage and send it east to do whatever it is they do with the stuff."

"Build more sraa," Revya said absently, scanning the horizon again.

"Don't they teach you that sort of the thing at the Academy?" Sark said.

"No, sir," Pahlu said, cheeks heating slightly. "Sraa studies are restricted." He allowed a hint of pride to enter his voice. "Only a tenth of the officer candidates are accepted by the Navy, anyway."

"They should teach everyone about them," Revya said without looking around. "Every child of five should know how to kill a scuttler. Every schoolgirl should learn their weak spots along with her letters."

Sark coughed and lowered her voice. "She can be a bit passionate on the subject."

"The Grand Alliance has been too soft for too long," Revya said. "We think that because we've gone a few decades without losing ground, we're safe. We let ourselves fall into familiar patterns." She laughed bitterly. "What's a decade to the sraa? What's a hundred years? Eventually—"

"There's the city," Sark interrupted, pointing. Revya, instantly distracted, peered in the direction she indicated. Pahlu looked too, more curious then he cared to admit. The Old Cities featured heavily in the tales that made the rounds of the Academy barracks. They were dark, haunted places, ruins ringed with trenches and barbed wire, silent monuments to futile last stands against the power of the Plague.

Some of that, he'd figured, was mere childish exaggeration. But he'd expected more than *this*. Pahlu leaned out to get a better look, and shook his head.

"There's nothing left!" he said.

Not *quite* nothing. Here and there a stone wall still stood, flanked by piles of rubble. Some of the debris was recognizable—flagstones, tarry chunks of asphalt, some carved stone pieces that might have been part of a statue. But there were no intact buildings, no trenches, nothing tall enough that he would have had to stand on tiptoes to see over it.

"They've been sifting through this place for years," Sark said. "Persistent bastards. They'll harvest anything but stone—metal, wood, bone, anything. They—"

"I see one!" Pahlu said.

He brought his rifle to his shoulder, peering over the iron sights, searching for the flash of movement that had caught his eye. It came again, the glitter of metal catching the sun. The thing moved in quick bursts, stopping as though getting its bearings, then dashing forward with startling speed. It was about the size of a dog, with a central oval body ringed by brass-mounted glass lenses and eight segmented legs. Even from a distance, the fluidity of its motion was disturbing. It moved as though it were truly alive.

"Well spotted," Sark said, shading her eyes with her hand.

Pahlu's hands were sweating. He shifted the rifle against his cheek. "Shall I fire?"

"Don't waste the bullet. It's only a scuttler. No danger unless he finds a few thousand friends. Quick, though, isn't he?"

Pahlu nodded, slowly lowering the weapon. The little sraa didn't so much walk as skate across the broken landscape, legs rising and falling neatly to match the ground so that the body barely stirred. He could see another one now, in the middle distance, poking its forelimbs into a pile of rocks.

Marilei's Wrath shifted underneath them, bearing to port. Revya turned to keep the sraa in view.

"The captain will circle the city to check for oxcarts," Sark said. "Too risky to try to go over all those rocks unless we have a good reason."

"The oxcarts are dangerous?"

"Not really. But they're valuable to the sraa."

"We think," Revya said.

"Why else come all the way out here to load them up?" Sark said. She shrugged. "Anyway, we try to destroy them when we can. Anything that slows them down can't hurt."

Revya muttered something under her breath, then froze. With one finger, she snapped a new lens into place on her scope.

"Find the captain," she said. "Tell him to reverse course *now*."

"Why?" Sark said.

"This is a trap."

The lieutenant smiled. "The sraa don't set *traps*. They just come after you like hungry animals."

"You don't—" Revya began.

Something shifted, stones falling away with a clatter. A mound of rubble, one of a thousand innocuous hillocks created by the sraa in their endless search for salvage, shifted slightly. Dull metal gleamed underneath.

"Gunspider!" Sark shouted. A brilliant flash obscured the mound of debris, hidden quickly by a plume of evil black smoke. A moment later, the *boom* reached their ears, and *Wrath* jerked underneath them. Soldiers grabbed the nearest rail as the ship slewed sideways, and Pahlu could hear the boiling-kettle whistle of escaping steam.

As if the shot had been a signal, the whole city came to life. Sraa rose up from the rubble in a clatter of stone and dust, gangly metal legs clicking into motion as far as the eye could see. The ground seemed to writhe with them.

Wrath rumbled under Pahlu's feet, turning her nose away from the ruined city and putting her stern to the sraa. A bell sounded with a single long buzz, and the engine sound rose to a new pitch. The landship leapt forward, jolting Pahlu's grip on the rail. At the same time, though, the whistle of steam rose to an unearthly shriek, and after a minute or so the hum of the engine fell away.

"Not good," Revya muttered. She leaned out over the rail, and Sark took hold of the back of her coat to keep her balanced as she peered down the side of the hull. "Leaking from the starboard strut!"

Sark looked at the pillar of steam that stretched behind the stricken ship. "They can't have lost all the pipes, or we'd be going in circles."

At that moment, the unearthly keening stopped. Pahlu could see the gushing plume of steam cut off, leaving a long, thin cloud dissolving slowly over the landscape.

"Did they fix it?" he said.

"They figured out which pipes were busted and closed the valves," Sark said. Her voice was grim. "But since they'll have to cut power to the port-side pod to compensate—"

"We'll be slow." Revya ran along the rail until she could get a look astern. "*Too* slow."

The leading edge of the sraa swarm looked like a wave, lapping gently over the land in a carpet of steel and brass. Thousands of scuttlers, skating smoothly over the broken ground on their multiply jointed legs, merged at a distance into a monstrous, unbroken mass of metal. Behind them were larger forms, spider-like shapes that hulked above the smaller sraa like horses in a pack of dogs. The time it had taken the sraa to dig themselves out and the brief, chaotic sprint had given the *Wrath* a lead, but only a small one, and it was diminishing fast.

"Eupater protect us," one of the soldiers at the rail muttered. A couple of others nearby touched two fingers to their eyes, a traditional Kotzi gesture of supplication and prayer. Pahlu looked between them and Revya, still pressed against the rail. A worm of fear had burrowed into his stomach, and he swallowed and fought it down.

Wrath surged forward at the best speed she could manage, massive caterpillar treads spitting out chunks of crushed earth and stone, accompanied by the distant keening of her steam tubes under tremendous pressure. The massive springs that supported the ship on its struts were unable to absorb every bounce and jolt of the terrain, and the deck began to shudder as though it were being shaken by playful giants.

The ship's bells blared another command, three short and one long buzz. *Prepare for action astern.* The soldiers, who had been lining both rails, converged on the rear of the ship. Revya went to follow.

"You should get below," Sark said in the tone of someone expecting to lose the argument.

"No," the professor said, pushing back from the rail and flipping her scope out of the way. "I have to see."

"Of course," Sark said under her breath. She grabbed Pahlu by the arm and hissed into his ear. "Remember, our job is to keep an eye on *her*, you understand? Don't get distracted."

He nodded and checked his rifle again. It was still loaded, but it suddenly seemed pitiful protection indeed against the mass of metal bearing down on them. What could a few bullets do against *that*?

Revya was headed to the raised firing platform that jutted off the after edge of the bridge tower, its rail already lined with riflemen. Just beyond them was the after six-inch gun, now turning frantically to bear on the swarm, and beyond that the stern rail and another line of armed soldiers.

"Coming into range, sir!" a rating said, clinging to a handle on the gun mount.

The officer in charge, a young woman with her hair in

a long, frizzy braid, peered through a pair of binoculars and then gave a decisive nod.

"Load high explosive," she said, prompting the gun crew to begin a frenzy of action. A few seconds later, the gun's breech slammed closed and they all stepped away. The officer took hold of a railing and slashed her hand in the direction of the enemy. "Fire!"

The sound of the gun seemed to fill the world, even over the roar of the engine and the scream of the steam pipes. Pahlu could see the shell as it arced out, crossing more than a mile of broken ground in a perfect parabola to fall, brutally fast, among the scuttlers at the front of the swarm. A flower of smoke and dust bloomed, and pieces of metal scrap pinwheeled away. The sound reached them a few moments later, a distant, hollow boom.

By the time the dust cleared, the carpet of scuttlers had closed up again, scurrying over the broken bodies of the fallen. It reminded Pahlu of tossing a stone into a lake as a boy, watching the splash and the ripples slowly settle back into a placid surface.

Domus protect me, he thought. Oddly, the instinctive, vestigial prayer sent a flare of anger through him that pushed back the terror. He'd turned his back on his father and his father's god. *I'm not going to give that up* now. *If I die, it will be as the man I want to be.*

Wrath's forward gun fired, and another fiery flower bloomed among the scuttlers. The after gun fired again, and again, an endless, hammering rhythm. Sraa bodies were thrown into the air by the force of the explosions, limbs flailing madly as they fell back to the earth. But the swarm came on. The guns had as little prospect of stopping it as Pahlu's boyhood stones had of emptying the lake.

Then there was a bright white flash from the swarm, smothered instantly by a plume of black smoke. A new flower of flame and flying dirt bloomed, two hundred yards short of *Wrath*. More flashes followed, and in between the cacophonous boom of guns Pahlu could hear the whistle of incoming shells. The explosions that marked their fall were always short of the ship, but marching closer, yard by yard, as the swarm advanced.

"Switch to armor piercing," the officer yelled. "Target the lead gunspider!"

Sailors raced to open another set of ammo chests, while two men cranked frantically on a large metal wheel to match the bearing a third was calling out to them. The gunspiders were the size of carriages, bulky creatures bearing a cannon that ran the whole length of their body, its bore like a single baleful eye. There were a dozen of them behind the mass of scuttlers and other sraa, walking in line abreast.

"Coming into range," Revya muttered.

"Scuttlers are getting close," Sark said. "We can't outrun them like this—"

Another round of flashes from the gunspiders, and another volley screamed down around the ship. This time the explosions bracketed *Wrath*, some falling ahead and some behind. One round went off practically in their path. The concussion rocked the landship on its springs, and Pahlu got one hot breath full of the smell of cordite.

The bell buzzed another signal. The soldiers at the

rail raised their rifles, and Sark thumped Pahlu on the shoulder.

"That's our cue." She braced herself against the rail and raised her own rifle. Pahlu followed suit, aiming down the iron sights at the leading edge of the swarm.

Three more long buzzes. *Fire at will.* Every rifle *cracked* at once, like an old-fashioned musket volley.

Pahlu had picked out one scuttler on the edge of the swarm as his target, and he saw it crumple and fall, but he had no way of knowing if it was his bullet or another's that had put it down. It didn't matter—behind it was another, and another. He lined them up and pulled the trigger, again and again, feeling the nerve-deadening *thump* of the rifle kicking against his shoulder and working the bolt back and forth to eject the spent shells. When his clip ran out, he turned and grabbed another from a box someone had strapped to a handle behind the line.

It wasn't going to be enough. The scuttlers were too fast, and there were far too many of them. He could hear a high-pitched whine as the engineers pushed the remaining steam tubes to the edge of their rated pressures and beyond, but the little sraa were still catching up. They were within a hundred yards now, spreading out, limbs a blur as they drove themselves forward at fantastic speeds. It made them easier targets, since they didn't take time to dodge and weave, but in spite of the efforts of the riflemen the gap slowly closed.

Pahlu sighted on a scuttler, only to see it vanish in a blast of fire and smoke. The sraa's shots were falling among their own now. Pahlu smiled, adjusted his aim, then was driven off his feet by a thunderous roar.

Two shells had landed on *Wrath* nearly simultaneously. One impacted just past the after gun, punching through the deck and exploding underneath. The force of the blast ripped a hole in the deck plating and twisted the gun and its mounting into scrap metal. The second shell hit the stern, just below the deck line. It failed to penetrate the armored hull, but the explosion sent a shockwave and shards of red-hot steel zipping through the riflemen gathered there.

When Pahlu raised his head, the deck was awash in blood. The man beside him had been chopped practically in half by a flying fragment, releasing a sea of bile and gore. Beyond him, a woman was curled up around an invisible wound, screaming wordlessly, while another sailor hung limply on the rail.

Sark grabbed Pahlu's shoulder and spun him round. It took him a moment to understand her through ears still ringing from the blast.

". . . you all right?"

"I . . ." Pahlu looked down at his uniform, which was spattered with blood. He didn't feel any pain. "I think so."

"Come on!" She pushed past him, leaping over the disemboweled body, her boots squelching in the pool of blood. Pahlu wanted to vomit, but he didn't have the time; he was already following, keeping his eyes glued to her broad back so that he didn't have to look down.

The deck shook with a metallic *clang*. He thought it was another hit, but there was no explosion, and the sound came again, and again. The sraa were *jumping* onto the deck, gathering down below the stern of the ship and hurling themselves into the air, limbs snapping closed like steel-jawed traps. For every three that tried it, two fell short or missed the mark and tumbled beneath *Wrath*'s treads, but a half-dozen had already made it and more were coming.

Pahlu skidded to a halt on the corrugated metal deck, bringing his rifle up to his shoulder. The soldiers who'd survived the shell blast were starting to pick themselves up, but the sraa were already on top of them. He picked out a scuttler closing in on a dazed young woman, one of its limbs already drawing back to deliver the killing blow. It was barely ten yards away—

—and Pahlu's shot caught it between two of its glass lenses, the bullet punching a neat hole in its carapace and emerging from the other side of its body in a spray of fine machine parts.

The soldier he'd saved rolled away, groping for her own weapon, as another sraa pulled itself over the rail and landed on the deck. Other rifles sounded, and scuttlers collapsed, but more of them were landing all the time. At the rail, Pahlu saw a young man grappling hand-to-limb with one of the things, the scuttler pushing one bladed claw into his stomach with piston-driven strength. A large woman with a deck sergeant's insignia delivered a two-handed blow with her rifle butt that shattered a scuttler's eye, sending it reeling across the deck, before another machine jumped on her shoulders and speared her neatly through the throat.

Sark, ahead of him, had discarded her rifle and drawn a large-barreled pistol of unfamiliar design. When she fired it at a scuttler, the weapon nearly kicked itself out of her grip, and the machine slumped to the deck with an inch-thick hole in its oval body.

She was running toward Revya, Pahlu realized. The professor had gotten down from the firing platform, apparently uninjured, but the lurching of the ship had tossed her against the rail near the hole in the deck. Sark reached her side, blasting another scuttler that had gotten tangled up on the rail and sending it tumbling out into the Waste. She grabbed Revya and pulled her to her feet just as another wave of sraa landed.

Two of the machines hopped down through the hole in the deck into *Wrath*'s innards, and Pahlu heard shots and screams. Two more headed for Sark. Pahlu raised his rifle, sighted, and fired, and one of them went down, but when he yanked back on the bolt, it gave the *clunk* that meant an empty clip. Sark had her big pistol broken open, pulling a pair of fat bullets from her pouch and struggling to fit them into the breech.

She's not going to make it. Pahlu was moving forward before he realized what he was doing, reversing his rifle like a club, the barrel hot in his hands. The second scuttler leapt for Sark, bladed forelimbs extended, and Pahlu caught it in mid-air with an overhand swing. Glass shattered, and the thing's carapace dented, but it was still squirming, forelimbs slicing at his shins. Pahlu danced backward. One of the blades scored, opening a long slice through his leather boot and leaving a shallow gash in his leg.

As the scuttler regained its footing, Sark grabbed his shoulder and pushed him aside. Her heavy pistol spoke again, blasting a hole in the little machine and putting it down for good. Rifles were barking all around them, catching the scuttlers as they landed and strewing the deck with mechanical corpses.

"Thanks," Sark said, pulling Revya to her feet. The professor's eyes were wide and unfocused.

"Is she okay?" Pahlu said.

"Just stunned, I think." Sark looked out over the stern, where the gunspider's heavy ordnance was still flashing. "I think we may be pulling away from them. May get out of this yet—"

The ship shuddered, armor plating ringing like a bell. Pahlu stumbled and grabbed the rail, while Sark held on to Revya. He braced himself for the shell's explosion, but it didn't come. Instead, two long, multi-jointed limbs reached over the stern rail. They were tipped with crescent-shaped blades, and the sraa punched the points into the deck, cutting easily through the steel. With this leverage, it hauled itself up and onto the *Wrath*.

This was no dog-sized scuttler. It was fully as tall as Pahlu, limbs stretching six feet or more, a hulking monstrosity of iron and brass. The lenses that ringed its body were the size of dinner plates. A dozen rifles fired at once, and the air was full of the ping and whine of ricochets as the bullets bounced off its armor like hailstones off a tin roof. It ignored them, picking its way through the bodies of its comrades with mechanical grace, and began to slaughter everything within reach.

The soldiers stood their ground, firing as it bore down on them. It opened the first man from throat to groin with a single, casual swing, the spray of blood coating its metallic hide in gore. The young woman Pahlu had saved fired her rifle from only a few inches away, with no more effect than the others. The sraa caught her with the point of its blade on the backswing, punching it into her chest. The momentum of the strike hurled her off the deck entirely, her body pinwheeling over the rail to fall to the broken ground below.

"Butcher," Sark growled, identifying the thing. She sighted carefully and fired, hitting it square in one of its lenses, but the heavy round from her pistol only cracked the thick glass. Tossing the weapon aside, she yanked something from her belt. *A grenade*, Pahlu realized as time seemed to slow to a crawl. Sark was running, pulling Revya behind her, and her free hand caught Pahlu and dragged him along as well.

The explosion shook the ship, as though the gunspiders had scored another hit. Sark threw herself flat, and Pahlu needed no urging to follow her. The concussion passed over them, a wave of hot wind and smoke. He twisted around to see the effects. The deck was blackened in a wide circle around the butcher, but the sraa was still there, burn marks searing its iron hide. At least one of its legs was damaged, dragging uselessly behind it, but that didn't seem to impede its mobility much. The surviving soldiers scrambled away as it came forward.

"Shit," Sark said, under her breath. "Shit, shit, shit. Rev, now would be the time for a good idea or two." But Revya, eyes still wide, was breathing fast and shallow and didn't seem to hear.

The butcher turned, and Pahlu saw the lens Sark's shot had cracked. The way was suddenly clear to him, as obvious as if Domus himself had dropped the knowledge ready-made into his brain. At the thought, his lip curled. *The hell with Domus. This is* my *decision.*

There was another grenade on Sark's belt. He pulled it free and rolled to his feet, ignoring her shout of warning. Hand grenades were a rarity, but they'd practiced a few times at the Academy, and the theory was simple. Yank on the pin to start the fuse, and get rid of it before it went off.

Pahlu got to his feet and aimed himself at the butcher. He pulled the pin.

The deck was treacherous underfoot, slick with blood and littered with scraps of scuttler. He ran flat out, leaping human and sraa bodies. As he came up to the butcher, it swung a forelimb in his direction, a lazy cut that would have decapitated him if he hadn't ducked. Popping up inside its reach, he pressed himself against the underside of its body, one arm extended. His right hand, holding the grenade, stretched up along the butcher's carapace until it found the cracked lens. He slammed the grenade against it, feeling the glass give slightly, and held it there with all the strength he could muster.

There was a long, strained moment of stillness. Pahlu, cheek pressed against the butcher, could hear the click and whirr of tiny clockwork through its metal skin.

Then the world went white.

Pahlu woke up feeling better than he'd ever felt in his life. He was floating on a golden cloud, staring up at the brilliant blue of the sky, his body a distant, numb anchor far below him.

A shadow fell across him, and he blinked. A brown blob resolved into the features of Lieutenant Sark Elb.

"Oh," he said. His throat felt raspy, as though he'd been shouting. "Are we dead?"

"Not yet," Sark said.

That's good. Pahlu's thoughts felt fuzzy. If he'd been dead, then this would have been Heaven, and that would have meant his father and Domus were right all along.

He sat up, or tried to. His muscles didn't seem to work the way they should. Sark reached out and put a hand on his chest, just a light touch. It stopped him as completely as if she'd lowered a thousand-pound weight.

"Lie still," she said. "Rev's still tying you off, and we gave you a pretty big dose of juice."

"Juice?" Pahlu said.

"A powerful opiod," Rev said from his right. "Useful as a painkiller in limited doses."

"Oh." He flopped his head to the right. She was on her knees, bending over him, working on a knotted bandage that swathed his right arm. There was something wrong there, too. He wasn't sure if it was the drug, but he thought there ought to be *more* of his right arm. He tried to wiggle his fingers, and silver pain lanced up into his chest, even through the comforting haze. His throat went thick.

"Oh," he said again.

"Good tactics," Rev said, finishing the knot. "Using the body of the butcher to shield yourself from the shrapnel."

Pahlu struggled to remember if that had been his plan. As best he could recall, he'd gone underneath the sraa because it seemed like the best way to keep from getting skewered and dropping the grenade. He hadn't really expected to *survive*.

"Did I kill it?" he said.

"Yup," Sark said. "Blasted its eye right in and sent nasty metal chunks through all its tender spots." She paused, with the hint of a smile. "I have to say: I'm impressed."

"Thanks." Pahlu turned his head away from his maimed arm, feeling dizzy. "What happened to the rest of them?"

"We got a little help." Sark pointed, and Pahlu flopped his head the other way to follow her finger.

He was on the deck of the *Wrath*, lying on a canvas stretcher near the rail. Beyond the deck, he could see the blasted ground of the Waste. And, a few hundred yards away, the looming shape of another landship.

Serrianople towered as high above the light cruiser as *Marilei's Wrath* herself did above a scuttler. The battleship looked like a mountain on the move, a solid wall of metal the height of church spire back home. Unlike *Wrath* and the cutter—unlike any other class of landship—it didn't have long, curving struts leading down to wheels and engine pods. Where the light cruiser was designed to keep the sraa at arm's length, the battleship was meant to confront them head-on; its hull was supported on enormous caterpillar treads, like *Wrath*'s rear pods, but they were concealed from view by a heavy skirt of interlocking steel plates that hung down from the hull and protected the engines from sraa. At the Academy, Pahlu had heard there was a whole twilight world under there, amidst the screaming, grinding steam pipes, and that each battleship had a corps of soldiers dedicated to hunting down any sraa that managed to sneak underneath.

On the deck of the battleship, high above, three triple-gunned turrets aimed their long barrels over her starboard rail. Men swarmed over them, tiny as ants, revealing their true, massive scale.

"The captain sent up a signal rocket as soon as we started our run," Sark said, looking at the battleship with a satisfied expression. "Fortunately for us, *Serrianople* was on the southern edge of her patrol area. The sraa turned away as soon as she came over the horizon."

"The sraa *ran*?" Pahlu said. The warm, cottony feeling was rising all around him again. He suddenly felt very tired.

"The sraa never go up against a battleship," Sark said. "They're smart enough to know when they haven't got a chance."

"Until today," Revya said softly, "the sraa had never ambushed a ship. They *are* smart enough to know better." She was staring up at the mountainous steel war machine, too, but her expression was more like regret. "And they never, ever give up. Someday . . ."

But Pahlu was no longer listening. He closed his eyes, and the black waters of blessed sleep closed over him.

★ ★ ★

ABOUT THE AUTHOR

Django Wexler graduated from Carnegie Mellon University in Pittsburgh with degrees in creative writing and computer science. Eventually he migrated to Microsoft in Seattle, where he now lives with two cats and a teetering mountain of books. When not writing, he wrangles computers, paints tiny soldiers, and plays games of all sorts. He is the author of the military fantasies *The Thousand Names* and *The Shadow Throne*, and the middle-grade fantasy *The Forbidden Library*. His website is djangowexler.com.

THE GRAPHOLOGY
OF HEMORRHAGE

★ ★ ★

Yoon Ha Lee

Rao Nawong, aide to Magician Tepwe Kodai, had not
been on the hillside for long with her. The sky threatened
rain on and off, and the air smelled of river poetry, of lakes
with their scarves of reeds. Water would make their
mission here, in the distant shadow of the Spiders'
fortress, more difficult, if not outright impossible. The
Empire's defeat of the upstart Spiders, whose rebellion
had sparked a general conflagration in the southwest
provinces, depended on the mission's success. At the
moment, Nawong found it hard to care. His world had
narrowed to Kodai's immediate needs, politics be
damned.

Kodai was scowling at the sky as she drew a roll of silk
out of a brass tube. She had clever hands, which he had
always admired, precise in every motion, as good with a

brush as she was with the pliers and hammers and snippers that she used for the gadgets that were her hobby. "I still think it's going to rain," she muttered. "But this has to be done."

Nawong hesitated for a long time before he said what he said next. "Does it?" he asked at last.

She looked at him sidelong, no doubt guessing his intent. Waited.

His hands tightened on the umbrella he had brought just in case. Stupid thing to carry in the field this close to the enemy, but the nature of graphological magic meant protecting Kodai's ink while it dried. He had once asked, when they were both new to each other, why the hell couldn't magicians use a pencil. She'd explained that the nature of the instrument changed the nature of the marks: you got different strokes and thicknesses and curves with a piece of graphite than you did with the traditional brush, and this in turn affected the spell framework in such a way that you'd have to discard centuries of research and start over with a completely new way of constructing spells. For the longest time he'd thought she was making this up to shut him up. Only gradually had he realized that this was not, in fact, the case.

"The spell-plague," Nawong said. "Don't do it this way. Use one of the traditional spells." One of the spells that wouldn't kill her in the casting, he meant. But he didn't say it outright.

Kodai began unrolling the silk, then stopped. Waited a little more. When he thought he would have to make another plea, she surprised him by speaking, in a low, rueful voice. "You know, you've spent years dealing with the fact that I cart around so many books and documents. Yet I've never once heard you complain about making the arrangements. Why is that?"

While it was true that he didn't believe in talking just to hear himself talk, he couldn't claim he never complained, either. "It's the nature of your work," he said.

Her eyebrows raised. "Be honest," she said, as though he was the one who needed sympathy.

It was Nawong's turn to be silent. He met her eyes, although he had a hard time doing so, trying to figure out what she wanted of him.

The Empire had developed a class of spells linked by their destructiveness: storms of fire, sheets of blading ice, earth swallowing cities. Such spells were not without their limitations. The performing magician had to know the languages of the region so they could bind the magic to its target, and copy out the spell, adopting a handwriting with the particular characteristics dictated by the spell's effects, whether this was the volatility of fast writing or the murderous intent of clubbed vertical segments or the fire nature of certain sweeping diagonal strokes.

The few other military magicians Nawong had met had little interest in reading their victims' writings after wielding fire or ice or earth to destroy their civilizations. Kodai was different, however. Kodai treasured her books and poems and crude posters, even if they belonged to the Empire's enemies. She'd carried them around even after the ability to read them was burned out of her, never to return.

This last mission, against the Spiders, was different. The Spiders' writing system was based on the Imperial writing system, which made it impossible to focus a spell on them without losing literacy in Imperial. It was a terrible thing to ask of a magician, someone trained to the nuances of writing and literature. But then, beyond being exiled to the military in the first place, Kodai being sent to this particular assignment—putatively on account of her brilliance—was a punishment. More relevantly, from her superiors' point of view, the entanglement of the two writing systems meant that anything that hit the Spiders would also hit the Imperials in the region, and a full evacuation would cede too much territory, enable too much mischief. They trusted that she would find a workaround.

Kodai's solution, if you could call it that, was to come up with a completely new class of spell. The difficulty, from Nawong's point of view, was that it would require her to sacrifice her life.

"Lieutenant," Kodai said. She had averted her eyes and was tensed as though she expected rain to fall like blows. "I have to do this one way or another."

"We don't," he said, meaning that *we*. "We could desert. I don't imagine you're very good at hunting or foraging, but my mother used to take me into the woods to gather greens and mushrooms. We'd find a way to survive, far from here."

"Just what kind of livelihood do you think there would be?" Kodai said. "Do you think the Spider rebellion is going to stop if we don't stop it?"

And it was true. It would be enormously risky to look for a hiding place elsewhere in the Empire. The disorder in the southwest might make it harder to track them into the outlying lands, but was a threat in itself. The Empire was little liked by its neighbors after the past decades of expansion. They would have difficulties wherever they went.

"It's a terrible chance," Nawong agreed. "But it's better than no chance. Which is what you're proposing."

"We are doing a terrible thing here," Kodai said. He didn't miss how she, too, said *we*: generous, considering the most he could contribute was to hold an umbrella for her, or carry her ink sticks. He wasn't the one with the specialist knowledge. "Maybe, if I carry through with it, other magicians will see just how terrible it is."

He wanted to shout at her. "That's a ridiculous reason."

"Someone has to fight," she said. "Even fighting with ink and brush. And some of the Spiders are as ruthless as we are." She was referring to the tactician who had taken out an entire division, which had included one of her old classmates. Nawong remembered how little she had eaten the entire month after that incident. "I will do this last thing, since it would disgrace my family for me to fail, and then I will be done."

Curiously, it was the mention of her family that stopped him from pressing the point. The Tepwe line was a proud one. She had spoken rarely of her family in all the time he had known her. The tremor of her voice when she mentioned them now did not escape him.

"Then you may as well get started," Nawong said, feeling each word like a knife.

Kodai smiled at him without smiling—her eyes shadowed but alert—and spread the silk upon the grass. Nawong weighted the corners with the ritual stones, heavy at heart.

* * *

Magicians in the Empire ranged from those who told auguries to the Empress's court to those who copied out charms for millers and farmers. Kodai's original trajectory should have been toward court. Magicianship was overwhelmingly the province of the nobility, and for all its importance, the military enjoyed much less prestige than the literati. So Kodai's parents, who had anticipated benefiting from their daughter's connections for years to come, reacted poorly when she enlisted.

It wasn't entirely their fault. Kodai's father had never quite understood his daughter, consistently giving her gifts, like sentimental adventure novels, that his oldest son would have appreciated more. (And did, actually. Kodai and her brother swapped books regularly.) On the other hand, their relationship wasn't so bad that he would have had reason to expect that she'd run off to the army.

As for Kodai's mother, she had romanticized visions of her daughter having erudite discussions on poetic forms in scented parlors while zithers played, or practicing calligraphy beneath gingko trees turning color. The fact that a number of court magicians led such existences didn't help. It came as quite a shock to her when Kodai broke the news to her.

What Kodai's parents never knew, and were never going to find out, was that the choice to enter the military had never been a choice. Sleeping in a leaky tent, picking at moldy biscuits, having to wear a uniform whose dyes ran in the rain, to say nothing of the run-ins with dysentery . . . no one would have considered Kodai, with her love of rhyme schemes and assonance, to be the sort of person who'd sign on for that if she could sit in a pavilion sipping tea and reading fortunes in people's pillow books.

At academy, Kodai and three mechanically minded classmates came up with movable type. They weren't the first in the Empire to do so, but the prior discoveries were classified, so they deserved credit for their ingenuity. Two of her classmates were also sent to the military as punishment. The third hanged herself.

Movable type seemed like a good idea at first. It would eliminate all the troublesome irregularities of human handwriting; it would replace personal deficiencies with a machine's impersonal perfection. Kodai and her friends worked out a simplified system for the Imperial script, reducing it to a much smaller set of standardized graphemes. It was moderately clever, and could, conceivably, be learned more quickly than the original script itself.

The head of the academy disapproved for entirely orthodox reasons, as had others before him, because of the democratization of literary magic that movable type implied. ("Democratization" was anachronistic; "vulgarization" might have been truer to the Imperial term.) It was one thing for the Empire's statutes to be enforced by the writings of ministers indoctrinated in the Empire's philosophies. *Think of the body of Imperial writings*, as one of Kodai's instructors often said, *as the living map of the Empress's will*. It was another thing for this to become available to people whose training consisted merely of combinatorial arrangement, rather than dedicated calligraphic toil.

On the other hand, the head of the academy was also a pragmatist. It wasn't that he didn't trust that the military sometimes accomplished useful things, but he recognized that Kodai was the most promising of the miscreants. Sending her to languish in a backwater unit would waste her skills. After her initial assignment, he had his agents keep an eye on her. When her initial performance in the military did, in fact, bear out her potential usefulness, he had a relative in the War Ministry pull strings to assign her to the problem of the Spiders.

Kodai collected letters, especially Spider letters. A love letter from Captain Arvash-mroi, for instance. Arvash was the Spider tactician who had come suddenly and unhappily to the Imperials' attention in general, and Kodai's in particular, when he arranged to demolish a dam on top of an Imperial army that was fatally certain the Spiders couldn't manage the trick so quickly. One of Kodai's three classmates had been part of that army.

She had obtained this love letter by bribing a Spider messenger. While all Spider captains used the same seal, Arvash consistently perfumed certain personal letters, which were delivered to a local town rather than his home city. The messenger endured hard days of riding and inadequate sleep in exchange for a salary that never went as far as it ought to. Kodai's agent, for his part, persuaded the messenger that some coin in exchange for the loan of a piece of personal correspondence was harmless enough. After that, it didn't take Kodai too long to copy out the letter—so close it could have been mistaken for the original—and substitute that to be given to Arvash's lover; like most magicians, Kodai was excellent at forgery.

Whether Arvash or his lover noticed the letter's delay

was an open question. If the Spiders' official messenger service was anything like the Imperial one, message delivery time varied anyway.

The fact of Arvash's letter suggested that his lover was also literate, although the man might also have had someone to read the letter to him. (It was not entirely proper for Arvash to take a man as a lover, but as long as he kept the affair out of sight of his wife, it was not a terrible sin, either, since there could be no child. A female lover would have been another matter.) While it was the case that the Spiders used Imperial writing, some of their calligraphy forms had diverged from the Empire's over time. Imperials argued over the interpretation of, say, the formation called the Swindler's Hook. Most Imperials said it should retain its meaning of an untrustworthy or vacillating personality. The Contextualists, a graphological school that had become politically irrelevant twenty-nine years ago, insisted that the interpretation should instead be drawn from the Spiders' conventions and community of use. Kodai had subterranean Contextualist leanings, but in this instance she was on the fence. The Spiders called the same formation the Widower's Hook. Maybe it pointed to a lack of interest in his wife.

Most magicians would have left it at that, but Kodai wasn't just a magician. She had been one of the best magicians of her class. And her mastery of graphological principles had only improved in her years of field practice.

So Kodai put together the puzzle pieces: the telltale leftward drift of the columns of text, the elongated water-radical and its association with strategic thinking, the slight tendency to roll the brush at the end of horizontal strokes (unattractive, but no one was perfect), even the preference for brushes too large for the size of the handwriting. The finicky attention to detail, with no smears or smudges or thumbprints. Kodai reflected that her instructors would have liked her to be this good with ink. Not that trying harder would have saved her from exile.

Captain Arvash-mroi's letter mentioned a gift of a fine bolt of cloth and (in surprisingly mawkish terms) anticipated embraces. It then launched into a tirade about how his boots pinched his toes. Interesting. Kodai would have expected him to be able to afford better than army issue.

More interestingly, the graphological signs in Arvash's letter spoke of conquests. Not just in bed, although Kodai saw that, too, especially in the vigorous club-ended downstrokes. But there was more, pointed at by forked marks and tapering lines and narrow diagonals: villages encircled and eaten by fire. Torched women. The lamentations of the drowned. The ugly seesaw balance of fire and water dominated his writing, as sharp as swordfall.

Kodai kept track of these traits, using them to focus her hatred of Arvash and writing them down in a notebook with dog-eared pages. Whenever she grew weary of her mission, she returned to the notebook and reread her notes, and went to the next page to write the name of her dead classmate over and over again in stab-shaped columns.

Nawong remembered the first time he had met Kodai.

She had been sitting in a precarious folding chair, lips moving slightly as she read a book and, occasionally, nibbled green tea cookies. He had been prepared to dislike her; he couldn't imagine that a daughter of the Tepwe family wouldn't be spoiled rotten. But instead, when he saluted, she waved him down and said, "Lieutenant, I trust you will consider it your duty to help me finish this box of cookies?" She added, "I used to love green tea cookies, but there's love and then there's being inundated with the things."

He was dying to find out what a Tepwe daughter had done to get herself exiled to the military, when she could instead be languishing amid silk cushions and (presumably) a greater variety of cookies. But it wasn't for him to ask. As much as she confided in him about everything from cookies to insect bites, she rarely dropped any hints about that part of her past.

So Nawong contented himself by making up stories, none of which he expected to have any relationship to the truth: Kodai was the reincarnation of a general who had died without winning their last battle (not that most people in the Empire believed in reincarnation). Kodai had followed a lover into the army—except she showed no signs of being lovesick. Kodai had fled an unhappy engagement—but would her family have permitted such a thing? All in all, he liked the reincarnation story best. If nothing else, it gave him an excuse to speculate about the legendary generals she could be.

He should have remembered that legendary generals rarely enjoyed happy endings.

★ ★ ★

Kodai collected books. One of them was a collection of military aphorisms, which she treasured. It wasn't the only such collection she owned, but it came from a country called Maeng-of-the-Bridges, which no longer existed. Maeng was conquered by the Empire half a generation ago and razed the way all things beautiful and defiant were razed. Kodai knew a little about Maeng, about its dueling aristocrats and its high gardens with the prized sullen orchids and the fabled crown of its king, set with seventy-six sapphire and aquamarine cabochons. (The rumor that nine of the aquamarines were in fact heat-treated topazes of much lower value was surely invention.)

She had carried it for the length of the Spider campaign, even when she was footsore and sleep-deprived and any modest decrease in the weight she was carrying would have brought her ease. Although no one had been able to teach her to read the dead Maeng language, she could still say a little about the calligraphic style. That was what mattered, not the book's fragile but exotic stab binding, in contrast to the link stitches favored in the Empire, or the book's cover, in fibrous dark red paper that was worn at three edges.

The book's aphorisms weren't organized in any useful manner, as though the unattributed author simply sat down to dinner and spilled out whatever came to mind. They were written untidily. Kodai got headaches when she examined the characters too closely. Both the Maeng and the Empire wrote with the brush, and in times past Kodai pored over the calligraphy style used in the book, which bore a distant resemblance to the Imperial one called The Stars Fall Slowly. Kodai's least favorite instructor in academy had used The Stars Fall Slowly, yet she couldn't deny the beauty of the script, with its deceptively relaxed spacing and dramatic, almost blot-like serifs.

Lately Kodai hadn't opened the book at all. In the evenings leading up to the ritual against the Spiders, Nawong had watched her sitting with her head bent, book cradled in her tense hands. *Open it*, he had wished her, but she refused herself that small comfort, as though she didn't think she deserved it.

When spoken indistinctly (and face it, drunken soldiers were a universal), the name of the nation of Pekti-pehaktuch sounded similar to the Imperial word for "spider." Thus the Imperials called the Pektis Spiders.

Kodai was familiar with the official Imperial maps of the region. The old surveys weren't as useful as she had hoped, given the cartographers' tendency to stylize topographical features and the fact that local roads were easily damaged. For military applications, she relied heavily on the scouts' investigations and on local informants.

Still, the official maps did hold some interest for Kodai, and this was in the realm of (what else?) calligraphy. Imperial cartographers were a conservative lot, and they wrote in what was called, unimaginatively, Cartographers' Hand. The characteristics of Cartographers' Hand had proved stable despite the ebb and flow of calligraphic fashion in the Imperial court and among the government's ministries.

Cartographers' Hand (according to Kodai's notes, terse but readable, and the few remarks she made to Nawong on the subject) had the following traits: extreme vertical alignment, as though the calligrapher labeled everything while being hounded with a knife-edged ruler. This signified rigidity, conformity, reverence for tradition. Minimal variation from the beginning and end of a brushstroke, in contrast, for instance, to the dramatic flourishes favored in Evening Flight of Swans. In fact, the permitted variation was so minimal that it made reading the script at small sizes difficult. The implication was of narrow vision and institutional incestuousness.

One final quirk of the cartographers' art was that borders were not drawn with simple lines (if any line, following the twist-weave of political entanglements, river boundaries, and the habitations of different ethnic groups, was ever simple). They were inked, carefully, with the same character repeated over and over, like textual bricks: *lio*, for Imperial jade. In other words, the Empire was being carved out of the substance of other nations, which existed for this purpose.

Kodai had her favorites in the collection of letters. Her interest should have been strictly military, focused on the task of reducing the Spiders to a name spoken only by the wind. But she was human, and anyway it was impossible not to take interest in the Spider soldier Gevoh-an's recipes when she spent so many days eating cold rice and longing for jellied anchovies, pickled lotus root, or beef braised in summer wine—any smidgen of flavor. She liked to talk about food with Nawong: specifically, she talked about food, and he made fun of her nostalgia for anchovies. They both took a certain consolation from this conversation.

Her favorite recipe was the one for shadow soup. Gevoh's instructions neatly paralleled those for some of the fish soups that they'd eaten in the past. Kodai hated fish, but not more than she hated starving. In any case, the concept was to catch a shadow in a pot with green onions, ginger, winter melon, and whatever other vegetables you could steal from stores or bully from the local peasants. If you boiled the shadow for long enough, it might become palatable. Or nourishing. Or something.

Gevoh's recipes had inconsistent letterforms, although in this case this indicated a partial education—he might even have been self-taught—rather than mental instability. His columns drifted right and left in the minor way that indicated humor rather than the major way that suggested a dangerous temper.

Kodai showed some of the recipes to Nawong from time to time, and they shared a chuckle over their fancifulness. But when she came to the one for shadow soup, her eyes darkened, and she murmured, "It may be a fake soup, but that's real hunger talking."

Kodai first explained the solution to the Spiders to Nawong on a cold, sleety night while the ruddy light of a full moon filtered through the clouds. They had been talking about something else entirely—the way local berries were mouth-puckeringly unappetizing, which guaranteed that the cook would incorporate them in desserts—when Kodai said abruptly, "If you think about

it, graphology is stratificational." Her voice was soft
but not drowsy in the slightest, above the soprano cry
of the frogs. "We've been focusing all this time on
characteristics, as though people and their cultures could
be factored into motes. But a person is more than the
sum of their traits, just as a grapheme is more than the
sum of its strokes. A person is a *character*, just as a word
is represented by a character. If you can specify people
entire, not just the traits, you can narrow the focus of the
spell. You can direct it against Spiders rather than
against Imperials. The Spiders won't know what hit
them."

Nawong wasn't a graphological theorist. But he wasn't
stupid, either, and he didn't like where this was going.
"You can't *say* that," he said more familiarity than their
relative stations would ordinarily permit. Except it was a
cold, sleety night, and they had come to know each other
well. "'Character,' like a person in a book."

"Oh, but everyone's in a *book*," Kodai said, suddenly
fierce, "if the whole damn Empire and its ever-growing
pile of decrees and statutes and declarations is a *book*."

Now, several years after that discussion, Kodai and
Nawong were on the hillside, hoping it would and
wouldn't rain. No frogs this time. Kodai was gnawing her
lip, not realizing it, as she wrote more and more
exactingly, approaching the knot of characters that would
complete and activate the spell.

She paused, withdrew her brush so it wouldn't drip
over the paper, grimaced. Nawong, recognizing the signal,
bent to massage her shoulders. She let him do this for a
while, then straightened. He backed off, resolved to

watch. For a moment, he thought she was about to say something. Then she lifted the brush and wrote the final few strokes with a sure hand.

Here's the final piece, the key, the piece you must have discerned from the beginning: ██████'s own hand, distinct from the style she would rather have used, itself distinct from the style she was originally taught by tutors in her parents' house.

Extremely crisp brushwork, as though chiseled. A broadening of the spacing of the characters as the text marched across the page. Vertical strokes like perfect spear hafts. Most of all, if you looked sideways at the page, diagonal spaces falling through the columns like rain.

██████ couldn't read any of this anymore. ██████, as she had known, and had explained to her aide, was gone. The side-effect of writing the Spiders into the narrative of their own destruction, even if she spared the Imperials, was that the author, too, was an implicit character in that selfsame narrative.

She had been obliterated along with them.

Everywhere the Spiders bled from punctures like crescent moons, in the villages, in the towns, upon the battlements of castles. Their bones burned up from the inside and candled the night. Their outposts ran red like hemorrhage and black like rot.

On the hillside, Lieutenant Nawong lingered beside the crumpled mass of charred meat that had once been ██████, knowing that he would never remember her name, and trying to anyway. After all, there was no hurry now. Then he gathered up the spell-pages, even if ████████ couldn't read any of them anymore.

Like the Spiders she had destroyed, she was no longer part of the story.

★ ★ ★

ABOUT THE AUTHOR

Yoon Ha Lee's work has appeared in *The Magazine of Fantasy & Science Fiction*, *Clarkesworld*, *Fantasy Magazine*, *Beneath Ceaseless Skies*, and *Lightspeed*. Lee's short story collection *Conservation of Shadows* came out in 2013 from Prime Books. Lee's stories have also appeared in the anthologies *The Year's Best SF 18*, ed. David Hartwell; *The Year's Best Science Fiction and Fantasy 2012*, ed. Rich Horton; and *The Year's Best Science Fiction 29*, ed. Gardner Dozois. Lee lives in Louisiana. Learn more at yoonhalee.com.

AMERICAN GOLEM

★ ★ ★

Weston Ochse

On Tuesday I stalked the old section of Kabul where the minarets stand impervious to the constant bombings. Men halted their chatter and peered at me as if they knew what I was about. Women sheathed in powder blue *burqas* hurried away. Even children scattered as I limped through their gaggles, worried at what seemed to be a white man trolling through their midst, his face wrapped in a black and white *shemagh*, body clothed in *Pashtun* long shirt and pants, but unmistakably American to those who would know the difference.

I ignored them. Purpose-made, I was on mission to kill the man who'd killed my brother. Not my real brother, of course, but the one from whom my existence derived. He, the child of Shira and Emil Drachman, me the man raised from the mud and sand of New Mexico—land of his birth, land of my birth, and the land where he was buried on the same day I was born.

My not-real-brother, Isaac, died three years ago while driving Massud Circle. One second he was in a vehicle bound for the airport for mid-tour R&R, the next he was eaten by the rage of a roadside bomb as it chewed through him, the three other American soldiers in his Hummer, and seven Afghan civilians, including a doctor, a student studying social work, and a child in the city for the first time for an operation on her lungs.

On Wednesday the military police chased me. I was AWOL from the Army. If they caught me, they were going to send me home. It was too hard to find my target behind concrete T-walls and armed sentries anyway. This way I was closer to the people, which also meant I was closer to him, wherever he was in this city of three million people.

On Thursday I witnessed a man on a bicycle ride into a crowd and detonate. He rained like hateful confetti at a nonexistent parade, the sound of his death ringing through the streets and on up into the Hindu Kush.

On Friday I met the woman from the embassy. It was an odd thing, her being there teaching a group of children to skateboard. I remember my maker whispering to me about Isaac and his love of Tony Hawk and his years living aboard a skateboard before he grew up to be a soldier. It was the skateboards that made me stop and watch. It was her eyes that made me stay. And it was her voice that captured my clay-made heart.

I wonder even now if it is my idea of what Isaac would have loved or if this love I felt was an invention of myself. Can a thing such as me have these emotions? I've felt anger. I've felt fear for others. So why not love?

"You're not from around here," she'd said, delivering the ultimate cliché once she noticed me sitting in the shade of a fig tree, only my eyes visible through the break in my *shemagh*.

I didn't answer her.

A moment later she asked, "Are you from one of the other embassies? It's probably not safe to have you out here."

"It's not safe for you, either," I said.

She grinned. "I have guards." She pointed to the six men deployed around the park, each wearing heavy body armor and Kevlar helmets and carrying HK 416s. "You sound American. If so, then you definitely shouldn't be outside the walls. What are you doing here?"

"Looking for someone."

"Who are you looking for?"

"I'd rather not say."

Her smile fell. "Why not?"

"I'd rather not say." I got up. One of her soldier guards was staring at me and seemed to be about ready to come over to investigate. I turned to go.

I'd gotten perhaps a dozen feet when she said, "I hope you find who you are looking for."

Me too, I thought. Then I said it aloud, but I was too far away for her to hear.

I have no memory of before. My first recollection was awaking fully formed in a Navajo mud hut that crouched in the shadow of the Chuska Mountains in New Mexico. My maker stood next to an ancient Navajo woman. She shook a bunch of burnt sage as she sang in a paper-dry voice. My maker drew the forefinger of his right hand across my forehead and traced on it the Hebrew word nqm, *which I knew meant vengeance. But the American English was truly inadequate to fully translate* nqm. *I felt it mark me—the idea of a community having been damaged because of an offense, something which could only be restored by a deed I was destined to commit.*

I sat up into a ray of speckled sunlight slanting through the window and breathed for the first time.

I had purpose.

I had knowledge.

I had a desire for nqm.

I found myself returning to the park where the children skateboarded. Half were girls, their bright headscarves stark against their black, white, and gray clothing. All wore elbow and knee pads; the girls wore pink and the boys wore blue. I read the signs posted garishly around the skate park. Although written in Dari, I could read them as easily as any other language.

Youth Empowerment.

Pride.

Take Charge.

Grasp Your Future.

Know Yourself.

Love.

Peace.

All Western ideas for an Afghani mind. It looked as if the embassy woman was using skateboarding as a mechanism for social change. Easier to change the children than to change the adults. I could understand this.

It was the third time back when I saw her again. She came and sat down beside me.

"I know who you are."

I looked at her. "I doubt it," I said finally.

"Corporal Isaiah Drachman, formerly of the New Mexico National Guard. Your tour ended three months ago. You're AWOL, soldier."

I glanced at her guards, who were in place and looking outward, then back to her. "You know me, but I don't know you."

"Call me Sam," she said, holding out a hand.

I took it, felt the softness, and shook it. Part of me wanted to never let go, to perhaps take it with me. She made my decision easy by pulling her hand free.

"Cold," she said, smiling apologetically. "Your hands are so cold."

"It's how I was made," I said, telling her more truth than she knew.

She rubbed her hands together as she spoke, watching the kids travel up and down the wooden ramps. "You have extraordinary eyes. I knew I'd seen them somewhere. We have a file on you at the embassy. Why didn't you go back when your unit rotated home? Why stay here? I have to say, you're one of the only people I've ever heard of who decided to stay. The others were at least Afghan-Americans."

"My mission isn't complete." That I said it surprised me a little. But I'd decided to be honest with her. After all, the worst that could happen would be she'd think I was crazy and not believe me.

"Your file says you were a truck driver. Are you trying to tell me you're on a secret mission for the government?" She flashed a smile.

"Not for the government."

"You said before you were looking for someone. Is that your mission? Who is it?"

"Mullah Vor Gul."

She stared at me. "Everyone's looking for him. What makes you think you can find him?"

"What makes you think I can't?"

"He's only one of the most wanted men in all of Afghanistan." Then her eyes narrowed. "I read in the report where your brother died in an incident a few years ago. That's it, isn't it? Vor Gul is a Haqqani leader. Did he claim credit?"

"He did."

She stared at me for a long while, then shook her head. "Jesus. You're going to kill him, aren't you?"

I nodded, but was beginning to feel uncomfortable. I started to stand, but she placed a hand on my arm.

"Can I see your face?" she asked softly.

I hesitated, then unwound the *shemagh*.

She appraised me, tilting her head slightly as she did.

Then I rewound the cloth around my head and face, stood, and hurried away. Now that she knew what I was about, I felt at risk. I kept my head down as I shuffled past the guards and into the gathering dusk.

My maker sat with me for two weeks before I was

ready to leave the sanctuary of my birthplace. The old woman fed us and kept fueling the fireplace with mesquite. His name was Yoram Drachman, and he'd been Isaac's grandfather. He explained to me that I was a modern-day gingerbread man. A golem of sorts. Not the rough-hewn simulacrum which had protected Prague so many centuries ago, but a finely crafted reincarnation of his grandson.

"I've spent my life working for the Israeli military, creating battalions of tools such as yourself, each one a little better than the rest. Until I decided it was time to make one for myself.

"The art came to our people from China a thousand years ago," he went on to tell me. "They'd been using golems for thousands of years, culminating in the creation of the Terracotta Army of the First Qin Emperor. But where the Chinese created their golems for defense, we create ours as hunters. And you, Isaiah, you will be my hunter."

Over the days and nights, he told me everything he knew of my not-brother and of his killer, Mullah Vor Gul. With the ability to never forget, the information built upon itself, until one day I was ready to leave. He'd had false papers made for me, showing I was a new transfer to the New Mexico National Guard.

I heard the name mentioned two days after Sam and I last spoke. *Mullah Vor Gul*, whispered by one man to another as they shared a cigarette in an alley. I was two blocks away when they said it the first time, but they were in sight when they said it a second time. Never more than a whisper, that name rang loud as a mission bell to me.

I followed them as they boarded a bus heading out to Shar-e-Now. When they disembarked, I did as well. They saw me, but I kept my eyes down and let them walk away. It took an hour, but I eventually found them again, homing in on their voices on the third floor of an old Soviet apartment building. I squatted with my back against the building and listened, my hearing so much more than any mere human could have.

They spoke of American soldiers. They spoke of the need to cleanse the earth of our stink. They spoke of bombs. They spoke of vengeance. I couldn't help but smile. I knew more about vengeance than they could ever hope to know.

I *was* vengeance.

The two men left the next morning. I followed them throughout the city, sometimes close enough to hear, sometimes too far away, until they returned once more. They spoke again of American soldiers and bombs. Then they mentioned Vor Gul. They said his name reverently. Then they said words which caused me concern. They spoke of skateboards, and they also spoke of bombs.

I went to them.

I broke the legs of the one and the arms of the other. I tied them to chairs and searched their meager place. I found maps taped to the wall of one room, along with a collection of prepaid cell phones-burners.

"What is it you want?" they asked.

"Vor Gul."

Their spines stiffened, despite their pain. "We won't tell you."

Then I broke the rest of their arms and legs. One passed out. The other whimpered gently, too tired to continue screaming.

"Tell me of skateboards," I said, squatting between them, staring at a cockroach scuttling across the floor. "Tell me of skateboards and bombs."

This they told me.

Then I killed them.

On the final day of my creation, my maker brought Isaac's parents in. Shira was in tears and threw herself at her father. Emil stood in the doorway, his face unreadable in shadow.

"You mustn't do this, Papa!" she cried.

My maker gripped her by her shoulders and held her at arm's length. "This is my choice. It must be done."

"Isaac wouldn't want this," she said.

"Isaac would understand this better than either of you." He stared hard at his son-in-law. "Take your wife."

Emil came over and put his arms around her shoulders. "Just let him do it, damn it."

My maker stood, towering over me as I lay on my back on the table. "Isaac understood the need to be a part of something greater than oneself. He knew the importance of protecting those things he loved."

"But this is America, Papa. Not Israel."

"We are not so different, our two countries. America is as surrounded by her enemies as Israel. Make no mistake that the oceans can protect her. They haven't before, and they won't now. The only way to protect is to find and kill your enemies."

Emil shook his head. "Enough of this, old man. Your daughter moved here with me to get away from such thinking."

My maker laughed. "And look what good it did."

"What is it you want of us?" Emil said.

"To bear witness to your vengeance." He placed his hand on my head. "Arise and introduce yourself, my American Golem."

I sat up and stared at the parents of the man from which I was made. My maker had burned him and ground him up, then had mixed his remains with the land. I felt a connection to these two people before me. I had memories of them that came fractured and chaotic.

"He lo-looks human," Shira said.

"He looks like him." Tears gathered in Emil's eyes. "Damn you."

"My greatest creation. He shall be Isaac's brother."

"Hello. My name is Isaiah . . . Isaiah Drachman," I said, for the first time speaking to someone other than my maker.

"Dear God," Emil whispered.

"Not God. A golem," my maker said.

I held out my hand as Isaac's memories swept through me like a storm. I couldn't help myself as I said, "Oh, Mother . . ."

Then she fainted.

I was drawn back to the skateboarders both because of my worry for their safety and because of something insatiable about Sam. The two low-level Haqqani militants had known only that the park was a target. They hadn't known when, but had believed the attack would happen soon. I felt the need to warn someone. I felt the need to save them, which felt strange, because I'd never felt the pull of something other than my singular mission. Even when I'd pretended to be a soldier, it had been in order to get here and find Vor Gul. Did I intrinsically know that this was something that Isaac would have wanted done, or was this *me*? Was there a difference?

When I arrived, Sam was working with the girls, posing them and taking pictures. I sat in my usual place beneath the fig tree. I'd been sitting there for three or four minutes when a man came and sat down beside me. He wore a polo shirt beneath body armor and 5.11 pants. He wore Ray-Bans and had blond hair cut too short to comb. He had a 9mm pistol in a cross-draw holster attached to the front of his body armor.

"I'm Scott," he said. He neither shook my hand, nor did he look at me. Instead, he kept his gaze steadily focused on the skateboarders. "I hear you're looking for Vor Gul."

Sam had told someone about me. Had my desire put my mission at risk? Was this what was meant to be human? I cursed myself.

As if he could read my mind: "Don't be nervous and don't worry. We have no intention of stopping you." He let that sink in for a moment, then added, "I work at the embassy, too."

"What is it you want?" I asked.

"The same thing you want. We don't care if you do it or if we get to him first. We just want to take him down."

Sam came over and sat on the other side of me. "I see you've met Scott."

I turned toward her. "Danger is coming."

Her smile fell. "What's that supposed to mean?"

"I found two men talking about Vor Gul and this skate park."

"When? Where?" Scott demanded, looking at me for the first time.

"No time frame. Soon, I think." I saw him exchange a look with Sam, and then I knew the truth of it. "You knew it. No, you planned it. This place, these children, they're a lure."

Embarrassment took root in Sam's eyes. She couldn't meet my steady challenging gaze. "We thought it might be too lucrative a target, especially after the *Time* magazine article that came out last week. But the children are safe. They were never in any danger."

"You're kidding yourselves if you believe that." Whatever it had been that had drawn me to Sam was now a phantom of what it was. She had commented about the coldness of my skin. That was no match for the empty cavern of her heart.

"Where are these two militants?" Scott asked.

I gave him the address. "They are no longer living," I said.

Sam's eyes widened. "You killed them?"

I watched as a girl of about twelve soared down a ramp, her knees slightly bent, her arms graceful as they caught air. "It's what I do."

"Can you explain to me why there's no record of you before last year?" Scott asked, his voice suddenly official.

"I'd rather not say."

"You're on record as being the brother of Isaac Drachman, but he never listed a sibling on any of his paperwork."

"I can't help that," I said.

Scott persisted. "Who do you work for?"

I laughed. He thought I was a spook. He'd never understand, so I just didn't answer him.

"You know we can bring you in if we want to," he said.

"I thought you said you had no intention of stopping me."

"That was before."

"Before what? Before I gave you a lead that might possibly help you find Vor Gul? Before I gave you information that would save lives?"

They exchanged glances. This wasn't going as they'd planned. So sad when reality intrudes on a well-planned idea. I decided to ask my own questions. "What do you know about Vor Gul? Do you know where he is?"

"We have reports that he left his safe house in Waziristan and is heading into Kabul." Scott reached out and grasped my wrist. "Let me see your face."

I pulled free of his grasp. "What is it you think you want to see?"

He grabbed my wrist again, and once again I pulled free. "I just want to see . . . You're not human, are you?"

The question floored me.

"What are you?" His eyes were fixed on me as he waited for the answer.

"I am golem."

His face froze. "Holy shit," he said finally. "You're one of them. Why were you made?"

"For Isaac Drachman."

"Are you free thinking?" he asked.

I shrugged. "How can one know such a thing?"

"Are you alone or are there more of you?"

I decided it was my turn to ask a question. "How did you know?"

He didn't hesitate to respond. "Isaac's grandfather is on our watch list. We know he traveled from Israel to America and stayed for several weeks. He's part of a special division of the IDF we've been trying to figure out."

The fact that he knew this left little doubt what section of the embassy he worked for.

"You're not real," Sam said, her voice filled with awe.

I turned and placed a hand on her cheek, feeling the softness, the warmth of living flesh. "Does this feel real to you?"

She pulled away from my hand. "I'm sorry, what I meant was you're not human. I thought Scott was crazy when he came to me with his idea."

Scott interrupted. "What happened to Yoram Drachman? We have no record of him leaving America."

"He's dead."

This gave him pause. "Did you kill him?"

"That's personal."

"Did he make more?"

"That's personal."

Now it was his turn to laugh. "A golem invoking personal privacy."

I shrugged. "Why not? I am as alive as you."

He shook his head. "We have souls."

"How do you know I don't have one?"

"Jesus," was all he could say.

I stood ready to leave.

Scott didn't say anything, but Sam stopped me and held out her hand. In it was a cell phone. "Here, take this." When I hesitated she said, "It'll let us track you and tell us where you are. We can also call and tell you if we have information about Vor Gul."

I took the phone and left. A mile later, I tossed it in the back of a donkey cart headed out of town.

They came at me the next day. All their talk about letting me continue my mission meant nothing. I noticed them following me in an up-armored SUV just after noon. I'd passed two Friday food markets where farmers brought in their own fruits and vegetables, often by donkey cart. I moved through the crowd slowly, like I was browsing. But like always, I was listening for any mention of Vor Gul. I could hear it even when whispered.

The SUV was at both locations. I decided to lead them to a place I knew. I acquired a limp as I shuffled down an alley and into a dead end that cul-de-saced between three four-story buildings. I waited until the SUV roared into the space. Four men leaped out of the vehicle and took up distance around me. They were operators. Probably TF 310 or 240. From their helmets to their knee pads to their body armor almost hidden beneath their one-size-too-large black shirts to the way they held their HKs all spoke to these men being pros. They exuded confidence. They'd clearly encountered a lot.

Too bad they'd never encountered a golem or they'd have known better.

"What is it?" I asked, deciding not to feign anything.

"Mr. Scott says you're to come with us." The speaker was a muscular black man who wore a scar down one cheek.

"And where are you going?"

"Some place where he can talk to you."

Study me was more like it. "Sounds like Parwan. I'll take a pass."

They shifted uncomfortably on their feet. They weren't prepared for my response. I wondered how much Scott had told them about me. I wonder how much he knew about golems.

Their leader spoke again. "I'm not going to tell you again, sir. You need to come wit—"

He never finished as I flowed toward him. Moving faster than any human, my limbs weren't held back by the mechanism of joints and muscles. I was a single entity. I was a human-sized amoeba.

I was death.

I grabbed his rifle and twisted it so quickly it broke both his wrists. I snapped the weapon in half and jammed one piece through his face. I moved on the next man as they fired, dozens of 5.56 rounds piercing my flesh.

I felt no pain. I barely felt the impacts. I reached the next man and broke him down. The others tried to run, but I wouldn't let them. I ripped them apart and left their pieces in a pile inside the back of the SUV.

When it was all over, I stripped and found where Sam or Scott had attached the tracking device to the back of my clothes. I left the device and my clothes in the SUV and walked naked for a time.

This was Kabul, so hardly anyone noticed.

The next day found me in the slums of Char Qala. I heard his name everywhere.

Vor Gul was back in town, they whispered. He had a target, they said prophetically. So many were talking it was confusing.

I spent the day moving from home to home, but no one knew anything further. It wasn't until after midnight that I heard his name only twice. Once from a young man who was praying to grow up and be like him, and the second time from a group of men on the eighth floor of an abandoned hospital, planning their next target.

I listened to them and waited for the man I had been made to kill.

After Shira and Emil left, my maker brought out a knife. "An interesting thing about golems," he said, "is that they are not so hard to make. Making them last, now that is the difficulty."

The ancient Navajo woman entered the room with two younger girls dressed in traditional garb. Their leather dresses had white and red beads sewn to make symbols I didn't recognize. The old woman turned to one of the younger ones, "Get a bucket and a towel," she said in Navajo. "There's going to be a mess."

One girl ran out, but soon returned.

"What are you going to do?" I asked my maker.

"A ceremony that can only be done once."

The girls began to finger paint symbols on the table while the woman scattered small white petals along the ground. When they finished, I made to lie down once more, but my maker stopped me.

"This is not for you. This is for me."

He lay down and handed me the knife. I felt a moment of panic.

"What is it you want me to do with this?"

"There's a way I can pass my art along that can let you live forever."

Isaac's memories of my maker flashed through my mind like a movie trailer of important events. An echo of an emotion sparked in my chest and I realized I didn't want this man to die.

My maker saw me and shook his head. "We're ready to begin," he said, then closed his eyes and began to chant.

I held the knife for a long time, then used it as I was told.

Vor Gul never showed that night, but the plan to attack the children was in place. Neither Sam nor Scott was at the skate park, which meant their guards were gone as well. Nine children played on the ramps, roaring up and down them on skateboards. Nine innocent children who were pawns in a political game that was going to get them killed.

Vor Gul.

I heard the name clearly and spun toward it. An up-armored SUV waited at the curb. Scott sat in the passenger seat. Two men in back and the driver stared at me with laser eyes.

I saw Scott's mouth move again. *Vor Gul*.

How long had they been waiting for me? How many of them were there? Or were they merely here to witness the deaths of the children? Nothing like the murders of children to spark humanity's rage against the militants. Families ensconced in their living rooms might not care about foreign men killing other foreign men, but when foreign men killed children, that was a different story.

Vor Gul. He said it again, and this time smiled. He made a motion with his hand, and the SUV roared away.

I'm not sure how long I stood there, but it wasn't until I heard the name spoken yet again that I moved.

Vor Gul.

I turned reluctantly, already tired of this game. But instead of another SUV or Scott or even Sam, I saw a young man walking unsteadily, clothed in a heavy jacket. He mumbled to himself. Both of his hands flexed and unflexed. I watched a moment, then realized what he was going to do.

I ran toward the children skateboarding in the park. They'd been promised a dream which was about to become a nightmare. My *shemagh* flew free and for a moment I was a bird, descending, wings out and flapping behind me. Then the wind took the cloth and I was once again a golem. The children were too far for me to reach, but not far enough away to be outside the kill zone.

The bomber reached into the pocket of his jacket and pulled out a cell phone. He dialed a number and began to speak into it as if he was FaceTiming. The Dari translated in my mind. "Vor Gul, I do this for you. I do this so people will see, so that they will attend, and know the terrible violence that has been brought upon us. Praise be to Allah." He held the phone out in front of him to give Vor Gul a view of what was about to happen, then began striding toward the skateboarding children. Any moment now and he'd detonate, sending shrapnel and hate into those whose only crime was to fall prey to a woman who'd taught them to skateboard for a foul purpose.

As a golem I fell upon him, bringing him down, flattening him, covering him with my body. For one brief moment I was a man with the courage to ignore my mission and do what was right. I was Isaac, the better part of him fueled by his desire to do good. I was Yoram, fueled with the ability to be reborn. I was the American Golem whose ability to avenge was unmatched. Then he detonated and I felt myself flung in a million directions as the pieces of me separated and rained down upon this small piece of Afghanistan.

I no longer had ears, but I could hear them scream. I no longer had eyes, but I could see them run. I was almost elemental, the blast having blown me into so many pieces I was indiscernible from what I once was.

I remained in place as the police came to investigate, then the military, then the Americans. They cleaned up the remains of the bomber, then put tape around the area I occupied.

Night fell. Then dawn came. Then night fell again.

I was present even though my body wasn't. But that was okay. The rains would eventually come, and when they did, they'd push pieces of me together, until one day there would be enough of me that I could reform. My maker had made sure I had the knowledge. His was my first murder. One day, I'd be the American Golem once more. One day, I'd have enough of me to resume my chore and exact *nqm* on Vor Gul—and Scott and Sam.

And until then?

Until then, I'd watch and wait, bearing witness to life from my low angle.

Yes.

One day.

One day soon.

When the rains come and wash me together.

★ ★ ★

ABOUT THE AUTHOR

Weston Ochse is the author of twenty books, most recently *SEAL Team 666* and its sequel, *Age of Blood*, which the *New York Post* called "required reading" and USA Today placed on their "New and Notable Lists." His first novel, *Scarecrow Gods*, won the Bram Stoker Award for Superior Achievement in First Novel, and his short fiction has been nominated for the Pushcart Prize. His work has appeared in comic books and magazines such as *Cemetery Dance* and *Soldier of Fortune*. He lives in the Arizona desert within rock-throwing distance of Mexico. He is a military veteran with 30 years of military service and recently returned from a deployment to Afghanistan.

WEAPONS IN THE EARTH

★ ★ ★

Myke Cole

*"The Mattab On Sorrah are but one of many
goblin clans that dot the endless plain. They are
villagers, farming outside their walls and
withdrawing into their fastnesses at night. But
goblinkind is as diverse and varied as mankind.
There are itinerant traders and fishing villages.
There are stone cities. The Black-Horns clan is
entirely nomadic, spending their lives on the
plain, finding one another by celestial navigation,
as close to their kine as they are to one another,
treating each cow like a member of the family."*

—Simon Truelove,
A Sojourn Among the Mattab On Sorrah.

Blackfly hadn't spoken a word since they had been
captured.

Twig surveyed their ragged band. A week in captivity had weakened them all. Stump's broad shoulders drooped; Hatchet looked impossibly thin; and Twig himself had lost the tip of his nose to the hungry frost. Blackfly was only a little girl, tiny and shivering. White-Ears's mind, clouded at the best of times, strayed deeper and longer into the fog, until Twig wondered if the ancient goblin would stare silently into the distance until the cold claimed him.

Worst of all were the kine. The twenty animals lowed and nosed in the frost-covered grass, desperate for forage that the winter had stolen from them. Bloodsuckers clung to their diminishing flanks as their bodies, weakened by hunger, could no longer resist them. It tore at Twig to see them so. The kine were food and milk and warmth to the Black-Horns tribe, the beating heart of Twig's world since his birth. They were family.

White-Ears extended a gnarled hand over a small rock, His skin looked like old leather long gone brittle. The white paint that marked him as a Sorcerer was long gone, a tracery of pale flakes the only reminder that captivity had not stripped him of his magic entirely. Old age and a feeble mind were doing a fine job of that on their own.

"You cannot force the flow," the old goblin wheezed. "You have to listen to it, feel it. Then you can . . . tell it what you want."

Twig felt the old Sorcerer's magical tide eddy erratically as White-Ears gestured at the rock. "You are too excited," White-Ears went on. "You have to be still."

The Sorcerer closed his eyes and breathed deeply, his stooped back straightening as his magical tide suddenly focused. The rock begin to shimmer, twist, stretching into the shape of a small knife blade that Stump could use to cut the bloodsuckers from the hides of the kine.

Twig caught his breath. White-Ears was the oldest goblin in the Black-Horns tribe. In his youth, White-Ears's magic had been legendary. When his mind was clear, it still could be.

But White-Ears's mind was rarely clear these days.

The Sorcerer grunted, farted loudly. His tide wavered and pulsed. The stone froze, half-formed, then the grass around it sprouted madly, stopped.

"Eh?" The old goblin blinked, looking at the half-formed stone knife as if it were the first time he'd ever seen it. "What's this?"

One of the kine—Clover, her belly huge with the calf growing inside—mooed softly and pushed White-Ears gently aside to crop at the sudden patch of fresh grass. She was hungry; all the kine were.

Stump would never disrespect an elder outright—none of them would—but disgust was clear in his eyes. He was one of the biggest of the Black-Horns. The short rations and cold nights of their captivity had done little to sap his strength. He tested the stone knife's edge, cursed at its dullness. "Let me get them gathered up before I try this."

He turned away, picking up the long stick he used to herd the kine, clucking as he drove them closer together. The Three-Foots would be along soon to check on their prisoners, and Twig knew that they would look for any excuse to beat them. Best to not be caught idle.

The huge creatures lowed plaintively, grudgingly taking a few steps only when Stump swatted them hard enough to nearly break the stick. The winter was coming in earnest, and the grazing was poor here. Earth Sorcerers like White-Ears could use their magic to coax the grass into new life, but White-Ears continued to blink at the half-formed rock, confusion written on his wizened face.

Clover finished the fresh grass, then pushed her broad black nose through the frost, glancing up at Twig, mooing a question.

A large bloodsucker had moored itself to her flank, its ridged back pulsing purple as it fed on her. There was just the one for the moment, but Twig knew that as she grew weaker, there would be more.

"There, girl," Twig said, patting her head. "We'll get you fed."

But his stomach twisted. He didn't know how he'd feed Clover and her unborn calf both. Clover ate for two, and that meant twice the forage. There was barely enough to go around as it was.

Twig felt his own magical flow, gathered it, reached out for the grass. He could feel the song of the earth around him, the secret language of the plants, the stones, the kine mooing and pawing at the frozen ground.

But he could not sing it. His Earth magic was weak, half-formed. The green below the icy curtain taunted him, its high joyful voice carried on the current of the Earth magic flowing through it. That song promised food for the kine. It promised shelter from the knife-tipped wind. It promised liberation from their captors.

But Twig's magic was not up to the task—"Soft," as the elders called it. He could only listen and seethe.

Blackfly clung to the ragged hem of White-Ears's robe, tiny, shivering and hungry. She was a dried-out husk of a child now, no tears left in her.

Hatchet sidled up alongside. His eyes darted inside a giant head that looked too big for his scrawny body. Twig would have thought him as starved as the kine if he didn't know that the goblin always looked that way. "You shouldn't be trying your magic." Hatchet's voice was thin, reedy. "And you shouldn't be encouraging that old coot, neither. You know it's forbidden. The Gibberer will have your guts."

Stump sucked in his breath at the contempt, instinctively turning and tapping his fingers against his eyelids toward White-Ears. Twig followed suit, adding a slight bow, his stomach turning over at Hatchet's rudeness to an honored elder. It was only a week since the Three-Foots had fallen on them, but that had been enough time to wear ruts in their sense of honor. White-Ears only looked up at their obeisance. "What? What's this?"

"Nothing, grandfather," Twig said, glaring at Hatchet, who suddenly looked at his feet, shame clouding his features.

"I meant no disrespect," Hatchet mumbled.

"Magic's our only way out of this," Twig said. "My magic's Soft. So White-Ears is our only hope."

"Soft?" White-Ears's eyes suddenly looked clear. "Not Soft. Fearful, angry. You cannot sing to the Earth until you are *still*, boy."

"We cannot wait on magic," Stump said. "We should run."

"The Three-Foots are the fastest runners and best

trackers on the plain," Twig said. "And us with a grandfather, a little girl, and herding twenty head of black horns? One near calving? They'd—"

"We'll get our fix by the stars!" Stump cut him off. "We'll find the rest of the tribe! We can stand and fight then, in numbers."

"They'd be on us before nightfall. We wouldn't have a chance to get a fix, much less find the others. And keep your yob closed on that, lest you want them torturing it out of us and taking the whole tribe unawares."

"Here we are," White-Ears said. The old Sorcerer held a perfectly formed stone knife in his hand, the afternoon sun glinting off the razor-sharp edge. "See, lad? You have to be still."

The wind picked up, carrying the heavy, wet chill that promised snow. It whipped over Twig's remaining ear. The Gibberer, the Three-Foots's greatest Sorcerer, had taken one, and the other had been numb for days, maybe past healing. But even if the remaining ear couldn't feel, it still heard the Gibberer's heavy footfalls across the frozen crust that was slowly winning its battle with the grass. Other Three-Foots warriors were with him.

Stump snatched the knife from White-Ears and thrust it into his ragged leather trousers.

Twig tried to look busy, hissing a warning to the others. The little knife couldn't do much, but it wouldn't do to let the Gibberer find them with it.

The crunching of the Gibberer's feet grew closer. Twig pretended not to hear, hoping against hope that the Gibberer was on some distant errand, that the footfalls would start receding. But the terrible huffing breath warmed his shoulders as the monster came to a stop behind him.

Worst of all was the pulsing of the Gibberer's magical current, the most powerful Twig had ever felt.

"Ey." The Gibberer's voice was the rasp of stone on iron. It burbled out of a throat twisted and stretched one too many times. Flesh Sorcerers were taught to never use their magic on themselves. It was madness to risk it.

But the Gibberer had abandoned sanity long ago.

"Ey," he rasped again. "Rat."

The Gibberer called them all rats. Stump was "Big Rat"; Hatchet was "Scrawny Rat"; Blackfly was "Little Rat"; and White-Ears was "Old Rat." Twig's esteem in the Gibberer's eyes must have been low indeed. He'd never earned an adjective.

"Rat," the Gibberer slobbered. His self-magicking had rendered his mouth unfit for speech. "Talking to you. Turn 'round."

Twig did as he was told.

The Flesh Sorcerer's magic had twisted him until he bore only the barest likeness to the goblin he'd once been. His body was swollen, rippling with lopsided muscle. Veins throbbed across the surface like wriggling tree roots, pulsing beneath patches of scraggly hair. His head and neck had vanished into the center of a powerful chest, below the arch of hulking shoulders. His eyes were misaligned: the lower one a tiny speck, the higher one as big as a raven's egg. He wore one of the human weapons around his neck as a talisman, the little L of black metal the human warriors called their "Glok." It could kill from afar if one had the metal arrows it spat, but this one looked bent, and Twig doubted it would work.

The Gibberer was named for his jaw. It hung to his knees, slavering, the gums rising over swollen purple lips. The Gibberer's teeth reared up nearly to his lower eye, yellowed tusks still crusted with the browning remains of his last meal.

"You look at me. I'm talking to you," The Gibberer gibbered. A long runner of slaver dripped from the corner of the giant, malformed mouth, leisurely making its way down to the frozen grass.

"I am looking at you," Twig said, trying to meet the thing's eyes. It was a task made considerably harder by the fact that they were practically in the Gibberer's armpits, different sizes and out of alignment.

"What you doing?" The Gibberer drooled. The bigger eye swept the surface of the grass. "Magic?" Twig froze, but the Gibberer only twisted his huge jaw up in a grim imitation of a smile. "You got no magic."

Twig could feel the Gibberer's powerful flow surging against his own.

"Ever meet a human, Rat?"

Twig knew better than to ignore the question. Not answering the Gibberer had earned him a beating once. The second time, the Gibberer had magicked his ear into a bloody, twisted antler. "Hear me now?" The Gibberer had asked. Twig had sobbed and screamed until the Gibberer had rolled his eyes and made Twig's ear fall right off.

"Ever meet a human?" The Gibberer asked again, his voice hard.

"No," Twig said.

"Call your magic 'rump,'" The Gibberer said. "Means arse. Your magic is human arse."

The Gibberer's magical flow intensified, and Twig felt the muscles in his buttocks clench painfully. He winced, his hands flying to his behind. The Gibberer laughed, a series of coughing barks.

"Arse rat!" Twig had finally earned an adjective. The Gibberer turned to Stump. "How's kine?"

"Hungry," Stump said. "This ground is freezing solid. We need to move them to—"

The Gibberer's arm extended, the magic making it elastic, the hand swelling into a distended paddle. He caught Stump on his ear and sent him sprawling. Stump managed to come up on one elbow, spitting out grass before the Gibberer reached him, his huge foot catching Stump on the chin, lifting him up and spinning him in the air. Stump landed in a heap beside White-Ears, who stared at him, confused. Blackfly began to wail.

The Gibberer turned to her. "Shut up."

She shook her head, biting down on her cries. The shrieks became muffled mewling. "Shut up!" The Gibberer snarled, pounding toward her.

The mewling turned to screaming as the Gibberer snatched her up by an ankle, dangling her headfirst over his gaping maw. She shrieked, beating against his fist with her tiny hands.

Twig launched himself at the monster, knowing it was useless, that the Gibberer could turn him to bloody rags with his magic, or beat him senseless without it.

Twig's feet slipped on the frost, made slick by the

Gibberer's slaver. He landed on his face, teeth clicking together painfully as the Gibberer lowered Blackfly, squalling, her head disappearing past the yellow-brown mountain range of his tusk teeth.

And then Stump was up behind the monster, whipping the knife from its hiding place, raising an arm to plunge the short blade into his back.

"No!" Hatchet shouted, colliding with Stump, sending them both tumbling in the grass, the knife clattering against a stone.

Stump sputtered while Hatchet rolled to his feet and backed away. The Gibberer spun, tossed Blackfly aside. She landed on top of White-Ears, toppling the old goblin.

"Wot?" The Gibberer asked, pinching the knife between two fat, malformed fingers, the blade tiny in his giant hand. "You little . . ."

He took two quick steps and snatched Stump up by the back of his shirt. The Gibberer growled and shook him. Stump flopped in his grip until the shirt tore, leaving The Gibberer clutching a scrap of filthy leather and Stump skinning his face in the grass for the third time in the passing of a few breaths.

The Gibberer panted. Twig got to his elbows, stayed there. Best not to let the monster see him on his feet. The Gibberer's breathing slowly evened, mismatched eyes narrowing, the light of thought entering them.

Twig caught his breath. An angry beast was bad. A thoughtful one was worse.

"You want knife?" The Gibberer whispered. He reached down, seizing Stump's wrist, slapping the blade into his open palm. Stump struggled weakly, but the fight was out of him.

"There," The Gibberer said, his voice suddenly soft, almost affectionate. "Knife."

Twig felt the monster's magic pulse, and Stump cried out as his hand melted around the stone.

The Gibberer seized Stump by his neck, dragging him over to White-Ears. The older goblin had gotten to his knees and was cooing to Blackfly, who sat shivering, eyes wide, seeing nothing.

"Now," The Gibberer crooned. "Cut."

Comprehension dawned across Stump's face. He shook his head emphatically. The Gibberer pointed to White-Ears. "Cut!"

"No." Stump's voice was edged with defiance.

"Kill you," The Gibberer promised.

"Then stop talking and do it." Stump bared his teeth.

Twig got to his feet, advanced, fists balled.

Hatchet sprinted to him. "Don't," the scrawny goblin whispered. "Don't make it worse!"

"Cut!" The Gibberer roared. His magic pulsed again, and Stump jerked like a string puppet, arm lashing out and plunging the knife into White-Ears's gut.

The old goblin exhaled in a rush, eyes going wide. Slowly he slumped forward, folding over Stump's extended arm. Stump knelt, his shoulders shaking as he wept.

The Gibberer grunted and turned away. He stabbed a finger at Hatchet. "You, good rat."

He spoke loud enough for all to hear, pointing at Hatchet again. "See good rat? All be good rat. Easier for you."

His eyes lit briefly on Blackfly, still beside White Ears, ignoring the ancient goblin's wound, Stump's sobs. "Not hungry," The Gibberer rasped. "Maybe tomorrow."

Stump's sobs coalesced into an angry shout. "You will die skewered on the Black-Horns! They are coming for you."

"Hope so," The Gibberer said. "Easier. Hard work, hunting you lot."

And then he was gone, the crunching of his footsteps across the frost fading into the distance.

Twig watched the hulking back recede. He knew he should help White-Ears, comfort Blackfly, but exhaustion overwhelmed him. He was conscious of his breathing, coming in ragged gasps, burning in his lungs. Wet cold kissed the bridge of his nose, and he crossed his eyes, watching the snowflake melt. Its cousins would be coming soon, and there would be no shelter from them save what warmth huddling with the kine could provide.

Stump's sobs rose, became shrieks, yanking Twig from his reverie. Twig shrugged off the fugue, shouldering Hatchet out of the way and dropping to his knees beside the big goblin.

Stump was bleeding freely from both hands. He grasped the knife blade with one hand, tried to twist it free of the melted mass of palm and fingers that clutched the handle.

"Leave it!" Twig shouted, grabbing his wrist.

"I stabbed him!" Stump shouted back, shaking off Twig's grip. "I stabbed a grandfather. I can't hold this cursed thing." With a final wrench, the handle came free, spraying both of them with blood, leaving a ragged groove in what used to be Stump's palm.

Stump clutched the hand to his stomach, doubling over. Twig tried to reach for it, but Stump turned away from him, cursing. Twig cursed too, called for Hatchet to help Stump while he went to White-Ears's side. The old goblin groaned weakly, lying on his side, curled up like a sleeping child. Blackfly sat as she had through the whole ordeal, silent and staring. Hatchet stood where he was, arms hugging his sides.

Twig eased White-Ears's body straight. "Easy, grandfather," he said. "Let me see."

White-Ears offered none of Stump's resistance and straightened out, exposing a small red hole surrounded by a spreading stain, the red made black by the filth ground into his robe. Twig widened the rent in the garment as gently as he could, revealing a small, neat slit in the Sorcerer's gut. Twig was no Healer, but he knew enough to know that all hinged on whether or not the blade had pierced the organs or slid between them.

Twig knew that Spadeleaf grew beneath the gathering frost. It could keep a wound from souring, but without Earth magic, he couldn't coax it to grow fresh enough to use. He sniffed the cut. When a goblin's guts were opened, there was usually a bad smell.

No Spadeleaf, no poultices, no Healing magic. There was nothing to do but stop the bleeding. Twig ripped a strip of filthy fabric from the hem of White-Ears's robe. He tied it tight over the wound, knotting it around White-Ears's back and cinching it up until the old Sorcerer groaned again. Twig leaned over White-Ears' face until he was sure the Sorcerer was still breathing, then returned to Stump.

Stump gripped bundles of frozen grass tightly. They soaked up most of the blood, tiny drips tapping onto the frozen ground. The knife lay in the grass, handle still encased in bloody meat.

"Let me see," Twig said, kneeling.

"S'fine," the big goblin said, getting to his feet and walking toward the scattered kine. "I'll see to the herd."

Twig turned and caught Hatchet's eyes. The scrawny goblin stood, arms still wrapped around him himself, shivering. His eyes widened with shame as he met Twig's glare, then narrowed in anger. "What'd you have done?" Hatchet asked. "I saved us all! He'd have killed us, that knife had gone in! I did right!"

"The knife did go in," Twig said. "Just not where Stump meant it to."

Hatchet held Twig's eyes as long as he could, which wasn't long. He looked at his feet, long toes flexing inside his sodden soft leather boots. "I did right," he muttered.

Twig left Hatchet, snatched up Stump's discarded stick, and jogged to the other side of the herd. He cooed and swatted, played to the kine's natural instinct to move together, and soon they had their twenty head milling in some semblance of order.

"Stump," Twig began.

"It's fine," Stump answered.

But it wasn't fine. The bundles of grass in Stump's hands had gone tacky from blood, fat drops still falling from them. White-Ears lay shivering in the grass, doubled over a wound that was likely going sour. Blackfly had found her tears again, curled up alongside White-Ears as if her closeness could make him well.

Twig felt another snowflake touch his nose.

Clover lowed again, her head poking up from the center of the herd. There was urgency in the sound, the pleading of a mother-to-be worried for her child.

"Aye, girl," Twig whispered. "I hear you."

He heard her, but what could he do?

Twilight came on. It brought cold with it, earnest, relentless.

Two Three-Foots warriors came when darkness fell.

Twig and Hatchet helped White-Ears, half dragging the old goblin along. The Black-Horns herded the kine, and the Three-Foots herded the Black-Horns, ready to hurt them should they slow.

And they were slow. White-Ears moved as slowly as growing grass at the best of times. His wound hadn't made him faster, and Blackfly refused to leave his side.

"Move!" grunted one of the warriors, the spear shaft punching into Twig's shoulders, sending him stumbling. Hatchet raced to keep up, and White-Ears moaned as his shoulders twisted. Twig checked his stride so as not to pull too hard on White-Ears. His sodden boot slid in the frost, and he fell to one knee.

"I said move!" shouted the warrior. He spear shaft shoved White-Ears now. The old goblin fell silently on his face, no strength left to cry out. Hatchet twisted away, breaking free from White-Ears's frail grip, and Twig dove to break the old goblin's fall, landing face first on the grass and filling his mouth with cold dirt. His head jarred painfully against something hard.

Twig lay for a moment, letting the stars clear from his

vision. But just a moment. Longer would invite a butt stroke from the spear that might exceed his endurance. He lifted his head, blinking, his scalp throbbing.

A metal stake was driven into the ground, the black iron surface dusted with ice, melting beneath his bright, fresh blood.

Even in his pain and humiliation, Twig was in awe of the Three-Foots skill at tracking. The plain looked the same in every direction, the green-white surface of the ground broken only by their footprints and the warm breath of the kine as they nosed in search of forage. He could always find the Black-Horns by the stars, but on the ground, he was useless.

Yet every night since the Black-Horns were captured, the Three-Foots hadn't failed to find their way back to this same circle of iron stakes. Twig didn't know how they were secured below the ground, but he and Stump had pulled and swore the first night the Three-Foots chained them there, manacles chaffing painfully at one ankle, the other end locked to the stake.

An old tree stump stood just outside the circle, a dogged reminder of the forest that once grew here before the grass reclaimed the land. Once the prisoners were shackled, one warrior trotted back to camp while the other settled himself on the tree stump, spear across his knees, huddling silently in his furs.

The kines' instincts were strong. They would not forage at night. For once, they drew closer to the goblins. Their thick coats stank, the softness tempered by the bones beginning to stand more starkly against them, but they were warm, and kept off the worst of the wind.

The darkness thickened, swallowing the kine, the thick black line of the horizon visible only through a forest of gently shifting legs. Clover was easy to pick out by the blot of her gravid belly. Twig clucked until she came to him, then dragged White-Ears over with Blackfly following. The three shivered, nestling close to the warmth of the pregnant beast, ignoring the chitinous feel of the bloodsuckers against their cheeks. Clover huddled closer, as eager for their warmth as they were for hers. Twig wondered if she sought comfort as well, the touch of a friend in the midst of this cold desert. If his magic wasn't Soft, he would be able to tell.

A spear butt swatted the side of his head, and he realized he had drowsed. Rough hands thrust a bowl at him, and he clutched at it, slopping hot broth over his lap. He was momentarily grateful for the warmth, his loins one of the few parts of him not numb, though he knew he would pay for it when the liquid cooled. He held the bowl close to his face, letting the steam touch him, feeling his muscles unclench ever so slightly. They had been given one such tiny bowl a day, not even enough to fill Blackfly's belly.

White-Ears clutched feebly at his bowl, sloshing in his trembling hands. Across from him, Hatchet crouched over an iron pot, at least double the size of the bowls. Something floated in the broth, peeking over the pot's lip. Twig couldn't tell in the dark, but it looked like meat.

Stump was already slurping down his meal as the guard strode off, and Twig turned to White-Ears as the old goblin managed to lift the bowl to his lips. Blackfly sat beside him, silently twisting the hem of his robe in her hands. The guard had forgotten her.

"You get what's given, and no more," the guard growled over his shoulder. "I catch you sharing it out, your head for it."

Hatchet picked the gobbets of meat out of his broth, licking the grease off his fingers. He froze as he felt Twig's glare.

The wind picked up, whistling in Twig's ears and freezing his wet lap. Hatchet lowered his head—in shame or to protect his food, Twig couldn't tell. He mumbled something so quietly the words were lost to the wind, but the insincerity of his tone rang as loudly as a thunderclap.

Twig shook his head. "No," he whispered across to Hatchet. "You heard the guard. Don't risk it."

Hatchet bent to his meal, eyes locked on the ground between his feet.

Twig struggled to his knees, his body feeling heavy, as if the chain at his ankle had cousins hauling on every inch of him. He coughed wetly in the cold, steadying the bowl as he knee-walked around White-Ears, who slurped at his food, bowl steadied on his knees, shoulders gently shaking with the rhythm of Clover's labored breathing.

Twig reached Blackfly and took her hand. He jerked his ankle, making sure the chain cleared White-Ears, and led the girl around to Clover's far side, where the bulk of the beast would hopefully screen them from the guard.

The girl stayed silent as usual, but only until her grip on White-Ears's robe was threatened—then she began to whine. The whining grew louder as Twig pulled harder, and threatened to turn to a scream, until Twig gave up with a sigh and pressed the bowl, already gone cold, into her hand. *Let* the guard see. He was too tired to care. If he was to be beaten, then he was to be beaten. Maybe the guard would beat him to death and end this misery.

But hunger's voice was more insistent, and Blackfly stared at the bowl of broth for mere moments before bringing it to her mouth and sucking it down so quickly Twig feared she'd be sick.

The cold creeped, icy fingers tightening around them as they shivered against Clover's side. Stump sat out in the open as long as he could, an act of defiance that didn't seem to impress the guard, huddled in his furs, a gray silhouette in the darkness. Hatchet joined them soon after. Twig didn't want to be close to him, but he couldn't deny the warmth the goblin radiated, no doubt increased by his full belly.

Whether he saw or not, the guard made no move to punish Twig for feeding Blackfly. Twig took advantage of the reprieve to check White-Ears's wound. The filthy binding stank, and in the darkness it was impossible to tell if it was the binding itself or the wound. White-Ears didn't stir, but Twig could feel the slow rise and fall of his shoulders, hear the dull whistle of his breathing. That would have to be enough for now.

The goblins huddled together in silence, too exhausted to speak, and nothing to be gained from the act anyway. After a moment, he heard Hatchet's soft snores. His big head lolled on Stump's shoulder, the bigger goblin too tired or too grateful for the warmth to push him away. Twig shifted his leg, trying to reposition his frozen arse, then paused.

A flash of something in the darkness, a broad patch of

black in the midst of the gray field the night had made of the frost.

He stuck his fingers in his mouth, gently sucking on them. It took a long time, but soon they began to answer, the numbness giving way to the fiery agony that told him they were still alive. He winced and endured. It would only be for a moment. He dragged his fingertips along the ground, the pain mingling with the brush of the frozen grass.

They stopped over a broader plant, a tiny cluster, shaped like knives.

Spadeleaf.

His first instinct was to pluck the plant immediately, but he bit down on the impulse. He could pluck it at any time, and such a small portion would be of little help. Far better if it could be magicked into more. Only White-Ears's faint flow resonated nearby; the guard had no magic, so he would never know.

Twig cupped his hands over the tiny plant and closed his eyes.

The song was there, faint, deep, but present: the hopeful trilling of new life, helpless against the timing of its birth, struggling against the great death that winter brings for all. Twig extended his magical current toward it, listening to his own breathing, trying to calm himself, to steady his shivering muscles, stop the chattering of his teeth.

The plant wanted to grow. It was desperate to live in spite of the frigid pall settling across it. Twig bent his magic toward that desire, coaxing the leaves to stretch themselves, the stalk to lengthen, to push free and rear its head above the frost. He fought to make every part of himself still, to be conscious only of himself and the song of the earth below him.

The wind picked up, gusting hard against his side, pushing up his shirt and pricking at his gut, now rimed with frigid broth. He shuddered, his jaw locking and his teeth grinding together. The song receded, the spadeleaf deaf to his entreaties, fighting on for survival on its own.

Twig knew he couldn't blame the wind. Even on a perfect high-sun day his magic was Soft, good only to make him aware of the talents of others—real Sorcerers who could affect the world. He cursed, biting his lip.

"I know what you're doing," Hatchet whispered across to him. "You just see what it gets you. What it gets all of us."

Twig wanted to scream, wanted to leap to his feet and knock Hatchet senseless, but all he could do was sink deeper into the pit of exhaustion. He had nothing left.

"It doesn't work anyway," Hatchet finished. That, Twig couldn't argue with.

Perhaps to spite Hatchet, or the guard, or the frost or even the wind, Twig kept it up for another torch-span. If it wasn't the wind, it was the hunger gnawing at his belly, or the angry burning of his frost-chapped backside. He could not find stillness in the midst of all this.

But it was no use. He let Blackfly's sniffling bring him back into the present. She curled against White-Ears, burrowing her head into his armpit, pressing so close it seemed she would crawl inside him. White-Ears bore it all stoically, despite the pressure it must be putting on his wound.

"There, there," Twig said, gathering Blackfly to him, but not so close that she would be forced to release the hem of the Sorcerer's robe. "Leave grandfather be for a moment."

She pulled away at first, but finally relented and gave herself into his embrace, one hand loosely clutching the hem while he stroked her hair. The smell of that hair comforted him. Even the filth that covered all of them couldn't mask the smell that all children have, the scent of fresh newness, of potentiality. Silent, sniveling Blackfly. Damned if she didn't smell like hope.

Twig found himself singing a herding song his father had taught him to pass the time on long marches, when the kine were moved from pasture to pasture:

Here are the hooves, two by two
Pairs of tails flicking
Eyes, ears, horns pricking
The kine in pairs
And paired with us, walking through.

The girl went quiet, snuggling against him, her breathing slowing, White-Ears's hem trailing loosely now from one finger. Twig breathed deeply of her hair as he finished the song, losing himself in the memory of the sun on his shoulders and his father's patient smile.

And there, unbidden this time, was the song again. The earth sang it now, the spadeleaf beside him, the grass beneath him, all thrilled to the calm wonder of the music. He felt the flow of his magic interlocking with it, his tide and the tide of the world around him matching course.

He sat upright, jolting Blackfly as he thrust his current forward toward the spadeleaf, trying to make it grow. The song drew away, the tenor of it changing back to the constant melody he normally heard, all trace of his touch on it gone.

Blackfly began to cry again, scrambling out of his lap and returning to White-Ears's side. She pressed against the old Sorcerer, and he stirred, groaning and pushing himself upright.

Twig helped him. "My apologies, grandfather. I hope I didn't wake you."

White-Ears leaned close, his eyes reflecting what little starlight penetrated the thick cover of clouds above. His voice was clear, lucid.

"I could feel you," he said. "That was very well done. All you need now is to be still, and you will have it."

The anger surged in Twig, moving his lips before he could still them. "How can I be still? We're freezing, starving. Blackfly is just a baby. Clover is pregnant, and she can't calve without a proper windbreak or the calf will freeze. Killing us slowly is still killing us. And Hatchet . . ."

"The Gibberer has to keep us alive," White-Ears said, unperturbed by Twig's rudeness. "He wants us to rear the kine."

"The Gibberer is crazy. Who knows what he wants?" Twig answered.

"Stillness," White-Ears said again. "Stillness in all things. Then you will have your answers."

But Twig had no stillness in him. He was quiet, and sat shivering, sleep a cruel stranger even as the sun lifted above the horizon, casting a pale and watery light over them, revealing a cruel landscape.

And it brought no warmth at all.

Clover brought him to his senses. She snorted and walked off, removing their bulwark against the biting wind. They pitched backward into the frost as she paced, lowing. As Twig watched, she lay in the frost, her tail lashing, then stood again, continuing her pacing in a tight circle.

A village goblin might not know what he was seeing, but Twig was a Black-Horn, born on the plain and walking with the herds since before his naming-day.

The calf was near.

It would emerge wet and weak. Without shelter, without food, without the thick coat the adults grew over years. Without the heat that the Flame and Wind Sorcerers of his tribe would normally provide, it would be dead within minutes.

Twig had seen fifteen winters, the calving coming at the cusp of each one. The Black-Horns had always stood by their sacred duty. They had never lost a calf. Never.

As if to remind him, the wind howled, boring between his shoulder blades.

Clover lowed again, heaving over onto her side and looking up at him. She looked scrawny, the bloodsuckers on her side had multiplied during the night, spreading up her neck. The rest of the kine fared no better. They couldn't resist the killing cold, the slow whittling of their reserves by the bloodsuckers. They needed strength. That came from good forage.

"Come," Twig gestured to Stump. Hatchet came with

him, unbidden, his eyes narrowing. White-Ears didn't move, huddling on his backside, arms wrapped around a shivering Blackfly.

Twig pointed to Clover. "The Three-Foots must want the kine. Else they'd have killed us long ago."

Stump nodded, his wounded hands wedged into his armpits. He looked exhausted, the tip of his nose unnaturally dark, frost clinging to it, unnoticed. "The horn fetches much in trade," he observed.

Twig nodded. "Clover and her calf are both doomed if we don't move."

"We cannot get far enough for good forage now," Hatchet said.

"No, we cannot," Twig agreed, "but we can find somewhere that will keep the wind off. And where there's rock, there's knife's-edge. It grows year round."

"Knife's-edge makes poor forage," Stump said.

"But it is forage, at least," Twig replied, "and with a boulder or two to block the wind? We can get the calf standing, at least."

"And then what?" Stump growled. "The calf dies standing, and us with her."

"You set your eyes on the horizon, and stumble on the stone before you." Twig used the age-old Black-Horns saying.

"Watch for winter," Stump replied with another, just as old. "Lest it catch you unawares."

"We cannot move." Hatchet hung his head. "The Gibberer will not permit it."

"That is because he is a warband goblin. He is no herder. We must tell him."

Stump looked up at him. "Your head has frozen. He will kill us."

"We are dead already. I will not go to the well-spring and join the flow wondering if Clover and her calf could have been saved."

They were all silent at that, shivering in the chilly dawn.

"I will go," Hatchet said at last. "He . . . perhaps he will hear me."

Stump bared his teeth. "You . . . ? You will . . . Why don't you just go stroke The Gibberer's—"

"Hatchet will go," White-Ears's voice cut through the wind.

Stump bowed and tapped his eyelids. "Yes, grandfather."

"What?" White-Ears said, his eyes suddenly losing focus. "I'm cold. Where is my bonded?"

Stump only looked sad now, his shoulders slumping as White-Ears began to mutter to himself, resting his pointed chin on top of Blackfly's head.

Twig began to feel a foreign magical current, growing stronger as it closed on them. "You do not have to go," he said to Hatchet. "The Gibberer is coming."

The Flesh Sorcerer appeared out of the freezing mist a moment later, two more Three-Foots warriors with him, all bundled in thick furs. One held a spear, the other, one of the human's barking weapons, their "Emm-For" fire-bows that killed goblins from across the plain. It was made for a human warrior, one of their green clad "soldiers" who rode in the belly of their giant iron insects. Twig had seen them flying over the herd once when he was a boy, buzzing angrily, their round wings spinning like a child's top. The fire-bow looked huge and clumsy in goblin hands, but the warrior was absurdly proud to carry it, his finger resting gently on the trigger that made the thing belch death. The soldiers' magic was weak, but their weapons more than made up for it.

Hatchet went to The Gibberer, moving as far from them as his chain would allow. The monster stopped as he approached, the misshapen eyes regarding him thoughtfully as he spoke in low tones. The Gibberer sprouted an exaggerated ear, the long top wrapping around Hatchet's shoulders as he listened. Hatchet kept his voice even, but couldn't suppress an involuntary shudder.

At last The Gibberer grunted, then casually extended a heavily muscled arm and swatted Hatchet aside. He stomped a few more paces toward the rest of the Black-Horns before barking, "No. Not time to move."

Twig could bear it no longer. Rage gave him courage, and he felt his magical flow surge, batting against The Gibberer's. "We will die here," he seethed. "*She* will die here, and her calf with her." He pointed a shaking finger at Clover, who had stood and begun pacing again, snorting in short bursts.

The Gibberer gave a shrug that could lift a tree trunk. "Then you die. Queen coming. We join her army." He pointed at the kine. "Food for army. They die, you die."

"We are *all* going to die, you fool! We need to find shelter and forage!"

The Gibberer's bigger eye narrowed, and Twig waited for the blow, or the focus in the magical current that would twist his head off. Instead, The Gibberer's eyes arched. His huge jaw came up, chewing thoughtfully on nothing. At last the little eye came back to him. "Tell me where your tribe went. We move there."

Twig froze. His bowels turned to water, shocked to find he had not yet plumbed the limit of desperation. Did The Gibberer know about the star maps? How the Black-Horns found one another by following it? If the Three-Foots fell on the rest of the tribe unawares, and in force . . . Twig's gorge rose just thinking of it.

"Tell me," The Gibberer said again. He looked at Hatchet, just beginning to rise. Hatchet opened his mouth, saw Twig's glare, closed it. Stump reached him in three steps and made a great show of helping him to his feet, but Twig saw the force in his grip, and the reminder it brought.

"We don't know," Twig said. "We were lost when you captured us."

But The Gibberer ignored him, his eyes locked on Hatchet's.

"We don't know," the scrawny goblin echoed, but Twig could read the lie on his face as easily as The Gibberer could.

"Eh," The Gibberer said. "Rats." His arm stretched, and Hatchet flew out of Stump's arms, skidding across the frost until the manacle brought him up short, digging sharply into his ankle. The Gibberer kicked him in his gut, sending him rolling, the chain clinking in the grass. Hatchet whimpered.

"Scrawny rat," the Gibberer said. "I like you. You can live."

"Thank you," Hatchet mewled, cringing. "Thank you."

There had been a lie in his voice when he denied knowing where to find the rest of his tribe. There was no lie now.

As he slipped further into weakness and hunger, the line between sleeping and waking blurred and Twig found he had lost the ability to control which side of it he stood on. As darkness fell again and the Black-Horns were chained up for the night, he stood beside Clover, trying to soothe the huge animal, rubbing her flanks and singing to her as she paced and lowed.

The next thing he knew, he was lying in the frost, a strange warmth settling over him. He smiled, nestling in the cold grass. Sleep beckoned, and with it, peace from the trials of this captivity.

"Twig." Stump's voice. His friend chucking his shoulder. Twig ignored him, reaching deeper into the drowsy warmth. Perhaps if he ignored the goblin, he'd go away.

"Twig!" Stump said again, shaking him. "Get up."

"G'away," Twig muttered, burying his face in the grass.

He whined as Stump grabbed his shoulders and hauled him upright, slapping his face. "Wake up, Twig!"

The warmth fled, taking the blessed cloak of sleep with it. Without its protection, Twig was back in the freezing hell, shivering again, his body suddenly reminded of every ache and wind-burned patch. He pushed Stump back, no more than a weak slap. "Damn you! Let me be!"

Then his eyes widened.

In one hand, Stump held a badly-notched spearhead. In the other, he held a broken length of chain. The manacle was still fastened around his ankle, but only a few iron links dangled from it.

"Eyeflower," Stump said. "Found a tiny bit yesterday, stuck to Rose's arse. Put it in my broth before that dung eater took it from me." He pointed to where the guard sprawled, unconscious across the stump, the broken shaft of his spear beside him. Stump planted the spearhead in between the links of Twig's chain, bent to pick up a rock. "Let me get this off."

"What are you doing!? This won't work!" he whispered.

Stump swatted Twig's hands away and set back to work. "It will. We will find the others. It is the only way we can live through this."

"It will not!" He fumbled against Stump's hands. "They'll run us down!"

"We can find them! We know how to find them! If we can get to them, they will defend us!"

"We won't reach them in time! And they won't be ready! We'll just lead the Three-Foots right to them!"

Hatchet roused at the sound of their arguing, limped over, dragging his chain. His face contorted when he saw Stump raising the rock to hammer the spearhead down. "You are a dead fool, Stump. I'll have no part of this." He turned and returned to his stake, gathering the chain into a coil and standing over it protectively.

Stump shoved Twig away, sending him tumbling. Twig lay on his back, too weak to resist, and felt a pressure lift from his leg as Stump parted his chain, then moved on to White-Ears and did the same. The old goblin looked up, perplexed, as Stump stalked toward Hatchet, spearhead in hand.

"Stay away from me!" Hatchet snarled. "I'll not die for your foolishness!"

"You will," Stump replied. He hefted the spearhead. "This goes in your chain or in your eye. Make your choice."

Hatchet was silent, glaring as Stump struck him loose.

Stump returned to White-Ears's side, helping the ancient to his feet. Twig joined him. The chains were broken now, and there was nothing he could do to set it right. When The Gibberer saw, he would heed no explanation. They may as well run now.

He hefted White-Ears's arm over his shoulders, amazed at how heavy the old Sorcerer seemed. He turned to Hatchet, who crouched by his stake, staring at his broken chain, horrified.

"Come now!" Twig said. "There is no choice any longer. We have to go!"

Short coughing barks sounded from the darkness.

The Gibberer's laughter. "Go? Run? With old cripple and a baby? Stupid rats."

Twig felt the Sorcerer's magical tide as he appeared beside the stump, his smaller eye regarding the guard. His torso sprouted a spindly leg that settled on the guard's head, shoving him experimentally. The guard gave a loud snore, but didn't move. "Good. Smart rats."

He came forward, his flow intensifying. "You want to run? Run," The Gibberer said.

Twig began to back away, White-Ears stumbling with them. The Gibberer reached out, snatched up Blackfly, her head disappearing inside his giant hand. He lifted her slowly, almost delicately to his mouth, his big eye closing, the little one half-lidded in concentration.

Then the giant jaw lashed out, snatching up Blackfly's tiny foot before slamming shut with a wet slap. The little goblin didn't cry out, but her eyes shot wide before rolling back in her head. She went limp, unconscious from the pain as The Gibberer tossed her back on the ground, her foot gone, leaking out her life's blood in a slowly spreading stain, black under the wan starlight.

"Go," The Gibberer said again, throwing the sleeping guard over his shoulder and returning to his camp. "Run."

Twig and Stump cried out, setting White-Ears down and racing to Blackfly. The girl's forehead was slick with sweat, and she moaned as Twig stripped off his ragged shirt and bound it around the stump of her ankle. He motioned for the spearhead, thrust it through the cloth, twisting it tighter and tighter until Blackfly screamed. She wept and howled, beating against his shoulder with her little fists.

But the dark stain in the frost stopped spreading.

"Stump! Get White-Ears and—"

Behind them, Clover gave a great bellow and froze. There was a wet splatter as her water broke, steam rising from the ground beneath her. She mooed again, and the kine gathered around her, lowing back in sympathy.

The calf was coming.

The wind shrieked across the exposed plain, howling loud enough to blot out both Blackfly and Clover's cries. It swept chilly wet kisses across Twig's brow that trickled down his bare back, a deeper cold than he'd ever known.

He looked up to find the sky pitch black, thick clouds blotting out even the little starlight they'd had.

It was snowing.

"Stump! Hatchet!" Twig shouted. The two goblins stood and stared, their faces invisible in the darkness. The snow swirled around them, coming thicker and faster now. Blackfly moaned in time with Clover's bellowing.

"Stump! Hatchet! By the flow that bore you!"

Twig saw their heads shake as they snapped out of their reveries, crouched in the sudden snow, now falling so thickly he blinked it out of his eyes.

"We must have a windbreak!" Twig shouted. "Dig, damn you!"

"The ground is frozen . . . ," Hatchet said. "We cannot . . ."

Twig snatched up a stone, scrambled behind Clover as the huge creature lay down, and lifted it over his head. His numb hands slipped on the slick surface, and he guessed the sharp edges were cutting him, but it didn't matter. The hard ground was barely scratched by the first blow, but the second and third yielded more dirt, and the fourth still more. Twig grunted, giving in to the chopping rhythm and the slowly building a mound of earth, grateful for something to do, an action that took his mind off the still forms of White-Ears and Blackfly, Clover's heaving sides.

He heard grunting and turned to see Hatchet and Stump, stones in hand, digging alongside him. Slowly, the mound began to build. He thought of Stump's wounded hands, but in the dark he could see no reaction on the big goblin's face.

At last the friction of the work broke through the numbness, and pain got the better of Stump, who dropped his stone with a curse. Twig paused, ready to go to his friend's aid, but the big goblin rose and went around to Clover's other side as she heaved and mooed, the ground steaming around her hindquarters, the high stink of her birthing reaching Twig's nose.

Stump gently lifted White-Ears, the ancient goblin tiny and frail in his arms, and tucked him in snugly against Clover's side, then returned for Blackfly, nestling her beside him. Then he returned to his digging, chopping away with the stone as if his hands were whole.

"They'll be warmer," he said.

Twig didn't answer, kept at his frantic digging, hoping Stump could feel his gratitude across the distance between them.

Soon there was nothing but the scraping of the stones, Clover's panting, the goblins' grunting breaths, and the gentle whisper of the snow. By the time the three goblins had built the windbreak high enough to rise over the creature's heaving sides, the snow had obliterated all traces of movement. Clover, White-Ears, and Blackfly were white lumps in the dark.

The thick snow was a blessing, as it formed a roof over the crust of frost. Twig began to dig through it, grateful again for his numb fingers. It took some doing, but soon he found what he was looking for: clots of kine dung, the bottom of which looked just dry enough to burn.

Stump squatted at his side. "What are you going to do with that?"

"Never you mind," Twig said. He pointed at White-Ears

and Blackfly where they lay curled against Clover's side. The animal was spasming now, shuddering as she pushed her baby out. "She'll be crowning soon. Get in there with White-Ears and Blackfly and keep them warm. Get Hatchet in there, too. It will help."

He expected Stump to argue, but the big goblin only nodded and rose, cuffing Hatchet and pointing to the white mounds that were White-Ears and Blackfly. Hatchet needed no convincing to lie down where it was warmest, and soon he was nestled in along with the other goblins, Stump alongside him.

It took him a good while, but Twig finally cleared a patch of ground, lit a corner of the dung patty with the sparks from one of the stones, and set it to smolder on a flat rock, feeding it with more of the kine dung until a tiny flame struggled against the winter coming on in force all around them.

Just as the fire came, Clover gave a great cry, heaved, and pushed out the calf. It came fast, pushing out of her in a torrent of the birth-blood, out into the world in a single pulse, as was the Black-Horn way. It scrabbled in the afterbirth, a wet, black, shriveled-looking thing, mooing plaintively.

The herd moved closer, drawn by instinct to the baby's cries, and Twig was hopeful they would do their duty, licking it to keep it warm, to clean its coat, to welcome it into the world.

But the kine were weak with hunger—from the predations of the bloodsuckers, from the cold. Their rhythms were thrown into confusion, and their behavior along with them. They sniffed tentatively at the calf, as if it were an alien thing pushed into their midst, a stranger who might harm them. They mooed in bewilderment, reminding Twig so much of White-Ears that he nearly wept.

A new mother always rose as soon as her calf dropped, showing her child the strength of the herd. But Clover stayed down, sides heaving, making no movement to welcome her new calf into the world.

Twig gathered the calf, slimy and squealing, and dragged it around to its mother's udders. They were smaller than they should have been, but she had been pregnant long before the Three-Foots had taken them, and there was still milk there.

Twig pushed the calf's mouth against the teat. The creature only bleated, eyes still closed, snowflakes mixing with the afterbirth that still coated its tiny body. It was shivering already. It wouldn't last long.

Since Twig had taken up his staff and gone to tend the herd, he had never lost a beast, and he would not now. Not to the Three-Foots. Not to The Gibberer.

He jammed his fingers into the corners of the calf's mouth, pressing until it opened. He squeezed the teat to start the flow of milk, then shoved it into the mewling creature's mouth, pumping the milk.

The calf choked, cried, tried to pull away. Twig held its head firmly in place. "Come on, curse you. *Come on.*"

At last the tiny animal shuddered, closed its mouth and was still.

Twig's stomach churned. Panic crept up his spine. Clover mooed plaintively, as if she knew.

He hunched over the calf. "Come on, little one. Come on."

Nothing. Only the soft patter of the snow, the flakes melting more and more slowly against the calf's cooling hide.

"*Come on, damn you!*" It could not be dead. He would not believe it. He made a fist and pounded it against the calf's side, as his mother had taught him to do with stillborns. She had told him that it could revive them if done right, but Twig could never remember a time when it had.

He paused, listened. Nothing.

Stillborns were one thing; a death was quite another. He pounded harder, fist hammering against the calf's ribs. "Come on! Come on! *Come on!*"

It was no use. Tears stung his eyes, mixing with the snow, making cold runnels down his frozen cheeks. There was no more strength in him. He had nothing more to give.

Twig bent double, resting his head on the baby's side, began to weep.

Stopped.

A tiny sound, a faint kissing.

Movement.

Tugging.

Suckling! The calf was suckling.

Twig suppressed a cry of joy and moved to get the dung fire, gently pushing it around on its flat rock and building it as high as he could.

"Stump."

The big goblin sat up. "I am sorry, Twig . . . I know —"

"Shut up. It lives. Get the others and curl up with it. Close to the fire as you can stand." The Three-Foots might punish them for building even a pathetic dung fire, but Twig was past caring now.

Stump's voice was incredulous. "It lived—?"

"Quickly, you fool! It needs warmth now."

Stump roused Hatchet, and the two moved White-Ears and Blackfly up against the tiny calf. There was no doubt it was suckling now, tiny neck jerking as it tugged on Clover's teat. The kine raised her head and sniffed at it once, huge eyes regarding Twig.

He could almost imagine they were grateful.

He huddled in with the other goblins, bundled around the calf and the dung fire, tiny threads of flame hissing defiance at the falling snow, already losing the battle, providing a sliver of heat that only the calf could feel. The tiny windbreak they'd dug did its work, the wind whipping over them to torment the landscape farther on.

The snow continued to fall, covering them all. Twig lay shivering, willing the warmth of his body outward, through Stump and the rest of them into the calf, willing it to keep suckling and breathing.

Willing it to keep living all through the night, as the snow kept falling, falling without end, shrouding all in peaceful, beautiful winter.

Twig could not remember falling asleep, could not imagine how he had managed it. Yet, sometime during the night, exhaustion had overcome cold and hunger and he woke with a sudden start as the weak sun bounced off the frozen crust, scattering diamonds across his eyelids.

He blinked, struggled to rise, cracking the ice over the snow that near buried him. The others were barely visible, indistinct white shapes in decreasing sizes, down to the calf and its mother beyond.

The calf. Clover was gone.

"Get up!" Twig hissed, rolling onto his knees.

The snow had stopped. The ground around them was an unbroken field of white. He scanned for the herd, saw them now, standing in a tight circle, heads hanging, more wretched than ever. But alive.

He saw a horn-tip among them, recognized it instantly as Clover's. If the mother had abandoned her calf, there was no chance it lived.

Twig swallowed and turned back to the lumps of snow, knelt to dig the tiny body out as Stump and Hatchet rose.

Twig bit back the tears and dug in the snow, his numb fingers scraping across the cold flesh beneath. Not the calf.

Blackfly. The little girl's eyes were closed and she shivered violently, but she lived. He lifted her up and she moaned, clinging to him, her forehead hot with fever. He let his eyes travel down her wounded leg to the tied-off stump of her foot.

The flesh around the wound had turned black, the edges still ragged and rimed with frozen blood. But the spearshaft held the rag twisted tight, and the wound was sealed. The girl would live a little longer, at least.

The calf was gone. Twig looked back to the herd and finally spotted it, standing and suckling, small black head darting and pushing at Clover's udders. The kine had decided the little beast could be trusted, and they licked steadily at its coat, though it was long clean and dry, the thick hair shining.

Twig gently laid Blackfly down and slumped forward in relief. Stump clapped him on the shoulder. "It will live."

"It will live." Twig nodded. "By the current, it will live."

"You are the best of us, Twig," Stump said. "When you go back to the flow, I will eat your eyes."

Twig knew he should say something, show gratitude for the honor Stump paid him, but all he could feel was exhaustion.

"Hatchet," he said at last, "see if you can find some—"

"He's gone," Stump said.

Twig turned. The big goblin's face was creased in sadness. He met Twig's eyes and jerked his chin in the direction of the Three-Foots camp.

Twig stood and squinted, shading his eyes against the sun's glare on the newly fallen snow. The Three-Foots huddled around their fire, big and blazing, snug in their thick furs. A smaller bundle showed where Hatchet sat, a warm leather blanket about his shoulders, pot of hot soup in his hands.

On the opposite side of the fire, Three-Foots warriors were arming, tightening the straps on their leather armor, limbering their legs as they did before long runs.

The Gibberer stood over Hatchet, meaty hands on his lumpen hips. He looked up at Twig, misaligned eyes narrowing, corners of the giant cave of a mouth rising in a smile.

"He told them," Stump said, spitting out the words. "The bastard told them."

The wide plain where the Black-Horns roamed, tending their herds, was an unbroken sea of waving grass. It changed color through the seasons, from green to brown to white and back to green again, but it was otherwise featureless. The Black-Horns found one another for generations by the stars, the Watcher, the Staff, the Horned-One, that unerringly spun through the heavens, a map that Black-Horns memorized from childhood.

A closely guarded map. For the secret of star-walking kept the tribe safe and hidden from enemies. To divulge it was to give up the tribe for dead. It was unthinkable.

Yet Hatchet sat, warm and fed, as the Three-Foots warriors finished arming and, with a final salute to the Gibberer, took off running with the speed they were famed for.

It had never been about the kine. The Gibberer had what he wanted.

"Maybe he lied to them," Twig said through numb lips, "told them a false path."

But even as he spoke, he knew he was wrong. Hatchet had betrayed them all. For a warm blanket and a pot of stew, he had sold his family into death. Had he magic, had he the ability to join the chorus of the earth singing all around him, he might have been able to do something. But his magic was . . . *Your magic is human arse*, The Gibberer had said. It was an apt description.

Twig turned back to Blackfly and White-Ears, his stomach twisting. If Hatchet had done what he feared, soon these might be all that was left of the Black-Horns. He swallowed hard and scrambled to them, suddenly desperate to hear their heartbeats, feel their breath against his face.

Blackfly lay on her back, still burning with fever, head

tossing. That was good. Movement meant life, no matter what affliction she now battled.

But White-Ears didn't move. The ancient goblin's little body lay curled on its side, just as Twig had left him, the thick blanket of snow unbroken.

Twig crawled to him, breath hitching in his throat, swatted at the snow covering the old Sorcerer. His numb hands suddenly felt heavy, dead, useless things, refusing to obey him. The thick crust of the snow resisted his touch, and at last he gave up and threw his shoulder into White-Ears's back, sending the goblin rolling clear of the drift, until he lay face up.

Twig reached him in a stride and put his ear over White-Ears mouth, willing the wind to silence, desperately trying to still the pounding of his heart enough to catch a faint whisper of the ancient goblin's breath.

But his numb ear could feel nothing, and the shriek of the wind would not let him hear anything.

It didn't matter. Twig knew the ancient Sorcerer was dead.

Stump knelt beside him. "I noticed just after we woke. I couldn't . . . I couldn't tell you. We will eat his eyes." The honor would give them his knowledge, show them all White-Ears had seen in life, ensure that his years and wanderings did not pass from the world.

Stump was speaking, but Twig could no longer hear him. The big goblin touched his shoulder as Twig slumped over White-Ears's cold body, tears refusing to come, tired past even that emotion.

Hatchet had given up the tribe. Their family, their herds, their legacy, all lost. Blackfly sprawled in the snow, slowly succumbing to fever. Stump's wounded hands festered and froze beneath their filthy wrappings. The kine circled and starved, eaten alive by the bloodsuckers burrowing deeper into their flesh, no strength left to fight them off. The calf shivered and starved with them. Young and weak, it would not last another night. And now, White-Ears was gone.

Try as he might, he could not save any of them.

The Gibberer stood at Hatchet's side, warm, fed, triumphant.

Twig couldn't even muster the energy to feel anger. He only lay, the heaviness of his body dragging him down over White-Ears's corpse, as if he might push through him and down into the earth, swallowed whole by the chilly darkness.

He welcomed the sensation, prayed the ground would swallow him up. It was better than this, better than living with his uselessness.

Despair blotted out all sensation, all sight, all sound, all thought. It fogged his mind, surged through his limbs. Stopped all process, all movement.

Twig was, at long last, still.

And into that stillness, the song of the earth came rushing, calling out its joy at all of the circle of existence, the winter that brought death so life could be renewed, the sickness that took the weak so the strong could prosper, dying and living and dying again.

Twig took comfort from that joy, let the music trill in his ears, his mind, his bones. He raised his voice, joined in the chorus, sang of his loves and his losses and his despair, gave them all up to the rhythm of the music, seeing them for the trifles they were—seed blown on the summer wind, landing to sprout anew far from home when the seasons came round again.

And this time, in his stillness, the song answered.

It carried him, washed through him. He felt it in his pores, his veins, he felt the current of his magic eddying through it, currents within currents.

He reached out experimentally, felt the individual notes of the life around him. Each rock. Each blade of grass. Each living root. Worms and insects and burrowing moles. The bloodsuckers.

The kine.

He reached out to the huge creatures, felt each one of them, their hunger and their fear. The calf's cold, Clover's aching fatigue, her knowledge that the child she had labored so long to carry was all but lost. He felt the wind burrowing against their hides, the bloodsuckers' endless biting at their flanks.

They sensed his presence, and he felt them draw close to him, seeking reassurance. His magical tide surged with excitement, and he felt the song recede, but he knew the stillness now, and calmed himself, retreating back into the song, letting it carry him.

Twig rose, opened his eyes.

White-Ears's body lay beneath him. Stump knelt, wounded hands in his lap, head hanging.

The kine had ceased their milling. They stood still, heads up and alert, staring at him.

Twig Drew his magic, reached into the song, Bound it into a command.

The kine tossed their heads and stomped past one

another, flicking tails and brushing noses, until they formed a line twenty long, disciplined as any warband.

As a single body, they lowered their heads.

The song had changed, responding to Twig's magic. The joyful trilling was gone. In its place was a warband's reel, a trumpeting horn, calling the spears to the banner.

Of the twenty kine captured with them, twelve were bulls, their long horns twice the length of their mates'. Starvation had weakened them, bloodsuckers had drained them, but they were still four times the size of any goblin, their horns as long and as sharp as any spear.

They were prized for their use as decoration, as the stuff of handles and pins and bracelets.

But on the living kine, they were weapons.

Twig turned to the Three-Foots who remained, surrounding The Gibberer, dipped into the current again, passed along to the kine behind him.

The animals dipped their noses farther, horns low.

The pounding rhythm of the song built, the tempo quickening, a tide building behind a dam.

The Gibberer looked up, sniffed the air. His misshapen eyes narrowed.

"Come on, Stump," Twig said.

The big goblin lifted his head. "Where?"

"To war," Twig said, and charged.

The kine charged with him. Their hooves churned the frozen earth, kicking clods of it into the sky, a spray of rocks and soil mixing with the drifting snow.

They parted around him, thundering past and toward the Three-Foots, who scrambled to their feet, shouting, snatching up weapons.

And then they were gone, swallowed by the rising and falling of the kines' giant shoulders.

Twig ran behind them, pouring his exultation into the song, willing strength and fury into the animals. "Black-Horns!" he shouted. "For White-Ears!"

"For White-Ears!" came Stump's shout as the big goblin ran past him, a heavy rock in his wounded hands.

They reached the enemy just as the lead bulls tossed their heads, sending Three-Foots warriors flying into the air, hands clutching at their opened bellies, purple ropes trailing from them. One of the kine lowed in rage, head dragged earthward by the Three-Foots warrior impaled on its horn, fingers scrabbling uselessly against the hard bone plate of its skull.

Another bull had stopped, throwing its weight to one side to arrest its charge, channel it in another direction, circling back into the fight. Screams echoed, the unbroken expanse of white was suddenly churned to black and red. Here and there a Three-Foots warrior stood his ground, drove his spear into the side of a charging bull. Twig could feel the agony of the metal grinding against bone, cutting through muscle and organ, felt the animal's desire to flee, to lie down and give up.

He Drew and Bound again, reaching into the song, amplifying it to even greater intensity, so that the wounded kine knew only rage, only a desire to charge and turn and charge again. All they knew of rival males, of endangered young, of the thousand cuts that at last would drive them mad, Twig channeled into the song.

The kine fought like ravening monsters, the song driving them, refusing to die.

Within moments, the Three-Foots began to throw down their spears, the warriors racing off into the snow in ones and twos, their legendary speed put to a different use.

Then one of the kine skidded to a halt, shivered . . . and turned inside-out.

Its hide unraveled, as if a skinner's knife had worked along the seams, showing the fat and gristle beneath as it rolled backward. Its bones followed, ribs tapering to sharpened points opening like a predator's mouth, then snapping inward to pierce its heart, its lungs.

Even the song could no longer sustain it. The bull fell, twitching. Beside it, another of the huge animals exploded, chunks of meat sailing through the sky to land at Twig's feet.

The Gibberer waded into the press, one arm grown horribly large, gripping a cow by the head, flailing the animal's body like a club, beating aside the others.

One of the Three-Foots raised one of the human fire-bows and aimed it at the advancing kine. It barked, louder than thunder, spat fire, but it was made for the bigger humans and sent the warrior tumbling, weapon flying from his hands.

Stump had snatched up a fallen spear, struck about him at the few remaining Three-Foots warriors, their courage failing in the face of the weakened prisoners who had suddenly become armed enemy.

Blood covered Stump's face, his bared teeth. The tip of one ear had been sliced off. He screamed at them, charging forward, the spear spinning about his head, trailing gore.

Twig marshaled his magic, turned the tide of the bulls against The Gibberer, forsaking the rest of the Three-Foots for the greater threat.

The Flesh Sorcerer knocked the first bull aside with the animal in his hand, then threw it aside. His giant arm pulsed, the flesh rippling as he added muscle to it, leaning deeply under the weight. The huge limb snatched up another bull, slammed it down, snapping its neck with a sharp crack that Twig could hear across the intervening distance.

The misaligned eyes roved, searching for the source of the magical flow. Twig crouched among the dust and spraying snow, driving the animals on, praying The Gibberer would not find him.

Then the uneven eyes fell across Stump as the big goblin lunged with his spear, skewering a Three-Foots warrior through the thigh, pinning him to the ground.

"Tricky rat!" the monster shouted, hurling the dead bull.

The animal's body flipped end over end, bouncing over the ground and catching Stump in the back. He shouted and fell, spear ripped free of his enemy's leg, flying from his hands.

Twig forgot his danger and stood, running toward his friend, who lay pinned beneath the animal corpse, wrestling to get free.

The Gibberer's legs thickened, rippled with sudden muscle. He crouched and leapt through the air, landing hard on the dead bull's ribs, cracking them over Stump. The big goblin screamed in pain, snarled something unintelligible.

The Gibberer bent, retrieved the fallen spear, small as a toothpick in his giant fist, raised it over Stump's face.

Twig ran with all he had, feet pounding the broken ground, kine heaving out of his way. He leapt as the spear came down, throwing himself against The Gibberer's giant arm.

The limb was as hard as stone. Twig felt something snap in his shoulder, cried out and fell at the Flesh Sorcerer's feet.

But the spear was knocked aside, the point driving into the frozen earth beside Stump's head.

The Gibberer snarled, looked down, the smaller eye narrowing into a slit of hate. He cursed, dropped the spear. Twig could feel the force of his magical flow focus, Bind, the tendrils of his magic worming their way into Twig's body.

Twig shut his eyes, praying it would be quick, desperately reaching his magical tide into the song.

Nothing. Twig opened his eyes.

The Gibberer stood over him, huge jaw open in shock. Just above it, Clover's bovine head pressed forward, forehead hard against the monster's chest. Her horns were shorter than a bull's, but just as sharp.

One of them was sheer through The Gibberer's center, so deep that Twig could just make out the far tip, dripping blood, streaked with tiny gobbets of purple meat. The shreds pulsed. Twig had butchered enough kine to know heartmeat when he saw it.

The Gibberer's strange eyes swiveled down, staring at the top of Clover's head as if he had never seen such a creature before. Twig felt the current of his magic reverse, turn inward to heal the damage.

Twig shouted, snatching up Stump's rock, raising it over his head and bringing it down on the Sorcerer's larger eye, feeling it pop and squelch, then something crunching beneath.

He raised the rock and hammered it down again, the steady rhythm he'd used to dig the windbreak, rising and falling, rising and falling, each blow cracking and digging. The Gibberer's flow grew wild, fluttering. The huge arm flailed, battering him, but Twig ignored the half-hearted blows, too confused and weak to throw him off.

Twig heard a cry as Stump broke free of the kine's body, snatched up the spear, and drove it under The Gibberer's armpit, leaning into the thrust, sinking into the monster up to his shoulder.

The other bulls turned, added their horns to the assault, piercing the Gibberer again and again, rearing and snorting and plunging.

The current pulsed, slackened. The flailings of the giant arm limped to a stop, and at last the bulk of the Flesh Sorcerer went still, the remaining eye turned upward, staring at Twig, seeing nothing.

Twig felt for The Gibberer's current. It was gone.

He slid down off the mound of dead flesh, so ragged with holes it could barely be recognized even as the misshapen thing it once was. He slackened his magical tide, let the tempo of the warsong relax.

The kine milled uselessly, pawing the ground, lowing in anger.

For there were no more enemy to fight.

The ground was a slushy mud pit. Torn bits of flesh and bone dotted the steaming puddles of blood. Three-Foots corpses lay gored and trampled, a few crawling weakly, crying out for water.

The only goblins standing were Twig and Stump, panting, blinking, unable to believe they had won.

"Hatchet—" Twig began.

"He ran off," rasped Stump.

They were both too tired to go after him, couldn't track him in the criss-crossing maze of footprints in the snow all around them.

Stump sank to his knees, head hanging, too tired to exult in victory. "What now?"

Twig marshaled the song again, reached out to the kine, the herd that had been his family from his birth. He grabbed a double handful of Clover's hair and swung up onto her back, Bound his magic, so that one of the bulls lowered its head and nudged Stump up onto it.

The big goblin looked a question at Twig, and then nodded, clinging to the bull's neck as the animal raised itself up and tossed him onto its back where he clung to it weakly.

Twig channeled the song again and moved the herd back toward Blackfly, where she lay beside White-Ears's body. He would gather them up and wait for nightfall, when the stars would twinkle brightly from their seat in the black winter sky.

The Watcher, the Staff, the Horned-One.

The Three-Foots were fast, but not faster than galloping kine. Forewarned, his people had a chance.

Twig looked over at Stump, lying across the bull's back

now, all strength gone, arms dangling limply. The creature steadied under Twig's magic, balancing the big goblin carefully.

He looked at the bodies of the dead bulls, turned away. There was no time to honor them as was their due. To delay would be to lose all.

The wind sighed across the plain, sweeping over Twig's shoulders, chilling him. He hunkered down closer to Clover's back, feeling the sharp ridge of her spine pressing up against his chest. She lowed encouragement and turned back toward the patch of ground where Blackfly and White-Ears lay.

Soft, cold touches thrilled across his ears, his head, as the wind died and Clover picked up speed.

The black and red of the shattered earth slowly began to fade back to white.

Twig looked up at the graying sky, blinking, shaking his head against the wet.

Snow was falling.

★ ★ ★

ABOUT THE AUTHOR

Myke Cole is the author of the military fantasy Shadow Ops series, which has been described as "Black Hawk Down meets the X-Men." As a security contractor, government civilian, and military officer, Myke Cole's career has run the gamut from Counterterrorism to Cyber Warfare to Federal Law Enforcement. He's done three tours in Iraq and was recalled to serve during the

Deepwater Horizon oil spill. All that conflict can wear a guy out. Thank goodness for fantasy novels, comic books, late night games of Dungeons & Dragons, and lots of angst-fueled writing.

HEAVY SULFUR

★ ★ ★

Ari Marmell

**Late autumn, 1916
The Western Front**

Amidst the roiling clouds of mustard gas, bilious and billowing, I could just make out the alchemancer positioned atop the hillock.

He stood tall, arms spread, apparently untroubled by the fusillades filling the air with lead, the bursting ordnance raising geysers of shrapnel and mud across the field of no man's land. Ritual robes of rusty hue hung open over an officer's uniform of the German Empire; unseen eyes glared through the lenses of a heavy gas mask, a hideous insectile thing that looked to have taken the place of the man's head. The carbine strapped to one shoulder hung unused, for his right hand was occupied by a rune-carved staff of oak, from which the impossible banks of flesh-searing gas flowed. He directed them, as an orchestra conductor, sending them against the wind, positioning them where he would. They rolled toward the trenches and the brave British defenders; far behind the alchemancer, I could see multiple squads of German soldiers preparing to rush any breach the mustard gas might open.

I wasn't meant to have spotted the poison-witch, none of us were. His occult defenses were far too strong. That, however, was why men such as I fought on the front lines. I could feel the faint wetness of the oil with which I'd anointed my own brow and eyelids, the charm that permitted me to overcome such protections.

"Smythe!" I hissed between clenched teeth. "Hamlin!"

"Sir, yes sir!"

"Top of that rise, lads," I told them. "No time to share the sight with you. Just shoot where I shoot."

"Understood, sir!"

Was a simple enough matter, that. So many of us were charging hither and yon across the battlefield, I was able to draw nice and close to the alchemancer before he realized I was approaching him directly, could see him where and for what he was. By then, there was little he could do. Even if the multiple rifle rounds I offered him from my Lee-Enfield hadn't cut him down right nicely, the burst of automatic fire from Hamlin's Lewis gun would have left him in tatters.

The mustard gas began dissipating almost instantly, broken apart by the encroaching winter winds, no longer bound by the will that had controlled it. The massed soldiers further along grew ever more exposed—as, of course, had been the point.

"Fall back, boys!" My team was already gathering about me as we retreated, weapons trained on the much larger force.

"Sir?" That was Waters, another of mine. "Should we not—?"

"Relax, man. We've known they were coming since last night's raid. Listen!"

And there it was, right on cue, the dull roar and heavy chop of a Sopwith Strutter. The biplane dropped from the low clouds, cutting a straight line over the enemy contingent. A bombing run on a battlefield objective was unusual, to be sure, but as I'd told the men, we'd known they were coming, and we'd decided to do for the whole lot. Artillery rained down on all sides, keeping the bastards from scattering, as the aeroplane drew closer. Any moment now and a bloody lot of Germans would be dispatched straight to—

"Um, sir?"

Oh, hell.

The dreary seasonal grey left little sun to speak of, and the pilot had released his weapon some distance across no man's land. Nonetheless, if one knew what to look for, the glimmer of the tumbling bombardment left no doubt that it was made out of something other than metal. Ceramic, most likely—and if so, it'd be a ceramic with intricate engravings over every inch of surface.

Engravings that would shatter when the pottery did, breaking whatever bindings they represented.

Bloody damn idiots in communications had gotten their wires good and crossed again. This was supposed to have been a *conventional* armament, not . . .

"Goetic payload!" I shouted at them. "Fall back to the trenches!" I was scrabbling about my person for various protective talismans even as I gave the order. Distance was probably still sufficient; surrounded by a whole array of Germans, the payload wouldn't likely turn its attentions to *my* lads.

But I wasn't about to risk their lives on "likely."

I located the amulet I wanted, raised it to my lips, and began muttering over it as I back-stepped. Made by a devout Anglican, this one was, and it showed in the charm's ritual of activation. Latin. Bloody hate Latin.

So there I was, reciting a ritual I only half understood, interspersed with psalms in a language I only half knew, in praise of a God I only half believed in.

Even with the talisman's boost, none of the charms I'd mastered would hide us for long, not against anything as diabolically potent as a front-line battlefield summoning. Still, if the entity were distracted when it glanced our way, should it chance at all to do so, this was better than nothing. Still chanting, I turned and rushed to join my companions in a retreat that I wouldn't have admitted to anyone else was one step short of a panicked dash.

By the time we were once more snug in the trenches, safe if not even remotely half comfortable, I was near as cross as I'd been since that Serbian malcontent with a cut-rate grimoire had sicced a demon on Archduke Ferdinand and sparked this whole bloody war to start with. I'm sure none of the lads appreciated my stomping through the trench, spattering mud as I went. If the officers' dugout had had a door to slam, I well might have, propriety be damned.

"He's waiting to speak to you, Corporal," the sentry barked with a salute before I could even demand to do so. That was a splash of cold water, but I wasn't about to let it stop me. I took the tight spiral stairs down at a rapid clip, barely seeing and only vaguely smelling the thick earth, held at bay by fat wooden supports.

The lower level of the dugout was one of the more comfortable chambers of this whole godforsaken network. Real tables, chairs, a chalkboard, electric lights run off a small generator, a smattering of anti-clairvoyance talismans, and a radio that even worked on occasion.

Major Grimes hunched over the table, reading some dispatch or other. The man had a tendency of muttering under his breath as he read, making his mustache bristle and twitch much in the manner of a dying anemone.

The Officer Commanding, of course, I recognized. The other two present, I did not. One was a woman in uniform not unlike the major's or mine, her features somewhat blocky and shoulders broad. The sort who, with a couple of decades on her, would fit the term "matronly" right perfectly, and probably proudly. The other was a tall, slender fellow in the gaudy and ludicrous—pardon, the *colorful*—cap and coat of a French officer.

"Stand easy, Corporal," Grimes ordered, scarcely looking up to acknowledge my salute.

"Sir," I began, only vaguely aware of the fury in my tone, and thus only vaguely able to manage it, "I wish to register a formal complaint. When my squad were dispatched to meet the German offensive—"

"You were far enough from the drop zone for a reasonable margin of safety," he interrupted.

"Still, sir, I should have been forewarned of any summoning to—"

"This will wait, Corporal."

I clicked jaw and heels together. "Yes, sir!"

Finally he stood straight, peering first at me, then at the others. "Corporal, this is Captain Shelby Hunter-Hughes, of his Majesty's Royal Channeling Corps. Captain, Corporal Peyton Cleary, the chap I was telling you about."

Royal Channeling Corps. A medium, then. Dead men *do* tell tales, when the right man—or woman—asks it of them. "Captain," I offered, saluting again.

"Corporal." Her voice was deep, rich without becoming masculine.

"This," Grimes continued, "is Major Ghislain Poulard, seconded to us for this particular operation."

"Major." Again, I saluted, though I'm fairly certain I couldn't keep the question from my tone.

"*Bonjour*, Corporal." Either the man had suffered in a gas attack recently, or he smoked enough to shame a foundry.

"The major has undergone all necessary checks and clearances," Grimes said, perhaps in answer to the question I hadn't voiced. "You'll speak clearly in his presence."

"Understood, sir! Though if I might ask . . . ?"

Grimes frowned, lips pressed together so tightly they all but vanished beneath his mustache. "Cleary, we have a Code Echo Rose."

It actually required a moment of me to recall what that meant. "My God. The chances against—"

"Are not zero, apparently."

"No, sir."

Our foreign guest politely cleared his throat. I cast a questioning glance at Grimes, who grunted an affirmation.

"Our magi," I told Poulard, "now and again attempt to conjure . . . entities with whom they can actually communicate."

Call them what you will . . . "Demons," "spirits." Use whatever occult or religious framework you like; Goetic, Hermetic, biblical . . . All of it is just even the cleverest of us trying to force ourselves to fathom entities that are unspeakably, incomprehensibly alien. We're not even certain how sentient they may be; what they are, how they think.

Most can only be commanded in a general fashion, by virtue of the spells or sigils used to bind them. A select few, however, are intelligent enough, and not *quite* so alien, that a magus can—with some patience, and sufficient nerve to risk madness—commune with them.

The Frenchman nodded. "We do ze same," he said in heavily accented English. "We preferably use such entities for espionage and intelligence. Divination, far-seeing, and ze like."

My turn to nod. "We do as well. We also have safeguards woven into our conjurations, meant to alert our magi should one of the demons they've summoned—specifically, one capable of direct communication—later be conjured by the enemy."

Poulard stared at me as though I'd abruptly *become* such a creature, and I could scarcely blame him. So far as we've ever been able to ascertain, the entities are infinite.

We've no way of discerning one from another, no way to call forth a specific being. The odds against a double-summoning of that sort—especially when limited to specific varieties of entity—were beyond astronomical. Most of the personnel in our occult divisions felt that the safeguards I'd just mentioned were an utter waste of time and effort.

Until perhaps two minutes ago, I'd been one of them.

"Are you saying zis has 'appened?" he demanded incredulously.

"I received both communication and confirmation this morning," Grimes said. "Even if the entity in question was never exposed directly to any sensitive information . . ."

He hardly needed to finish. Even if nothing else, it would know the name, the *true* name, of the magus who had conjured it.

"The summoner," he continued once he knew the severity was lost on none of us, "was one of His Majesty's Grand Magi."

God! If the Germans or their allies got hold of *that* . . .

"Do they know what they've got?" Captain Hunter-Hughes asked.

"We don't believe so, and odds are they'd never think to ask. We cannot, however, rely on 'odds,' especially given the circumstances.

"Corporal Cleary!"

Here it was, then. Why I'd been brought in on this. I thought about reminding the major that my occult training was fairly limited, that even countering the battlefield wards of an enemy such as the earlier alchemancer was pushing my limits.

I decided against it. If he'd chosen me, it was because I was better suited than anyone else—or at least anyone else readily available, which amounted to the same thing.

"Your job is to banish or destroy the entity in question," he said, confirming my suspicion. "Obviously, we can't tip the Germans off to its importance, so this'll happen under cover of an assassination attempt against the magus who conjured it. Said magus is, in this case, one of our opposite number in the enemy trenches, not far from here."

Well, that partly explained why I was the best bet, then. I nodded. "Do we know who or where he—?"

"Captain Hunter-Hughes has already penetrated the postmortem defensive conditioning of several of the raiders killed in last night's attack. Thanks to her interrogations, we have the magus's name, his most probable location, and the German sentry pass-phrases currently in use."

And there was the *other* reason he'd chosen me. I could pass for, and was fluent in, German.

Ancestry, linguistic skill, *and* some measure of occult mastery. No wonder he was making do with someone of my education.

I looked first the major's way— "Guess I'm to report to you, sir, if I make it back." —and then the captain's— "And to you if I don't."

Gallows humor at its finest, but neither one of them showed so much as a twitch of the lip. They could stand to be a *bit* less dour about the whole endeavor, after all; it wasn't as though *they* were being dispatched on an almost certain suicide mission.

"We'll be staging an insertion offensive," Grimes continued, as though I hadn't spoken, "including your own squad. Am I correct in understanding none of them speak German?"

"Afraid so, sir. Pickens has some fluency, but never enough to pass."

"Right. Just you, then, while your boys and everyone else keep the front line occupied."

"Sir, if I may . . . ? I'm afraid I don't understand Major Poulard's place in all this. No disrespect, sir," I added to the man in question.

"None taken. I am wondering about zis myself."

"The major is a skilled, military-trained magus," Grimes said. "We have none of our own available nearby, not of sufficient proficiency, anyway. So he's been seconded to us for the duration."

This time, the look I directed Poulard's way was incredulous. He shrugged. "Better to dress to blend in, when ritual garb is unnecessary, *oui*?"

Sensible, that, but I still was uncertain why we required a magus at all. When I returned my attentions to Major Grimes, though, I saw something. Something in his eyes, something I'd rarely seen there before.

Reluctance.

"Cleary . . . You understand there's a good chance you won't live to complete your objective."

"Always a possibility, sir."

"Indeed, but this is too vital a task to fail, even if you fall. We've . . . This operation has been designated Heavy Sulfur, Corporal."

"Ah. That's how it's to be, then, sir?"

"It is. Cleary, you understand, if it were up to me—"

"No bother, sir." I hoped I sounded far more confident than I felt. "Just another duty for king and country. We'd best get started then; time's short enough as it is."

And now it felt shorter, to me at least, than ever it had.

We began with two separate bombardments of artillery, starting on the target zone and then spreading outward, clearing the path of barbed wire, land mines, and of course German soldiers. Hundreds of us had then charged across the no man's land between their trenches and ours, foundering and stumbling in the mud, making for the newly weakened position. Flames rose over this way, thrashing tentacles of a hue somehow fleshy pink and rotting gray at once over that. The air was soup-thick with cordite, brimstone, and blood. My left ear still rang; my right had gotten well and truly sick of the whole affair and sat in sulky silence.

And of course, I was still in pain, my entire body chafing under my uniform thanks to the requirements of Heavy Sulfur. It had been well over twenty-four hours since Poulard had completed his part in things, a process which itself had taken almost a whole day; it would be far longer before I no longer felt the discomfort.

Our forces would sweep in, turning left behind the enemy lines and surrounding what had long been a troublesome artillery battery, taking it out before German support could move up from the next row of trenches to secure the breach. Standard infiltration tactics, but in this case, also a diversion.

All for me.

The German uniform, scavenged from the dead, then mended and cleaned, would never have sufficed all on its own. Someone would have spotted me emerging from a British contingent. Nor would my charms of misdirection have worked, not if any of the German sentries had even the slightest training in penetrating such glamours. The both of them together, however, in conjunction with the bedlam of the offensive, was enough to carry me unnoticed behind the forward position. Once there, it was a simple matter of diving into the nearest trench and sheltering with my "fellow" German soldiers.

As we huddled, backs pressed to walls of packed earth, everything roaring and exploding all about us, I couldn't help but almost feel at home. The world these men occupied was scarcely different from my own. Oh, the precise design of the trench might differ—the shapes and curves more extreme, the walkway of boards layered in the wrong pattern, the buttresses of different widths and materials—but in the end it was still just a trench. A manmade gash in the earth, boasting few comforts save the occasional dugout or other underground chamber. It boasted the same rats, growing ever more bold and contemptuous of us invaders. The same puddles of filthy, stagnant water that would rot boots and even feet if soldiers proved too incautious. The same stench of the latrines, enough to make a dead man wince.

And, though the language differed, the same constant shouts and cries and orders and prayers.

I wound up ensconced between a pair of soldiers; a young man, one Karl Dreesen, who was serving in his first week on the front line, and an older, more hardened fellow called Neubauer. (I never did get his Christian name.) After I'd identified myself as a runner from the nearby *Infanterie-Regiment* 49, we spent the next hours in idle chat while waiting for the bombardment to ease. I told them a bit about a fiancée in Stuttgart—only after confirming that neither was from there, of course, it turning out that Dreesen was from Graudenz and Neubauer from Berlin—and while my entire life's story was spun from whole cloth, neither seemed to note anything amiss with it.

I hoped they were equally oblivious to my discomfort as I leaned against the walls, my inability to find a comfortable posture—or at least, if they noticed, that they thought it the effect of a nervous disposition.

The barrage finally ended as darkness neared, as I'd known it would. I excused myself to the latrine, both as cover for my departure and because I needed the facilities, such as they were. The other soldiers I passed by on my way tossed the occasional salute or nodded greetings, but otherwise paid me no heed at all. And why should they? I looked as though I belonged.

Frankly, and all things considered, this had been remarkably easy. If any operation that requires a frontal military assault by an entire battalion, to serve as a diversion, can be considered "easy," I suppose.

At which point—after I completed my necessary ablutions at the edge of a pit, at the end of a short side-trench, that could as easily have stunk of English piss as German—I discovered that it wasn't to be *quite* so easy as all that.

"A moment," Neubauer said in German from behind

me. I felt a grip on my arm, turned to see a young soldier who was, had I to guess, probably on sanitary duty for this latrine. Neubauer stood behind him. "Roll up your sleeve, please."

As God is my witness, I've no idea how he'd discovered me. My uniform coat had remained on and buttoned up at all times while we were together. Had the cuff slipped back at some point? Had I at some moment bent or hunched in such a way as to allow the collar to gape? I've no idea.

Clearly he'd seen *something*, and a look at my bare arms would only confirm it. The fresh tattooing—Poulard's esoteric work, intricate patterns and hair-thin swirls, still enflamed and seeping—covered my entire body from wrists to neck to ankles.

Thank heaven he'd caught me while the day shift stood their watch against a dusk assault, and the night hadn't yet been awakened. In the latrine, there were only the three of us.

A quick blow with one hand to the young soldier's throat, ensuring he could not call out, while I drew a heavy trench knife with the other. Neubauer was good, experienced, but—though generally suspicious of me—had not recognized me as an immediate threat. I was able to lunge in under his guard, my knife taking him in the solar plexus. An ugly warmth drenched my hand.

I saw movement, twisted desperately away as the other soldier, though rasping for breath, slashed at me with a bayonet. The fabric of my coat sleeve parted, but not the shirt beneath—nor, thank God, my skin! *That* would have proved a right mess, and no mistake!

As the soldier was off his balance, watching for a thrust of my bloodied knife, I instead put a boot to his gut, kicking him into the foul pit.

He rose, gagging, struggling for a handhold, and I drove my blade down into his skull. Given his predicament, it seemed the only decent thing to do.

I dumped Neubauer's body in there with him, and then kicked in a bit of mud to cover them. It would stand up to no true observation, but given the fading light and most men's tendency not to stare too long into a reeking latrine, I hoped they'd go undiscovered for a trice. Time was definitely against me, though, even more now than it had been.

I dashed out into the trench, choosing to make use of—rather than seek to conceal—my urgency. I approached the first soldier I spotted, tossing off a hasty salute.

"*Oberstleutnant* Erdmann Vossler!" I demanded of him, breathing hard. "Where might I find him?"

"I'm not . . . I believe he's meeting with the other officers," came the puzzled response. I nodded my thanks and set off, grateful to Captain Hunter-Hughes that I had at least a working notion of the trench layout.

As I approached the dugout that I believed to be the officers' command center, however, I was intercepted by a pair of sentries.

Again I inquired after the lieutenant colonel and occultist. "I've an urgent message for him only!"

These two, however, were not so readily convinced. "From whom?" the man on the left demanded.

Bugger. I didn't have the time for this! "For him only," I repeated.

"I didn't ask to see it, fool, just to know who it comes from!"

"I've been instructed not to say even that much."

"Then we cannot allow you to pass. Procedure demands—"

I drew myself up straight. "If you would like to register a complaint with the *zaubertruppen*," I informed him, referring to the Germans' own military occult division, "I will be happy to stand and wait with this *urgent* communiqué while you do so. May I have your name, *mein herr*, so I may ensure my report is free of inaccuracies?"

Grumbling something about witches, they stood aside for me.

Summoning all my willpower not to fidget with pages of the banishing ritual I carried in my coat, I slipped into the officers' dugout.

It lacked the chairs to be found in Major Grimes's "office," but the table and boards were similar indeed. Of the four officers gathered around that table, I could not be sure which was the magus, Vossler.

There was, however, no doubt whatsoever as to the entity.

It sat at the head of the table, *floating*, bobbing as if on a gentle sea. I saw angry flesh, such as might result from abrading a hound bald with sandpaper. Limbs that I hesitate to call legs hung, limp and loose, lightly coiling where they reached the floor. Smaller limbs, jointed far too many times and also backwards—again like a dog's— wobbled as they stretched out over the table. Its head . . . God! I can best describe it as a hound's or wolf's snout—

just the snout, no eyes or forehead—splitting open to resemble a blossoming flower.

"Yes?" one of the officers barked as they all looked irritably up at me. "What is it you—?"

The *thing* howled, or maybe hissed; steam through a trumpet, perhaps. It pointed at me with one arm, which unfolded, joint after joint, ever narrower, impossibly long, until it aimed a single gnarled digit at me. And within that unholy sound, a smattering of syllables came together to make a horrid sense.

"Ennng . . . lishhhhhh . . . mannnnnn . . ."

I dove aside, hand darting for the ritual, but I wasn't remotely fast enough. No man could have been. I heard the crack of pistols, felt agony blossom across my body. The wounds were tiny pits of fire, but the night had gone so very cold.

"Call for a channeler," I heard one of them say. "We'll find out why he's come, what the English thought to achieve . . ."

The voice—indeed all the sounds—faded away. All sounds but one, that is; a faint chorus in my ears, a growing unhallowed chant.

I do not know if you can hear me, Captain Hunter-Hughes. My final thoughts may amount to nothing, this final report shouted uselessly into the void. But I can feel the pain of my injuries turning into something else, the agony falling away even as it grows worse, as though becoming . . . distant.

The ritual of binding loosens, the lines of the great sigil tattooed across my flesh now broken by the bullets that shredded my skin.

Heavy Sulfur. If a man should fail, what better way to wreak havoc amongst the enemy? How better to kill a demon . . . than with a *greater* demon?

I feel it rising within, tearing free, preparing to rid itself of the prison of blood and bone that is Peyton Cleary. I feel it coming, and I am content.

For king and country.

★ ★ ★

ABOUT THE AUTHOR

Ari Marmell would love to tell you all about the esoteric jobs and wacky adventures he had on the way to becoming an author, since that's what other authors seem to do in these sections. Unfortunately, he doesn't actually have any, as the most exciting thing about his professional life, besides his novel writing, is the work he's done for Dungeons & Dragons and other role-playing games. His published fiction consists of both fully original works and licensed/tie-in properties—including *Darksiders* and *Magic: the Gathering*—for publishers such as Del Rey, Pyr Books, Titan Books, and Wizards of the Coast. His most recent creation is the Mick Oberon series, urban fantasy/noir set in Gangland Chicago. Ari lives in an apartment that's almost as cluttered as his subconscious, which he shares (the apartment, not the subconscious, though sometimes it seems like it) with George—his wife—and a cat who really, really thinks it's dinner time. Find Ari online at mouseferatu.com and on Twitter @mouseferatu.

STEEL SHIPS

★ ★ ★

Tanya Huff

"Kytlin! Look outside! That's Commander NcTran!"

Kytlin lifted her gaze just far enough from her beer to frown across the scarred, wooden table at the newest member of the Royal Navy's Special Forces. *When*, she wondered, as Harrin directed her attention to the courtyard outside the window, *did we start accepting children?* She glanced out at the bundled figured crossing toward the admiralty, and her frown deepened. The figure was one of theirs, that much was certain—their people were nearly as bulky on two legs as they were wearing their sealskins—but with a cape draped over the uniform, she couldn't tell gender let alone rank. "How can you tell that's NcTran?"

"I can see his empty sleeve flapping in the wind!"

Young eyes, she thought, but said, "He's not the only shifter missing a limb."

"It's him. I'm going to —"

"Sit, Harrin." Kytlin grabbed his wrist, hauling him back onto the bench, counting on the swirl of smoke from the clay pipes clenched between every other set of teeth and the flickering shadows from the hanging oil lamps to cover the motion and maintain the boy's dignity. The storm had filled the mess with men and women trying to escape the weather and it wouldn't take much to tip a room full of bored sailors to mockery. "We're off duty," she growled. "If NcTran needs us, he'll find us."

"But . . ."

"No."

Harrin shook off her grip, but remained seated—however reluctantly. "I swore in over a month ago, and I've done nothing but harbor patrols." He picked at a gouge in the tabletop with his thumbnail. "I can do more."

"There's a war on, there'll be more to do. Count on it."

"Yeah, but something . . ."

His voice trailed off, lost in the noise of the Royal Navy drinking and dicing, but Kytlin could read the last word off his face. *Something . . . important.*

Harrin had been too young to face the serpent and that defeat had come to define Special Forces. Kytlin had been in the first group of decoys. She remembered one cousin dead and another maimed. She remembered blood in the water. Three years later, their numbers still hadn't recovered. "There's bugger all glory in dying."

"More glory in dying than sitting around here doing bugger all," Harrin muttered into his beer.

★ ★ ★

"Steel ships?" Kytlin glanced around the boathouse at those members of Special Forces who'd been available for the briefing and saw her disbelief mirrored on nearly every one of the two dozen familiar faces. "Ships made of steel?"

"The Hawkeye wasn't willing to commit a hundred percent," Commander NcTran admitted from where he stood on an overturned dory. "The shipyard is camouflaged, and they know we have birds in the air . . ."

"How . . . ?"

"*They* have birds in the air, Dugald." NcTran's tone shut down further argument.

No surprise he'd recognized the voice; Dugald had fathered two of the commander's nephews. Well, two that Kytlin knew of. All the members of the RNSF were tied by blood—brothers, sisters, cousins. When one of them bled, all of them bled.

"They've put archers in towers, so her bird had to move fast," NcTran continued, "but she's certain she saw metal and she's certain the Navreen have covered at least two ships in it."

The boathouse filled with speculation. The Hawkeyes—blindfolded and safe behind the front lines—didn't see what their birds saw; they saw through the eyes of their birds. It was a subtle but important distinction. And if the Hawkeye saw metal ships . . .

"It could be mage work," she heard NcTran say in answer to a question she'd missed, "but the Hawkeye doesn't think so. Said it looked too *useful*."

That brought a unison snort from everyone present. The Most Wise were seldom useful.

"So we have surveillance that puts the shipyard eight to ten hours up the Treel River." The commander leapt off the dory and motioned Jeordie NcMarin, his Second, forward. "The Treel's not deep," he continued as NcMarin unrolled a map of the North Sea's eastern shore against the dory's curve. "They're building shallow-draught boats, made for rivers. They're planning something big, and not only because they're trying so hard to hide it. Now, given that we've recaptured the mines, unless the army's been lying to us . . ."

"Like that's never happened," Eoin NcMarin called from the back. He was the Second's first cousin and Kytlin's second cousin, and the gesture Jeordie tossed at him was rudely familial.

". . . using this much steel has to have emptied the Navreen's iron reserves. They're gambling big, like they did when they brought in the serpent."

It always came back to the serpent, Kytlin acknowledged silently. The Navreen had emptied their treasury when they hired a Mer to negotiate with the serpent. The Mers' services did not come cheap. If they'd covered two boats with steel . . . Two *river* boats . . . "Commander! Could they be planning a run up the Atanent to the capital?"

NcTran nodded. "High Command believes that's their intent, yes. And they'll have a clear run. If we block the Atanent, we'll have to pull horses and men out of the army and off the lines to get wood to our own shipyards. The queen won't agree to that, not when there's a river right there. If we leave a dreadnought in the bay"—he smacked his palm against the map—"their Hawkeyes will spot it and they'll engage it as a distraction, we'd be playing right into their hands. The Navreen will slip around close to shore and across the estuary under cover of darkness."

"And once they're in the bloody river," someone called from the back, "incendiaries'll be useless and there's bugger all we can do to slabs of metal."

"Then we take out the sails!" Kytlin thought that was Dugald.

"Or the oars!" Fyona, probably. Though it might have been Selen.

"If they plan a run up the Atanent," the commander snapped, cutting the argument short, "then we have to assume they've come up with a fast and quiet method of propulsion."

"And that their mages are more useful than ours," Jeordie muttered.

"Couldn't be less useful," Commander NcTran agreed.

Eoin pushed forward and frowned down at the map. "And if that isn't their plan?"

"If you can think of a way that the enemy building ironclad ships will benefit us, Eoin, I'd like to hear it." NcTran waited until Eoin finally shook his head. Then he turned his attention back to the company as a whole. "If you'll recall, the Hawkeye's description was *have covered* not *are covering*. Whatever they're going to do, they're close to launch. Dark of the moon's in eleven days: High Command assumes they'll move then, so we're running out of time. Our orders are to take out those ships—and the shipyard if possible."

"And do what against steel?" Kytlin asked as the noise level began to rise again.

Before NcTran could answer, the small door in the north wall opened and a tall, skinny young man blew in on a gust of wind and rain. He flipped his hood back, revealing pale skin, a scattering of freckles, bright red hair, and only one eyebrow. Given the red and blistered skin on his forehead, it looked as though the other had recently been burned away.

Mage, Kytlin realized. When skirmishes had turned to war, Queen Isabella had gathered all six of the mages within her borders under one roof and ordered them to turn their attention to the defeat of the Navreen. Kytlin knew three people running book on when they'd blow that roof off.

"Listen up, people!" NcTran stepped forward and took the mage's arm, pulling him into place beside the dory. "This is Alaster Grant. Those of you who were on the *Vixen* when she sailed the strait know him. For the rest of you, yes, this is the Most Wise who came up with the spell that destroyed the serpent."

The room erupted into cheers and barking. None of them were in their seal-shape, but sometimes that didn't matter. Alaster blushed scarlet.

NcTran let them sound off for a moment then raised his hand for silence. "The Most Wise is here today because he has a way for us to destroy the steel ships. Most Wise . . ."

"Right. Yes. Well . . ." Alaster looked up, then down, shifting from foot to foot, and Kytlin realized he couldn't be much older than Harrin. He drew an oilcloth bag out from under his cloak, set it carefully on the dory, and opened it.

Everyone in the boathouse leaned forward, then back again when he pulled out a small clay bowl wrapped in waxed cloth, a large piece of rock, and a hammer.

"The rock isn't for the ships," he explained, unwrapping the bowl and setting it facedown on the rock. "We were trying to speed things up, to get more iron out while we control the mines, before the Navreen take them back again."

"Takes them *away* again," Dugald called. "Not back. They were on our side of the border to begin with."

"Were they?" When the commander nodded, Alaster sighed. "I've lost track."

The war had started when the Navreen took the mines. Kytlin couldn't decide if she was annoyed the mage had forgotten or was envious that he could.

"Anyway, we made this spell for the miners, but they couldn't use it." Shifting his grip, he hit the bowl with the hammer. The bowl shattered, the rock shuddered, and gray liquid ran from the rock, down the side of the dory, to puddle on the floor. "That there, that's the iron's final state. It can't be heated or worked or turned into weapons. It's pretty much useless."

Kytlin stepped forward, squatted, and poked the puddle. It felt like warm water. "Will the spell work on steel?"

"Absolutely. I've got a lot of clay bowls left over, bigger ones, and it's just a matter of adding the parameters of the carbon to the spell before I paint it on the inside curve. When you get where you're going and you need to use them, you just wet the edge of the bowl with a finger"—he licked a fingertip and mimed a circle in the air. ". . . and stick them to the ship above the waterline. Then, before you break the bowl, you strike the ship to align the spell. With the hammer," he added. "Because of the added carbon content."

Kytlin sighed and straightened. "What part of covert," she asked over the rising profanity, "do you not understand, Most Wise?"

He blushed again. "Oh, you don't hit it hard. Just a light bonk."

"Bonk?"

The blush deepened.

"How many spells to dissolve a ship?" Eoin asked, moving to crouch at Kytlin's feet and poke the puddle himself.

"Four should do it." The mage sketched ships in the air. "On the bow, the stern, and one about the middle of each side. Once I've worked out the changes, I can have a dozen ready in two days."

"Three days," NcTran said, waving Kytlin and Eoin away from the dory. "Two dozen bowls."

Alaster opened his mouth, closed it again, frowned, and finally nodded. "I can do that."

"How many teams, Commander?" Harrin looked as though he was one step away from waving his hand and shouting, *"Pick me! Pick me!"*

"Three teams," NcTran replied. "Four to a team. Strong, fast swimmers who can make it from the estuary to the shipyard under cover of darkness with no idea of the defenses along the river."

If the commander wanted twenty-four bowls, eight bowls to a team, four bowls to a ship . . . each team would have enough firepower to complete the mission. That was more than redundancy. That was expectation.

Kytlin looked around the boathouse. It looked as though everyone else had also done the math—although Eoin was still counting it out on his fingers.

"Well, that's why we're Special Forces," NcTran said into the silence. "If it was easy, everyone would do it."

"There is, uh, one small problem." Alaster flinched as everyone's attention snapped back on to him. "Because the spell's painted on the inside of the bowls, you can't get the bowls wet."

Kytlin pulled herself up out of the water onto the gravel beach, shrugged out of her sealskin and into a long sheepskin robe. Temperature change effected shifters a lot less than non-shifters, but there was no reason to be stupid about it. "The harness works," she said, nodding out to where Harrin and Aiden dragged covered coracles around the harbor at full speed, their seal-shapes barely visible in the chop, "but we need to improve the waterproofing at the join." Made of willow and hide, the coracles were light, and it had been Kytlin's idea to protect the spell bowls by joining two of the small, round boats together gunnel to gunnel—like a walnut shell. "Tar's a pain in the ass in the amount we need and the wax has gone brittle enough to crack."

"Wax is faster to remove than tar, particularly if it's pre-cracked, and you'll need to work quickly when you reach the ships. The bowls will be wrapped in waxed cloth," Commander NcTran continued before she could respond. "And you'll spend a minimal amount of time in the sea. There won't be chop enough to crack the seam on the river."

She made a noise halfway between a grunt and a seal's bark. It could've meant *Yes, sir.* It could've meant *Fuck you.* It usually expressed a sentiment somewhere between the two, and they both knew it. The commander was a solid, familiar presence at her back as they stood and watched Aiden swim in a wide circle as Harrin tried to submerge his coracle. "He's very young," she said after a moment. He. Harrin. Although Aiden wasn't much older.

"What choice did we have?"

A rhetorical question, she assumed. Twelve swimmers—four strike teams strong enough and fast enough to reach the shipyard before dawn—meant Harrin had to be on the list. "He's too young to believe he'll die."

The commander's turn to grunt. "And you?" he asked.

"How long have we been at war?" That was as much of an answer as she had to give him.

"The Navreen emptied their treasury to pay for the Mers' services; they've emptied their iron reserves for this," NcTran said quietly, his voice barely carrying over the sound of the waves and the wind. "If we can take out these ships, this shipyard, there's a chance they'll have lost enough to sue for peace."

How much of a chance, she wondered as she beckoned Harrin in to shore, then answered her own question as Commander NcTran met him at the highwater mark with a robe. Wars were won by a throw of the dice as much as strategy, tactics, and attrition. The Navreen were ready to throw. Time to pick up the dice.

★ ★ ★

The next night they were in a fast sloop heading south; black sails, black woodwork, metals dulled to prevent reflection. Jeordie NcMarin—the commander's eyes and ears at sea, cleat on the bottom of his wooden leg digging into the deck—alternated with one of Kytlin's cousins at the wheel. No siblings shared this mission, but her people were too tied to avoid all family connections. Aiden's cousins Boyd and Fyona stood by the starboard rail; Euan and his cousin Shuard were at the bow; Harrin and the other five still asleep below deck were tied back for generations. Even with minimal losses, every family on the coast would mourn. Kytlin stared down into the water, the surface as black as the ship and considerably colder. If no one made it to the shipyard then the whole country would end up mourning. Perspective was everything.

She bent her knees as the schooner rolled, sails snapping taut in the rising wind. On the one hand, the storm coming in from the east would provide cloud cover and keep the defending dreadnoughts busy. On the other hand, storms at this time of the year were more than dangerous: they could be brutal.

"A polite enemy would fucking wait until spring," Boyd growled, half slamming into the rail beside her. "The Navreen must want the war over before freeze."

"*I'd* like the war over before freeze." She'd like the war over before morning. Bracing herself, she glanced toward the helm where her cousin had hung his considerable body weight off the wheel to hold the course. They planned for the schooner to slip into the estuary and drop anchor to unload teams and equipment. They'd slip out again when the tide turned, spend the day avoiding the enemy, and return the next night for extraction. The sea had a way of rewriting plans. "We go in any closer, we risk losing the ship. We'll have to go over the side in deep water."

"The wax . . ."

The waves had swelled in the last couple of minutes, troughs grown deeper and darker. "No choice. Wake the others."

By the time they were assembled on deck, the storm had gone from promise to howling wind and freezing spray.

"Trust the Navreen to use a river just over the border when they control the whole fucking south sea," Travis grumbled, settling the heavy leather harness around his neck. "They should shove their shipyard somewhere warm."

"River ships can't spend much time at sea," Harrin reminded him. "Not enough keel."

The big man's lips twitched. "Somewhere warm where the sun don't shine."

"That's . . . oh."

"Estuary's not large, but even you lot should be able to find it." One hand holding the coracle in place on the top of the slide, Kytlin flicked sleet off her face with the other. "We'll form up in the river. First team, go!"

Heavy robes hit the deck to a chorus of profanity. Three men and a woman went over the side in long low dives, powerful legs pushing them away from the ship. Skin in the air, seals when they hit the water. Ropes attached to the two harnesses disappeared into the black glass curve of a wave, snapped tight, and the coracle dropped.

It didn't shatter on impact, so Kytlin counted it a win.

"This could end the war!" NcMarin shouted from behind her.

She could barely hear him over the wind. Hadn't heard him approach. "That's what they tell me. Second team! Go!"

"Commander NcTran says the brass are calling this the Coracle Raid."

She turned to face him then. "Why? Was Operation Suicide taken?" Before he could answer, she turned again. Eight of her people and two coracles in the water. "Third team!" Robe off, she tugged the leather harness into place on Harrin's shoulders, adjusting it so he could change within its circle. "Go!"

She was the last into the water, and, even in seal-shape, the water was as cold as it looked. Without the coracles, they could have gone deep and, at the very least, avoided a pounding by the waves. Tethered to the surface, Kytlin stayed close on the left while Shuard guarded the right and Euan and Harrin threw themselves forward, struggling to remain far enough apart to keep the ropes from tangling.

The surf got harder to fight closer to shore. They were in enemy water, and the water was the enemy.

The coracle slammed against her shoulder then tipped up on one side. If it went over, it'd twist the lines, so she dove far enough to slap it back level with her rear flippers, scraped her chin along a rock shelf bottom, and surfaced in time to see Harrin flung out on shore, Euan right after him. If the coracle hit with that force . . .

She slid under it, brushing against Shuard's flipper as he had the same idea.

Bones wrapped in seal-shape were harder to break, but slamming down onto the rocks still knocked the breath out of her. Harrin staggered close on legs, skin wrapped around his waist, and bent to drag the coracle off her, looking as though he worried about her age as much as she worried about his youth. Rolling out of her skin and onto her back, she gasped up at the scudding clouds and tried to work out how long they had until the storm hit land.

"Commander?" Harrin had never sounded so young.

Right. Commander. That would be her this trip. Except for NcTran, rank had little permanency among their people. "I'm okay. Shuad?" A flipper and a curve of fur extended past the shell of the coracle.

"Hit his head," Euan grunted. "Should be fine in a minute."

"Not sure we have that much time." She stood, shivering in the cold, missing the layer of fat she'd lost. So far they'd attracted no attention from the enemy, but that couldn't last. No one gambled so deeply and left the dice undefended.

"River's that way." Harrin pointed northwest.

Seals had excellent night vision. Not as good in skin, but still better than non-shifters. Harrin's, it seemed, was better than hers. Young eyes. "Faster on foot," she said. "Sling the coracle."

They were fisherfolk when they weren't fighting wars. If this worked, maybe they'd be fisherfolk again. She helped Euan tie the tow ropes off into a loose net while Harrin got Shuad onto his feet.

"Commander? Should I unstrap the knives?"

There were four sheathed on each of the coracles' lids. Kytlin glanced across the rock to the dark line of trees. "Leave them. If we're attacked, get back in the water."

The footing was slippery and uneven. They moved recklessly fast to keep from freezing.

When they reached the river, bruised and shaking, they found the second team already in the water, Fyona bleeding from a cut across the top of her right shoulder. "Blades," she ground out through clenched teeth as she came up on shore, sealskin dropping into her hand. "Spears with long sharp points set just under the surface and angled to catch anything coming in. Coracle skimmed over them. I didn't."

In the center of the river, where the water was merely rough, not wild, two blunt heads bracketed the coracle. Eoin and Mykal. One short.

"Dugald never met up with the team."

They turned together to look out to sea. He might have been swept south. He might still be working his way toward land.

He might not.

They weren't the only predators in the water.

Kytlin waved her team into the river as she squinted across it at the stretch of gravel beach that made up the estuary's north arm.

"There!"

Harrin's young eyes again. "Get in the water before you freeze." He had less body fat than any of them.

First team carried their coracle slung between them. Even at that distance she could see Boyd favoring his left leg; otherwise, they seemed fine. Stone rolled smooth made easier walking than the shore to the south, but with the beach rapidly disappearing under the storm surge, the team was farther from the safety of deep water. Travis spotted them and waved, his team picking up the pace.

The wolves attacked without warning. Six, no . . . seven silent shadows separating from the treeline. Large, heavy shoulders, dark gray fur that blended with the night.

"Not wolves," Fyona snarled.

Shifters.

When they reached the first team, Aiden screamed.

"Eoin!" Kytlin's voice jerked him to a stop, halfway to the far bank. She understood his need to help, but they couldn't stop a wolf pack. At best, they'd become part of the slaughter.

She dove, changed, and when she surfaced in the center of the river saw that Aiden and Boyd were down. Travis charged toward the sea in sealskin, coracle bouncing behind him, tangled in the net. Beside it, Selen swung one of the big knives. The wolf stalking her leapt back, jaws wide. The coracle tipped and broke open. Two of the wolves darted in between Travis and the water. He reared and roared, a bull seal not easy prey, but the closer wolf rose onto two legs, pulled the single shot crossbow strapped to his side and fired. The quarrel slammed into Travis's mouth, and two wolves leapt in to rend and tear. Selen fell onto the coracle, one forearm caught in a wolf's jaws, one hand reaching back . . .

. . . then rising above the wolf's head, the wind licking sparks from her fingers.

Kytlin slapped Harrin with a flipper to get him moving, and the seven of them raced upstream, the tidal current lending speed.

Three.

Two.

Selen had been sprawled out over the coracle. Igniting one incendiary would ignite them all. *Take an honor guard with you*, Kytlin told her.

One.

Heat. Light. Smoke rolled up the river after them, stinking of burning blood and fur. One less wolf pack. One less seal team. Two coracles and seven hands to hold a hammer. Enough to do the job.

When they were far enough from the sea that the water barely tasted of salt and the storm had become a roiling gray cloud against the horizon, Kytlin brought them to a halt and searched both shores for signs of pursuit. Nothing—although she thought she could hear howling in the distance. Her flippers were unwilling to give way to legs, sealskin and water combining to wrap around and stop the change, but with wolf packs on patrol they couldn't risk their scent on the ground. Eoin changed with her.

"We've been made," Eoin grunted, eyes wide, the sudden death of four of their number lingering on the surface. "They'll have sent word to the shipyard."

"Probably," Kytlin agreed, "but it'll take time to get the word through. Non-shifters barely trust *us,* and these are wolves."

"They trust them to guard the river."

"They use them, but they won't trust them. There'll be a shitload of hoops they'll have to jump through before they can pass information on." Teeth clenched to keep them from chattering, she watched heads nod, then she bared them. "And if they've sent word, we'll beat it." It was as close to a speech about not allowing the five they'd lost die to in vain as she planned to make. She held Eoin's gaze until he nodded. Pain and grief pushed down, denied until the job got done. "All right." She let the current drag her sealskin back around her. "Let's go end the war before we have to do something this stupid again."

All twelve of them had been chosen for their ability to maintain speed over distance, so that's what they did. Bruises driven into Kytlin's arms and legs during impact with the shore ached as she slipped through the water—a shadow among shadows. When she took her turn in the harness, she hissed at the press of the leather against her shoulder. When Harrin and Fyona, who had the least protective bodyfat, began to look glassy-eyed, their strokes stuttering, she sent them deeper to the warmer water—although warmer was relative and distance from the surface added distance to the swim.

They ate on the move, small fish snapped up without slowing, blood and scraps of flesh left to swirl away toward the sea. Just past a weir, Shuad grabbed a young salmon and forced Harrin to eat half.

Twice, warned by the change in currents, they cut their way through weighted nets, the top cable just below the surface, invisible in the dark even to their eyes.

"If the net moves too far in any direction, it sets off a spell. Don't know what kind, but I doubt the Most Wise are working in our favor." Face barely breaking the surface, Kytlin swam back to the center of the river. She'd had to stand ankle deep at the shore before she could see the cable ends and had nearly frozen her tits off. The water'd actually felt warm when she'd submerged. "Coracles will clear it with a little help, but we'll have to go through. Cut it carefully about an arm's length down. Carefully!" she repeated as Eoin changed and yanked a knife free.

With the stars masked by thick, gray clouds, time became defined by the ache of joints, the burn in lungs. Remaining at the surface, Kytlin weighed colder water against her increasing need for air. She noted each ache, each pain, and knew they had to be close. Might as well spend it all on the way there; time enough to rest when the shipyard burned.

They'd rounded a bend and headed south when the taste of the water changed.

Acids. Metals. People. If not *the* shipyard, then *a* shipyard.

Then visibility dropped; the water suddenly murky.

She surfaced and could see only another bend and what might have been unnatural angles through the trees—if they were still in leaf, she wouldn't have seen that. Eoin surged past her, powerful rear flippers slamming up and down. If she'd had a hand, she'd have grabbed him, but all she could do was slide below the surface and bark out a warning.

The currents changed, broken into eddies.

She tasted blood in the water.

Beckoning Shuard forward, the two of them sped through the murk. Speed. And caution. One of Eoin's rear flippers slapped the side of her head, and she froze. Shuard stopped dead beside her. Eoin stilled at her touch, and she worked her way up his body until she found . . .

Blades. Spears angled to catch anything moving upriver. Fyona had been injured on a similar set; Eoin had been impaled. Instincts had taken over and he'd fought to get free, twisting the blade in the wound.

Together, they worked him back off the spike. A gush of blood darkened the water further as they carried him to the surface and rolled him onto his back. More blood as he coughed and gasped for breath. The blade had cut through skin and fat and into muscle. He couldn't have hit it hard enough to damage bone, no matter how sharp it was, but it could have slid across his shoulder, cutting tendons.

They were harder to kill in sealskin, but easier to treat out of it.

If he changed, and the change didn't kill him, if she packed the wound and bound it, he couldn't change back. He'd drown out in the river, and he'd freeze on the shore. With Shuard tucked under him, sculling gently, Kytlin led the way to the shallows. It took a few moments to find a protected area with water deep enough to hold Eoin's weight. Then she shifted. This needed fingers.

"Stay here," she growled, packing weed against the wound. It was cold enough that blood in the water shouldn't call the wolf packs, but this close to shore she wasn't taking the chance. "We'll pick you up on the way

out." When Eoin snorted, dark eyes rolling back in his
head, she tugged on a handful of whiskers with fingers
nearly numb from the cold. "Don't die. That's an order."
Now, two people short, she couldn't leave anyone with
him.

Skin draped around her neck, she rode Shuard back to
the center of the river. Harrin stared at her as she slid into
the water, eyes wide, nostrils flared. "We'll pick him up
on the way out." If she said it often enough, she might
believe it. "Fyona, Mykal, those blades will have to be
lowered to bring a boat out—they can't have covered
every boat they own in steel—find it and flatten them."
She wanted to add, *as fast as you can*, but they knew that.
If she could smell dawn in the air, they could, too.

If the lives lost were going to mean anything at all, they
had to reach the shipyard while night still provided cover.

While they waited, she checked the wax sealing the
coracles closed. Cracked in multiple places, there was no
way to tell if the water had gotten inside until they opened
them.

Fyona surfaced and sneezed, blowing water out of her
nose.

Mykal surfaced beside her.

They stayed close to the surface, swam over the blades,
rounded the bend . . .

The steel-covered boats were in the water, docked
diagonally, bows jutting halfway across the river.
Camouflaged from the air by poles and branches, the
sides of the shelter were mostly open except for where it
looked like two trees had been torn up and shoved down
in the water. Kytlin ground her teeth and hoped there

were no giants around. Usually giants stayed in the mountains, throwing boulders at each other, but if the Navreen thought this important enough, they might have pulled a couple off the front lines.

Still, camouflage from the air meant nothing from the river. Unfortunately, there could be a whole division camped beyond the shipyard, ready to board, and they wouldn't be able to tell from the water.

They crossed the last open area and tucked in under the shelter of the bows. Long and shallow draft, completely closed in, painted in patches of grays and black, the boats would be as hard to see slipping up a river in the dark of the moon as their coracles would. Had been. But these boats were large enough to hold troops.

Death, like life, needed hands. "Euan, port side. Mykal, starboard. Fyona, Harrin, stay here at the bows." Fyona was injured; Harrin was going home alive. The bows were the farthest from the enemy and offered the most cover. "Shuard, you're up the middle under the dock. Once your spells have been set off, join me at the stern for the incendiaries. The rest of you, the moment the things start to burn, haul ass back to Eoin. We'll join you there."

When they cracked the first coracle, two of the spells were wet. Three out in the second. Eleven left; they needed eight.

"Two on each on the outer hulls, then. Might as well use them if we have them." She held up a hand, ignored the way it shook, and began the count. "One."

Moving silently, a ripple in the water, a shadow

following, Harrin pulled the coracle to Euan's position. Euan changed, set the spells on the ship, changed again, hammer held in his mouth. No point freezing.

Starboard side, Fyona and Mykal swam the same pattern.

Thirty.

Bowls set on the bow.

Forty.

All the incendiaries were loaded into a single coracle and Shuard dragged it under the dock.

Fifty.

With his set, she dragged it to the stern.

Sixty.

Starboard first.

Seventy.

Then port.

At eighty, everyone was to be in skin.

Ninety-nine.

One hundred.

They'd practiced this on unspelled bowls.

Strike the hammer against the ship.

It actually went *bonk*.

The steel began to sag the moment the bowl broke, the light seeming to sag with it.

Light. Dawn.

She could hear voices approaching, and there were two bowls still to break. An incendiary tossed over a pile of cases at the end of the dock acted as a distraction as she swam to the other ship, slow and clumsy in skin, rose up, and broke the second bowl. Turning back to the coracle, she saw Shuard crouched on the end of the dock, muscles in his arm and back bunching as he threw incendiaries deep into the shipyard.

There was smoke, plenty of smoke, but not much flame.

Then Euan screamed. Back in sealskin, she rounded the stern, past steel sliding off the boat like silvered water, to find three long black arrows nailing Euan's dead body to the exposed wood. And she remembered what else the Hawkeye had seen. The Navreen had archers in a tower.

She could see it now she knew where to look. At the edge of the shore rising out of the trees, light glinting off an upright. A metal tower? They'd expected incendiaries then, thus the lack of flame. They hadn't expected the spell on the steel, though. No one ever expected the Most Wise.

The archer had a clear line on the river, but if they went deep . . .

An arrow hit the water.

The river lit up, the water suddenly crystal clear and bright as day.

Another arrow hissed past her shoulder and sped straight and true to the bottom. That was impos—

Fucking mages! Kytlin flattened against the ship. A clearwater spell of some kind on the first arrow to remove any cover the water provided and something directly applied to the arrows as well so that they moved through the water like they moved through the air. It seemed the Navreen mages *were* more useful.

Then Harrin was out of the water and running for the trees, bare legs flashing white through the smoke, the ninth bowl in one hand, a hammer in the other.

"Fyona! Mykal! Keep the archer's attention on the river. Shuard, forget the yard; burn the boats!"

Euan would burn with them, his ashes returned to the water.

Boots pounded against planks, men and women shouted orders, the shipyard's defenders held back by the smoke. The smoke that shielded them from any archers on the ground but not the tower. As long as that tower stood . . .

The tower began to fall.

Instead of diving straight into the river, Harrin ran back toward the boats. Smoke swirling around him, he became a target the archers on the ground could hit.

He stumbled as the arrow slammed through his leg. Staggered on, coughing. The second arrow creased his forehead and he froze, blinded by the blood pouring into his eyes.

Kytlin was half up on the shore when Fyona raced past her, grabbed Harrin's arm, and all but threw him into the water as a crate exploded and her body jerked back and forth, splintered pieces of wood tearing her apart until she collapsed, half in-half out of the river, her blood absorbed by the clearwater spell as it fell.

Her sealskin slid off her shoulder, into the water, and dissolved. Dead, then.

Shuard surged up, broke the surface and roared. Kytlin changed and dove deep. With Mykal already at Harrin's side, the four of them raced downriver.

The clearwater ended just before the blades. Had the blades not been down . . .

Eoin wasn't happy when they reached him, but,

against all odds, he was still alive. He groaned and bled sluggishly as they got him back to deep water. Then, with his back resting on hers and Shuard's—his belly to the sky—three sets of rear flippers churned the water. It wasn't stealth, but it worked; her right front flipper and Shuard's left kept them on course. Mykal and Harrin took point.

A wolf pack waited by the first net. Fortunately, they were wolves, not archers; hitting a moving target on a moving river needed both luck and skill, even in daylight. Even when their targets slowed to pass the injured through the hole in the net. They'd have been better off using the net as a weapon, but they were army, not navy, so what did they know.

Between the nets, they met the storm that had chased them off the schooner. The sleet kept the wolves pacing them in fur and destroyed their aim when they changed to shoot.

They'd caught the current and, even at the surface, were moving fast. Mykal and Harrin went deep and moved faster.

She'd lost track of how long it had been since she'd seen them rise to breathe when she tasted salt.

There were blades at the mouth of the river. By the time they reached them, Mykal had them laid flat.

As they spilled out into the estuary, a wolf pack howled by the black scorch on the northern shore.

Kytlin pointed her nose toward the ocean and barked to pull Harrin into formation. They'd destroyed the ships, burned them to the waterline, but if the shipyard was protected by the Most Wise, well, that had nothing to do with them. She had five out of twelve to get home, a long way still to go, and there was bugger all glory in dying.

★ ★ ★

ABOUT THE AUTHOR

Tanya Huff has a degree in Radio and Television Arts and spent the late '70s in the Canadian Naval Reserve. She has been translated into eleven languages and won the Constellation Award for her work on *Blood Ties*, the television series based on her five Vicki Nelson novels, and the Aurora Award for her novel *The Silvered*. Her recent titles include the mass market edition of *The Silvered*, DAW Books, November 2013, her next will be *The Future Falls*—a third Emporium book—out in hardcover from DAW in November of 2014. She's currently writing a new military space opera in the 'verse of the five-book Valor series which is under option at Breakthrough Productions.

SEALSKIN

★ ★ ★

Carrie Vaughn

Richard's hand was shaking. The noise, the closed space, the lack of easy access to the door were all getting to him. He pressed the hand flat on the polished, slightly sticky surface of the bar. The webbing between his fingers, mutant stretches of skin reaching to the middle joints, stood out. The hand closed into a fist.

Doug noticed him staring at his own hand. "Ready for another one?"

"No, I think I'm done." Richard pushed away the tumbler that had held Jack and Coke.

"This is supposed to be a celebration. I'm supposed to be congratulating you."

"I'm thinking of getting out." He hadn't said the words out loud before now.

Richard appreciated that Doug didn't immediately start arguing and cajoling.

"Can I ask why?" Doug finally asked.

He offered a fake grin. "Well, my knees aren't going to last forever."

"Fuck that. Why?"

He shrugged. "I don't deserve the promotion."

"Richey, that's exactly why you deserve it. Nothing's worse than an entitled asshole in command."

It was nice of him to say so, but Doug had been on that last mission; he knew what had happened. Richard stared at the empty tumbler, trying to figure out what to say to make his friend understand.

Doug kept talking. "You didn't screw up. It could have happened to anyone. Besides, what'll you do if you get out? You have some kind of plan?"

He didn't. His skill sets were highly developed, but highly specialized. He could spend ten minutes underwater on one breath. He could infiltrate and escape any country on Earth undetected. He could snipe a Somali pirate on a life raft from a hundred yards on rough seas.

He said, "Private sector? Make a fortune while the joints still work, then find a beach somewhere to retire to?"

Doug gave him that "bullshit" look again. "Sounds like a waste of meat to me. Maybe you can buy an ice-cream stand." He smiled, indicating he'd meant to tell a joke. But he kept studying Richard. "That last trip out really spooked you."

His team was on call to mobilize for rescue operations. The four weeks of boredom and two days of terror routine. This time they'd been tasked with rescuing hostages from pirates in the Arabian Sea. The target he'd shot had been fifteen years old. At the time, all Richard cared about was that the guy had an AK-47 pointed at a boatful of civilians.

The people he was killing were younger and younger, while he was feeling older and older. He didn't know where it ended. When it was his turn, he supposed. So what was the point? Just do as much good as he could until then. By shooting teenagers.

Yeah, it had probably spooked him.

Doug's phone rang. "I have to take this. My sister's been in labor all day, and Mom said she'd call with news. I'm going to be an uncle." He grinned big as a sunrise.

"Congratulations," Richard said as Doug trotted out the door. Richard was happy for Doug, and Doug's sister, the whole family. But that left him sitting alone, staring at the rows of bottles on the back wall.

"Can I get you something else?" The bartender was an older woman—Richard couldn't guess her age, either a worn fifty or a youthful sixty-something. Not the usual young and hip type of bartender. She might have been doing this her whole life.

He gestured with the empty tumbler. "Naw, I'm good."

"Looks like you got left."

"He had a phone call. He'll be back."

He must have looked like he was in need of conversation, because she kept going. "You stationed out at Coronado?"

"That obvious?" he said.

"We get a lot of you boys out here. You have the look."

"What look is that?"

"Let's just say we don't get a lot of trouble here, when you and your friends are around."

It wasn't his build, because he wasn't that big. It was the attitude. You spotted guys like him not by the way they looked, but by the way they walked into a room. Surveyed the place, pegged everyone there, and didn't have anything to prove.

Doug came back in and called out to the room, "It's a girl! Seven pounds eight ounces!" Everyone cheered, and he ducked back out with his phone to his ear.

"Well, isn't that nice?" the bartender said.

"I wouldn't know." It just slipped out.

"No siblings? No kids in the family?"

"No family," he said. "Mom died last year. I never knew my dad."

"Well, I'm sorry."

"It's just how it is." He shrugged, still staring at his empty glass, trying to decide if he needed another. Probably not.

"Then you're all alone in the world. The soldier seeking his fortune."

Is that what it looked like? He smiled. "I know that story. You're supposed to give me some kind of advice, aren't you? Some magical doodad? Here's an invisible cloak, and don't drink what the dancing princesses give you. Or a sack that'll trap anything, including death." He'd have a use for a sack like that.

"Got nothing for you but another Jack and Coke, hon. Sorry."

"That's okay. I'll tip big anyway."

"You change your mind about the drink?"

"Sure, I'll take one more."

Doug came back in then. Richard expected him to start handing out cigars, but he just slapped his shoulder.

"I'm an uncle! I'm going to head up to L.A. this weekend to see them. Can't wait. I have no idea what to bring—what do you give baby girls?"

"Blankets and onesies," the bartender said. "You can never have too many blankets and onesies."

"What's a onesie?"

Richard raised his fresh drink in a toast. "Congratulations, brother."

"You know what you should do?" Doug said, and Richard got a sinking feeling. "You should come with me. You're going on leave—get the hell out of San Diego, come to L.A. with me."

"I am not going to hang around while you visit a baby." He couldn't borrow someone else's family.

"You have to do something," he said. "You can't just stay around here. You'll go crazy. *More* crazy."

A soldier seeking his fortune. He didn't even know where to start. He didn't want to look at his hands.

"You think I'm crazy?"

"I'd be lying if I said we weren't worried about you."

God, it was the whole team then. "Right, okay, I'll find a place to go on vacation. Do something normal."

"Good."

Normal. As if it could be that easy.

He didn't remember learning to swim—he always knew. He did remember the day he noticed that none of the other kids at the pool had webbed feet and hands. He counted it a stroke of profound good luck that he never got teased about it. But everyone wanted him to hold his hands up, to look at them, to touch his fingers, poke at the membranes of skin, thin enough that light showed through, highlighting blood vessels. He loved to swim, and for a long time didn't notice how sad his mother looked whenever he asked to go to the pool of their low-end apartment complex.

They didn't have much money growing up, and he joined the military because it seemed like a good way out, a good way up to better things. He was smart. ROTC, active duty, advanced training, special forces—it all came easily to him, and he thrived. He was one of those masochistic clowns who loved SEAL school. They trained underwater—escape and survival. One time, their hands were tied behind their backs; they were blindfolded, weighted, and dumped into the pool. They had to free themselves and get to their scuba gear. Terrifying, a test of calm under pressure as much as skill. Richard had loved it. He'd gotten loose and just sat there on the bottom of the pool for a long minute, listening to the ambient noise of everyone else thrashing, taking in the weight and slowness of being submerged. He'd been the last one out, but he'd been smiling, and his pulse wasn't any faster when he finished than it had been when he started.

"He's half fish," the trainer had declared, holding up Richard's hand. "Your feet like that too, Fishhead?" They were. He'd graduated top of his class. His teammates still called him Fishhead.

★ ★ ★

Richard got on a discount travel website and searched under "Last Minute Deals." Belize—intriguing, but sounded too hot and too much like the equatorial places he'd been to recently for professional reasons. San Diego, ironically. Las Vegas, not on a dare. Ireland—ten days, rock-bottom airfare and rental car.

Cool, green, quiet. He could have sworn he heard his dead mother whisper, "Do it. Go."

Luck had gotten him back into the country in time to be at her bedside when the cancer finally took her. That was enough to make him believe in miracles. It wasn't much of a stretch to imagine her spirit pushing him on. He booked the trip and wondered why doing so made his heart race.

His mother only ever said two things about his father: he was Irish, and he was like something out of a fairy tale. Richard had figured this was a metaphor, that she'd had a wild fling in Dublin or Galway with some silver-tongued Celt who'd looked like a prince or a Tolkienesque elf. Gotten knocked up and came home. When Richard was young, he'd urged her to go look for him, to try to find him. He'd desperately wanted to meet this fairy-tale father. When his mother said it was impossible, he'd taken that to mean the man was dead.

Ireland, then. Not because he thought he could find his father or get sentimental at some gravesite, or even because he wanted to. But because his mother must have been there, once upon a time.

It would be going back to where he started.

★ ★ ★

What he loved most about Ireland: how green this country was, and how close the sea was, no matter where he went.

Dublin was a city like any city, big and cosmopolitan, though he found himself having to adjust his thinking—a hundred years was not old here. History dripped from every corner. He didn't stay long, ticking off the tourist boxes and feeling restless. He picked up the rental car and headed down the coast on his third day.

Ireland was having a heat wave. He rolled down the windows, let the smell of the ocean in, and arrived in Cork. Found a B&B at the edge of town, quiet. Went for a walk— these towns were set up for walking in a way few American towns were, a central square and streets twisting off it, all clustered together. Cork was a tourist town, shop fronts painted in bright colors, signs in Gaelic in gold lettering, just like in all the pictures. He still somehow found himself at a bar. Pub, he supposed. The patrons here were older. Locals, not tourists. No TV screens in sight. Low conversation was the only background noise. He ordered a Guinness, because everything he'd read had been right about that: Guinness was better in Ireland.

"You American?" the barman asked. Two stooped, grizzled men who must have been in their seventies were sitting at the bar nearby and looked over with interest.

Richard chuckled. Everyone had been able to spot him before he even opened his mouth. Maybe it was his jeans or his haircut or something. "Yeah."

"You looking for your roots? Family? Americans always seem to show up looking for their ancestors. Every single American has an Irish great-uncle, seems like."

"I'm just on vacation," he said. "Enjoying the scenery."

One of the old men said, "What's your name, son? Your family name?"

"My mother's name was Green."

"Huh. English. Could be from anywhere. Your father?"

"I don't know." He gave a good-humored shrug. "He was supposed to be Irish. But I don't know his name."

The barman snorted. "Most folk looking for family at least have a name to go on."

"Sorry. Mom liked being mysterious."

"Hey," the second grizzled old man said. "Hold up your hand there, son."

He got a sudden thudding feeling in his heart. The back of his neck tingled, the sort of thing that would normally have him reaching for his sidearm and checking on his teammates. But it was just him and the curiosity of some old men.

He lifted a hand, spreading his fingers to show the webbing.

The room fell quiet. Richard squeezed his hand shut and took a long drink of beer.

"Son," the second old man said, his voice gone somber. "You're in the right place."

"The right place for what?" Richard muttered.

"You know the stories, don't you?" A couple had come over to the bar, the same age as the two men, their eyes alight; the woman had spoken. "The stories about hands like yours?"

"It's a genetic mutation."

The woman, short white hair pressed close to her head, shook her head. "It's the *stories*."

"Can I get you another?" the barman said. He'd finished his drink.

"No, it's okay. I think I'd better get going—"

The first old man put a hand on his arm. Richard went still. He felt trapped, but he couldn't exactly shove the guy off. The man said, "Go south from here, past Clon and out to Glandore Harbor. That's where you start."

"But what's there—"

"It's very pretty," the woman said.

Nobody would say more than that.

He knew the stories. He got a degree in English with his ROTC scholarship, he'd taken classes in folklore and mythology. Maybe looking for that fairy-tale father.

It was a genetic mutation.

Irish back roads were harrowing in ways Richard thoroughly enjoyed. Barely enough room for cars to pass, no markings, curving right up against hedgerows or stone walls, or to the edge of cliffs, promising a rolling plunge down if he missed the turn. Never a dull moment.

The landscape was searing green, and the sea beyond was a roiling, foam-capped gray. He kept having to draw his gaze back to the road ahead.

He approached Glandore, and the directions he'd gotten from the man at the bar and the actual available roads he encountered didn't quite match up. But he could see the ocean the whole way down.

That gave him his compass.

The town itself was ridiculously picturesque, a perfect sleepy fishing village. Sailboats dotted the harbor. Richard kept driving to the far side of the harbor. Anticipation

welled up. He thought he was going to keep his eyes open
for a B&B, one of the cute little houses-turned inns that
seemed to cover the island. But he kept going. He wanted
to see if the roads ever stopped.

He wanted to get away from people, away from
buildings and boats and civilization. Go someplace where
he could be sure to be the only person for miles around.
Then maybe he'd be able to think clearly. But the
farmland, cultivated squares of fields and pastures, went
all the way to the coast. People had lived on this island for
a very long time.

Eventually, he parked the car on the verge and walked
out to where the roads and farmland couldn't get to—
broken cliffs where the waves had eaten away at the rock.
There wasn't any room for him to move, between the
water and the land. That was all right. He made his way
over stone ridges and crevices where he could, letting the
spray of breaking waves soak him. A big one would wipe
him right off the cliff side. He wouldn't even mind. He
could get washed away here and no one would ever know
what happened to him. No one knew where he was, no
one would look for him—

Instead of letting himself fall toward the comforting
waves, he inched farther along the rocks until he found a
spot where he could lean back, rest a moment, think.

There were seals in the water. They were smaller,
sleeker than the hulking sea lions living off the California
coast. These creatures were elusive, blending into the
color of the water. Domed heads would peek up from the
surface, revealing liquid dark eyes and twitching,
whiskered noses, then vanish. This—this was what the

world might have looked like a million years ago, before people.

A little farther on, the cliff curved sharply into an inlet. He'd continue on, explore what was there, then maybe climb up to the top to see where he'd ended up. Maybe find a village and start asking around to see if anyone knew of a guy who'd knocked up an American tourist some thirty-five years ago.

A hopeless quest for the fortune-seeking soldier.

In the inlet, cut not more than twenty feet back, he found a boat. It must have been set on a narrow ledge of rock during high tide and left dry when the tide went out. A standard aluminum rowboat, the kind you'd take fishing on a lake. A niggling in the back of his mind was sad that it wasn't one of the hide-bound *currachs* Ireland was famous for. Just as well. That would have been too perfect.

He looked around for the boat's owner, thinking maybe someone had come out here to fish, had gotten in trouble and needed help. Nothing—just him, the waves, and a couple of seals glaring at him from afar. He got to the boat and looked it over—it had been here awhile. A pool of brownish water filled the bottom; a film of green scum clung to the sides. Algae, along with salt and water stains, discolored the outside of the hull.

But a pair of oars still lay inside. The pool of water suggested the thing didn't have leaks and was still seaworthy. However it had gotten here, the boat now looked to him like a challenge.

With a lot of awkward bumping and banging, he managed to get the thing unwedged from the rocks and let it slide down to the water. He kept hold of the edge, scrambling over the crumbling outcrop to hang on to it while nearly falling over, and, getting smashed up by the waves in the process. It was a fight, but a satisfying fight, and in the end the boat was in the water, drifting away from the cliff, and he was inside.

No oarlocks for the oars, but that didn't matter. First thing was to get away from the cliff. The waves helped. Once he was out and drifting, he made a perfunctory effort to bail out some of the water. He was already soaking wet; sitting in the stale pool didn't seem to make much difference.

Felt good to be out on the water, though. Out on the water with no job to do, just the sun and sky and the gentle rocking. He stretched out on what passed for a bench, lay back with his arms under his head. Maybe he'd take a little nap, see where the waves took him.

That would be an adventure.

The boat thudded, and he started awake. That was a collision, something hitting the hull from underneath. Doug or one of the other guys playing a prank during training, he thought. Except he wasn't off Coronado; he was in the Celtic Sea off the coast of Ireland.

It happened again, something slamming into the hull hard enough to make the boat jump. Dolphins playing? Maybe some of those seals. Some whale species lived in these waters as well. He leaned over the edge to look.

Just gray water, chilled and opaque. He touched the surface, splashing his fingers in the sea.

Hands reached up and grabbed hold of him.

The hands came with powerful arms that pulled him over the side before he could take a breath. He splashed into the water.

There were more of them, many hands grabbing his shirt, clamping around his arms and legs, and brushing fingers through his hair. He could just make them out underwater, like looking through a fogged window. Women, muscular and graceful, with flowing hair fanning around them in the water like seaweed. They surrounded him, curling their long, scaled tails around him in weird embraces.

One of them, black hair rippling in streamers, wrapped her fists in the front of his T-shirt and pulled him close. He squinted to see her, but human eyes weren't meant to see underwater. All he could see were their shapes, and feel them diving and circling, rubbing against him as they passed.

He was dreaming. He'd fallen asleep and was dreaming. Or had fallen overboard and was drowning. That was okay, too.

When she kissed him, he didn't really care what happened next, but as his arms closed around her, the kiss turned into a bite, sharp pain on his lower lip that stopped being fun awfully quick. He made a noise; heard laughter, like the chittering of dolphins. When she pulled away, he tasted blood. Bubbles from his last breath streamed away from him.

She shoved him away and dived straight down. Her sisters followed her, ivory and silver bodies falling into the depths, propelled by muscular tails, stray bubbles trailing behind them. Then they were gone. Loose, limp, his body drifted up of its own accord. He broke the surface and took a reflexive breath.

He didn't appear to be dreaming. His lungs burned, and his eyes stung with salt water.

He had no clue how far out he was. Treading water at the surface, bobbing with the waves, he looked around to get his bearings. That far-off strip of land, dark cliff topped with an edge of green, was where he'd been climbing. The boat was gone. Like it had been set out as bait and he'd taken it.

In the other direction lay the low, rocky profile of an island, a spit of rock so low he couldn't see it from the mainland, of a slate gray that blended with the color of the ocean, the skin of seals. This was closer, so this was what he aimed for, just to get out of the water and catch his breath.

The rock wasn't comfortable. It wasn't even that dry—likely, high tide would submerge it. At least the sun felt warm. He peeled off his T-shirt and wrung it out. Pausing, he looked around.

The rock inlet was covered with seals. Writhing bodies humped across the rocks, slipping into the water then lurching back out, grunting, squeaking, barking. Dozens of seals, all looking across the rocks at him, blinking with large wet eyes, studying him. Out across the water, heads bobbed among the rippling waves, eyes and nostrils just above the surface. The mermaids were there too, black and brown-haired, mischievous smiles flashing.

He was sure if he tried to make a swim for it, the mermaids would force him back if the seals didn't. He was trapped. Captured. He smiled a little because training never covered a situation quite like this. Maybe he could wait them out. If he could hunt for a weapon, maybe he could make them back off.

Then the seals on the inlet parted. With raucous barking, the crowd of them moved away, some of them sliding into the water, some of them waddling aside and looking back, as if staying to watch.

Three men appeared, standing on the inlet's highest point. There wasn't a boat around. They might have been hiding behind the rock outcrops. They couldn't have swum here; they were dry—and naked, unselfconscious about their lean, tanned bodies. They looked like California surfers without the swim trunks. Muscular, rough hair, pompous smirks. Young guys with something to prove. And they held weapons—spears of pale wood tipped with what might have been broken shells, the jagged edges threatening, and bound with green fibers of seaweed.

Richard wondered exactly what he'd fallen into here.

"Hi," he said, making the word a challenge.

Two of the guys dropped their spears and ran at him. So that probably meant they didn't want to kill him, at least not right off. Small comfort.

Richard was ready. They would go for his arms, hoping to restrain him, so at the last minute he swerved, shoved the first aside, twisted to get out of the reach of the other. Threw his shoulder into a punch at the closest, rushed to tackle the second. They were strong, and fast, dodging and countering all his moves. He'd underestimated them.

But they'd underestimated him as well.

One stuck out his leg to trip Richard, a move he should

have seen coming. He fell on the rocks and felt a cut open on his cheek, blood running. From the ground, he grabbed a loose stone, big enough to fit in his hand, with sharp edges. He saw his target's eyes widen as Richard swung up. The guy ducked, which meant Richard caught his chin instead of the forehead he'd been aiming for. The spatter of blood was still satisfying, and the target had to pause a moment to clear his head. This guy's partner was smart enough to stay out of range, so Richard threw the rock at him instead. He didn't think he could lay the guy out, but it might buy him time.

He was reaching for another rock, his only available weapon, when the first guy grabbed his arm—his right arm; they'd paid attention to which arm was his strongest. Richard changed direction, tried to leverage himself free—didn't work. The second guy grabbed his left arm and pulled the other direction. They stretched him out between them, forced him to his knees. He made a token struggle, but he had nothing to fight against from this position. When he tried to swing a kick at one of the guy's naked, unprotected genitals, the man swerved out of the way. Their muscles were taut, straining—at least they had to work to keep hold of him.

The third guy hadn't joined in, not even when Richard did damage to his companions. He stood before them, leaning on his spear, regarding Richard with a clear sense of victory. He was the leader of the gang—and he had an agenda, a reason for all this. He was studying Richard. Sizing him up.

"Think he'll do, then?" one of the henchmen said in the thickest brogue Richard had heard since arriving in

Ireland. The man might have grown up not speaking English at all. "He can surely fight." He sounded impressed, but the compliment only annoyed Richard. If they'd wanted a fight they could have asked for one.

The leader, Richard assumed—the one who'd kept his hands clean—said in an equally thick brogue, "What are you, then? Not so big as all that, not so tough. And I'd heard you were a big, bad man." Richard grinned back in an attempt to piss the guy off, but the man ignored him. "There's some that think we can use you—a strong man with the sea in his veins, even if it's just a little of it. A warrior with skills that none of us have, that might be useful in our battles. There's some that think that blood calls to blood and if I called, you'd answer."

Richard's mind raced to keep up with the words and the tangle of meanings. "Who are you?" he demanded.

"Show me your hand," the leader said. Richard didn't move, because he couldn't.

Clamping his arm against his side to keep him still, the goon on the right forced Richard's hand up, squeezing his palm to straighten and spread his fingers.

"Webbed," the leader observed. "You know the stories?"

Richard struggled, mostly on principle, and the two guards gripped him even harder. His hands were growing numb. "Yeah."

"Tell me the story."

His mother met a handsome stranger under circumstances she never talked about. He'd always lived by the sea, and his mother would always look out at the waves as if she was searching for something. It was just the waves, he thought. How could anyone not look at the waves with a sense of longing? It was just the way things were.

"Tell me the story," the naked man repeated, stepping forward and lifting his spear to threaten.

Richard was sure the guy wouldn't actually hurt him. *Pretty* sure. "The story goes, the child of a selkie and a human will have webbed feet and hands."

"You believe that? You think it's real, those stories you've heard?" the man asked.

Just a mutation. Richard's jaw tightened. "Yes."

The man smiled like he'd won something. "Well then. Why are you here, selkie's child?"

"I don't know," Richard said, suddenly tired. "I don't even know." He'd wanted to find something, but he hadn't known that he'd been looking. He'd wanted an answer, an origin—but this wasn't quite it. "I think it's fate."

The leader nodded, and his two guards let go. Richard's arms dropped. He wiped blood from his cheek and stared up at this man with salt-crusted hair. "Do you know who you are, selkie's child?"

"I have a feeling you're going to tell me." Richard chuckled, letting go of good judgment, of trying to make sense of this. He ought to be thinking of escape—he was sure he could swim to shore. But he couldn't swim faster than seals or mermaids.

"You're the son of the seal king. And so am I."

The statement was no more outlandish than the fact of him sitting on these rocks, talking to these men in the first place, all of them slipped out of time and reality. He studied the man standing before him, trying to find any part of himself: eyes, nose, build, or manner. He couldn't see it.

"How do you know?"

"The sea hears. The sea tells stories. You know it. You've listened."

He'd been watching the sea the whole drive down the coast. He parked because it seemed like a good spot. He'd been looking for something, or following something. He'd been trying to drown.

He spread his hands, felt the membrane of the webbing stretch. A crowd of seals had gathered, staying a respectful distance off, but they watched, looking back and forth between them with an eerie awareness.

The man—who somehow seemed at home on the rocky outcrops, even as he seemed terribly out of place, bare-skinned and primal in a modern world—moved to a spot and reached into a hidden depression. With his free hand he drew out an object, a folded weight of something, thick and wide, almost too large for him to lift. He held it up like a prize. It was gray, sunlight reflected off a rubbery sheen.

Sealskin.

Richard almost reached out to touch it, but stopped himself. His hand was shaking again.

"My father—our father—sent me to find you," the leader said. "I don't like it at all—there should only be one Seal Prince. But I see why he did. I see the wisdom of it. We need warriors—"

"Why?" Richard said, laughing outright. "What kind of wars can you possibly have to fight, when all you have are spears and seaweed—"

The Seal Prince's two guards tensed, and the damp seals around them grumbled and shifted.

The Prince merely smiled. "There are other tribes of our kind. They raid our fishing grounds and we raid theirs. We defend our territory. But you—you don't understand what it is to have a home, do you, selkie's child? Would you like to learn? I can give you this." The sealskin was a limp, still version of the creatures gathered around him.

Richard had a flash of a vision, a lifetime encompassed in a beautiful moment, sunlight streaming through green-gray waters, nudged by a current as he dived along rocks, his body curving and twisting with the shape of the surf, clothed in the smoothness of the skin he'd been given, the second skin he'd longed for all his life without knowing—

But it would be a borrowed skin, an act of charity. He wasn't born to the water, not like these men were. He was born at the edges, in the surf, half of him in each world. He could swim like a fish and hold his breath for ten minutes. He could fight and kill—and was that all they needed him for? What then, when the war was over?

"He left us. My mother and I—*he left us*. Why should I think that he, that any of you, care about me now?"

"He's been listening for you all this time, hasn't he? We know about the boy you shot, the hostages you didn't save. The feeling of fear and of failure, and how you haven't had a good day since."

He didn't need to be told. Being told made him angry, and it put him back there. That chaotic moment when your thinking brain didn't know what the hell was going on but your training knew exactly what to do, and you already had the target in your sights. Enemy shots fired, and when your captain yelled, "Take it, take it!" you were already breathing out and squeezing the trigger. The Somali boy's head whipped back. A crack shot on rough seas and a rush of triumph. This was the kind of shot they gave medals for. He didn't really see the kid when he shot him. He saw the gun, he saw the enemy, he'd felt very rational about the whole thing. When it was all over, the water he'd swum in looked just like this. When they arrived at the skiff and examined the aftermath, the rush died. The pirates were dead. So were the three hostages. The pirates had been trapped, so they lashed out, took a stand the only way they could, and if Richard had made the shot two seconds earlier, the aid workers he'd been trying to save would have survived. Nobody's fault, no reprimands needed. Just the bad odds of a bad situation. Two sides with guns face off, people get killed. But he should have taken that shot two seconds earlier. And this shouldn't be a world where fifteen-year-old kids carried AK-47s and killed hostages for a living. That moment your training takes over becomes the moment you play in your memory over and over again, wondering what happened and if you could have done it differently.

"The sea is in our blood, and our blood is your blood. We felt the shock, even so far away," the Seal Prince said. "We felt you return home, felt you swimming straight out from shore as far as you could, thinking you'd swim so far out you couldn't get back and so not have to make a decision to keep going at all. You thought maybe one of the white sharks would take you, but they know better than to hunt the son of the Seal King. And now here you are 'cause you've nowhere left to go.

"Take it, Richard. Come with us." He knelt, touched the skin, nudged it forward.

Well, he'd told Doug he might try going freelance.

The water was the only place he felt safe. He was born for the water, webbed hands that worked best when he was swimming. But he wouldn't be a true seal any more than he was a true human.

A mutant in both worlds.

At least when his teammates called him Fishhead, they did it with love. What would they call him here?

Richard chuckled. "I know this story, too. The soldier home from war, who gets advice not to drink what the dancing princesses offer him. He doesn't drink, so he stays awake, and he sees where they really go at night."

The Seal Prince snorted. "Do I look like a princess to you, then? Does this look like poison?"

"No. Are you really my brother?"

"I could say yes or no, and you wouldn't believe me either way."

He was right. Richard smirked. "I have a place waiting for me back home." He wasn't born for land or sea. He wanted to keep a foot in each place. That, he could do. He wanted to go home.

The Seal Prince studied him, and Richard couldn't read his expression, if he was surprised or disappointed or full of contempt. He had a feeling he could have known this man his whole life and he still wouldn't be able to read him, to understand him.

"Don't you even want to meet your father?" the Seal Prince asked.

"If he'd wanted to meet me, he would have come himself," Richard said. His half-brother didn't deny this.

"Go then, selkie's child," the prince said, gathering up the borrowed sealskin. "Go back to your world. We'll be watching you."

Richard said, "Tell the Seal King—tell him that my mother died last year. She never stopped looking at the waves."

The Prince's smile fell. The two guards, henchmen, whatever they were—they looked to their leader. None of them had expected him to say what he'd said. His news had shocked them. They might have known many secrets, but they hadn't known this.

"I'm sorry for your loss," the Seal Prince said.

"Thanks."

The three men, tanned bodies shining, disappeared behind the same outcrop of rocks they'd emerged from. As a mass, a rippling mob of shining mottled skin, the barking seals lifted themselves, scooted on blubber and flippers and heaved into the waves, splashing a wall of water and mist behind them.

And suddenly the world was quiet. The barking and belching ceased, leaving only waves lapping against the rocks. Richard looked back to the mainland. The audience of seals and mermaids was all gone. The stretch of waves between here and where he'd started was unbroken. He sat there, nothing more than a man who'd lost his boat in an ordinary world. He turned his face to the sun and grinned.

He had a long swim ahead of him.

★ ★ ★

ABOUT THE AUTHOR

Carrie Vaughn is the bestselling author of the Kitty Norville series, the most recent of which is the twelfth installment, *Kitty in the Underworld*. Her superhero novel *Dreams of the Golden Age* was released in January, 2014. She has also written young adult novels, *Voices of Dragons* and *Steel*, and the fantasy novels, *Discord's Apple* and *After the Golden Age*. Her short fiction has appeared in many magazines and anthologies, from *Lightspeed* to Tor.com and George R.R. Martin's *Wild Cards* series. She lives in Colorado with a fluffy attack dog. Learn more at carrievaughn.com.

PATHFINDER

★ ★ ★

T. C. McCarthy

Hamhung, Korea
2 January 1951

Hae Jung frowns at the smell but shakes her head because
it isn't an odor as much as it's a sensation—that something
irritates the inside of her nose. The way hot peppers burn.
Her inner alarms ring, and before she can show any sign
of fear a litany scrolls through her mind, the words
keeping her nerves from firing. Once she regains control
Hae Jung looks up to turn her head from side to side. It's
gone; the smell disappears as if it were never there and
she makes a note to remember everything, to tell Dae
Nam that something may have followed the last batch of
wounded into the caverns.

Lanterns hang from the rock ceiling. They cast a warm
light on the injured soldiers to distract her with an illusion
of peace, and Hae Jung wonders why it's quiet before she

remembers what happens at night, the time when injured sleep instead of scream and her chest feels lighter; this is when many of the dying let go. *Maybe the stars draw them out*, she thinks.

The last time Hae Jung went outside her wet hair froze and she had trouble breathing in the wind, but the American Marines hadn't yet lit Hamhung on fire and more stars than she could imagine emerged to make the sky glow. They had spoken to Hae Jung. She smiles at the memory and imagines that stars are candles of her ancestors and wonders if her mother waits for the time when Hae Jung herself will make the trip across. The thought makes her happy enough that she almost misses it when the wounded man next to her sighs with rattling lungs.

It's his time; Hae Jung imagines she can see his spirit and rests a hand on his chest before leaning over to whisper. "Your ancestors have been told. They will welcome you, so do not be afraid, because your grandmother asked me to show you the way."

Hae Jung wants to tell him everything but she can't because this is an important moment, a procedure that requires concentration so she can find the path, a road home that makes all fear melt into nothingness. She meditates. Within a second her hands begin to glow and then the man smiles because he sees something; it is invisible to her, but his joy is infectious and Hae Jung grins without realizing. This means his ancestors are laughing. She feels his existence in the hospital start to fade, which means it's the last stage, and she prepares to light the way by going deeper into her trance.

Hae Jung is about to do it when the smell returns. Now

it's clear, a scent of burning cinnamon that makes her eyes water at the same time she feels her heart race because she had hoped that whatever it was had moved on and it's her first time in the presence of *this*, the kind of thing she's been warned of but hasn't yet experienced. She waves her hands over the soldier; Hae Jung tries to fan something away but now she's crying and confused because the gesture is useless and what comes for the man can't be stopped with a wave. The path slips, forcing the man's eyes open. Then he tries to scream but his breath is already gone and so he looks at her with terror and she nods while wiping tears from her cheeks.

"I'm sorry," she says. "I didn't know. I didn't know this would happen and it wasn't supposed to; I will tell your ancestors so they can pray for a way to bring you out of darkness."

A second later it's over. The man stares at the ceiling and Hae Jung has to turn away because she feels the anger and sorrow of his dead mother, a rage and a blame that somehow it's her fault—that his soul is lost because Hae Jung is weak.

Someone puts a hand on Hae Jung's shoulder and she jumps. One of the other nurses asks, *Who are you talking to?* and she shakes her head but then smiles because it's only Mi Yae and seeing her makes the cavern feel safe again.

"To him." Hae Jung points at the dead soldier. "To his ancestors, to ask for forgiveness."

Mi Yae shakes her head. "If you are religious, hide it. You know when this is over, they will return to the ways from before, and even in this place there are informers, Hae Jung. You are my best friend and we are good little soldiers. Remember?"

Hae Jung says *I know* at the same time the bombs fall. She feels the rock vibrate under her feet and detonations shake the wooden cots; dust rains from the walls and ceiling while the things land far overhead, against the mountainside, with deep booms. The lanterns still cast a dim yellow light but some of them wink out because of falling pebbles that smash their glass and Mi Yae grabs her friend's hand, pulling Hae Jung through the maze of cots where some of the Chinese soldiers are now awake, reaching to touch their hands. One asks, *Are we safe here?* But the girls are already gone by the time Hae Jung understands the man's words.

Mi Yae guides them in a winding path. She moves so fast that it takes some time before Hae Jung realizes they have a candle, its light barely enough to keep her from stumbling on rocks, but soon it gets slippery because water trickles down the walls, so *any* light helps. Finally, they arrive at their bomb post: a tiny alcove with two wooden stools and two buckets of sand.

Mi Yae flinches at the distant blasts. "Even this deep you feel them."

"American bombs must be very large. My brother is lucky because he was posted with the Chinese in Dandong; the Americans fear war with China and won't bomb across the border."

"When this is over, I will marry your brother."

Hae Jung sees Mi Yae's grin and from her voice knows that she tells the truth.

"He asked?"

Mi Yae nods. "When you and I were up north. He stopped by our camp for a day and told me not to say anything because there was no time to see you and he wanted to give the news himself. I'm sorry for keeping it secret, Hae Jung."

"Don't be!" She hugs her friend and feels tears roll off her cheeks while she laughs. "I am so happy. Remember we used to pretend we were sisters when we were little? We were so good at it that the old men at the police station thought we really were."

Mi Yae nods again and smiles. "I know; I was thinking the same thing. You will help me plan the whole thing— my entire wedding!"

Hae Jung lets go, unable to stop smiling. Even with only the candle for light she sees that Mi Yae is beautiful and knows why her brother chose her for a wife, recalling how the two would stare at each other all those years and how he never had the courage to speak in Mi Yae's presence. She is a year older than her brother. Even now that they are *all* older, it still would have taken him courage to ask Mi Yae to marry, and Hae Jung wishes that he were there because now there are so many questions and so much to plan and nobody knows how long they will be stuck underground—or how long the war will last.

"Hae Jung," Mi Yae asks, "why do you spend all your time with the hopeless?"

"What are you talking about? Who is hopeless?"

"The wounded Chinese. You always tend to the ones who have no chance, the ones who are sure to die."

Hae Jung says nothing. She had forgotten about the

dead and the thing that now haunts the tunnels, the thing that until now only existed in stories, and Mi Yae's question erases the joy that a second ago had felt so promising. There are no words to explain it. Even if there were, her friend wouldn't believe any of them because this is the People's Hospital 157 and there are no Pathfinders because people like Hae Jung don't exist—not officially.

"Because they need me the most," Hae Jung says, which is at least part of the truth. "The dying are alone, Mi Yae, and far from their homes in China, so they deserve attention because they all seem so lost."

Mi Yae sighs, and Hae Jung hears that she's crying. "I am tired. They stand no chance even if we *could* treat their wounds."

Hae Jung doesn't know what to say and rests her back against the wall, not caring about the dampness because exhaustion now begins to wash her brain of memories, its temptation of sleep sending feelers into the deepest parts of her mind, scrubbing it of details; she almost forgets the thing's smell. But just as her eyes shut, a blast sends sharp pebbles to fall on her leg, forcing Hae Jung awake so that her thoughts land in a place where the dying soldier waits, his eyes staring at her as if asking *How can you just sit there?*

Hae Jung grabs Mi Yae's arm. "Have you seen Dae Nam?"

"I don't know. Maybe he is with the equipment section. I heard someone say that 'the crazy monk' is working on boots and refurbishment, and only Dae Nam is called that. Why do you want *him* all of a sudden?" When Hae Jung stands and begins running, Mi Yae shouts after her, "Where are you going? *This is an air-raid, Hae Jung, stay at your post!*"

But Hae Jung can't grasp the words. All she hears are her own boots slapping on the rock and the sounds they make when she splashes through puddles, and even in the pitch black she doesn't slow because she has spent almost a year in the tunnels and knows the way. Plus she needs to speak with Dae Nam as soon as possible; *he* will know what to do.

"You are a Pathfinder and haven't met the enemy before?" Dae Nam asks, and when Hae Jung shakes her head he sighs. "From your description, I would say this one is different from those in the stories, Hae Jung, so abandon that idea. Let me fix more shoes; we need information."

Hae Jung watches. On one side of the small rock chamber is a pile of shoes and boots, some of them still blood-soaked from the injuries of their former owners. Dae Nam picks out a canvas sneaker. To her it looks like a ritual, where he first soaks the shoe in dark water for a few seconds, letting it penetrate the fabric before he submerges it to the bottom of a deep pan, pressing the sneaker down and then bringing it up, repeating it until he's satisfied that its canvas is clean. Then he inspects it under a lantern. Dae Nam runs his finger along the seam joining the sole to the fabric, and where it begins to separate he takes a thick brush and pushes glue into the gaps, pressing the sole downward for a few moments so it re-seals. He then tosses the sneaker into another pile.

"So many shoes," Hae Jung whispers. "And none of them suited for snow and ice."

"But each one has history, and we need it. And it is worse where you work, where you see the ending of the story, the failures of men. I am lucky to have been assigned here. The research suits me and we need the intelligence."

Hae Jung shakes her head and slides to the floor near his side, where she stares at a wall but sees nothing. "I don't mind the hospital, Dae Nam. When I succeed in finding the way, I get to see them rejoin their families, and often the dead are met by friends forgotten—not to mention the fact their pain is gone." Hae Jung wipes a tear from her cheek, but she is smiling, and what she says is true. "Still, it does hurt sometimes. . . . What have *you* learned since our assignment to Hospital 157?"

"You mean besides the fact that your friend calls me the crazy monk?"

Dae Nam smiles, but Hae Jung feels bad. His head is shaved and the man seems older than she remembers, but then Hae Jung thinks it might be the fact that his lantern is dim and the soapy water prunes his hands. He wears a stiff rubberized-canvas apron that resembles the robe of a monk, and she knows they are lucky to have him.

"I am sorry, Teacher."

"Do not be sorry; I like the name." Dae Nam picks up a boot and frowns. "Let me see what this one has to tell me—there is something here, Hae Jung; this was worn by one of *our* warriors."

Now his hands glow. Hae Jung watches in fascination as he holds the boot over his water, and the glow expands around it at the same time Dae Nam's eyes roll back to make them white and inhuman. Hae Jung looks away. This is her first time seeing him work, and even though she knows his specialty it disturbs her to watch his face contort. If the boot was worn by one of their kind—maybe a boy who trained with Hae Jung and who Eastern Command sent to fight both men and spirits, or maybe a master magician who had achieved the rank of full warrior but whose luck eventually ran out—the fact that he's dead makes her sad. She is in the war within the war; Hae Jung is glad she is a nurse, glad she doesn't have to share what Dae Nam now experiences: the last images of the man who wore those boots, and his last feelings at the moment of death. Dae Nam is crying when he drops the boot into the pan.

"This is too much," he whispers. "Too much for us, and they think they can control it. The Americans have gone mad."

Hae Jung stands. "Control what?"

"That thing in your hospital ward; they have done something, brought a thing here."

"What is it?"

Dae Nam grabs her shoulders and forces Hae Jung to lean over the pan where she sees the boot more closely, and the burn marks are clear and Hae Jung notices that it has been clawed by something that melted the rubber sole to form a twisted handprint. She pushes away.

"What is this?"

"It isn't evil," he says, "not in the sense that this is a thing driven by hate; it is nothingness. A being from the empty place, which feeds on the material and the spirit, and it has nothing against any of us because the thing has no understanding of humanity at all and would just as easily go after the Americans and British; it wounded the warrior who wore this boot and then tracked his soul here. Had you succeeded and finished showing your dying man a way to his ancestors, this thing would have detected the signatures and *you* would have been killed and *your* soul dissolved into nothing, too. It hasn't seen us yet, Hae Jung. But it's only a matter of time before it does."

Hae Jung's heart races. She feels like crying and wants to tell him that she's only eighteen and that this is a terror beyond her, but then she realizes that there isn't any choice because the war is all around and there is no leaving it. Whether she's ready for it or not, it doesn't matter; there's no safe place anywhere.

"What will we do, Teacher?"

Dae Nam grabs the lantern and then her hand, and he guides her from the chamber, down a winding passage where the darkness seems to absorb almost all illumination and she has a vague sense of passing other soldiers and doctors. They nod to the monk. Most get out of his way and bow their heads, even officers, and Hae Jung wonders if she really knows who the man is, how great someone has to be to deserve this level of respect. Finally they arrive at another chamber entrance, where Dae Nam lifts a curtain; he ushers her in and drops it behind them.

"Do not speak loudly," he whispers.

"I am scared."

Dae Nam hugs her, and she sobs into his chest. "There, there," he says. "It will be all fine. Somewhere there is a plan, and you should know more than anyone that your ancestors watch over everything, protecting you as best they can."

"What will you do?" she asks.

"I will do nothing. You will help me pack my things because it's time for me to report to the Eastern Command in Shenyang and brief them on what we learned. They have to know about this threat as soon as possible—to make sure Beijing begins conjuring a counter-demon."

Hae Jung pulls away and her hands tremble so she pushes them into her pockets. "You said that if I try to guide the dying, it will destroy me."

"It will *devour* you; there is a difference. Hopefully I will return with information that will help us deal with this, Hae Jung, but there's something you should know."

The bombs have stopped. Hae Jung isn't sure if they just ceased this second or if she's been so scared that the air raid ended long ago and she never noticed, but now that Dae Nam is silent the quiet soaks into everything.

He grabs a rucksack and tosses it onto a cot. "All of us have had to deal with something like this; it's part of the process, because in a way learning never stops. There is always something new and dangerous, something that threatens the world in a horrifyingly different way, and for some reason it came here and into your hospital ward."

"What are you saying?"

"This task may already be assigned to you, Hae Jung; fate sent it to *your* patient. Meditate. Recall everything you learned in training and then determine your actions based on what we know of the past. And don't be stupid, because if you are meant to face this one alone it means you already have the way to destroy it."

Hae Jung almost faints at the words. She backs toward the curtain and Dae Nam watches without speaking, filling his bag with spare uniforms and shirts. She has to get back to the ward. The implication of his words is too much and Hae Jung ignores it in favor of a false idea that she shouldn't have left Mi Yae alone; thinking of something else, anything else, helps her avoid the crushing mental weight. She *needs* Mi Yae.

"You expect the impossible," Hae Jung says.

"I'm not the one who's asking for this, child, but those who watch over us *are,* and they think you can handle it or this wouldn't have happened; the empty thing would have tracked one of us to another hospital. *Fate* has involved you."

Hae Jung shakes her head and ducks through the curtain, breaking into a sprint as soon as she makes it into the corridor. Someone asks, *What's wrong, Hae Jung, why are you crying,* but she ignores the man and pushes past, hoping that Mi Yae is safe.

A new batch of wounded streams in just as Hae Jung arrives; she can't find Mi Yae. She stares at the river of soldiers in brown uniforms that flows into the ward as doctors shout for orderlies to push existing cases into as tight a space as possible to make room for the new ones, some of which scream for help as their comrades drag them out of the cold. Hae Jung can't move. A nurse in charge grabs her and pulls her toward an operating table and then forces a dirty gown on her front, tying it off in the back before she realizes that any of it happened, and then a doctor shouts that she should apply pressure to a leg wound and *Wake up, Hae Jung, we need you to be on top of all this*, but she can't; the air itself smells like burning cinnamon. Hae Jung holds the leg, from which blood spurts so she knows that this one might not make it because the wound is to an artery, but she squeezes anyway and while the surgeon prepares his tools Hae Jung looks around—searching for any sign of *it*, anything visible on which she can focus.

At first there is nothing. A metallic smell of blood overpowers the cinnamon and Hae Jung looks down to see the surgeon at work and she now holds a handful of gauze near the wound, trying to soak up blood. There is so much. It has stopped spraying, but now it flows over her hands, making them hot, and Hae Jung feels the room start to spin until it's there again and she senses the thing as if an electrical charge fills the air to make it sparkle and crackle around her.

"Do you see that?"

"Hold the gauze closer," the doctor says. "See what?"

Hae Jung steps away. "The air; the colors."

"Get back to the patient!"

Then the soldier on the table opens his eyes and mutters something to the doctor, who adjusts his lantern to get more light, his hands so fast they almost blur. She wants to tell him not to bother. The look on the dying soldier's face is one they should *all* recognize, and although she can't see the demon, she knows it's wrapping itself around him, waiting for the moment of death. A second later Hae Jung thinks she hears the thing speak with the voice of a little boy: *"So many of them."*

"I am not a coward," Hae Jung whispers. But she's shaking and deep down knows that she won't act because maybe as long as she hides her power the thing can't reach her soul and Hae Jung pretends to be a normal nurse, looking on with concern.

The doctor throws his clamps to the table and drops a cloth over the dead soldier's face before motioning to the orderly. "Next one."

"Have you seen Mi Yae?" Hae Jung asks.

"No, not since yesterday."

"Where are all these wounded coming from?"

The doctor shakes his head and dunks his arms into a bucket of alcohol next to the table. It is pink with blood. He shakes his hands off and then does it again while the orderlies collect the corpse.

"A Turkish unit moved into this sector yesterday, taking the place of the American Marines. They are fierce. Our Chinese boys are having a tough time keeping up with them, and the Turks snuck into their trenches early this morning to massacre almost an entire battalion."

Hae Jung shivers. The uniforms bring another wounded soldier to the table, heaving him up and then dumping him in place where she sees the man's charred chest, a nightmare of burned uniform and cloth that merge to form something surreal. The surgeon doesn't pause. *Get over here!* he shouts at Hae Jung but she shakes her head and backs away, nearly knocking over a nurse at the table next to them; the wounded have surrounded her. This is a feeding ground and every death will make the thing bigger, stronger, and soon none of them will be safe because she suspects that it might recognize the souls of the living if allowed to grow.

"I have to find Mi Yae," she says.

The surgeon yells at her again but Hae Jung is deaf from terror and she dives into the wall of brown uniforms around her, imagining that Mi Yae is just on the other side of it.

When she reaches the main tunnel exit, Hae Jung thinks the bombers have returned but then realizes that these blasts come from artillery—American naval shells that hit Chinese positions a few kilometers south of Hamhung. The shells explode, and cover the Hungnam factory in smoke. Their factory is *already* gone. Hae Jung doesn't understand why the Americans have to hit it so many times, over and over again, and she marvels at the amount of equipment they have, wondering if it explains their willingness to summon a spirit so powerful and beyond control; they seem to worship destruction.

"Has anyone seen Mi Yae?" she asks.

The walking Chinese wounded crowd against each other on the cold rock, sitting with knees pulled up to their chests and with blank eyes that stare as if they've all been shocked into a kind of waking coma. She asks again, this time in Chinese. A few of them look at her and shake their heads but most seem gone and one starts screaming before he heads up the slanting tunnel, toward the sunlight and artillery shells, which are now close enough that they vibrate the rock. The man disappears through the opening and Hae Jung turns back toward the ward—not wanting to see if he returns.

She picks her way through the sitting soldiers. It reminds Hae Jung of moving through a swamp, maybe the one outside her school in Songbo where the mud and grass grab at her bare feet and lock themselves around her ankles; Mi Yae and her other friends laugh on either side, all of them locked in a filthy race to see who can cross the fastest. But there isn't any laughter here and in the early morning the men don't resemble swamp grass at all. And there's a new smell. At first she thinks it's the demon because it makes her hold her nose, but then Hae Jung realizes that the tunnel is warm enough that the soldiers' feet and hands thaw to send the odor of gangrene everywhere; they are warming up, and the warmth will rot them all to death.

She screams Mi Yae's name now. Part of her wants the words to hurt the silent Chinese men and she would be happy if they clamped their hands over their ears or yelled for her to shut up, but they do nothing, and none of them seem to notice her, even when she steps on their dead feet in an effort to get through—to get away from the odor and sadness.

Before she knows it she's returned to the main ward and operating chamber. Something is wrong though because the room is silent and the doctors and nurses have backed everyone up as far as they can, opening an empty circle in their midst.

"Hae Jung!" Mi Yae shouts.

Hae Jung is about to run forward when someone grabs her arm and holds her back. She can't grasp what's happening. A haze of smoke fills the area and mixed with the scent of cinnamon is the smell of cordite and there are several people on the ground, all of them dressed in dirty medical gowns, all of them dead. Hae Jung knows that something is wrong with her friend but the horror of it prevents her from believing that Mi Yae is almost certainly gone. She laughs; it's absurd that a human being can survive like this, legless and on the ground crying, reaching out for help.

Hae Jung pulls against a doctor's grip, but he refuses to let go. "The rocks overhead," he says, pointing. "A patient came in with unexploded ordinance lodged in his gut; it detonated when they began operating. Now the rocks are coming loose and your friend is beyond our help. We have to evacuate."

"Let me go," says Hae Jung. The artillery comes closer and a boulder falls, smashing into the floor near them and sending shards against Hae Jung's legs. Despite the danger, she pulls again. "Let go!"

"Suit yourself."

The doctor releases her and follows the rest of the crowd, helping to wheel patients out of the large chamber and deeper into the tunnel complex, deeper into the mountain. He calls out to Hae Jung, telling her, *You're an idiot; wait for the engineers to come and then you can collect the body*, but instead Hae Jung kneels beside her friend and hugs her; the girl's skin feels wet and cold.

"I have you," says Hae Jung. "I am here."

"I am very thirsty."

She nods. "You lost your legs above the knees and there is much blood."

Hae Jung ties tourniquets and then begins arranging her friend so she can carry her and Mi Yae laughs. "What are you doing?"

"There is a smell of burned cinnamon here," says Hae Jung. "Can't you tell? I want to get away from it, and we need to move quickly."

Mi Yae shakes her head and looks down. "I can't smell anything. My legs are gone; do you think your brother will still marry me?"

Hae Jung grunts as she lifts Mi Yae and there is a wash of warmth as blood covers both arms so that Hae Jung begins crying. "He will marry you; you are still the prettiest girl in Hamhung."

"Don't be sad, Hae Jung. I smell the cinnamon now so things must be getting better; my nose is working again."

Hae Jung knows that it is close. The air turns heavy and once more begins to spark so that Mi Yae mumbles . . . *The colors are so pretty, Hae Jung, I wish you could see this* . . . and Hae Jung wants to scream at the nothingness to go away but it knows too much and is moving in. The thing must sense her, she figures; as she stumbles through the tunnels, barely able to carry Mi Yae, she hears its footsteps and then starts to pray—opening the way for her friend to pass.

"*I see you,*" it says.

Mi Yae rests her head on Hae Jung's shoulder. "There is a little boy following us and I think it is my brother but how can this be? He died when we were very young. He wants us to stop and talk."

"It is not a boy or your brother," Hae Jung says. The tunnel brightens and she can see the rocks in front of her, and the glow from her hands resembles the one she saw when Dae Nam worked on the boots, a soft blue that helps light the way. Smells of rot and cinnamon push up the tunnel from behind. Hae Jung can sense Mi Yae's willingness to make the journey and there is a fuzzy sense of warmth that makes her think it will be fine, a familiar feeling because it means the path is opening and that Mi Yae's ancestors are waiting—happy to welcome her home. But juxtaposed against it is horror. Hae Jung's back feels cold and now the spirit is close enough that she hears its wheezing breath.

"There is nothing," it whispers.

The tunnel exits aren't far. Hae Jung ducks into a side passage, one empty of wounded and staff, but it takes her closer to the city, and the artillery blasts are so near that they vibrate her jaw.

"I'm tired," Mi Yae says.

"You have lost blood."

"Am I dying?"

Hae Jung nods and a tear falls from her cheek. "Yes."

The pathway opens with a jolt. It is strong, and the will of Mi Yae's ancestors almost overpowers her own subconscious, threatening to make Hae Jung blind with their desire to see through her eyes and look at their daughter, their granddaughter and their sister, and they can feel Mi Yae through Hae Jung's hands and they want more, but they worry because they sense the presence of something horrible.

Hae Jung wills them back.

"Slow down," the spirit says, but it's laughing and Hae Jung glances over her shoulder to see the little boy break into a sprint, his speed impossible.

She struggles to remember what Dae Nam taught her—that some spirits can't resist the offered soul of a Pathfinder. But to offer it is forbidden. In this case she counts on the thing's hunger and hears the little boy sing as it closes the distance, so Hae Jung feels a sudden sense of relief when the tunnel fills with sunlight and she decides that for Mi Yae it is fine to break the rules, that for Mi Yae she will be forgiven if her plan fails.

"Is it time?" Mi Yae asks.

Hae Jung nods, trying to keep from sobbing. "Yes."

"My mother says you are very special, and that you have a secret but that it's a good one and it's one that you use to help the dying, but that you are risking a lot for me. She says to say *Thank you.*"

"Tell her that you are my sister."

A moment later, Hae Jung breaks into the morning light. She is low on the mountainside, but high enough that Hamhung spreads out below her in a panorama of ruin, within which American bombs and artillery have ripped buildings off their foundations. Naval shells scream in. The projectiles are slow enough that Hae Jung watches in fascination as they arc into the ruined factory and then detonate in silence, sending geysers of black and gray smoke upward before the sound hits a second later. She shivers. But the sun feels warm on her face and there is nothing to worry about because she knows what will happen next and can tell from the thing's laughter that it has forgotten the old dangers and can only focus on her soul.

It has forgotten about sunlight.

"Tell them to say hello to my grandmother," Hae Jung says, but it's too late; Mi Yae hears nothing. The pathway closes and Hae Jung feels the warmth of her friend's passage and almost laughs at the sense of happiness that her ancestors managed to radiate from the other side. She turns to the tunnel entrance then and waits.

The little boy springs from the exit and at first grins to show blackened teeth, but then a scowl forms on his face and Hae Jung looks away, not wanting to see any more. A cloud of dust hits her. Hae Jung feels like throwing up at the smell, and she coughs as it fills her lungs and nostrils, but when she opens her eyes the last remnants of the spirit float off the mountainside, clouds of ash that formed under sunlight and soon disappear into nothingness.

She puts the remains of Mi Yae down on the pathway by the tunnel exit and says one more prayer before sighing and moving into the mountain. Part of her thinks it's too soon to return. The night and morning sucked most of her strength and with Dae Nam gone all of the special missions will fall to her, but then she wraps both arms around herself, hurrying away from the artillery and the winter with a smile, and remembers something else Dae Nam once told her.

"Without war, we wouldn't be needed."

"Someday I will see you again, Mi Yae," she whispers. Then Hae Jung picks up the pace because somewhere, deep in the mountain, there are dying soldiers.

* * *

ABOUT THE AUTHOR

T.C. McCarthy is an award-winning and critically-acclaimed Southern author whose short fiction has appeared in *Per Contra: The International Journal of the Arts, Literature and Ideas*, *Story Quarterly*, and *Nature*. His debut novel, *Germline*, and its sequel, *Exogene,* are available worldwide, and the final book of the trilogy, *Chimera*, was released in August 2012. In addition to being an author, T.C. is a PhD scientist, a Fulbright Fellow, a Howard Hughes Biomedical Research Scholar, and a winner of the prestigious University of Virginia's Award for Undergraduate Research.

Bone Eaters
The Black Company On the Long Run
★ ★ ★
Glen Cook

Whittle and Fall Woo led the trigger gang: four unreliable brothers with a decrepit, covered goat cart, two broke-down mules, a moth-eaten burro dragging an open cart, plus some refugee slatterns and associated brats.

Out of sight behind, the Company stretched for miles along a track locals called a road, crossing stony hills whiskered with brush and scraggly young pines. Wildfire had passed through, years back. Charred adult tree corpses still tilted drunkenly.

I rode with the hidden guard posse supporting the scouts.

The brigands were new to the trade. Only one was mounted, aboard a nag that might not last another month. The rest were kids armed with rusty knives and farm tools.

The barefoot boy on horseback gobbled a stanza of "Stand and deliver!" in the local dialect. Another waved a sharp-ended stick and pranced. The rest approved with less enthusiasm.

A brown something materialized beside the rider's ear. He squealed. The thing looked like a monkey with too many legs, each tipped with a claw like a pruning knife. It had too many yellow eyes, too.

Hiding in the goat cart was that nasty toad of a wizard, Goblin, who loved crafting revolting illusions.

Whittle disarmed six youngsters, injuring two. The boy on the horse galloped off, squalling.

Ranging ahead, I caught up first—and saw nothing to elevate my esteem for humanity.

Whittle had left the captives with Rusty and Robin. Rusty was a waste of meat, a coward, a bully, a shirker, and a scrounge. Only Robin liked him. Everybody thought somebody ought to put Rusty down.

Whittle left Rusty in charge because he wanted to be rid of dead weight. He lacked the imagination to see a potential problem in leaving Rusty self-supervised.

Rusty had a bandit bent over a boulder. Both had their trousers down. Rusty was having no joy. Little Rusty was not interested. Robin sprawled nearby, aching in body and soul, tangled up with a couple of bound, gagged, and extremely agitated male captives. He had tried to interfere. He met my eye, gasped, "Croaker! Please! Help her."

I spurred my mount.

Rusty stayed lucky. A low branch ambushed me as my valiant steed lunged forward. Over her tail I went.

Pants held up left-handed, Rusty gave me a case of boot rash while letting the world know that he had had it with my holier-than-thou, candy-ass whining. "Croaker, grow a set! Act like a godsdamned real soldier."

Hoofbeats approached.

Rusty went white behind his freckles.

His victim moaned and tried to crawl away.

Darling and the sorcerer Silent dismounted. Silent fixed Rusty with a venomous glare. Rusty saved the excuses. He always had some but knew they would be wasted today. Darling always knew the smell of bullshit. Rusty would fool himself before he fooled her.

Darling's sad disdain was palpable. Rusty wilted. Darling was no longer younger, was never pretty and never available, was ice hard outside but suffered from a soft heart. We all love her. And her good regard is precious even to the worst of us.

Was Rusty smart enough to realize how lucky he was, having Darling show up before anyone else? Even in a situation so similar to her own first brush with the Company, back in another age? Death had stalked him for months already. Only Hell's luck and Darling's grace had kept him on the weather side of the grass this long.

Silent's evil eyes said he would happily give Rusty a painful nudge along the downward road, were Darling not there to stay him. His sorcery will not work around Darling. No sorcery will. The Lady herself would have no recourse but mind and muscle in Darling's presence.

★ ★ ★

Darling set me on the girl. I brushed auburn hair aside. The kid was pretty under the grunge. I saw no physical damage. Darling tapped her own forehead, belly, and signed. Silent shrugged. He could not tell from inside the magical null.

Darling feared the girl might be pregnant, not thanks to Rusty, who had suffered another of his life's numerous disappointments.

She had me check Robin and the male prisoners next.

Robin would heal. That idiot kid was more worried about Rusty than about himself. Some friendships just never make sense.

Rusty now had his arms wrapped around his knees, his head tucked. He rocked slowly, knowing he was well and truly screwed—and probably did not understand why.

No captive was smart enough to speak a language any of us knew. Talking loud or slow did not help.

More Company men arrived. Rusty rocked faster.

His behavior had not been extreme. Rape was weather. War weather. And good men do not join the Company. His big problem was, he was "that asshole Rusty" that everybody loved to hate.

Darling held Robin's hand briefly. The kid took that as a divine dispensation. Then she made a round of the prisoners. One boy met her eye stubbornly, not defiant but definitely determined. He kept an eye on the pretty girl always.

They would be siblings. Maybe twins. They were of a size and looked enough alike.

His glances toward Rusty were not kind.

Rusty rocked.

Robin moved the bandit girl without touching her, distancing her from the scene of her embarrassment. I stayed close. She was scared but neither defiant nor resigned. She observed, calculated, abided her time.

Then she groaned, clutched herself as though kicked in the gut, and puked.

Darling had come close enough to touch her.

Bandit girl was not knocked up despite having run with an all-male gang.

Sporadically, randomly, unpredictably, I am intuitive. She was a witch. A menarche-onset wild talent who did not yet understand what she was. She would not respond to Darling so violently, otherwise.

Wild talents seldom prosper. They scare the mud out of people. Evil sorcerers begin as local nuisances who grow to become regional afflictions. The worst then begin raising wicked armies and putting up dark towers. So why not burn them before they set the earth to shaking?

Me, I reckon any pretty young sociopath can create chaos without injecting magic into the mix.

Darling flurried signs at Silent, telling him to teach and protect the girl and make her keep her distance. When the girl hurt because Darling was close Darling hurt because the girl was close. Darling had me spread the word that the girl was not to be touched even if she sprinted through camp bare-ass begging for male attention.

The girl and her friends became not quite prisoners who were not quite guests. Silent sloughed their care and feeding off onto Robin. The girl seemed comfortable with him.

Rusty got busy being an invisible man. He stayed far away from the girl.

Some of our tagalong refugees spoke a dialect related to that of the bandits. Darling offered the bandits an opportunity to participate in our great adventure. They would be expected to pull their weight, of course.

They owed us for several meals before they fully understood the peril they had put themselves into. Our one-time employer, now our great enemy, the near-goddess the Lady, was a traveler's tale in these parts. Her hunting dog sorceress, the Taken Whisper, was a complete unknown. Too late the newcomers learned that our pursuers were determined to convert us all into acres of feasts for ravens, flies, and scavengers.

The girl's name was Chasing Midnight. She was scary smart. She picked up enough language to get by in just a week. Though officially Silent's problem, she stuck to Robin till she learned that I was educated enough to be Company physician and Annalist. Literacy is sorcery itself in the hinterland. Plus, smelly old Croaker looked easy prey for pretty girl manipulation.

She definitely had an unconscious talent, proven by her having run untouched with that gang of boys. It explained Rusty's disappointment, too. Males who got close could not sustain an interest.

Darling had a similar aura.

Midnight's twin brother was Chasing Moonlight, not so bright but loyal to a lethal fault. She was twelve minutes older. Their story was familiar. Bad weather, pests, poor crops, relentless tax collectors. Many of us played a turn in a similar drama once upon a time.

"They fear me," Midnight complained. She was underfoot all the time, now, two weeks on. She meant the refugees traveling with us.

"They think you're a witch. They lost everything because of a witch."

"Stupid thinking."

"Never any shortage of stupid, girl."

She muttered something in her own language, which I was having trouble picking up. She was no help, of course. As long as only she and her boys spoke the tongue, they could share secrets. She was their leader now.

The cavalier who ran from Goblin's devil was an older brother, now first on her contemptibles list. He had wakened her keep-off-me talent. His fierce cowardice was sugar on the biscuit. She only hinted at the ugly. I did not pursue it. That is not done in this tribe.

I did press her on her personal habits. I want clean, neat, healthy people around me. She considered the pressure absurdist humor. "Why bother? You do not expect to escape your Whispering Doom." She meant Whisper, who certainly planned to be our doom.

"The Company has faith in Darling."

"The black man that does not talk. He is dangerous?"

"Only if you're a threat to Darling."

"Not I."

I shrugged. She could be the Lady's plant. The old terror would not scruple against using a child. "He's our strongest wizard." She had not yet met Goblin or One-Eye. One-Eye had been missing for more than a month. "Just don't make him worry about Darling."

Moonlight and pals rolled up. They were FNGs with attitude now. No longer hungry, they objected to having to do shit jobs just because they were new. They wanted Midnight to wiggle her ass and get them easier jobs.

People. Saints and philosophers tell us to love them. No doubt anchorites who never suffered the everyday mob. I seldom see anyone actually deserving of brotherly love.

But I have been here in the Company most of my adult life.

I do hope that karma is the keystone of the universe— even if I have to come back as a banana slug myself.

Nerves frayed. This was the Company on the long run, a flight already years in duration. We had luck out the wazoo, every day, like it was going out of style, and most of it was bad. Which we expected.

Only . . . Whisper's scouts faded away, which made no sense. They ought to be pressing harder than ever, to repay the hurt we had done them not so long ago. But they lost interest instead. Or they lost the trail.

Our flight slowed. Some days we moved only a mile or three. Other days we did not move at all.

The villages we skirted became less bristly. We paid for supplies rather than make new enemies. Some villages adopted the less repugnant of our female hangers-on. I did not mind. I would not miss having all those children underfoot.

★ ★ ★

My apprentices were exasperating. They were competing to see who was laziest.

"One of you is going back to the ranks at the end of the week." That got their attention. "Midnight, who is showing some actual interest, will take his place."

She had overtaken them in the last month. She did not evade fatigue details. She worked hard, wanted to learn, never complained. And she was killer cute, a skill with which no boy can compete.

I looked Joro in the eye, he being the most useless. "Since Moonlight and his gang left us there are openings in human-waste management." Of which I was lord and arbiter. I do not get my own paws dirty. I do decide who does.

Midnight's friends had vanished one night, several back. Nobody missed their whining. Only Midnight's feelings were hurt. I wondered why they had not taken her along.

I wondered to Darling, the Lieutenant, Silent, and Elmo. Elmo and the Lieutenant did not care. Darling would see no evil till it bit her. Cynical Silent figured Midnight was behind the desertion even though she stuck with us herself.

By being helpful and pliable she became increasingly suspect to Silent. His reasoning was impossible to follow.

Then One-Eye turned up, which complicated things considerably.

"The Lady called them off," One-Eye reported. "For their own safety." He was tired and hungry. The rest of us thought he needed a bath, something he would not undertake voluntarily. "Two Taken were killed when Whisper attacked that castle. She and the other Taken got hurt, too, but our luck held. She didn't die. She's *almost* dead, but we'll eventually see her back with the last ounce of mercy boiled out. Her troops, after fighting us and suffering what I've been putting them through, are used up."

He meant their fighting spirit was gone, not that their number had been exhausted. There is never any shortage of men willing to take the Lady's coin. She is a reliable paymaster—who purchases your soul and conscience as well as your time.

So with the surviving Imperial sorcerers concentrating on staying above ground, our less potent wizards could serve their minions misery in epic portions.

"You shoulda been with me," One-Eye told Silent. "I ain't never had so much fun since . . . Since before buzzkill Croaker signed up! Mice in a barrel!" He grinned, flashing terrible teeth, trying to flirt with Midnight, who had come along to get a look at a living legend. Said legend was older than dirt, often hard to distinguish from dirt, and when not engaged in criminal activities, about as ambitious as dirt. It was a certainty that he had lined his pockets somehow during his independent venture.

He held a cherished position on every brother's shit list but never soared up where he might be at risk like Rusty. He did occasionally make himself useful. He could do amazing things if the notion took him.

Midnight hunched deeper into my shadow, pressed her fists against my back like she was terrified and needed protection. All contrived. She was raw but definitely an actress, all the world her stage.

Nothing like a hundred-and-some-year-old, shriveled-up little black wizard making eyes at a pubescent girl to get the boys sneering.

One-Eye was calculating himself, of course. His world is a stage, too, his life performance art.

He gave the remnants of his disgusting old black hat a quarter turn, winked again. "I'm in love. You want to sell me that one, Croaker?"

Midnight's squeak might have indicated real concern.

Darling signed almost too fast to follow. Had One-Eye not been as dark and wrinkled as a worn out-boot, he might have turned pale.

Ages have flown since the Company rescued child Darling from some Rebel Rustys when she was years younger than Midnight now. Many who were with us then have gone on to darker worlds. But Darling remembers. Darling does not suffer anyone making light of horrors she endured herself.

She was grimly uncomfortable, anyway, with so many sorcerers so close by.

Midnight was uncomfortable, herself, but stubbornly insisted on slaking her curiosity.

One-Eye said, "Here's the story. The Lady told them to back off, rest up, and get healthy. She'll keep the Eye on us. She'll send new Taken if Whisper can't get healthy. She'll come out here herself if she has to." He winked at me, pumped his left thumb between the first two fingers of that hand.

I was once a captive in the Tower, while the Company

was in the Lady's service. She turned me loose eventually. I have been taunted about being the old horror's bed buddy ever since.

Customers awaited me at the clinic. "Twiller, my man, tell me, how does a guy get the clap in the middle of a godsdamn desert?"

True desert it was not, just dry scrubland that went on and on and on.

"Never mind. I know. You got it from some woman who got it from Swain who got it from some other woman who got it from you the last time you had it."

Twiller had the grace to look sheepish. His behavior would not change, though. He was still that young, and none too bright.

Robin was my other customer. His ailment was one no physician has ever cured. Sometimes Midnight seemed interested back. Her stay-off-me aura weakened when he was around.

The kid was the gentle soul that Rusty could never be, which did not serve him well with a girl. He needed more push.

Midnight mused, "The old black man did not tell us everything."

"No." I had seen the tells. One-Eye was shifty. If a potential score was out there we might hear nothing solid till the fallout set in. If it touched on the safety of the Company, though, he would be whispering with Darling and the Lieutenant now.

I asked, "You know anything about what's ahead of

us?" I had a suspicion about why the Lady had leashed her hounds.

"We approach the bounds of fable already."

We had covered little more than a hundred miles since her ambush. With no pressure on we slowed despite a consensus that we ought to grab all the separation we could.

"You can't be that ignorant. The bounds of fable sounds like something somebody avoiding the subject would blat. Meaning somebody had something she didn't want to talk about. But that wouldn't make sense. She'd be strutting into the shit storm with the rest of us."

"I know fairy tales. Only fairy tales. I never heard of anybody who ever actually saw the Village of Hungry Ghosts." She paused. I said nothing. The vacuum moved her to fill it. "My da would say that was because nobody who did ever came back."

Her words for Village of Hungry Ghosts were unfamiliar, but the concept was not. I had encountered it long ago, while we served the Lady in the east reaches of the Empire.

Hungry ghosts are not regular spooks, the spirits of dead folks that cannot move on. Legend described hungry ghosts as being more like vampire phantoms. They would possess the living and consume them slowly from within. They would never move on to heaven or hell or wherever because their earthly business was never done. They would migrate from host to host till something somehow annihilated them.

Where did they come from? The stories do not explain. Like monkeys and crows, they are. Likely an ancient sorcerer was involved, or a cruel, mischievous dawn-time god.

Great communal sorcery was required to effect a migration from a dying body to a fresh one, at least in the hungry ghost stories I had heard.

I told Midnight. She shrugged. She had nothing to add. My information fit with what she knew.

I left her to Robin, went to talk it over with those in charge.

Fantastic as a village of hungry ghosts seemed, the behavior of our enemies made more sense in that context.

We should expect an occasional Imperial nudge intended to keep us hopping toward disaster.

I am destined to be in the wrong place at the wrong time when shit happens. I turned up while Rusty was trying to plug Midnight. Then . . .

I was two rods from the latrine when someone inside squealed in surprise, pain, and terror. The moon's light showed me nothing because Darling insisted that the pits be masked by canvas to preserve the modesty of the females among us.

I hollered as I charged.

Two kids came out to see about the noise. Both had deserted with Chasing Moonlight. They owned no combat skills. I laid them out as quick as it takes to tell it.

Canvas did not mask the latrine from the eye of the sky. The half moon shed light enough to show me what I expected: Midnight's brother and friends swarming Rusty, who was in serious trouble, having been caught seated on logs with his trousers down.

Punch! Grab! Sling! Prod, poke, and jab! Punch! I am no master infighter, but I have stayed in one piece for years. And the idiot kids had not posted a lookout, or said lookout had been unable to resist joining in on the fun.

Give them this: they hit their man at the exact perfect moment. But we need to knock off points for not having brought the tools to make quick work of the job.

My yells brought help fast. Quick response is something we do well, our lessons learned in a brutal school. There is still a Company.

Nobody got dead. Not even Rusty, though he might wish for worse luck when he woke up and began to enjoy the pain. His chances would be iffy for a while. He lost a lot of blood, one weeping shallow wound at a time. The boys cut him a lot, inside a shithouse. Sepsis was almost certain. Also, in time, a spider's web collection of thin new scars.

Only a double handful of cuts needed stitching. The rest I cleaned with alcohol and swabbed with an astringent. I made Midnight assist though I was sure she had had nothing to do with the attack. The lesson was that medicine and surgery leave no space for personal feelings.

I know. I make exceptions. I am dumb enough to have recorded a few in these Annals. Sic a lawyer on me. I will borrow some black on his hair-splitting ass, too.

So. Do as I say, child, not as I do.

She amazed me. Rusty naked and painted with dried or jellied blood troubled her very little. She did not interfere with his hunger for breath. She might have considered elevating him to eunuch status but let that go, too. She followed instructions precisely. Scary, a kid her age having that much control. What next? Conquering armies and new dark towers?

I was halfway in love when we finished, not with the girly girl but with the unflappable surgeon's assistant.

All the others did was keep Robin away while Midnight and I fixed Rusty. Then, tired as she was, she took over wrangling Rusty's only living friend.

During that was when Chasing Midnight finally admitted to herself that she might be the wild talent the rest of us said. She began flirting with all of our wizards. They all, Silent included, took her on as a kind of smart, pretty pet.

She started winning the hearts and minds of the soldiers, too. She recruited herself a platoon's worth of adopted, protective big brothers.

Definitely a menace to tomorrow, this Chasing Midnight.

Darling got a little jealous.

She never had any competition before.

I stretched out aboard a cot a parallel yard from Rusty's and fell asleep halfway hoping I had not gotten every wound completely clean. The regular guy suppressed by the physician wished "that asshole Rusty" all the joys and complications of protracted gangrene.

Darling's judgments were neither harsh nor unpopular. Moonlight's boys got extra duty. Moonlight himself got extra extra for fomenting. Darling overlooked their desertion completely.

Oh. The boys had to carry Rusty's litter when we were on the move. That pained them more than any other punishment could.

"We have a problem," the Lieutenant told the assembled officers. Darling sat to one side, leaving it all to him. She washed me in disapproval. I had brought Midnight. She wondered if something untoward was going on with us. Croaker might be a good man, generally, but he *was* a man.

My thinking was, the kid ought to start learning now because she could end up running the show someday. She had that much going on.

Silent disapproved, too, but only because Darling was hurting. He agreed with my long-range assessment despite what having a sorceress in charge might mean.

"We have fallen under a glamour," the Lieutenant told us. "It keeps us from going the direction we want." No secret, that. Whatever we tried, come sundown the sun would be directly ahead. Come sunrise it would be directly behind. Darling's talent was too localized to resist any sorcery beyond a hundred feet. Those she could not shield shambled on like zombies.

Our wizards would fight it but still had to trudge on along with the other hundreds.

So there it was. The Village of Hungry Ghosts, where immortal souls, perhaps once human, lived on in old but epic squalor. I was reminded of a bat cave occupied for ten thousand years. The immortality of the hungry ghosts produced neither prosperity nor any form of sanitation. A commentary on the essential wickedness of willful circumvention of natural order.

Our wizards sat in a row, inches separating their shoulders. They stared at ruins so ancient they were barely recognizable as recollections of human construction. Midnight rested on her knees behind the gap between Goblin and One-Eye, determined to observe and learn. The rest of the Company were supposed to be setting camp a half mile away, beyond a narrow defile of a dry wash, beside a bitter pool fed by a marginally less bitter spring that once must have served the village. Remnants of an aqueduct ran to the memory of a town. Darling made herself an anti-magic plug in the defile, at a point where she could both watch and protect the handful of us who had assistants who could set up our part of the camp for us while we did something we found more interesting.

I was inside Darling's null, barely, feeling the siren call of the village, which was as relentless as gravity itself. Whatever our efforts, sooner or later somebody was going to break down and go sprinting in.

Goblin said, "They're bound here. They can't leave without a body to carry them. But if they do leave and their host dies, they'll die, too."

One-Eye said, "They do generate one hell of a siren call, don't they? We can barely handle it."

"The Lady knew," I told the Lieutenant, who relayed my comment to Darling.

She nodded. She seemed unconcerned, there inside her null, keeping scores from marching toward personality death. Did she not get the horror?

Of course she did. She was Darling. Darling always understood, better than any of us.

Silent signed that he sensed six hungry ghosts but thought there might be more so long separated from flesh that they had become undetectable. He warned that those would be more dangerous than those that he could sense. They would be the hungriest. They would be able to seize living flesh. Elaborate ceremonies were necessary only for abandoning used-up flesh, not for taking new bone.

Silent seemed remarkably well informed. I did not ask. He would tell us if he thought we needed to know.

Goblin and One-Eye muttered. Silent signed. Midnight watched and listened. She read sign well enough now to eavesdrop on Silent's dancing fingers. She was not good at signing herself, yet, though.

She would learn. You have to sign to deal with Darling or Silent. Darling is deaf and dumb. Silent is bone stubborn about not talking. And signing is handy when we are sneaking around on people we mean to hurt or who plan on hurting us.

Darling beckoned. I needed to fall back to where she blocked the defile, restraining glassy-eyed, confused shamblers who wanted to go make love with the hungry ghosts.

Sometimes our most potent resources conflict. Darling's null, though, never spread out enough for general use in battle. We employed her in ambushes and where sorcery-capable antagonists were unaware of what they faced.

Our antagonist here was hunger incarnate, or would-be incarnate. The hungry ghosts had no other drive. Normally they did not need to be anything else. Lure a victim with the siren call, devour him from within, slowly, while the flesh withered, then find another host, always where there were fellow incarnates to help with timely migrations.

Speaking of. If these ghosts snagged enough Company people they could migrate physically, collectively, the lot of them, somewhere with a rich supply of replacement flesh.

Did anyone else realize that? "Are any of them still incarnate?"

Silent raised three fingers and flurried signs that said something about asses.

Goblin translated. "There is one old woman and two wild asses."

"They possess animals, too?" I conjured an image of possessed killer box tortoises. Tortoises were common in this almost desert.

"Higher order vertebrates."

"What do we do now?" Midnight asked. Very young, untrained, yet confident that she belonged to a "we" that included only her and the men she knelt behind, not our broader gang.

Chasing Midnight never lacked confidence or self-esteem. Neither did she own an inflated notion of who and what she might be.

No one but the Annalist, who worries about secret meanings hidden within words, studied her question. The Annalist relayed his curiosity to Darling. Darling was in a mood because people kept piling up and jostling her as they tried to see what was going on out front. She signed back, "Is it possible to kill the hungry ghosts?"

Unsentimental and pragmatic, our Darling, in the hard places—especially where somebody was preying on weaker folks. She disdained painful revenge but lacked all qualms about cutting throats she deemed in need of cutting.

Rusty had that in mind back when he was doing all that rocking. He had it in mind, still. He was putting in his longest streak of good behavior ever.

I relayed Darling's question aloud. Maybe because of the "first do no harm" oath from when I was too young not to have a caul of idealism across my eyes, I do have one of the softer hearts in the Company.

They tell me it will get me killed. No doubt they are right.

Once again Silent had the answer. "Yes."

Darling signed, "Then get killing. I cannot block this path forever."

The null is part of her, always. When it goes active against sorcery it sucks the energy out of her the same as the sorcery sucks it out of the sorcerer.

It was obvious immediately that there was a sad gap between knowing that a hungry ghost could be killed and knowing how the killing could be managed. Even Silent had no suggestions.

"Oh, Sweet Billi Afi!" One-Eye blurted, in a flat voice. "I guess it had to happen."

Four people oozed toward the Village of Hungry Ghosts. They had circumvented Darling by clambering over a ferociously rocky barrier hill between the ruins and the bitter oasis. All four had bloodied themselves during the crossing. Two were refugee kids. One was a mildly retarded cook's helper named Thorodd Asgeir who had been with the Company for years without capturing the attention of the Annalist. The last was one of the Chasings' boy bandits.

I shouted. Goblin and One-Eye shouted. Silent gripped Midnight's arm and kept her from charging her doomed cousin. None of the four heard a word. They walked faster as they got closer to the village. Their expressions said they were marching straight on into heaven.

Goblin and One-Eye groaned. One-Eye began a muttered countdown. Silent shivered, angered by all the stupid. Midnight mostly looked puzzled. Unlike the old men she had no idea what was about to happen.

She had not yet seen the true bleakness of the world. Hunger, cold, and human bad behavior were the only ugliness she knew.

"Two, one, and . . ." Seconds passed. One-Eye was not quite in rhythm today. "And there she goes."

The screaming started as a dense and intense shimmer enveloped the four. One refugee kid's head exploded. All four came apart in tiny, bloody fragments. The insanely hungry ghosts knew no restraint.

The shimmer intensified as ropes of twisted light streaked into the bloody scrum.

One-Eye told Silent, "There were more dormant ones than you thought."

Silent grunted, which proved how rattled he was.

Midnight gasped once, then just watched. Her face lapsed into the grim hostility that had shone there whenever she looked at Rusty back on that first day. She was scary, there, for a while.

Meantime, One-Eye declared this shit to be all Croaker's fault because he disappointed his honey in the Tower so bad that she wanted him and his friends hooked up with horrible deaths.

I called across, "I would sincerely appreciate you giving that crap a rest."

He grinned a grin full of nasty teeth and gave that foul hat of his a full half turn. He was thrilled. He had gotten under unflappable Croaker's skin.

I said, "I guess we can assume we were pushed to these hungry ghosts. But might there be more to it than just trying to put the hurt on us?"

The wizard crew looked up in militarily precise cadence as a shadow rippled across the ground. I looked up, too, in time to see a smaller vulture join a pair already circling. A young one, not long out of the nest, now an apprentice to mom and dad in the carrion clean-up business.

"Suppose the Lady can control hungry ghosts once they occupy somebody's body?"

"She might see this as a kind of Taking?" Goblin asked. "She could get control of the Company?"

"Just thinking out loud."

"It would friggin' fit!" One-Eye bellowed. "For the gods' sake, Croaker, you sure can pick them!"

I had some trouble keeping my temper. "What happened to those four idiots maybe says I'm all wet, but she *is* a long ways away. Maybe she don't know how starved those hungry ghosts are."

Darling's hands danced. I relayed. "The call is getting weaker and confused. The feeding frenzy broke their concentration."

Chasing Midnight now sat between Silent and One-Eye, with Goblin moved to the apex of a triangle. The girl did all the talking. Filthy old gray heads bobbed. Then Silent headed my way.

Silent and Darling may be soul mates at the heart of the romantic tragedy of our age. They are what they are, doomed never to touch, but all their years of yearning have narrowed the distance they have to keep between them. They can stay close for hours sometimes, so long as they do not touch or make eye contact.

They manage, however painful that must be. To quote our fallen Captain, "You do what you got to do."

Darling and Silent would cuddle up as much as nature allowed. They denied that any such thing was going on, of course, but even dim thug Rusty saw the untruth in that.

Which signified only because Silent approached Darling close and signed in a blur, presenting a suggestion on behalf of Chasing Midnight. At the same time he offered arguments against Darling subjecting herself to the risks.

Darling entered the Village of Hungry Ghosts in measured steps, that dumb-ass Company Annalist Croaker beside her on her right. He carried a seldom-seen

bow that had been a gift from the Lady on his release from
the Tower. He was pretty good with that bow.

Along for the stroll was my favorite sergeant, Elmo,
and two old soldiers named Otto and Hagop. Also with
us, at Darling's behest, speaking in tongues with terror,
was Rusty.

There was no popular support for his presence, but
Darling insisted. He needed a chance for redemption.
Even he understood, but, still, he looked like hammered
shit as we headed into the ruins.

We were about to execute a scheme bought instantly
by Darling when Midnight proposed it. Darling had us
drafted and rolling as quick as it took the buzzard family
to complete a couple circles around the sky.

Darling eased through the ruins, each step careful. We
saw some dressed stones still topping other dressed
stones, but I suspected that the original structures would
have been mostly mud brick. Rain would not be a
frequent problem here.

We smelled decay and saw some bones, but nothing
like what I had worked myself up to expect.

Hagop grumbled, "This reminds me of someplace we
used to be."

Otto bobbed his head. "Aloe, five, six years ago."

I recalled, "That country was flatter. And civilized.
There were people. Mostly nice people."

Hagop said, "It had the same feel, though. All the time
like the shit was gonna come down any minute."

Yes. True. There was a sense of imminence. I became
shakier. Hard not to suffer the heebie-jeebies when what

looked like snakes of water slithered and splashed in the air on all the fringes of Darling's tightened null. They would strike instantly if any crack opened.

She grew more bold. That crack would not develop. She *was* the null. It did not turn on and off, though she could control its range and intensity a little. A very little.

Looked like she knew where she wanted to go.

The advancing null scared up a skeleton ass draped in mangy, saggy hide. It shambled out of a dark place, set out to put distance between us and it.

Darling made an impatient gesture my way. Why was I just standing there, gawking?

"Hungry ghosts," I reminded myself. There was no moral ambiguity.

The black arrow hit the air immediately. The frightened animal inside this being with a capacity for moral anxiety *could* get things done. Better to be alive tomorrow to whimper about what got done today.

The arrow wobbled through the fuzzy bounds of the null. The spells on it took life. It struck behind the animal's head, skipped off bone into brain. Rusty charged. Otto and Elmo yelled at him to hold up, it was too dangerous to get so far ahead. But nothing happened. When we got there Rusty was jabbing his spear into the carcass repeatedly.

Otto stepped up with his big ax and removed the wild ass's head, after which good buddy Hagop began trying to recover my arrow for me.

Darling signed, "The brat was right." Not entirely pleased to admit that. "That was a crippling shock to the monsters. Let us move on quickly while they are panicked." She walked on, again looking like she knew where she wanted to go.

We took our places, Rusty now seeming all twitchy. There was a long difference between bullying and cold killing.

The watery ropes around us were fewer and more randomly behaved. They stuck with us out of inertia, not purpose.

Darling's confidence soared. Her step quickened. Thirty yards onward a long, sad moan of despair from under a stone slab brought us to a halt. Shaking, Rusty took a knee, looked underneath. "It's hollowed out under here. Somebody is in here."

Elmo, Hagop, and Otto took hold of the slab and heaved. Three men were not enough. Rusty and I joined them. Darling stood by, shielding us from the raging mad terror of the discorporate hungry ghosts.

The hidden woman had been unable to keep quiet when the null touched her. She was not old in years lived, she was just starved to where her bones were brittle and her weight had shrunk to nothing. Were she not possessed, she would be dead already.

We looked to Darling. Somebody had to act. She should pick.

Ticking and twitching, Rusty started to step up but then thought better. Darling might figure he was sucking up.

Darling used Otto's ax to do it herself. She was muscular, but that ax was heavy. She damaged the blade badly.

Was I alone in seeing the moment of human terror

and pleading in the woman's eyes as the ax fell? I did not ask. Something else we do not talk about with our brothers.

The head rolled away. The body jerked once and stopped moving forever. Not much blood got loose. What did smelled diseased.

The impact was instant. Insanely despairing emotion soaked into the null. The siren call collapsed completely. The rest of the Company picked up the next phase of Midnight's plan, which began slowly because people had to shake the wool out of their heads before they could understand.

Our intrepid band pressed on, looking for the wild ass being worn by the last incarnate hungry ghost.

That hungry ghost did not want to get caught. It wanted to stay out of sight till we messed up and exposed some of our people to seizure.

A few of our idiots tried, but Midnight, with stubborn help from Goblin, One-Eye, and Silent, kept the suicidal stupidity in check.

The discorporate hungry ghosts never recovered enough to regenerate their call. Midnight kept their madness boiling by having livestock paraded outside the confining boundary. All reason fled the ghosts. Midnight and the wizards began to expose livestock carefully. The animals fought, futilely. They calmed instantly once a hungry ghost got inside.

I asked Silent, "Can you keep track of which ones are infected?"

Staring into nothing, in the general direction of where

Robin and Rusty were watching, he signed, "I can. We can."

Those animals would be slaughtered and eaten first.

Practical, pragmatic Darling and Chasing Midnight! Darling's harshness did not trouble me. I had seen it for years. I was comfortable with how her head worked. Chasing Midnight, though, did worry me. She had so much potential and was still so young. She might make bad decisions. She might be nudged onto the shadowed path by another's bad behavior. She could end up a victim of her own adolescent humors.

Darling smirked when I mentioned that. "Smitten, are we?"

"No! Not that way. But I do like the kid. In a fatherly way. She's brilliant. I don't want to see that wasted."

Darling nodded, reflected, most likely the only member of the Company who would not serve me a ration of shit about incest. She signed, "You fuss too much. She is fourteen. She is already who she is going to be. All you can do is set an example that she will want to follow."

Parenting advice from somebody twenty years my junior.

"All right. I'll try." But I had my reservations. I feared that there was a shadow inside Midnight that she had kept well hidden.

I went walking in the ruins, thinking they would be choked with loneliness and silence. I reexamined recent events repeatedly, sure that I was missing something.

The ruins were neither quiet nor lonely. The hungry

ghosts had been replaced by every vulture and carrion eater in nearby creation, all squabbling over the remains of two wild asses and one old woman whose dying eyes I could not get out of my head.

It did not come together for weeks, during our talks with the Magistrates of Rue, who wanted to pay us to discourage the predatory behavior of their neighbors, the Dank. Both sides had heard wildly exaggerated tales of our work for the Lady, years ago.

What I finally noticed, like a sudden slap to the back of my head, was that now always twitchy Rusty hung around Midnight more than Robin did. And Midnight put up with that dickhead.

The last piece clicked. Rusty was no longer an asshole. Since the Village of Hungry Ghosts he had stopped being true to his nature. He had become, in fact, almost Chasing Midnight's dog. And Midnight appeared to have no problems with him anymore.

The same could not be said for her brother and the other surviving bandits. Moonlight still got that look when his gaze chanced upon Rusty.

The Magistrates argued almost not at all before they made a deal. That guaranteed that they would double-cross us as soon as they felt safe from the Dank. We understood. It was nothing new. Evil in its own time. Meanwhile, we could take a break from traveling, in a place where people did not know us.

I set up my clinic inside an actual building. We handled a few cuts, scrapes, and malingerers looking to get out of work. Caught up, I told Midnight, "Go fetch Rusty for me. I want to take a look at him."

She pouted prettily, not pleased. "Robin says he has been having stomach troubles. So, I guess, yes. You should check him out." She left.

I waited, appreciating my new digs. They were part of a small barracks. I might stay warm and well-fed all winter. Fingers crossed. Let us stretch out the war with the Dank.

Rusty arrived. Twitchy, pale, watery-eyed Rusty, not at all pleased to be so close to the Company sawbones. I said, "Have a seat here."

"What's up?"

"I've noticed . . ." and I explained my professional interest.

Where was Midnight? I heard Robin talking in the waiting area. Maybe she was out there with him.

Rusty began to relax. This was all routine. Yeah. He was having trouble with his guts. Maybe he got himself a ulcer. He had an uncle once; he got him a ulcer. Uncle used to puke up blood sometimes.

I got behind Rusty, rested my hands on his shoulders, leaned, whispered, "I know you're in there. And everyone else knows, too."

Rusty lapsed into the worst twitches, tics, and shakes yet.

The hungry ghost had him only under partial control.

I would start checking local sources right away. There might be an exorcism that could save the man—even though haunted Rusty was better liked than Rusty his own self ever was before.

★ ★ ★

I never saw Chasing Midnight again. She, Moonlight, and their friends stepped off the face of the earth. Not so difficult in a city. Darling would not let me waste time and energy looking for someone who did not want to be found. Darling wanted to be our unchallenged princess. Moreover, we had soldier business to handle.

The skirmishes with the Dank all ended badly for them. Local fighters on both sides were amateurs of abysmal quality led by fat old men who got their jobs because they were the sons of privilege. And we had Silent, Goblin, and One-Eye to give us that extra edge.

Rusty disappeared a week after Midnight did. Robin did not vanish with him. That boy went half crazy with worry. Nobody else cared. Rusty carried a hungry ghost that could not migrate unless he found another colony. The tacit popular choice was to let nature run its course.

One winter night a partially recovered Whisper slipped into Rue to hand the senior Magistrates a plain directive from the Lady concerning the Black Company. The Magistrates agreed to her terms but failed to execute their promised treachery because clever One-Eye had rat spies keeping watch on all of Rue's most important men.

We did considerable selective damage before we left town with pockets sagging.

I got the final word on Rusty as we cleared Rue's eastern gate. His mutilated corpse had been found in the mud and water along the edge of the river that ran through Rue. The rats and crayfish had been at him, but they had not done a tenth of the damage that he suffered at human hands before what was left of him was dumped.

I knew then, for sure, why I had grown ever more uneasy with sweet, pretty little Chasing Midnight.

Maybe there will be those new grim armies and fresh dark towers someday, after all.

★ ★ ★

ABOUT THE AUTHOR

Glen Cook was born in New York in 1944. He grew up in northern California and served in the U.S. Navy, spending time with the Force Recon unit of the 3rd Marine Recon Battalion. He attended the University of Missouri and the Clarion Writers' Workshop. His only job has been with General Motors. Recently, he retired and is devoting more time to his writing. He is best known for his Black Company series, but has also written many other novels, such as those in the Garrett P.I. series, the Dread Empire series, as well as many standalone novels and stories.

BOMBER'S MOON

★ ★ ★

Simon R. Green

April 1944
Spring, in Bomber County

A lovely evening in the English countryside, not far from the coast. Rob Harding, bomber pilot, stood alone at the edge of the air field, looking out over the open fields, at the dark and moody woods beyond. So peaceful. The last hours of the day, before it gives itself up to the night. Rob smiled at the sounds of living things moving through the wood, birds and beasts settling down, or waking up to the night's possibilities. The pleasant sounds came clearly to him on the quiet evening air, along with the smell of grass and flowers. He breathed in deeply.

He looked up at the darkening sky. A full moon hung fat and heavy, gathering its light for the night. Rob looked for the man in the moon, but couldn't see him anywhere.

Rob Harding was tall and lean, with a calm thoughtful face, and a hawk's fierce eyes. Barely into his mid twenties, he had the look of a much older man. Flying bombers will do that to you. Out of the corner of his eye, he saw his navigator heading determinedly towards him. He didn't look round. Chalkie White: big and broad and always cheerful. Not because he didn't think or didn't care about what he did, but because he didn't let it get to him. Chalkie moved in beside Rob, and the two men stood together for a while, looking out on the world in companionable silence.

"Full moon is a bomber's moon," Chalkie said finally. "A clear way out, and a clear way back. A hunter's moon; if you like."

"The full moon is a two-faced friend," said Rob. "It shows us the way, but it also shows us to our enemies."

"You've always been a glass-half-empty kind of guy, haven't you, Rob? For me, the glass may be half empty, but I am half full."

Rob smiled, briefly. "Any idea how much longer?"

"We're still on hold, because the new priest isn't ready yet."

Rob shrugged. "Can't go up without him."

Their old priest, Father Alistair, had been rushed to hospital with suspected food poisoning. They were lucky to be getting a replacement at all, at such short notice. Rob turned his back on the woods, and looked at his plane, waiting patiently for him on the air field. Not a bad crate, the Hampden. Old enough, even old-fashioned, but the big brass had dragged every available craft that would still fly out of mothballs for this very special Op. The two men looked out across the ranks and ranks of planes, lined up and waiting for the off. Lancasters, Wellingtons, de Havillands . . . most of them already crewed, just waiting for the word. Dozens of planes, carrying hundreds of bombs, for the biggest raid of the war. The city of Dresden wasn't going to know what hit it.

"A big one, Chalkie," said Rob.

"Aren't they all?"

"Could end the war, they say."

"We've heard that before. And here we still are."

A cheerful voice called out to them. They looked round to see their main gunner, James Ross, limping painfully but steadily toward them. Short and stocky, with a uniform that fit him where it touched. No one ever said anything. James was always ready with his fists, to avenge any perceived slight, and he didn't care what rank you were. Everyone made allowances, because it was either that or take him out back and shoot him. Which had been seriously discussed, on more than one occasion. The rear gunner, David Stuart, came bustling along behind, careful to match his pace to James's. Even though he was clearly bubbling over with enthusiasm. David was young, eager, and ready for anything. Just looking at him made Rob feel like an old man.

"Why are we still hanging around?" said James, slamming to a halt before them. Just about keeping the pain from his ruined feet out of his face. "Everyone else is boarding!"

"The new priest is still in with the CO," said Chalkie. "Father John. Don't know him, myself. Any of you fellows . . . ?"

There was a general shaking of heads, and some shrugging. They all liked Father Alistair, but in the end any priest who could do the job would do. They couldn't get into the air without one, but beyond that, he was superfluous.

Rob looked fondly at his waiting plane. The Hampden was a mess, but she was sound. Rebuilt and repaired so many times there probably wasn't an original part left in her, but she was strong. Reliable. And that counted for a lot on a bombing mission. The old leather and canvas exterior was gone, of course—replaced by pages from the Bible. Stitched together by a local order of nuns, the holy sisters praying over every stitch. The holy words wrapping the plane in sanctity.

Father John came hurrying forward, finally. A tall skinny presence in shabby black robes, with a prematurely bald head and a tense, fretful face. He handed Chalkie the CO's latest maps, and introduced himself. The crew just nodded. There would be time to get to know one another, once they were up.

Rob strode out onto the airfield, and the others followed him. James was soon left lurching along in the rear, but he still kept up, refusing to be slowed down by his crippled feet. The others didn't look back. James hated anyone to make allowances for him.

They boarded the plane and slipped into their accustomed positions with the ease of long practice. Pilot at the controls, in the cockpit. Navigator strapped in below him, studying his maps and calculations. Main gunner at the center, checking his big brute of a gun. Rear gunner at the far end, checking his water reserves. The priest dithered about, uncertainly, before finally settling onto a folding chair beside the navigator.

Rob checked out his controls, running steadily through the regular routine, and then glanced back over his shoulder. "Say the words, Father."

The priest nodded quickly, and began the invocation. The familiar chant sounded loudly inside the plane, the holy words soaring up and out. A growing presence manifested, filling the Hampden, as something old and powerful descended upon them from every direction at once. A great and terrible presence, sinking into every part of the plane, suffusing it with power from Above. The holy sentences in the Bible pages blazed up with a sudden fierce light, illuminating the plane's interior. The whole aircraft shook and shuddered as the angel settled in, possessing the plane.

Hello, my friends. I am Uriel.

The words sounded in their heads—warm as honey, strong as steel. Rob nodded, pleased. He'd flown with the angel Uriel before. A friendly, pleasant sort—calm and dependable. Unlike some. The light from the Bible pages winked out, replaced by a gentle golden glow that didn't pass beyond the plane's interior. Some angels had to be reminded to do that, on the grounds that a plane which glowed in the dark wasn't too likely to reach its target. Angels might be old and wise, but they were often inexperienced in the more practical aspects of the material world.

Rob looked out his side window. Row upon row of planes flared briefly into life up and down the field as a host of angels descended on the squadron's planes and possessed them. Holy fires, blazing against the falling night. Signs of hope and judgment day, come at last.

The forces of Light, set against the Darkness.

Ron spoke quietly on the radio to mission control. At least that was still there, still needed. Part of the old craft, along with the basic controls. Most of the rest had been ripped out, as unnecessary. A calm voice from mission control gave him the go-ahead, and the Hampden's crew braced themselves.

"Operation Shadrach is go," said the CO. "Good luck, everyone. Go with God."

There was no taxiing into position, no racing down the runway building up speed; the Hampden just rose suddenly into the sky, leaping up into the darkening skies in one swift, easy movement—as though the Earth and its dull gravity no longer mattered, no longer had any hold over the possessed plane. Rob's stomach fell away for a moment, as it always did, and he had to fight to hold on to his last meal. Cold beads of sweat popped out on his forehead. Man wasn't meant to travel like this, he thought. And then the plane steadied, and so did his nerves, and his hands moved surely over the controls, taking charge of the plane. He never asked the others if they felt the same, on takeoff. It was none of his business.

Plane after plane rose up into the air all around him, filling the sky, each taking its designated place in the formation. The biggest squadron of possessed bombers ever assembled; on their way to bomb the shit out of a whole city, and destroy its entire population. In the name of a greater good.

Spitfires shot up into the air, in ones and twos, to fly

alongside them. Ready to run interference against attackers, and protect the planes from flak. Spitfires: individual men and women, each possessed by an angel. Only a few were strong enough to hold an angel within them. The few, the brave, and the pure. They could fly, were supernaturally strong, and the fierce cold and thin air of the upper reaches didn't bother them at all. But they didn't last long. Even the most dedicated souls tended to burn out quickly. Because men and women were never meant to blaze so brightly.

"Why do they do it?" said Chalkie. "Agreeing to become a Spitfire is like signing your own death sentence."

"They do their job, so we can do ours," said Rob. "They're all volunteers."

"Aren't we all?" said James, running one hand lovingly over his gun. Everyone managed some kind of smile.

Rob prayed quietly, under his breath, as the last few planes slotted into position. They all did, all the crews. They'd been told it wasn't necessary, that the angel would protect the plane and its crew from Hell's power . . . but they all prayed anyway, quietly, on every mission. Every man felt the need to make his own peace with God, in the face of death.

The possessed planes moved forward, out across England and then over the Channel. Heading for Germany—and Dresden.

"Why Dresden?" Father John said suddenly. "Sorry . . . I only skimmed through the briefing on the way here. What's so special about one German city, to justify so many bombers?"

"Intelligence says something really big and really nasty

is going on in Dresden tonight," said Rob. "Most of the head Nazis will be there, the real top ranks; everyone from Goebbels to Himmler. Not the Fuehrer, of course. He never leaves his bunker in Berlin anymore. But the word is, these particular higher-ups will be holding a summoning in Dresden, to call up more—and more powerful—demons. The highest ranks in the Pit. The Nazis are going to sacrifice every man, woman and child in the city, to power that summoning—and pay for the help they're expecting. We can't allow that to happen."

"So we kill them all first!" James said cheerfully. "Bomb the city back and forth and up and down, until there isn't a single living thing left in it. Stop the summoning, and maybe wipe out the top Nazi bastards too, if they haven't protected themselves properly."

"It's hard to remember, back when the war was just a war," said Chalkie. He didn't look up from his maps or his calculations. The angel knew where to take them, but it was up to the navigator to select the best route. "When it all started, when it was just armies fighting armies . . ."

Till Adolf Hitler realized he was losing, said Uriel. *Realized there was no way he could win. And so he made a pact with Hell: human sacrifices in return for power, after he called on Heaven for help and was refused. Rather a shock for the Fuehrer, I understand. To finally know, beyond any doubt, that he was not on the side of the angels and never had been. That God was not with him. Some say that was what drove him insane, made him crazy enough to sell his soul—and his country—to the Devil. In return for the demonic forces he needed to win the war.*

Of course, once Hell entered the war directly, so did

Heaven. As demons rose up, angels came down. There are limits to our intervention, on either side. Or the world—and all its peoples—would be destroyed. Men can be helped—even empowered—on both sides, but you must still make your own decisions, do the fighting yourselves. Or victory . . . would be meaningless.

Rob thought of a great many things he would have liked to say in response to that, but he kept quiet. Uriel was quite a chatty sort, for an angel, but it still didn't pay to press him. Angels did God's work, and followed His wishes; there was never any point in arguing with them. They would do what they would do—no more, and no less.

"I prefer riding in this kind of crate," said Chalkie. "So quiet without the engines. Remember the old days, Rob? The terrible deafening roar of the engines, the vibrations that shook you from head to toe . . . the awful cold, and the need for oxygen? With Uriel providing all the speed and power we need, it's like the dreams of flying I had when I was just a kid. Gliding carelessly and effortlessly, on the roof of the world . . ."

Rob just nodded. He found the silence eerie, if anything. Still, the angel could move a plane far more quickly than even the most advanced engines. They'd be across the Channel and into Germany in under an hour. Which reminded him . . .

"Check your positions, everyone. Sound off."

"Navigator, aye," said Chalkie. "Course plotted. Just follow the directions I give you, and try not to get lost."

"Main gun, locked and loaded," said James. "Firing fifty-fifty: tracers and blessed bullets. Lovely, lovely."

"I'm sorry?" said Father John. "What are . . . blessed bullets?"

"A cross carved into the nose," said James with open relish.

Father John pulled a face. "Ah. Dumdums. Nasty things. Some might even say dishonorable."

"The purpose of a bullet is to kill the enemy, Father," said James. "The more efficient a job it can do, the better. A wounded man can always recover and come after you again. The only good Nazi is one with his head blown right off."

"Keep the chatter to a minimum," Rob said mildly. "David?"

"Rear gunner, aye. Cannon ready to go, water tank full to bursting. Holy water is as good as a flame-thrower, when you're going up against demonic forces, Father."

"Thank you, David," said Rob. "What about our payload, James?"

"All bombs primed and ready to drop," said James. "And I'll say it again: if I have to pull double duty as main gunner *and* bombardier, I should be pulling double wages. For double responsibility."

"Take it up with the CO when we get back," Chalkie said cheerfully. "Go on—see how far it gets you."

"Are the bombs blessed, too?" said Father John. "Have you worked some blasphemy on them, as well?"

James winked at the priest. "Bombs are just bombs, Father. They blow up and kill people who need killing. Who could ask for anything more?"

The priest shook his head slowly. "This is my first mission. First actual combat mission. I have been briefed, prepared, trained. I have read the official proclamation from the Holy Father in the Vatican. But there's still so much to get used to. I still have . . . doubts. Problems, with this whole idea of a Holy War. I find it hard to accept that my loving God wants one group of his children to murder another."

"We won't be killing the people of Dresden, Father," said Rob, as kindly as he could. "We'll be setting them free. Saving their bodies from suffering—and their souls from Hell. Better a clean death at our hands . . . than the horror of human sacrifice to the powers of the Pit."

"You believe that?" said Father John.

I have to believe it, Rob thought but didn't say.

"Pay attention, Rob," said Chalkie, his voice sharp. They were a friendly crew, but the closer to a target they got, the more professional they became. "We just crossed the border into Germany; we are now heading into hostile territory." He looked over at the priest. "We have to fly around demonically possessed areas and cities that have been given over to Hell. Where Satan's influence has become so strong, so ingrained, it could rise up and override Uriel's protections. By avoiding these infernal territories, we avoid malign influences. Move on up into the cockpit, Father, beside the pilot. Take a look out the window. Look down and see what kind of hell the Nazis have made out of their own country."

Father John squeezed up into the cockpit, beside Rob, and peered out the side window. Rob didn't need to look around; he could see the awful countryside spread out before him. Huge areas of dead land, the earth soaked with blood and sowed with churned-up bodies. Great swathes of land so blighted, so damned, that nothing natural would ever grow in them again. It was said terrible beasts roamed through the dark forests now—things the Nazis *only thought* they controlled—searching for what innocents remained, that they might consume them.

Whole towns on fire, burning with blood-red flames, their populations slaughtered on the Fuehrer's orders. Because some Germans mattered more than others. The Nazis had been sacrificing their own people for almost a year now, ever since they ran out of prisoners and victims and subjugated peoples.

"Some of those towns will burn forever," David said quietly, from the rear of the plane. He had an unblocked view of the land behind them. "Even if we win, there will be a limit to what we can do to restore this land and its people. Hitler has poisoned the wells of Germany—forever."

"Does bring a whole new meaning to the phrase 'scorched-earth policy,'" said James.

The Nazi hierarchy know they're losing, said Uriel. *It has made them desperate. They believe they can do anything, anything at all, because they have nothing left to lose.*

"I still don't get it," said James, leaning on his gun as though it were an old friend. "Why can't you and all the other angels just go storming into Germany, with great flaming swords, and put an end to all this? Or send down the old Biblical plagues? Strike down the Nazis and their demons and bring any survivors to justice!"

It's not that simple, said Uriel.

"It is from where I'm standing," James said stubbornly. "How many more good men have to die—"

He broke off as the Hampden bomber and everything in it disappeared—the angel Uriel was showing them a vision: of giant winged creatures, angels and demons, huge and potent beyond bearing. Big enough to fill the sky, clashing together. Powers and presences so vast they broke the world, just by manifesting in it. Stamping through cities, treading great buildings underfoot as they went head to head, the human inhabitants less than ants at their feet. The vision only lasted a moment, but when it was gone and the familiar details of the Hampden returned, every man on board was chilled to the bone— and the soul.

Is that what you want? said the angel Uriel. His voice was calm, almost kind. *The more Heaven does, the more Hell is permitted to do. We must maintain the balance.*

"Why?" Father John said fiercely. "What is the point of these rules? Why does our good and just Lord allow Satan to make deals with the Nazis? Why doesn't he just strike the Devil down, as he did in the beginning?"

Because this is not the beginning, said Uriel. *There was no world then, no natural order of things. There are rules, for your protection.*

The priest put his hands together, bent his head over them, and prayed silently.

"I never feel more alive than right now," James said happily. "Flying off to death or glory, risking my life to do something that matters."

"Really?" said David. "You never feel scared?"

"Not any more," said James. "I was part of the

original D-Day landings last year. I was scared then. But after that . . ."

"Was it bad?" said David. "In France?"

"It was bad, young Davie," James said quietly. "Fighting the Nazi armies for every mile of land, head to head and sometimes hand to hand. Forcing them back foot by foot, and paying for even those small victories with the blood and bodies of good friends. In that awfully cold winter.

"I ended up with frostbite in both feet. Lucky not to have them amputated. Sent home and invalided out, of course. But I still wanted to fight, so I volunteered for this. Always a need for fresh volunteers on bomber duties. And it's not like you need whole feet to fire a gun or drop a bomb."

"But . . . why?" said Father John, his head coming up to stare uncomprehendingly at James. "You were out of the war! You did your duty, you'd done your bit . . . Why would you go back to killing again when you didn't have to?"

"Because I *did* have to, Father," James said steadily. "Because of the things I saw in France. Long lines of crucified Resistance fighters. Whole towns reduced to rubble and ashes, their populations burned alive in giant Wicker Men, down to the last man, woman, and child. Rivers thick with blood, and bodies, and bits of bodies. I'm not done with killing Nazis yet, Father. Not just yet."

The priest looked down the length of the plane, to David. "And you're no more than a boy. Why did you volunteer?"

David turned right round, so he could smile at the

priest. "I wanted to fly, Father. And they were never going to let me be a pilot with eyes as bad as mine."

"Now he tells us!" said Chalkie. "Just remember to point your cannon away from us, Davie boy, when the fighting starts."

There was quiet laughter in the plane—from everyone except Father John.

The Hampden lurched suddenly to one side, and everyone grabbed on to something to steady themselves.

"Sorry about that, chaps," said Rob. "We seem to have drifted into a bad area . . . Powerful winds are hitting us from one direction after another. Compass is spinning round like a mad thing . . . Chalkie: do us all a favor and check your maps, please. We do seem to have drifted away from the other planes . . ."

Chalkie quickly checked his maps and his calculations, and then got up to squeeze into the cockpit next to Rob. He peered quickly out of the side window and winced at the blood-red clouds surrounding them, full of flaring hell lights.

"The maps say we're on course, Rob, but I don't think I trust them. We've been this way before and it never looked like this. We're way off course."

"Can you see the ground anywhere?" said Rob. "Anything you recognize?"

"I can see a river," Chalkie said steadily. "It appears to be on fire. Get us out of here. We shouldn't be here."

"Give me a direction," said Rob.

"Give me a minute." Chalkie thought hard, doing rapid mathematics in his head, and then gave Rob a new heading. Rob swung the Hampden around, and after a few moments the rest of the squadron appeared again, in an open night sky full of stars, under the gleaming full moon. The land below was devastated, but still recognizable. Rob allowed himself a quiet sigh of relief.

"We're back on course, everyone," he said mildly. "Back in the pack, back in position."

"How the hell did that happen?" said James. "How can the maps be wrong?"

"They were supposed to be the most up-to-date maps," said Chalkie. He climbed back down out of the cockpit and looked at the priest.

"Those are the maps I was given by the CO," said Father John. "I'm afraid one map looks much like another to me."

"Military intelligence," snarled James. "A contradiction in terms."

"Stick with the other planes, Rob," said Chalkie. "They'll get us there. Hopefully by then I'll have worked out a safe route home for us."

"That would be nice," said Rob.

Soon enough, the Hampden reached the outer edges of Dresden air space. Flak came flying up almost immediately, vivid explosions bursting in and around the planes, from hundreds of heavy guns set out in defensive positions all around the city. The night came alive, lit with fire and rocked with detonations. Shells burst and planes blew up, falling back to earth like burning birds. The rest of the squadron pressed on, moving to their designated positions over the city. There were hardly any lights below. Dresden was dark. The guns blazed away, firing blindly into the night skies, hitting targets more through luck than accuracy. Because with so many planes they were bound to hit something. Angels could protect the craft they possessed from supernatural threats, but not from German guns.

"Heads up!" Rob said sharply. "We have visitors! *Ubershreck*!"

Just the name was enough to put a chill into all of them. The RAF had Spitfires, men possessed by angels; the Nazis had their Ubershreck: stormtroopers possessed by demons. They came howling up into the night sky like shooting stars, burning fiercely with crackling demonic energies. The Spitfires went swooping down to meet them. They fought hand to hand in midair, striking terrible blows and tearing at each other like animals. Punches ripped heads off bodies, and unnatural strength tore arms and legs out of sockets. Blood and bodies fell out of the air, tumbling toward the city below. Both sides fought with unflinching ferocity, driven on by the forces within them.

There were far more Ubershreck than Spitfires, and many of the howling shapes got past the defenders to attack the planes. They couldn't touch the Bible-page fuselages, so they concentrated on tearing off wings and punching through cockpit windows to get at the pilots.

James manned his gun, sweeping the long barrel back and forth. It took a lot of bullets to take out an Ubershreck, but hit them hard enough and often enough and they would go down. Plummeting back to earth, leaving long bloody trails in the air behind them. All the guns on all the planes were firing now, but the Ubershreck shot back and forth so rapidly it was hard to target them.

James fired and fired, until the mechanisms heated up and the barrel glowed red hot. The grips burned his hands, even through thick leather gloves. Smoke curled up, from burning leather and burning flesh, but he wouldn't stop. His teeth were clenched in a ghastly smile and his eyes were feverishly bright.

David kept up a steady stream of fire from the rear gun, a water cannon, firing blessed holy water. Where it touched the Ubershreck it threw the possessing demons right out of them and sent shocked stormtroopers screaming back to the earth. But the cannon's water tank had only a limited capacity. David had to save his shots for where they would do the most good. Knowing it would only take one Ubershreck, speeding in from a direction he didn't see, to smash through his cockpit and put an end to him.

The skies over Dresden were full of burning planes and accelerating supernatural figures, death and horror everywhere. And still the squadron pressed on, spreading out over the city, to do the maximum possible damage. Possessed men and women flew between and around the planes like angry bees, while glowing tracers chattered across the night skies.

"How much further to the target, Chalkie?" said Rob, raising his voice to be heard over the din. "Some of these demon chappies are getting awfully close, you know."

"Almost there! Almost there!" Chalkie crouched over the open bomb-bay doors, looking down through his aiming mechanism. "James! Leave that bloody gun alone and get over here! Bombardier! *Get here now! That's an order!*"

James turned away from his gun. He had to pull his hands off the grips. Charred leather and meat clung stickily to the grips for a moment, but James never said a word. He crouched down beside Chalkie and waited patiently until the navigator gave him the signal. James hit the lever hard with his elbow and bombs tumbled away from the Hampden, one after another after another.

"Die, you Nazi bastards, *die*," said James, almost reverently.

"Language, James," Rob said mildly. "You're not at home now. We have a priest on board."

James slammed the bomb-bay doors shut and went back to his gun. He grabbed the barely cooled grips with both wounded hands and bared his teeth in the old familiar grin. The gun bucked and heaved, pumping out tracers and blessed bullets, fifty-fifty.

All across the city of Dresden, planes were dropping their bombs. Long streams of certain death, falling with almost casual ease. Buildings exploded. Fires rose up. Black smoke everywhere. Whole streets disappeared, blown apart, as the center of the city became a great inferno, a firestorm whipped up by overheated winds. Dresden became a raging hell, with hardly a trace left of where the city had been. People were dying, too, of course. But they were too far below to see.

The surviving planes peeled away to every side— bombs gone, job done, heading home. The Spitfires and the Ubershreck were gone, all dead. Flak was still coming up from guns on the perimeter, not yet affected by the spreading fires. Planes were still being hit, plummeting from the sky, falling into the inferno they'd made below.

The Hampden rocked suddenly, slapped to one side by a terrible impact, and the plane dropped like a stone. Something had blasted a massive hole through the left-hand side, leaving a ragged gap big enough to drive a car through. So many Bible pages gone in a moment. Fires broke out down the whole left side of the plane; whipped up by the air blasting in through the hole.

"We've been hit!" yelled Chalkie, beating at the nearest flames with his gloved hands.

"I noticed, thank you," said Rob. He fought the dead controls with all his strength, struggling to bring the nose back up. "Uriel! Anything you can do?"

I can only possess this plane as long as the fuselage survives, said the angel. *There is enough left for me to remain—for a while. I will stay with you for as long as I can.*

The nose came up slowly, reluctantly, as life returned sluggishly to the controls. Rob found he was breathing a little more easily. James and David left their guns to try and help Chalkie put out the spreading fires. David struggled forward with the plane's only fire extinguisher, but ran out of foam long before he could make any real impression on the flames. David threw the empty canister aside and turned back to the rear cockpit. He ripped the water cannon out of its mounting through sheer desperate strength, turned it around, and used the last of the holy water on the flames. It helped, but not for long. David dropped the cannon and went to join Chalkie and James, beating out the flames with his gloved hands.

The Hampden left the burning city behind and headed on, back across Germany and into France. Burning ever more fiercely, and sinking ever lower in the sky as the angel's power weakened. Half the plane was ablaze now. Rob finally looked back over his shoulder.

"Hate to say it, chaps, but I really don't know if the Hampden will hang together long enough to make the French coast. Never mind the Channel. We're losing more Bible pages every minute, and once enough of them are gone, so is Uriel. And a Hampden with no angel—and no engines—has roughly the same glide ratio as a brick. Chalkie, where are we, precisely?"

"Still over Occupied France," said the navigator. His face was blackened and scorched from the heat and the smoke.

"Then everyone check your parachute—and jump," said Rob. "Take your chances below. I'll hold the plane steady."

"No!" said David. "I won't leave you!"

"I have to stay," said Rob. "Try and nurse the Hampden home. We're short of planes, you know. Especially after all the craft we lost tonight. But you can go. You've done your duty."

"But . . ."

"We go," James said roughly. He stood stiffly on his ruined feet, clutching his burned hands to his chest. "Pilot's right. Better to risk a landing in Occupied France than a splash in the Channel. Those waters are cold enough to kill you in minutes. Let's go. Help me check the straps, Davie boy."

David checked James's parachute, and then his own. They moved over to the open bomb-bay doors, and peered down at the ground rushing past.

"Will you be able to pull the ripcord okay?" said David.

"Bloody well have to, won't I?" said James. "Sorry, Father."

James jumped, with David right behind him.

"You're next, Chalkie," said Rob.

Chalkie shut the bomb-bay doors and staggered back down the plane, wincing away from the roaring flames he passed.

"How are you going to get the Hampden home without me to guide you? If I keep fighting the fires, there's still a chance this old crate will hang together long enough."

"Lot of ifs and buts in that," Rob said mildly.

"No buts," said Chalkie. "We're going home."

"No," said Father John. "I don't think so." He squeezed up into the cockpit and jammed the barrel of his pistol into Rob's ribs. "Land the plane, Mister Harding. Put us down, anywhere. You've done enough."

"What's this, Father?" said Chalkie. He wanted to jump the man, wrestle the gun away from him, but he was too far away.

"It would appear our new priest is a traitor," said Rob. Looking carefully straight ahead, not down at the gun in his side.

"I am not a traitor! I am a pacifist." The priest's voice shook with the strength of his emotions, but his gun hand remained steady. "I am what I'm supposed to be: A man of peace, as all good Christians should be. I cannot believe my God wants so many people to die. I cannot believe my good and just God approves of this . . . madness! No. It has become clear to me that Hell is on both sides of this war.

"I came aboard this plane to do my duty. To sabotage your mission. I poisoned Father Alistair; I pray he will recover. I supplied you with altered maps, to steer you away from your target. I may be only one man, but I wanted to stop one plane at least, tonight."

"But you stood to be killed along with the rest of us!" said Chalkie.

"I am ready to die, to put an end to at least some of this madness, this evil," said Father John. "The Church has always been strengthened by the blood of martyrs."

"Who got to you?" said Rob. "Who have you been listening to?"

"My conscience," said Father John. "No more talk. Land the plane. There have been enough deaths this night."

"How can you not believe God is on our side?" said Chalkie. "The plane's possessed by an angel!"

"Hell is full of fallen angels," said the priest. "No more arguments! I will do as my conscience and my God commands!"

You are wrong, said Uriel. *Everything that happens, happens for a purpose.*

And once again the Hampden disappeared as the angel showed them a vision, this time of what the Nazi Hierarchy had been doing in Dresden that night. Afterwards, Rob would only remember some of the details in his worst nightmares. Blood and horror, slaughter and suffering, on a scale almost beyond comprehension. The massacre of an entire city's population, in horrid and vicious ways, to open the Gates of Hell, for a time. For those still left alive in the city, the falling bombs had come as a blessed release. For the Nazi

Hierarchy, distracted and caught off guard, it was judgment day.

Father John cried out miserably as the vision disappeared and the Hampden returned. He fell back out of the cockpit, the gun dropping from his hand. He dropped down on both knees, wringing his hands together, tears streaming down his cheeks.

"I'm sorry! I didn't understand! I didn't know . . ."

Now you know, said Uriel.

Holy fires burst out of the priest, blasting from his eyes and mouth as they consumed him from within. He burned up in a moment, unable even to scream, as the terrible heat sucked the air out of his shriveling lungs. And all that was left was a charred and blackened shape, curled up on the floor of the plane. Chalkie retched and turned his head away.

"Why did you do that? Why did you have to kill him? He said he was sorry!"

Penance isn't good enough, said Uriel. *We're at war*.

"Why didn't you know he was a traitor?" said Rob.

I knew. But things must play out as they must. Men must save or damn themselves. I can only aid in human affairs; not meddle.

"That doesn't make any sense!" said Chalkie.

The angel was silent.

Chalkie looked back down the length of the plane. Half the fuselage on the left side was gone. Fires burned fiercely. Bible pages blackened and curled as they were consumed. Chalkie could see the night sky rushing past, through the remaining struts and supports in the tattered gaps. He lurched down the plane, stamping out flames on the floor, beating out fires with his charred and smoking leather gloves. The heat inside the plane was almost unbearable now. His bare face smarted, and then burned. Until he couldn't force himself forward into the heat any more and he had to fall back and stand below the pilot in his cockpit. Rob concentrated on the controls, and the way ahead, ignoring the heat as best he could, nursing the Hampden along.

"How much ammo do we have left, Chalkie?" he said. "Be a bit of a bad idea if the heat got to it."

"The ammo!" said Chalkie. "If it explodes inside the plane . . ."

"Better do something about it, then," Rob said mildly. "I've rather got my hands full up here."

Chalkie braced himself, and made himself go back down the plane, into the awful heat, foot by foot. Until he reached the ammo cans stacked below James's gun. He grabbed them up in his burned hands and tossed the metal canisters out through the holes in the open left side. Any one of them could have exploded at any time, from the raging heat, but he wouldn't let himself hurry, determined to do a proper job. He got them all away and then hauled the gun up off its mounting and threw it after them, just in case it still had ammo up the spout. He staggered back to the front of the plane. His eyes were streaming with tears from the thickening smoke and he hacked and coughed violently.

"Well done, Chalkie," said Rob. "We're over the Channel now. Coast up ahead. Almost home. The Hampden will get us there. She's a good crate. Uriel . . . Uriel?"

My hold on the plane is weakening, said the angel. *Soon, I must leave you.*

"There must be something more you can do!" said Chalkie.

Perhaps. One last, small miracle. For two good and brave men who did their duty.

The Hampden passed over the coast, sweeping over the English countryside, driven on by the last of the angel's power. Under a full moon, a bomber's moon. And a great shimmering path of silver moonlight suddenly appeared on the ground below, pointing the way back to the airfield. Showing them the way home. Rob laughed out loud and pointed the Hampden down the glowing moonlit path.

Good luck to you both, said Uriel. *God be with you.*

And just like that, Rob and Chalkie felt the angel's presence go. The plane was just a plane. No longer possessed, the Hampden dropped suddenly, all power gone. Gliding over the English countryside, limping on toward the airfield up ahead. The shimmering, shining path hung on to the very last minute, right up to the edge of the runway, before it finally faded away.

An angel's gift, from a bomber's moon.

They came down hard, at the end. More a series of controlled crashes than a landing. But the plane finally skidded to a halt on a mostly deserted runway. Ambulances and fire trucks came rushing forward. Rob and Chalkie left the plane through the bomb-bay doors and staggered away from the Hampden, leaning heavily on each other. They looked back at what was left of their plane. Half destroyed, half still on fire: a battered and charred frame, never to fly again. It didn't matter.

The Hampden had brought them home.

★ ★ ★

ABOUT THE AUTHOR

Simon R. Green has written over forty books, all of them different. He has written eight Deathstalker books, twelve Nightside books, and thinks trilogies are for wimps. His current series are the Secret Histories, featuring Shaman Bond, the very secret agent, and The Ghost Finders, featuring traditional hauntings in modern settings. He acts in open-air productions of Shakespeare, rides motorbikes, and loves old-time silent films. His short stories have appeared in the anthologies *Mean Streets, Unusual Suspects, Powers of Detection, Wolfsbane and Mistletoe, The Way of the Wizard, The Living Dead 2, Those Who Fight Monsters, Dark Delicacies III,* and *Home Improvements: Undead Edition.*

IN SKELETON LEAVES

★ ★ ★

Seanan McGuire

"He was a lovely boy, clad in skeleton leaves
and the juices that ooze out of trees . . ."
—J.M. Barrie, *Peter and Wendy*

The sun rising over the lagoon tinted the water in shades of red and gold. Nothing moved, not even the wind, which had ceased blowing sometime after midnight, stranding the ships at sea and the rafts on shore. It was a moment of rare peace, and while it held sway, it was almost possible to pretend nothing had changed: that this was still a place of endless summers and endless games, where growing up was a choice and not a foregone conclusion. This was still Neverland.

Then the sun finished rising, and the red streaks on the surface of the water remained behind, the blood marking the places where the dead had fallen. This was still Neverland, but it was no longer suited for bedtime stories.

"I don't think I can betray her."
"Do you ever want this war to end?"

The ragamuffin army gathered in the shadow of the oaks drooped, their thin shoulders weighed down by birch-bark armor, their arms exhausted from the strain of holding swords and shields against the enemy. Those who had been lucky enough to stay behind and miss the night's battles moved through their ranks, offering cups of water and wiping blood from split lips and bruised foreheads. Only whimpers broke the silence; whimpers, and sighs as Wendy after Wendy found one of their charges on the verge of collapse.

"This can't go on much longer," murmured one of the Wendys, whose name had been Maria before she came to Neverland. She barely remembered the life she'd left behind. She knew there'd been a man who had hit her, and a woman with sad eyes who had never intervened, but more and more she found herself wondering if that was really worse than this endless parade of dead and dying children.

"It will go on for as long as the Pan wills it," said another Wendy stiffly.

Invoking the Pan's name ended all attempts at conversation. The Wendys scattered like so many birds, the blue ribbons in their hair and tied around their upper arms standing out like brands in the gloom beneath the trees.

The sound of distant crowing alerted them that their time was almost up, and they worked faster, trying to bandage every wound and wipe every eye before the inevitable happened: the curtain of branches at the far end of the clearing spread wide, and the Pan floated inside, her feet drifting a foot above the hard-packed ground. Her Wendy walked after her, hands folded behind her back, and the Pan's three lieutenants followed. They were the children who had survived the most battles, and their eyes were dead and dark with too much dying.

"Five Lost Children died last night—rejoice, for we killed twice that many pirates." The Pan's voice was jovial, as it always was; she announced death as if it were just another game. "Their bodies have been given to the mermaids, as apology for the three mermaids who were also killed in last night's fighting. Our alliance continues strong."

Each of the Wendys looked to their own charges and then, with pleading eyes, to the Pan's Wendy. There was not a one of them who was not missing someone, but that could mean their children had been sent to scout, or were out gathering ripe apples and fresh strawberries to feed Pan's army.

The Pan would never think to give the names of the fallen—forgot them, in fact, as soon as each Lost Girl or Boy breathed their last. Dead things held no interest for the Pan.

Her Wendy sighed and named the dead: "Christopher, Agnes, Jimmy, Minuet, and Xio."

One of the male Wendys cried out before muffling his sobs with the heel of his hand. The other four who had lost children managed to keep themselves under tighter control. It was too late: the Pan's eyes had found the

Wendy who dared to cry aloud. She loosed herself like an arrow across the clearing, stopping to hang in the air before him as she demanded, "What's wrong? Why are you crying?"

The Wendy swallowed, trying to take back his tears. It didn't work, but he pressed forward all the same, saying, "Minuet was one of mine, Pan. I didn't realize . . . I'm going to miss her."

"Miss her? Miss who? All your children are here!" The Pan shook her head, pouting petulantly. "It's like you don't *want* us to have any fun, Wendy. You're a stick in the mud. Why, I bet your children never get to play any good games."

The Pan's Wendy took a sharp breath as she grasped the danger. She stepped forward, forcing a laugh as she said, "Why, that's not so! I've seen his children playing *lots* of games. He's an excellent mother, Pan, one of the best. I wouldn't be surprised if he's crying only because Minuet is going to miss playing with her brothers and sisters, like any good Lost Girl."

The cornered Wendy nodded in rapid agreement. "Yes! Yes, Pan, it's just as she said. We play such lovely games, it's a pity Minuet won't be able to play them with us anymore."

"Ah," said the Pan, starting to turn away. "You must have the best games in Neverland, then."

"Oh, yes," said the Wendy carelessly, thinking that the danger was past. He didn't see the sudden tightness in the eyes of every other Wendy in the clearing.

The Pan whirled back toward him. "Liar!" she crowed. "*My* Wendy is the *best* Wendy, which means *I* get the best games, and not your children at all! And if you lied about *this* then you must have lied about *that*, because that's what liars do! Snips! Gantry! Take this Wendy's children to the enlistment tent. They need to learn how to play properly."

The Pan's two lieutenants began grabbing the younger children, collaring them by ones and by twos and dragging them out of the clearing. The Wendy started sobbing in earnest, blubbering incoherent pleas for the Pan to leave his children alone. The Pan's hand caught him across the cheek, sending him crumpling to the ground.

"You're not a Wendy," said the Pan. "You're just a scared little boy. Follow Gantry to the tent. We'll teach you how to play yet." She raised her head, looking around at the carefully composed faces of the other Wendys and the remaining Lost Children. "Enlistment is open for another two hours, and then we'll play at sword practice, and then? Back to war." Her smile was almost bright enough to make up for the darkness in her eyes. "Beautiful war."

Somewhere in the back row of Lost Children, a little girl began to cry.

The Pan made yet another grandiose speech about the glories of the great game of war before she turned and flew out of the clearing, off to do whatever it was she did when she wasn't terrifying Lost Children or challenging pirates to fights she couldn't win. The Wendys began calling their children to them, counting noses and tweaking ears when necessary to get them to fall into line. There was a time when this process would have taken hours, with the youngest Lost Ones needing to be cossetted and cajoled into lining up and quieting down. That time was in the past, and as every single one of them knew, what was past was beyond recovery. Past was even more inaccessible than the bottom of the lagoon, with no helpful, hurtful mermaids to dive down and bring things back to you once they were lost. In a matter of minutes, the children were lined up and the Wendys were leading them away, leaving the Pan's Wendy standing alone and looking at nothing.

"Cecily." The name was accompanied by a small hand on the side of her arm. The Pan's Wendy turned to see a girl who looked scarcely seven years of age standing beside her. The girl was wearing a much-mended cotton dress, and had her cottony hair tied into two puffballs on either side of her head, each secured with a blue Wendy-ribbon. "We need to speak of things, you, and I, and the other Wendys."

Cecily—who was called Wendy by all except her fellow Wendys, because they had to have some way of differentiating themselves, didn't they? At least when they were alone together, with no sprawling families of ever-shifting children to count or mind—shook her head. "I'm sorry, Edith, but I can't," she said, without real regret. "The Pan might need me."

"She's flying the lagoon's edge, flirting with mermaids," said Edith. "We lost five children tonight, Cecily. *Five.* Can you continue putting this off?"

"Yes," said Cecily flatly. "I am very good at delaying things."

"Angus says the apple trees have stopped bearing fruit,

and no one's found a ripe melon in days and days," said Edith. "Can you delay that? The land is failing. We water the sea with our blood. The only ones who eat well are the mermaids, and that's the only reason they still fight with us. Even the fairies have started to disappear! I don't care how good you are at delaying things, Cecily. Some things refuse to be delayed."

Cecily hesitated, reaching for excuses, and finally offered the only one she could think of: "What about the children? Someone has to stay with them." She had no children of her own to watch over—the Pan demanded the whole of her attention, and her heart—but she knew that she was an aberration amongst her kind.

"Angus has offered to take all the youngest children while we have our conference, and the older ones have already gone to train for the Pan's war," said Edith. "Come."

Cecily sighed. The rules of the fellowship of Wendys were clear: if the other Wendys wanted her, she had to go, unless she had reason to think they were leaving their Lost Children in danger. Angus was a good mother. He would care for all the children like they were his own.

"All right," she said. "I'll come."

Edith smiled.

The places of the Wendys were safe and secret, bolt-holes carved out of the fabric of Neverland to allow them the brief moments of peace their hearts required if they were going to keep on loving the Lost Children like their own. Cecily had long suspected that the love the Wendys gave wasn't really mother-love, which was selfless and strained but couldn't be broken; Wendy-love was selfish, demanding tribute and loyalty in a way she couldn't imagine mother-love would need to, and revoked as soon as its targets strayed too far. Mother-love was given freely and without constraint, and while Wendy-love might aspire to that great height, it could never quite achieve it.

There were four other Wendys waiting when Edith led Cecily down the ladder and into the safe, cool space beneath the roots of the old sycamore. Belinda, Michael, Sara, and Pike sat on the narrow benches. Cecily felt suddenly as if she had walked into a snare. Those four Wendys were among the eldest of their fellowship, second only to herself . . . and to Edith. Edith had been there long enough see five Pans come and go while she remained a Wendy under the grace of Neverland's eternal summer sky. This was something more than just a gathering of mothers.

Edith closed the door, turned to Cecily, and said without preamble, "The Pan is not keeping us safe. What say you, sister, who flew here first by this new Pan's side?"

Cecily bristled, pride and caution warring in her belly. "This 'new' Pan has kept Neverland safe for days and days," she said. From talking to the new children who sought Neverland's shores, she knew that it had been more than a hundred and fifty years. Words like "decade" and "century" were forbidden, but even as the Pan had outflown her predecessor, so had Wendy outloved and outlasted all but Edith, who seemed as untouchable as the ocean tides.

"Days without counting, yes, but days end," said Belinda, somehow making the statement sound completely reasonable, when Cecily knew in her heart that it was anything but. "Twilight comes when night is falling. The land is failing. Our children are dying. We are suffering for this Pan's frailties."

"The Pan is heartless and cruel," said Cecily pleadingly. "She keeps us safe. She keeps these skies safe."

"I remember when you first came to Neverland," said Edith softly. "You were a beautiful child, and you have grown into a beautiful mother."

"But not a woman," said Cecily. The pleas were gone from her voice, replaced by a hard core, like steel. "I'm a child. I'm a *Wendy*."

"You were a child when you came to us, and you're a Wendy now, but you didn't arrive alone, did you?" Edith looked around at the blank, bewildered faces of her sisters and brother, and sighed. "I hate this part. This is a difficult part, and I hate doing it." She stomped her foot, for just a moment looking like the child she'd been when she flew away from home. "I don't want to."

"Then don't," said Cecily. "The Pan is tired, that's all. The tide of war will turn. It always turns, and we'll drive those blasted pirates out to sea just like the last time, and the time before that, and the time before that."

"But there has to be a time when Neverland loses," said Edith. "There has to be a time when the pirates sail on valiant tides, because otherwise there would be no way of losing this game, and a game that can't be lost isn't worth playing anymore. Some Pans lose on their own. Some Pans lose because they can't keep a Wendy with them long enough to learn to depend on her. And some Pans . . ."

Cecily's eyes widened. She shook her head. "No," she said. "No, you can't make me do this."

"You didn't come to Neverland alone, Cecily."

"No."

"I'm sorry, but what are you talking about?" Michael frowned, standing as he asked his question. "I know Cecily is the Pan's Wendy, but how can she change whether or not the pirates win? Why would we *want* the pirates to win?"

"So the game can go on," said Edith. She watched Cecily as she spoke, and her eyes were sad. "The game *is* Neverland, and Neverland is the game. The game is the war unending, the battle unrefused, and it must be fought, or Neverland will fall."

"I don't care," spat Cecily. "I know what you want me to do, and I won't do it, I *won't*. This isn't right. This is . . ." She paused, fumbling for the greatest condemnation she could think of, and finally said, "It's *against the rules*."

"Why would Edith ask you to break the rules?" asked Sara, frowning.

"It doesn't break the rules, because this is in the rules. I'm sorry, but it is." Edith shook her head. "There have been Pans before this one. None of you remember them, but I do. Franklin, Amanda, Wesley, Padraig . . . and Peter. He was my first Pan, although I was never his Wendy. That honor, and that burden, fell on other shoulders."

"What would make a Pan want to grow up?" asked Belinda, sounding shocked and slightly disgusted by the idea. The others murmured agreement.

Cecily wanted to scream. Growing up was the only end

any of them could conceive for a Pan's tenure in Neverland, even with Edith right there, talking about losing, talking about letting the pirates win. They were Wendys to the core, and they couldn't see the truth even when it was standing right in front of them, waving its arms in the air and screaming.

Maybe she had never really been a Wendy after all.

"Edith isn't talking about Pans going home and growing up," she said, and sighed. "She's talking about Pans letting the pirates win.

"She's talking about the ones that have died."

Silence fell across the room, and Cecily allowed herself a brief, cruel moment of satisfaction. If they were going to put this on her, at least they could understand what they were doing—and what they were asking her to do.

"The Pan didn't come to Neverland alone, and she wasn't the Pan when she came," said Cecily. "Her name was Sheila. And she was my sister."

They flew to Neverland with hands clasped tight, following a boy they barely knew who said that he could take them to a place where they would be children—and together—forever. What he didn't tell them was that he was recruiting soldiers for his private war; what he didn't tell them was that inside of a week, they would have swords in their hands and blood in their hair, and be fighting for their lives against a pirate crew straight out of a storybook.

Cecily had cried and flailed with her sword, barely hitting anything, but Sheila . . . Sheila had laughed and flown to the highest mast, daring the pirates to follow her. Cecily remembered the look in her sister's eyes, like she was drunk on something more powerful than brandy, more addictive than laudanum. The boy—the Pan—had seen it too, and Cecily had expected him to yell for Sheila to come down and fight properly, but he'd only smiled.

He'd been dead by morning, and Sheila had flown away, surrounded by a chiming cloud of fairies, only to come back in a gown made of skeleton leaves, with a crow in her throat and a wild new light in her face.

That was the first time she had called Cecily "Wendy."

That was the day that Cecily had lost her after all.

The Pan flew to the edge of the water and landed, her feet touching down with the familiar faint buzz that was Neverland welcoming her home. She'd felt it every time she'd touched the island's hallowed soil, even back to the first time, when she and Cecily had flown in from—where? She didn't really remember where they'd started their lives, but she remembered Cecily was her sister, and that seemed like enough of a past to be burdened with. Neverland wanted her. Neverland had welcomed her with open arms and a gown of skeleton leaves peeled from the body of a dead boy with too many freckles and a smile like a Tuesday morning (not that she knew what a Tuesday was; not that she knew the boy's name, then or now or ever). Neverland would never let her go.

Pirate ships with storm-cloud sails bobbed on the horizon, waiting for the wind to pick back up and the tide to turn around, allowing them to resume their endless assault on the island's shores. They'd been fighting this war for as long as the Pan could remember—had been fighting it when she first arrived, when the Lost Children were led by that freckle-faced boy in his vest of skeleton leaves. But it had never been like this before. It had never been so unending and so . . . so *vicious*. The pirates would attack, a few people would be injured, leaving them with interesting scars to brag about at night, when they lay in their hammocks under the trees, and that would be that; the pirates would go away again, leaving the Lost Children to more important concerns, like rabbit hunts through the thorn briars or moonlit swims with mermaids. But not this time. This time the pirates were fighting to kill, and they just kept coming and coming, like waves against the shore, and people were dying, and the Pan didn't know what to do.

No one was supposed to die in Neverland. That wasn't the agreement. That wasn't the way.

A fairy zipped in from the side, hanging in the air in front of the Pan's face and ringing softly. Her wings cast a soft pink glow over everything around her. The Pan had heard some of the newer Lost Children scoffing at her Wendy's fairy, calling it too "girly" for the Wendy attached to their Pan. The Pan didn't quite understand that; when Vinca had first attached herself to Wendy (*Cecily*), the Lost Children had laughed and said a proper girl would have a blue-glow fairy, leaving the pink fairies for the boys where they belonged.

The Pan didn't understand much about the newest wave of Lost Children, if she was being honest, which was a thing she hated to be. Pans should be liars and fliers, that's the rule. But these Lost Children came in as wide-eyed and scarred by the adult world as all the boys and girls who came before them, and then they turned their attention to questioning *everything*. Some of them had even refused to accept the authority of the Wendys! They said they'd come to Neverland to escape adults and their stupid adult rules, and they weren't going to accept a new set of guardians that they'd never asked for. The Pan had insisted they divide themselves appropriately, sending them to the Wendys who would be their caretakers, but it was strange, and it was wearying.

The Pan was tired.

Vinca rang again. The Pan frowned.

"I don't know what you want, Vinca," she said. "I speak Pan-fairy, not Wendy-fairy."

"She's telling you not to go for your sword when you hear me creeping up behind you," said a familiar voice.

"Wendy!" The Pan turned, beaming at the sight of the girl who made everything better just by walking into a room. She looked sad. The Pan didn't like that much— Wendys should be joyful things—and so she skipped, leaving the ground, and flew the few yards to land nose-to-nose with her Wendy. "Have you come to keep watch with me?"

"I have," said Wendy, with a small smile. She reached out, brushing the Pan's hair out of her face, just like a mother should. "I also wanted to talk to you, Sheila, if that's all right."

The Pan flinched, her feet touching down. "I don't like that name. That's a before-name. I'm the Pan."

"Pans have names," said Wendy calmly. "Remember? Franklin was Pan here when we came. He came through our bedroom window, and he told us if we came with him, we could be children forever, and free forever . . ."

"Pans have names, but that doesn't mean we have to *use* them," said the Pan petulantly. "Franklin wasn't a good Pan. He lost. Remember? He led his lieutenants against the pirates, and he *lost*, and he *died*, and I became Pan in his place. He wasn't a good Pan. So why should I follow his example?"

"Because you're the Pan and I'm your Wendy, but you're also Sheila, and I'm your sister," said Wendy gently. She put her hand against the Pan's cheek. "Remember? Neverland loves me too much to make you forget *that*."

"Of course I remember," scoffed the Pan. Then she hesitated before admitting, slowly, "I'm just not sure I remember what a sister *is* . . ."

Wendy pulled her hand away. "It's nothing important," she said. She stood up straighter, looking at the Pan, and said, "I want to come with you when you attack the pirates tonight."

"What? Why? Wendys are only good for getting themselves kidnapped and tied to the mast."

"I know. Having me there will confuse the pirates and make it easier for you to win, and then we can get home in time for the feast." Wendy smiled. "I trust you to rescue me."

"Of course I'll rescue you!" said the Pan, her feet leaving the ground again. "I'm the Pan! Rescue is what I do!" She turned cartwheels in the air, crowing, and Wendy watched her, and said nothing.

There was nothing left for her to say.

★ ★ ★

"This is how it goes. The Pan plans battles, and the Wendys win the war."

"It isn't fair."

"Cecily." Edith frowned at her. "Whoever told you that childhood would be fair?"

Time passed; the tide turned. Time and tides were dependable that way. The sails of the ships on the horizon grew pregnant with wind, and the pirates of Neverland began the trek to shore. Their decks were packed with men bristling with swords, and their cannons were loaded, ready to unleash hell. At each ship's helm was a pirate captain, grim of jaw and dead of eye, steering them inexorably toward battle.

On the shore, the Pan flew back and forth before her gathered army, her feet pointing straight down and hanging inches above the shore. All of the Lost Children big enough to hold a knife or a spear were there, and their Wendys were with them, leaving only a few behind to keep watch over the younglings. Mermaids bobbed in the surf, their multicolored fins breaking the surface in brief flashes, like captive rainbows, and the sky overhead glowed with the aurora of ever-moving fairy wings.

"The pirates have grown bold of late—too bold," said the Pan. "They dare our waters even on the days when their passage is forbidden; they steal our stores and raid our berry bushes. Six of our newest Lost Children have been lured out to sea, forsaking play for piracy. We are gathered here today, we are players in this greatest game, because this! This ends tonight!"

The Lost Children roared their approval. The

mermaids slapped their fins against the water, and the fairies chimed as loudly as they could, a hundred bells proclaiming the need for war. Of the Wendys, only the one who looked so very much like the Pan stayed silent, her eyes fixed on the surf at her feet. No one paid attention to her, or to the deep sorrow in her eyes.

"We have lost friends! Brothers and sisters! Remember them! Fly for them! Make vengeance in their names, and then do them the greatest honor that can be done in Neverland: forget them. Today, we have mourned. Today, we grew a little bit older, because you need a heart to grieve, and that which is not heartless can age. Tonight, we avenge. And tomorrow, we will be joyful and heartless once more."

This time the roar was louder, because all the Lost Children knew that this was the way of things: when the Pan made a stirring speech, you cheered. Only the Wendys held their silence, because to be a Wendy is to be other than heartless, and so they were already on their way to being older than everyone around them.

"We fly for Neverland!" proclaimed the Pan, and this roar was the loudest of them all.

They left the shore by air and by sea, those who could not fly—either because they feared falling or because they had never quite caught the knack—clustered in coracle boats towed by mermaids as they made their way unerringly toward the distant pirate ships.

Most Wendys *could* fly, although Neverland etiquette dictated that as mothers, they should keep their feet on the ground as much as possible, to show that they provided the stable center for the chaos of the Lost

Children. Cecily had been in Neverland for more than a hundred and fifty years, and still her flight path was shaky and uncertain as she tried to keep pace with her sister, the Pan. As she flew, she stole sidelong glances at the Pan's face, looking for traces of her twin. Sheila had all but disappeared as the decades slipped by, blurring away into the features of a legend. They still looked exactly alike if you measured only in hair color and eye shape and height, but those were just fripperies—they didn't *matter*. Cecily looked like warm fires and hot milk and bedtime stories. Sheila looked like cold winds and wild forests and stolen children coaxed out of nursery windows by the promise of something bigger and better than what they had. They didn't look anything alike.

But they had, once. Before Neverland, before the old Pan died and the new Pan seized his sword.

Who will the new Pan be when you fall, Sheila? Cecily wondered, and shivered.

Until that moment, she hadn't been sure that she would really do it.

"Pans aren't like the rest of us," said Edith, her eyes never leaving Cecily. "We live in Neverland, we play the parts Neverland asks us to play, but we're just residents. The Pan is Neverland. The Pan is every leaf that falls and every flower that blooms. The Pan is every one of us, from the youngest Lost Child to the oldest Wendy, and without the Pan, everything would fall to pieces and be forgotten. But when the king is the land, sacrifices must be made. There are costs to keeping things in balance. Do you understand?"

"No," said Cecily, and yes, said Cecily's heart, and she knew what she was going to do. Not because she loved the Pan, and not because she loved Neverland, but because she loved her sister. It had been a long, long time since two little girls followed a boy clad in skeleton leaves out their bedroom window, fleeing from adults who raised their hands too quickly and hit too hard. They had flown to Neverland, both of them expecting nothing more than to be welcomed. Instead, they had been torn apart, Cecily gone to the Wendys, and Sheila . . . Sheila gone to something more. Being the Pan had eaten her up, swallowing her bit by bit, like she was drowning. If she lived much longer, she wouldn't be Sheila at all. She would just be the Pan, and Cecily would be alone.

"She needs to lose," said Edith.

And Cecily nodded.

The pirates were ready when the Lost Children arrived, notified of the oncoming attack by Edith's message even before their sentries spotted the oncoming line of flying children, all led by a flaxen-haired little girl whose gown of skeleton leaves gleamed pale against her tan brown skin. She crowed. The pirates thrust their swords into the air, jeering, and the battle was joined.

Even in Neverland, even in a place where bedtime stories can go on forever and no one is ever told to go to bed or wash behind their ears, there are some things that are not pretty: were not meant to be pretty, because prettiness would steal their essential power, rendering them impotent and useless. So swords clashed against swords, and steel bit into exposed flesh, and children fell out of the sky like raindrops. Pirates fired arrows up at the Lost Boys and Girls who soared overhead, or down at the mermaids who flashed through the waves, trying to break the rudders and snare the anchor lines.

The Wendy who had been forced into the war by the Pan took a knife in the chest. He died choking on his own blood and was kicked overboard into the surf. Two of the mermaids seized his body and dragged it under, the fight forgotten in favor of a ready meal. Still the battle went on, the smell of gunpowder and blood wiping everything else away.

Cecily hung at the edges of the battle, waiting for the sign that Edith had promised her. A hand grasped her wrist, spinning her around, and she found herself looking into the tired, bearded face of a man she almost knew, if she looked at him just right.

"You . . . you were Franklin's Wendy," she said, her words tumbling into the space between the cannon fire. "I remember you."

"Yes," he said. "Are you here to pay the cost of war?"

No, cried her heart, and "Yes," said her mouth, and he nodded and pulled her close, flipping her around so that her back was against his broad pirate's chest. He pressed his sword to her throat.

"Do not be afraid," he murmured, and bellowed, "*Pan*! Come and face me, girl!"

The Pan jerked toward the sound of her name, eyes going wide as she saw her sister captive in a pirate's arms. "Let my Wendy go!" she shouted, darting across the battlefield toward the pirate who held Cecily. "Fight me like a man!"

"Ah, but lass, it's never a man as kills a Pan," said the pirate. His hand did something clever at his belt, and suddenly Cecily was holding a knife, small and sharp and wicked.

She remembered this, remembered Franklin shouting and diving for the pirate who held his Wendy. But the pirate had stabbed him in the stomach like a coward, and Franklin had died. Wasn't that what had happened?

The knife's hilt was patterned with the whispery bones of skeleton leaves. Cecily felt it with her fingers, and felt the story shift around her, finally coming clear.

"I love you, Sheila," she whispered, and the battle still raging all around them took her words away as her sister dove closer and closer, shouting all the while.

In the end, Cecily didn't even have to stab her.

All she had to do was hold the knife.

Sometimes a war isn't about how many casualties can be piled up on both sides; sometimes it's about one. One body falling as gravity suddenly remembers that it has a claim here. One body striking the deck of a pirate ship. One little girl overwhelmed with grief and rage, turning to bury a knife in the throat of a pirate captain who doesn't resist, because he's been where she's standing, he's felt what she feels, and he knows that in the moment that the knife slid home, she grew a heart so big and so broken that Neverland can no longer hold her. She'll grow up, this girl, until her feet fit perfectly in his boots and she steers the armada away from land, a pirate leading pirates, to wait for the day that Neverland needs to make a sacrifice once more. She doesn't need to know what a Fisher King is. Neverland knows for her.

Sometimes a war isn't about an army. Sometimes it's all about one person. But which one?

Does Neverland go to war for Wendy, or the Pan?

The death of the Pan filled the Lost Children with rage, and seeing the Pan's Wendy kill the pirate that had killed the Pan filled them with strength. They *could* win this, and they *would* win it, for Neverland. For the Pan.

Bit by bit they beat the pirates back, until the horizon was free of those foul sails, and the Lost Children—the ones who survived—turned their eyes toward home.

"Where's the Pan's Wendy?" asked a little boy.

No one knew the answer.

"She must have died," said Gantry. He'd been one of the Pan's lieutenants, and so his words carried a certain weight; what's more, there was a wild new light in his eye, one that spoke of flying, and lying, and never, never growing old. He was not yet dressed in skeleton leaves, but he may as well have been. "Poor Wendy."

"Poor Wendy," murmured the other children.

"Now come on—let's race back to shore," said Gantry, and took off like a shot, laughing as he flew. The others flew after him, the war and its costs already beginning to fade from memory. The blood on the water would take longer to disperse, but given a little time that, too, would be gone.

It was a beautiful morning in Neverland, and it would be long and long before anyone thought that it might be fun to go to war.

★ ★ ★

ABOUT THE AUTHOR

Seanan McGuire was born and raised in Northern California, resulting in a love of rattlesnakes and an absolute terror of weather. She shares a crumbling old farmhouse with a variety of cats, far too many books, and enough horror movies to be considered a problem. Seanan publishes about three books a year, and is widely rumored not to actually sleep. When bored, Seanan tends to wander into swamps and cornfields, which has not yet managed to get her killed (although not for lack of trying). She also writes as Mira Grant, filling the role of her own evil twin, and tends to talk about horrible diseases at the dinner table.

THE WAY HOME

★ ★ ★

Linda Nagata

The demon, like all the others before it, appeared first in the form of a horizontal plume of rust-red grit and vapor. Almost a kilometer away, it moved low to the ground, camouflaged by the waves of hot, shimmering air that rose from the desert hardpan. Lieutenant Matt Whitebird watched it for many seconds before he was sure it was more than a mirage. Then he announced to his squad, "Incoming. Ten o'clock from my position. Only one this time."

But even one was deadly.

Sergeant Carson Cabuto, some six meters to Whitebird's right, huddled against a jut of rock, black as obsidian, a stark contrast to the gray-brown camo of his helmet and combat uniform. "Okay, I see it," Cabuto said. "That's fifty-six minutes since the last one. I was starting to get worried."

"Just starting?"

White teeth flashed in a round face tanned dark by the sun as Cabuto glanced at the lieutenant, his eyes invisible behind black sunglasses. "Now we know the rules, bring it on."

The squad—what was left of it—had taken refuge atop a low plateau, one of several that punched up through the desert plain. Ten meters high and maybe twenty at its widest point, the plateau's black rock was cracked and fissured, skirted by sharp-edged fragments that had fallen from the walls. The squad had spread out around it, so they could watch the desert in all directions.

Their combat training had neglected to cover a situation in which they were alone in an unmapped desert with no GPS, no air traffic, no vehicles, no goats, no sheep; where the radios worked, but there was no one to talk to; where the enemy emerged from churning dust wielding glittering, lethal swords—but they were learning.

There was no sun above this desert, and no real sky, just a dust-colored glare so bright it was impossible to squint against it for more than a second or two, but though there was no sun, there *was* heat. One hundred twenty-one degrees Fahrenheit according to Whitebird's weather meter. He sucked in the heat with every breath. Belly-down on the black rock, he soaked it in, an exhausting, brutal heat that seeped past his chest armor and the heavy fabric of his combat uniform, heat that got inside his brain, making him think thoughts that never would have entered his mind if he was still in the world. Thoughts like, *If Goodfellow breaks down one more time I'm going to shoot him* and *I'm more than halfway sure we're already dead*.

Whitebird knew that in all likelihood he had simply gone mad.

"This one's coming fast," Sergeant Cabuto warned.

"Roger that."

Madness was not an assumption he could work with. It offered no way out. It demanded that he give up the fight, retreat from the battle, wail at a soulless sky, and pray for a rescue that would never come.

Fuck that.

This was real, for whatever value of real might get defined along the way.

He licked at the salt tang of blood seeping from his cracked lips, wondering if the demons smelled it, or just felt the presence of their souls like an invisible lure, undetectable by any human measure.

Whitebird turned his head, projecting his voice across the rock. "Estimated forty-five seconds until the next dust bunny gets here. Foltz, any more showing up on your side?"

"Not so far, sir!" the specialist shouted back. "But if I spot one, is it mine?"

"This isn't a game, Foltz. Alameri, how about you?"

"Negative, Lieutenant!"

Assurances came back from Fong, Keller, and Cobb that no other demons were in sight.

Last of all, Whitebird turned to Private Goodfellow, down on his belly five meters to the left. The eighteen-year-old was not watching the horizon as he'd been assigned to do. Instead his worried gaze was fixed on the thing of sand and vapor, his gloved fingers clinging so tightly to his assault rifle Whitebird wondered if he intended to use it as a club. "Goodfellow."

The private flinched. He turned to Whitebird. Dust coated the dark skin of his cheeks; behind his protective glasses his eyes were red-rimmed. All the warrior accoutrements—combat uniform, helmet, boots, safety glasses, body armor, backpack, assault rifle, grenades—could not make Goodfellow look like anything but what he was: a scared kid, overwhelmed by the unknown and the unexpected.

"Still with us, Private?"

"Yes, sir," he whispered, not sounding too sure of himself.

"This one is yours."

His brows knit together in abject worry. "Sir, please no, I—"

"You're going." Whitebird didn't want to send Goodfellow. He had more worthy soldiers, but Goodfellow was the weak link and Whitebird didn't want him around. "Stay down," he instructed. "Don't move until I tell you and *do not* use your weapon."

With Goodfellow, the worst-case scenario was all too likely: at some point the kid would panic, and then his friendly fire would be more dangerous than the demons that hunted them. "When I say go, you jump down that ravine. You're only going to have seconds to get to the bottom, so move fast. You got it?"

"Yes, sir."

"Lieutenant," Cabuto warned, "it's here."

Whitebird looked down in time to see the train of dust boil up to the base of the plateau. He could hear the burr of unknown forces swirling within it . . . or maybe that was just the sound of sand rubbing against sand, and maybe the sparks of electricity flaring and dying within the cloud were caused by friction, too, or maybe they were generated by magic—he didn't know. He only knew it was a waste of ammo to shoot at the demon while it was in its sand and vapor form. The squad had learned that early. So Whitebird leaned over the edge of the shallow precipice, his M4 carbine aimed at the demon's churning mass, and waited. Sergeant Cabuto did the same.

Seconds passed, and then the skein of sand drew itself upright, a snake raising its head.

"Here we go," Cabuto whispered. "Show yourself, dust bunny."

To Whitebird's shock, the demon's sand form shot up the cliff face. It burst over the top between him and Cabuto, showering them in a storm of grit that crackled and pinged against their helmets and eyewear. Whitebird rolled onto his side, his weapon aimed up as the demon congealed from the cloud.

It came dressed in a gray-brown desert combat uniform, with an M4 carbine clutched in its long, black-clawed fingers.

That was new.

For eight weeks, ever since his unit had transferred to their combat outpost, Whitebird had been haunted by a sense of disaster lurking just out of sight in some unknowable direction. Every night he'd awakened in a rush of panic, sticky with sweat in the aftermath of some monstrous dream. He had told himself it was the altitude, the unrelenting aridity of the high-desert air that made it hard to breathe hemmed in as he was by the bare plywood walls of his little bunkroom.

On most nights he had wound up outside under a blazing firmament of stars, the soft purr of the outpost's generator the only sound in the world—and when the generator cut out, silence enfolded him, silence so deep his brain hallucinated noises and he would imagine he heard a susurration of sand-on-sand, a crackle of electricity, and a haunting, hungry wail that made his hair stand on end—and his heart pound with fear.

He imagined other worlds brushing up against the one he knew.

He never spoke of these imaginings—who would?— and when the generator kicked on again he would go back inside and prepare for the day's assignment.

That day the squad had been patrolling on foot, chasing down numerous reports of insurgents in the district. At the end of a brutally hot afternoon they were returning to the shelter of the outpost—a haphazard collection of plywood buildings surrounded by sand-filled barriers and barbwire situated at the crown of a low hill. They were five-hundred meters out and Whitebird was looking forward to food and e-mail when a missile came screaming out of the north.

"Get down!" he yelled and dropped to his belly.

He watched the missile hit. It missed the outpost, striking instead the hill beneath it. That hill proved to be made of ancient, weathered, rotten stone. Afterward, Whitebird would conjecture that the slow pressure of a cosmological intrusion had seared and heated and cracked the stone within that hill until it was shot through with dimensional faults and fractures. A blistering weakness, it shattered at the missile's impact, collapsing into roiling clouds of dust and fire . . . and the demons slipped loose—boiling, vaporous plumes sweeping toward the squad with all the deliberate speed and inherent purpose of charging predators.

More than fear, Whitebird felt an instinctive repulsion. He didn't know what was going on. He only knew he didn't want to be touched by it, or caught up in it. Turning to his squad, he screamed at them to run.

Too late.

The land rejected the intrusion. It trembled and heaved and folded in on itself, crushing the demons in the seams of that transition, pinching off their shrieks and wails as day turned to night. Whitebird felt himself falling without ever leaving the ground as if gravity shifted around him . . . and then the sky ignited into an unbearable glare and he was here, his squad with him, prone in the heat and the red dust of a lifeless plain, without a blade of grass or a fly buzzing anywhere around them.

Cast out.

No longer in the world.

They had been delivered to a desert plain as flat as an ancient lakebed. Heat shimmers rising from the clay surface bent and blurred the air, limiting clear sight to just a few tens of meters. So they heard the first demon before they saw it—a murmuring of blowing sand though there was no wind, and then a sparking snap of electricity as a train of dust charged into their midst where it congealed into . . .

. . . a glimmering white sword—that was the first thing Whitebird saw, a curved weapon nearly a meter long looking like the tooth of some monstrous *T. rex* or a slaughtered dragon. It was held in long-fingered hands, red-brown like the desert. Behind that primitive weapon was a manlike figure—if a man could be seven and a half feet tall with eyes like asymmetrical black fissures slashed into a white-bearded face with red lips around sharp teeth and its tongue a cluster of tentacles glimmering with moisture as it darted in and out, in and out, the creature wearing only a low-slung belt of what looked like human finger bones, with an exaggerated stallion dick dangling flaccid between its legs.

The sword swung, severing Yuen's neck, sending his helmeted head tumbling from his shoulders. Blood fountained just like in the movies. It showered the squad. Screams erupted as everyone fell back, separating themselves from the collapsing body and the long white sword. Whitebird brought his M4 to his shoulder, at the same time dropping to one knee, a move that let him aim up so his rounds wouldn't hit his soldiers who were behind the monster.

He put three quick shots into the demon's chest.

No one knew where the demons came from or what they wanted, but it was now clear that they could learn— and adapt. The creature presently looming above Whitebird was no naked warrior with a sword. It was modernized, weaponized, and far more lethal—assuming it knew how to use the carbine that it held. It hooked a finger over the trigger and started experimenting, firing a string of rounds that hit the rock behind Whitebird. Stone and metal fragments pummeled him as he returned fire, shooting it in the face. Cabuto punched holes in it from behind, shots aimed outside the protection of the armored vest it wore, hitting both shoulder joints and rupturing its neck.

Fire erupted from every wound. Roaring, sinuous streamers of yellow-orange flame, the energy of the demon's existence maybe, bursting into this dimension from some lower world.

The thing arched its back in agony as the fire enveloped it. It shrieked and it shook, but it did not go down.

They never did.

In the twisted landscape of his exhausted mind, Whitebird was more disturbed by the demon's refusal to collapse than he was by the hellfire, or by the creature's inexplicable appearance out of blowing grit and vapor.

The reality he once knew had been stolen away. The rules were different now.

"Can you see it?" Cabuto shouted over the demon's keening. "Is it opening?"

Whitebird vaulted to his feet, backing away from the searing heat. "Not yet!" But it *would* open. "Goodfellow, get your ass over here!"

"Sir, I—" He backed a step away. "Let Foltz go first. He really wants to go—"

It wasn't a debate. Whitebird had made his decision. He just hoped like Hell—

Ah, fuck that. He needed to cut that phrase right out of his vocabulary. He hoped *to God* he was sending the kid home and not to Hell.

Holding his M4 in one hand, he grabbed Goodfellow's arm with the other and marched him up to the fire while the demon's shrieks faded as if its voice was retreating into the distance.

Cabuto circled around to watch.

The demon's shape could no longer be seen. The fire that had consumed it became a thin sheet that expanded into a pointed arch seven-and-a-half feet high. As soon as the arch formed, it split in the middle, opening along a vertical seam, the fire drawing back until the shimmering flames framed a passage that had been burned through to the world. Whitebird could see through the passage, to home. He knew it was home because he could see the proper color of the sky. He could see figures in the distance in familiar uniforms; he could see vehicles, and helicopters circling the collapsed ruins of the outpost.

Cabuto called it Death's Door.

Whitebird longed to pass through it. So did Cabuto. Everyone wanted a chance to go—except Goodfellow. "Now or never," Whitebird warned him. "You will not be given a second chance."

He shoved the kid hard, and when that failed to convince him, he brought his weapon to his shoulder and trained the muzzle on Goodfellow's face. "Go now, or die here."

For a second, Goodfellow was too shocked to react—but then he stepped through, a moment before the fire burned itself out. When Death's Door closed, he was on the other side.

Whitebird intended to get everyone out, but it was a

slow, dangerous game, and it had taken time to learn the basic rules: that a door only opened if they killed a demon, and then only one soldier could pass through.

No one knew why.

No one knew who had made the rules: God or the Devil or an ancient magician or random chance. It didn't matter. "We know how to get home. That's all that matters."

Whitebird knew—they all knew—that the longer any of them stayed in that place, the more likely they were to die there. The demons might kill them or, worse, the demons might stop trying to kill them. If the demons didn't come hunting them, if there were no demons to kill, there would be no passage back, and whoever was left behind would die of thirst.

So in his mind Whitebird weighed the merits of each of his soldiers. He balanced the potential of their unknowable futures against the immediate needs of the squad, and he developed a list in his head that prioritized their lives.

"Keller!"

"Yes, sir," she answered from her position on the opposite side of the little plateau. Specialist Trish Keller, who had a year-old daughter and no support from the dad.

"You're going home next, Keller. Be ready."

"Lieutenant, who goes after Keller?" Foltz wanted to know.

Foltz was a good, determined soldier, but not a selfless one. He'd been putting himself forward at every opportunity, pushing hard to be the next to go home— but Sergeant Cabuto didn't approve of his lobbying.

"Knock off the chatter, Foltz! Keep your eyes on the desert. The lieutenant will let you know when it's your turn."

Whitebird squinted at the glassy haze of heat shimmers rising above the dust, going over again in his head the evacuation list he'd developed. Foltz was going to be disappointed, because after Keller he planned to send Private Bridget Cobb, who was an only child. Then Private Ben Fong, who would make an excellent non-com if he lived long enough. Only after that would he let Omar Foltz go, and after him, Private Jordana Alameri, who was basically a fuckup and didn't have much of a future to go home to. Once his soldiers had all made it back, then Sergeant Cabuto would be willing to go.

It was a tentative schedule, subject to revision. Whitebird considered moving Cabuto up the list, ordering him to follow Keller. He didn't want to have to get by without the sergeant, but Cabuto had a wife and three kids. Or maybe he should send Alameri next. After this tour of Hell's suburb, she might be ready to walk the strait and narrow.

There was only one position on the list that Whitebird was sure about, and that was his own. He would go last, which meant that for some unknown interval of time, a few seconds or forever, he would be here alone—and what *that* would be like?

It didn't bear thinking on.

After Yuen died and Whitebird killed the first demon, Death's Door had opened for the first time. Foltz had been nearby. He'd seen through to the world and had tossed a rock into the passage to test the way—but the rock bounced back.

Specialist Jacobs had a different idea. "Let's try something from *our* world." He moved in close to the searing fire, tossed a cartridge—and it passed through. The squad pressed in around him despite the heat, watching the glittering cartridge shrink with distance and then silently strike the ground on the other side, bouncing and skipping across the familiar gray grit of the desert they used to patrol.

There was a nervous catch in Jacob's voice when he announced, "You know what? I'm going home." Then he stepped through.

Whitebird had been badly startled. He'd grabbed at Jacobs, tried to catch him, to pull him back out of harm's way, but Jacobs was already on the other side, a distant figure seen in utter clarity as he turned to look back at them. His mouth moved with words Whitebird could not hear as he gestured emphatically for them to follow—but Whitebird could not follow. The passage pushed at his mind and he could not move his limbs in any way that would take him through it.

"Foltz, *go!*" he ordered, and Foltz was willing.

He pushed past the lieutenant and tried to push on into the passage, but it was closed to him too. When he realized it, he turned on Whitebird in an explosion of frustration. "Goddamnit, Lieutenant! What the fuck is going on? Is this some kind of crazy experiment? Yuen is fucking *dead*. What the Hell did you get us into?"

Jacobs was still looking back at them from the other side when Death's Door closed.

★ ★ ★

What did you get us into?

Whitebird had no answer for that or any of the other questions the squad lobbed at him:

What is this place?

Why are we here?

Is this Hell?

"I don't know!"

They clustered around him, Cobb and Goodfellow weeping, Keller praying quietly, her folded hands pressed to her forehead, the rest clutching their M4s, their gazes flitting from him, to each other, to the heat-blurred horizon—scared, suspicious, angry.

Whitebird forced himself to use a matter-of-fact voice: "I don't know what happened. I don't know why we're here, but we *are* going back. Sergeant Cabuto!"

The sergeant stepped up, stern, determined. "Sir!"

"Set up a perimeter guard."

"Roger that, sir."

Foltz still had questions. "I don't get it, sir. Why the hell did Jacobs get to go back? He did go back, didn't he? It looked like he went back."

"He went back," Whitebird confirmed. He was not going to allow doubt on that—it was all they had to hold on to—but the question that really mattered was, could they do it again? Could they send someone else back?

He put Keller to work inventorying their supplies, and then he helped get Yuen's head and body wrapped up in an emergency blanket. When that was done, he conferenced with Cabuto. "If it happens again, we need to be ready."

"Agreed, sir."

They pulled Private Lono aside, selecting him because he was their strongest man.

Whitebird asked him, "If the chance comes, are you willing to try it? To follow Jacobs?"

"Roger that, sir. I sure as fuck don't want to die here."

Whitebird nodded. "I want you to carry Yuen's body with you when you go. We'll follow if we can."

Out on the open plain Whitebird felt too vulnerable, so he directed the squad to make for the nearest plateau. They would take turns carrying Yuen's body.

They'd been walking only a few minutes when the second demon came. The soldiers out front started shooting when it was still churning sand. That drove it back, but only briefly. It charged in again, congealing into existence only inches from Fong, who fired his M4 point-blank at its belly and then fled as fire erupted. The passage back to the world opened just like the first time, and Lono escaped with Yuen's body. But though Keller tried to follow, she could not.

The next demon came just as they reached the rocks and it got LaBerge.

After that, two demons came together. One was killed. Fernandez used its death to return to the world with LaBerge over his shoulder. After he left, Cobb got all weepy, claiming she'd seen LaBerge's soul seeping through the passage— "Like a glowing light cleaner and brighter than daylight" —which convinced Whitebird that she was full of shit because there was nothing clean and bright about LaBerge's soul.

But that didn't mean he'd deserved to die here,

halfway to Hell, with his head cut off by a lunatic demon.

They spread out once again around the top of the small plateau, waiting for another demon to appear. Five minutes crept past, and then ten before Cabuto spotted a sand plume, far out on the desert and barely discernible above the heat shimmers. It churned up against the wall of another low plateau a kilometer and a half away, and disappeared.

Fong spotted another, but it too failed to come after them.

It had been six hours since the squad dropped out of the world, but there was no sign of nightfall in this place and the heat remained constant. They'd been low on water from the start. Soon it would be gone and then they'd have only a few hours before they succumbed to dehydration. They needed to find more demons before then.

Whitebird turned to catch Cabuto's eye. "We're moving out. The dust bunnies didn't have any trouble finding us on the plain."

Cabuto turned to look again at the next plateau, a black island rising from the shimmering red-brown flat. "We saw one disappear over there."

Whitebird nodded. It was as good a direction as any.

They made their way down from the rocks and then set off across the hard clay surface. Every footfall sent a puff of fine red dust into the still air. Sweat leaped off their skin, evaporating as soon as it formed. Whitebird sipped at his remaining water, but the relief it brought was wiped out by the next breath of hot, dry air.

They stayed ten meters apart. Whitebird and Foltz marched in front, Cobb, Alameri, and Fong formed a second rank, and Cabuto and Keller held the rear, keeping watch behind them.

They couldn't see far. Hot air rose in shimmering columns, reflecting distant plateaus while hiding what was really there so that again, like the first time, they heard the demon before they saw it. "Three o'clock!" Whitebird called out, turning toward a faint rustling white noise.

"I can hear another," Cabuto warned. "Five o'clock."

"Fucking *two* dust bunnies?" Alameri grumbled. "Again?"

"Two tickets home," Whitebird reminded her. "Fall back if they materialize between us—and stay alert for more."

"I see it!" Foltz shouted. "Three o'clock!"

"Fall back!"

"Incoming from behind!" Cabuto warned.

The two plumes of sand and vapor churned past their outer ranks, converging in the middle where Cobb had been standing. She tried to get away. She plunged right through one of the sand plumes, but the other curled around to cut her off. Both demons transformed. Giant figures, they stood back-to-back, dressed in desert camo and armed with carbines. Cobb was caught between them as gunfire erupted from all sides.

Whitebird dove for the ground. Bullets chewed through the hot air as demon howls broke out, competing with the racket of the weapons. The demons had been hit.

Whitebird rolled, coming up on one knee to see the two creatures on fire, their weapons burning and useless in their hands—with Cobb sprawled and bloody on the ground between them.

"Cease fire!" he screamed. "Cease fire!"

The shooting ended, and Whitebird charged toward the two flaming figures. As he did, he saw Foltz move in the corner of his eye. "Foltz! Help me get Cobb!"

"But, sir—"

"*Now!*" He crouched beside Cobb. Her jaw was shattered. Blood soaked her right arm and thigh. Grabbing her pack strap, he dragged her away from the fire.

Goddamn. Goddamn.

The demons couldn't have shot her where she'd been standing.

"Foltz!"

Whitebird looked up to see Keller, Fong, Foltz, and Alameri, all waiting near the flames.

"Keller goes next!" Whitebird ordered. He strode into their midst, grabbed Foltz, shoved him away, shoved Alameri. "And you, Fong, go."

Foltz and Alameri looked mutinous, so Whitebird kept his finger just above the trigger of his M4 and watched them until Keller and Fong were gone.

Foltz cursed into the quiet that descended. "Goddamn *shit*. Why the fuck do I have to stay here? Why? We are going to fucking *die* here."

From somewhere behind Whitebird, Cabuto spoke. "Lieutenant, Cobb's not going to make it."

"I know that."

"I can't get a heartbeat. We've lost her." And then, "*Holy shit*. Lieutenant, you have to see this."

Whitebird turned.

Cabuto was backing away from Cobb as a black shadow, utterly dark, seeped up from the ground beneath her body. It spread out to surround her, and as it did, Cobb sank into it, her shattered corpse dropping slowly away—into some place worse than this one?

"Don't let her go."

"She's dead, sir."

What did that mean, here? LaBerge had died here. Yuen had died. This had not happened to them.

Whitebird rushed to Cobb's side, went to his knees and grabbed for her, but though she was only inches away, he couldn't touch her. A twist of geometry had placed her out of reach as she lay cradled in darkness, her eyes hidden behind sunglasses, but with the mangled flesh and shattered bone and broken teeth of her jaw exposed.

He didn't exactly see it happen. He couldn't point to the moment, but the pliant geometry that held her stretched and shifted and she was suddenly away, lying on rocky soil among tufts of grass with a moon rising over sharp peaks, spilling a yellow light.

Whitebird knew the place. "That's home. That's right by the outpost." He looked up at Cabuto. "Go. Follow her. Follow her through."

Pale dust frosted Cabuto's dark face. "No, sir. We've got two soldiers who need to go ahead of me, sir."

"*Goddamn it*," Whitebird whispered. "I want *you* to go."

"Not before them, Lieutenant. No fucking way."

Whitebird stood up, furious. Cabuto was worth more than Foltz and Alameri together. He had a wife and kids. Arguing, though, would only waste the chance.

"Foltz!"

Foltz was still steps away, cursing his luck, but Whitebird discovered that Private Alameri had come quietly to his side. She looked up at him from behind her dark sunglasses. He nodded. "*Go*. And don't waste your fucking life."

No hesitation. As Foltz came charging up, she stepped into the shadow and then she was standing on the other side, standing beside the body, an infinite distance away but still close enough that he could see her as she turned, looking up at the three of them gazing down at her. Then searing desert light infiltrated the shadow, destroying it, leaving only hardpan covered in red dust.

"What the fuck just happened?" Foltz screamed, probing at the ground with the butt of his weapon and then hammering at it. "Why did that happen?"

"Death's Door," Cabuto said.

Foltz turned on him. "It didn't happen when Yuen died! Or LaBerge! What was different this time?"

"Leave it!" Whitebird snapped. He already knew what made this death different. "It just fucking happened. You are going to make it home, Foltz."

"Yeah? Alive or dead?"

"Alive if you can hold yourself together. What happened to Cobb doesn't need to happen again. It was an accident."

Whitebird regretted the words as soon as they were out, because they pointed Foltz to the truth.

He backed a step away, eyeing Whitebird with a guarded expression. "The demons didn't kill her, did they? *We* killed her."

"Friendly fire," Cabuto affirmed as he turned in a slow circle, eyeing the terrain.

"But it's not going to happen again," Whitebird added.

Foltz nodded, though he was thinking hard.

Thinking the same thing Whitebird was thinking: that Death's Door opened every time they took a life . . . and not just a demon's life. They knew that now, but it was a poisonous knowledge.

"We're in this together," Whitebird emphasized.

Foltz nodded again, though he did not seem convinced.

They went on, deciding that it was more likely another demon would notice them if they kept moving. Or maybe more than one would come. There might even be three. Three would be enough to get them all home, and then Whitebird wouldn't have to stay here alone.

He'd kept his fear locked up for hours, but they were close to the end now and his dread of what that meant was rising up to choke him. Foltz would get to go home next, and then Cabuto. Whitebird would make sure of that. It was his duty. He swore to himself he would make it happen.

Then only he would be left behind, left here, alone.

And if the demons killed him, then what? There was no one to take his body back. What would become of his soul?

He wasn't sure he believed in a soul, but he worried over it anyway.

A faint susurration reached his ears, barely audible over the crunch of their boots, the creak of their packs. He stopped and turned, scanning the plain—and this time he saw the demons at a distance, reflected in the heat shimmers so that their plumes of dust appeared elevated above the ground. One snaked toward them from two o'clock and another from four o'clock, two came from behind, and a fifth raced in from their left.

"Ah, *fuck*," Cabuto swore.

Whitebird said, *"Run."*

Their packs banged against their backs as they sprinted for the rocks. Cabuto took the lead with Foltz on his heels. Whitebird followed. If they could get behind the fallen boulders with their backs against the black cliff, then they could make a defense, hold the demons at bay, reduce their numbers . . .

But they were already too late.

More than an hour ago they'd watched a plume of sand and vapor wander the plain before disappearing into these rocks. That demon was still there, waiting for them. Dressed in desert camo with an M4 carbine in its black-clawed hands, it crouched behind the shelter of a massive, angular boulder lying like a black prism on the ground. They were fifteen meters away when it started shooting.

The first shots went wild. Then a burst struck Cabuto in his chest armor, knocking him over backward. Foltz caught a round in his hip. It spun him, dropping him ass-first to the ground. Whitebird jumped over him, jumped sideways, pulled a grenade from his vest, and hurled it behind the rock as a bullet chewed past his helmet.

He dove for the ground. The grenade went off.

The explosion blasted a cloud of dust into the air and shook the cliff hard enough that an avalanche of sharp stones dislodged, tumbling down with a roar. The body of the demon ignited on the edge of the debris.

Foltz saw it and heaved himself up in an act of will that somehow got him to his feet. Under the incandescent light of the false sky, the blood that soaked his hip blazed red. He took a step and his leg gave out. He sat down hard again. "Goddamn it! Goddamn it, Whitebird, you got to help me!"

Cabuto, a few meters behind Foltz, had recovered enough to make it to his hands and knees. He rocked back to a kneeling position, his weapon aimed at the oncoming assault. The storm front of demons was a hundred meters out, five plumes that blended into one, bearing down on them with a low whisper of sand on sand, punctuated by the sharp crack of arcing electricity.

"Help me!" Foltz screamed.

Whitebird ran past him, ran past Cabuto, and lobbed another grenade, heaving it as far as he could in the direction of the oncoming cloud. It went off ahead of the churning sand, with no effect that he could see. He looked back over his shoulder.

The burning demon swayed like a balloon afloat on hot air, its feet just brushing the hardpan as flames spread over it in a blazing sheet: the prelude to Death's Door opening. Foltz was trying to drag himself toward it, but for him, it was too far.

So for the last time, Whitebird mentally updated the order of his evacuation list. "On your feet, Sergeant," he said, rejoining Cabuto. "This one's yours. You can make it if you run. Now, *move!*"

Cabuto didn't. He scowled past dark sunglasses while keeping his weapon trained on the oncoming cloud. "Take Foltz, sir!"

"Goddamn it, there's no time! Get on your feet and go!"

Foltz had stopped his slow crawl. He twisted around, his M4 gripped in two hands. Past the blood-smeared lenses of his safety glasses, Whitebird saw fury and a sense of betrayal in his gaze. "Foltz," he said, trying to reassure, "I'm staying with you."

But a decision had already crystallized in Foltz's eyes. A calculation born of logic and desperation: there was still a way for him to go home.

The demon storm was eighty meters out when Foltz raised his weapon, training the muzzle of his M4 on Whitebird, and on Cabuto, who was still kneeling with his back turned.

Whitebird screamed *"No!"*—but it was already a meaningless protest, an empty aftermath to a decision made and acted upon. Deep in the pragmatic layers of his battle-trained mind, he'd concluded a calculation of his own. His conscience continued to wrestle with the choice even as his own weapon fired in a drawn-out peal of hammering thunder, dumping slugs into the midline of Foltz's chest armor, stitching a straight line to his throat, through his face, shattering his glasses and his skull. His weapon flew out of his hands, tumbling, caught in a shower of blood.

Cabuto lunged to his feet. He spun around, eyes wide with horror, his mouth a round orifice of shock as he held his M4 tucked against his shoulder, contemplating Whitebird over its sights.

Whitebird shook his head, gesturing with his own gun at a black shadow seeping up through the desert floor, enfolding Foltz's body. "*Go.*" Already, the body was subsiding into darkness. "Go, Sergeant. Follow him home."

"You killed him!" Cabuto screamed. "Why? Just to buy a way out?"

Whitebird answered, saying what Cabuto needed to hear: "He was aiming to kill *you*. Us. We were his passage out of here. You saw him before. You know what he was thinking. I had no choice." But that wasn't the whole truth. "I fucked up and called it wrong. He was never a hero—and I let him think he could be left behind."

Cabuto looked like he wanted to argue more, but what was left to argue?

"Go *now!*" Whitebird shouted, knowing that neither of them—no one who had been in that place—would ever really leave.

The sergeant's gaze shifted to the burning demon, transformed now into an arch of flame framing a transient passage back to the world. "You better get your ass in gear, Lieutenant. You better fucking *run!*"

Cabuto turned and stumbled into the shadow, dropping out of Whitebird's sight.

The swirling sand storm was almost on him when Whitebird took off, sprinting for the fire. The demon-driven sand swept past him and then spun around, encircling him to block his way but he plunged through it, the grains hammering in tiny, painful pricks against his cheeks and pinging against his sunglasses, his helmet, his clothes. Demon figures resolved out of the red-tinged chaos, some armed with white swords and others with guns.

Whitebird started shooting. He emptied his magazine at half-seen shapes until he felt the fire's searing heat radiant against his face. Only then did he look at it, and within the encircling arch of flame he saw familiar stars spangling the moon-washed night sky of home—a step away or an infinite distance, he didn't know.

In the dusty air above his head the whistling passage of a demon's white blade sounded, descending on him.

He dove.

★ ★ ★

ABOUT THE AUTHOR

Linda Nagata is the author of *The Red: First Light*, a near-future military thriller nominated for both the Nebula Award and the John W. Campbell Memorial Award. Among her other works are *The Bohr Maker*, winner of the Locus Award for best first novel; the novella "Goddesses," the first online publication to receive a Nebula award; and the story "Nahiku West," a finalist for the Theodore Sturgeon Memorial Award. Though best known for science fiction, she also writes fantasy, exemplified by her "scoundrel lit" series Stories of the Puzzle Lands. Linda has spent most of her life in Hawaii, where she's been a writer, a mom, and a programmer of database-driven websites. She lives with her husband in their long-time home on the island of Maui.

ACKNOWLEDGMENTS

★ ★ ★

Publisher/Editor: Jim Minz, for acquiring and editing the book, and to the rest of the team at Baen Books.

Agent(s): Seth Fishman for being awesome and supportive (writers: you'd be lucky to have Seth in your corner), and also to my former agent, Joe Monti, the agent who sold this particular anthology but is now a book editor whom I plan to sell many other anthologies to.

Cover Artist: Dominic Harman, for the wonderful, spot-on artwork.

Cover Designer: Jason Gurley, for taking Dominic's art and turning it into a beautiful cover.

Mentors: Gordon Van Gelder and Ellen Datlow, for being great mentors and friends.

Colleagues: Ross Lockhart for a little behind-the-scenes editorial assistance; Myke Cole for answering a bunch of stupid military jargon questions for me; Kate Galey for vetting my Tolkien references; and Andrew Liptak for title consultation and steering me toward that great Eisenhower quote I riffed on in my introduction.

Titlers: I had a hell of a time coming up with a title for this anthology, so I held a little title contest on my website. I got somewhere in the vicinity of 750 title suggestions (!!!), but big thanks go to J. P. Behrens, who came up with the winning suggestion of *Operation Arcana*. And Steven Howell, who almost came up with the same thing (*Arms & Arcana*), deserves an honorable mention for his suggestion of *Runes of Engagement*, which I also liked a lot.

Family: my amazing wife, Christie; my mom, Marianne, and my sister, Becky, for all their love and support.

Interns and First-Readers: Lisa Andrews, Britt Gettys, Bradley Englert, Amber Barkley, and Jude Griffin.

Writers: Everyone who wrote stories for this anthology, and all of my other projects.

Readers: Everyone who bought this book, or any of my other anthologies, and who make possible doing books like this.

United States Armed Forces: Thank you for being real-life heroes and inspiring so many of our fictional ones.

ABOUT THE EDITOR
★ ★ ★

John Joseph Adams is the series editor of *Best American Science Fiction & Fantasy,* published by Houghton Mifflin Harcourt. He is also the bestselling editor of many other anthologies, such as *The Mad Scientist's Guide to World Domination, Armored, Brave New Worlds, Wastelands, The Living Dead,* and The Apocalypse Triptych (*The End is Nigh, The End is Now,* and *The End Has Come*). Called "the reigning king of the anthology world" by Barnes & Noble, John is a winner of the Hugo Award (for which he has been nominated eight times) and is a six-time World Fantasy Award finalist. John is also the editor and publisher of the digital magazines *Lightspeed* and *Nightmare,* and is a producer for Wired.com's *The Geek's Guide to the Galaxy* podcast. Learn more at johnjosephadams.com and follow him on Twitter @johnjosephadams.

Epic Urban Adventure by a New Star of Fantasy

DRAW ONE IN THE DARK

by Sarah A. Hoyt

Every one of us has a beast inside. But for
Kyrie Smith, the beast is no metaphor.
Thrust into an ever-changing world of
shifters, where shape-shifting dragons, giant
cats and other beasts wage a secret war
behind humanity's back, Kyrie tries to control her inner animal and remain human as
best she can....

"Analytically, it's a tour de force: logical, built from
assumptions, with no contradictions, which is aston-
ishing given the subject matter. It's also gripping
enough that I finished it in one day."

—Jerry Pournelle

1-4165-2092-9 • $25.00